Mer'edrynn Book One

Warping the Weave

by
Stephy Dewar

*To my husband and family
with many thanks
for all the love, respect, and laughs you've given me.*

This is a work of fiction

All names, characters, places and events created by the author are used purely fictitiously .

Text copyright © 2018 Stephy Dewar
All rights reserved

No part of this book may be reproduced, stored or transmitted in any form or by any means , electronic, mechanical, photocopying, recording or otherwise without express permission from the author.

ISBN: 9781724058997

A map of Mer'edrynn by the author. (forgive me, I'm no artist!)

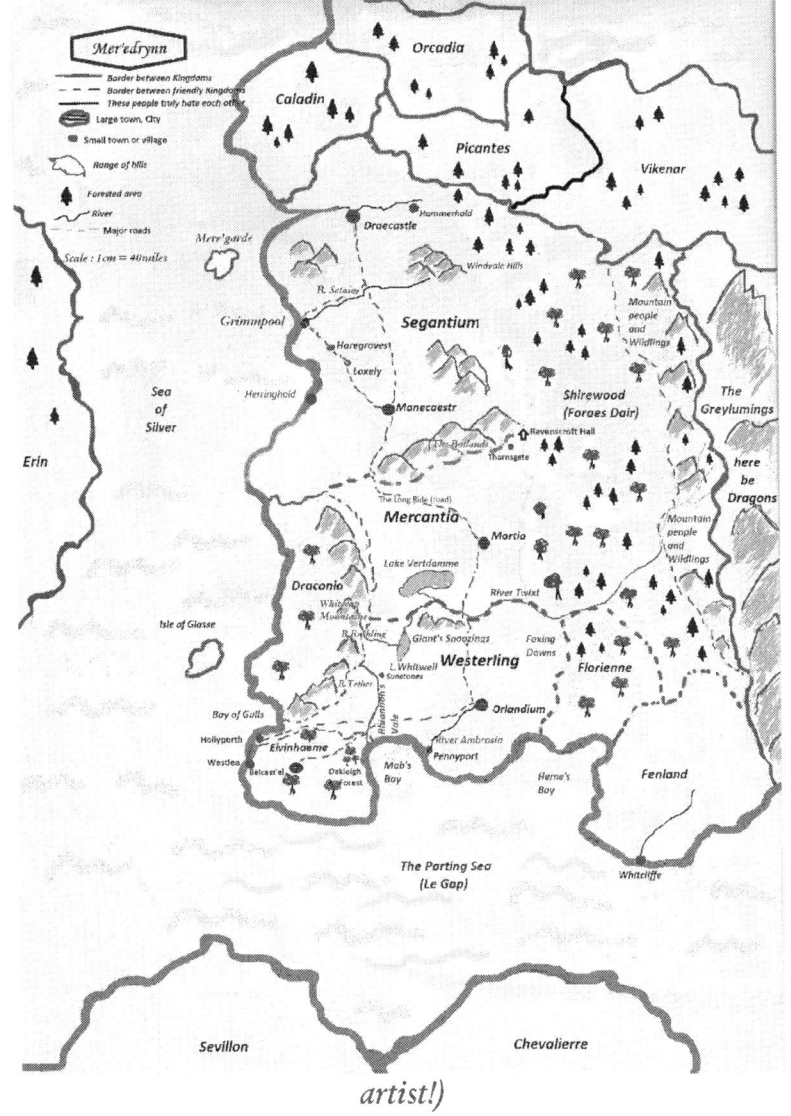

Part 1

For Merrie's Sake ...
A theft, an invasion and a gathering of the four.

Prologue:

Place: The Vaults, Floriénne   Time: Beltane, aeon of the Lady Merrie.

With considered care and a quantum of skill, he slipped silently through shadowed, hallowed halls. His measured breaths drew air stuffy with the fusty taint of age and the blackened flecks of sooty torchlight ... light enough to see by ... or unfortunately, be seen. Warily, he trod the gloomy passageways with the trepidation that only a thief can feel; these vaults held guards aplenty, all no doubt alert and watchful. To his favour however, few others were down here, not on this day, this special day.

Upstairs held a wealth of life and fun, the bibulous chatter of feasting and pleasure, the Lady Merrie's own spring festival. Love and romance were in the air and the folk upstairs would dance, sing and party until dawn, Merrie's way, *live life... love life*. He too enjoyed a good festival, but would take no part today, it was simply fit for purpose. Nay, if anything he was the spectre at the feast, the bringer of doom. No pleasure then ... this had to be done, and today was useful.

Let them drink their fill upstairs, all the better for his mission. Does a drunkard remember a shadow's passing?

He was no mage, but he had grace enough to tread quietly, invisible in the flickering torchlight; flames wavered in the draft, the only signal of his crossing. The art of concealment had been assiduously practised for years in the unforgiving Foraes Dair, now it served him well. Many guards, many passages, many stairs, downwards and on, thus far he advanced unchecked. Once or twice a guard looked up curiously as, with surreptitious stealth, he crept softly by.

The elf stole onwards, ignoring rooms full of treasures and weapons, mementoes of war, talismans and harbingers of death, all carefully classified and codified. He sought only that which was in the final vault, the deepest and most sacred: his sole goal.

He halted briefly as a mouse squeaked and ran across his path, almost standing on its tail. He hid against the shadowed wall, barely breathing until the rodent disappeared down an arid, dust-filled hole to seek its family. For some moments he stood rigid, listening for movement from guards, before creeping onwards.

He was amazed at the size of this underground treasury; room after room burgeoning with spoils of war, the loot of centuries, the wealth of a nation. He touched none.

Instead, he followed his instinct to the final vault, their most precious treasure. The air this far down was damp, miasmic with age. He paused briefly to consider his next move, a mere momentary hesitation for contemplation, before solemnly pulling back his shoulders, determined to finish this task. His face wore no emotion, neither excitement nor anxiety, merely a mask of concentration. He quietly continued his mission to the lowest level.

A guard stood idly in front of the last doorway, a little miffed at missing the Feast Day pleasures upstairs - down here was boring, tedious work. Chilly down here too, the cold seeped into his veins, a glass of mead would go down well later. It was supposed to be an honour to guard the vault, but he would be glad for his shift to be over. Few nobles ventured this far down, except once or twice a year; a mage or two, the Dûchesse, her duty to inspect the glass case, to see and worship the relic.

The elf moved with soundless assurance, melded and moulded twixt dark and light. Cloaked and camouflaged, he remained unseen until he stood solemnly by the side of the bored and clearly oblivious guard. He gave a muttered apology as he knocked him out with a swift blow to the head and took the keys hanging from his belt; the guard was only doing his duty and he had no quarrel with him. He took from his pocket a small vial of softened beeswax, oiled the lock as well as the hinges of the door, waiting for a few moments before unlocking it. The door to the final vault now swung silently, it would not betray him.

Inside was lit by a single flame; a small room - smaller than he thought, almost cave-like - but then, it held only one item, that which he sought.

One oblong oaken table, the legs wrought with fine elven carvings, leaves and vines. One large glass case on top, extremely simple in style yet immensely heavy, *no visible openings*.

It was clear he could not take the case, nor did he wish to.

The elf gave a deep sigh of satisfaction as he gazed at the relic, surprised that it wasn't better protected. It looked naked inside the crystal glass, open to the world. Surely there should be locks, perhaps chains? There were none, not locks, handles, seams or hinges. The case seemed complete, whole, perhaps it had to be broken open? *'In emergency, smash glass'?* But he was neither tradesman nor craftsman, he carried no axe or hammer. True, he'd brought glass cutters and lock picks with him, although somehow, he had not expected the need of them. He wasn't even that sure how to use them.

He examined the seamless crystal case thoroughly, shaking his head under his hood, how had they put it in there? More to the point, how to get it out?

He tried the glass cutter on the top of the crystal case: nothing happened, not even a scratch. *Hmm*, magically warded then, no ingress that way. In that case, even a hammer would do nothing. This relic was meant to stay here forever.

Time was going by, how much longer could he have before the unconscious guard outside was discovered? Frowning now, slightly worried. he stretched out his hands to touch the cold glass, feeling perhaps for pressure points. It was smooth, so smooth, not a ridge or an indentation anywhere, certainly nowhere for a lock. He shook his head once more, he had come many miles - in more ways than one - for this, he would not return empty handed. How in Mer'edrynn did it open?

But then he smiled with relief as the case suddenly sprang open at his touch revealing a previously hidden seam, the glass connected together so perfectly - and obviously magically - as to be invisible, and he gazed with relish at what lay on the bed of faded purple velvet. Another quietly satisfied sigh escaped him, mingling oddly with a strange sound - a brief echo perhaps, a movement of age-old air? - from within the case.

For a moment his face was bright with pleasure.

Ah ... it was beautiful, more so than he imagined. But his triumph was followed by a brief moue of *dis*satisfaction; with shaking head he realised the ancient relic had been vandalised at some point, reducing its power.

Regardless, he quickly secreted his prize in the leathern cloth he had brought with him for the purpose, and left as silently as he came.

*

Hollyporth port, Elvinhaeme: month of Oestra, one month earlier.

They rolled in on huge carracks from their island stronghold of Glasse, north west in the Sea of Silver, not so many miles away from Hollyporth. The massive ballistae faced landward, war weapons designed to terrify the natives. Also very useful in the port, make some damage down at the docks, not too much, but enough to hurt.

Who could stop them? There was no navy to fight these ships, not necessary, no-one had invaded for hundreds of years and the elves of Elvinhaeme were on good terms with the humans of Westerling just to the north, sharing a land border between them. In any case, King Alexis' wife, Queen Neria, came from their own Court. King Alexis kept a small contingent of boats armed against smugglers bringing contraband from Sevillon or Chev'alierre across the Parting Sea; wines, coffee, perfumes, leafroll, expensive stuff. Sometimes the Sevillain came to fish illegally in their waters, King Alexis' small fleet of warships kept them at bay. The elves of Elvinhaeme in their south west corner of Mer'edrynn were grateful to the human Westerling king and paid him a sum towards upkeep.

But no one had a real navy, and no one had a large army, except maybe King Kyneweth far north in Segantium, sharing the borders with Caladin and Picantés, his troops patrolled regularly. He kept the wild tribes down too, Bregantines and Alderfolk of the far north in Shirewood. He was a long way off though, nigh on nine hundred miles by road. Here in Hollyporth, a few guards kept the port clear of louts and drunkards, and the special ones, experienced and mature, guarded Merrie's Temple.

No, the peace-loving elves of Elvinhaeme weren't ready for this, nor were their gentle human friends. Humans lived in Elvinhaeme too, side by side, artists, writers and poets were usually inspired by the beauty. They came to enjoy the University of Arts at Belcast'el, the music, the camaraderie; many intermarried, or just stayed. Life was pleasant here. They weren't ready either, and in any case, none were fighters.

The invaders arrived on a lovely spring day, just the sort the elves loved; a blue-sky day in this small city by the sea. Wide, white streets, pink with flowering cherries lining the roads. A city full of blossom, for the elves were great gardeners and farmers, the city blooming with spring, as bonny as a bride on her wedding day. Attractive buildings too, the local stone so pale as to be almost white. The buildings sparkled in the bright clean light, a rainbow radiance.

It was one of those days that made an elven heart sing, perhaps bring out a lute to play a tune, watch the elf maidens dance their welcome of spring. A time to take part in the age-old ritual of life; summer and sunshine just around the corner.

But the black-clad soldiers poured off the ships, fully armed and well trained, years spent in training on the Isle of Glasse for this day, the first foray onto the mainland. They held their metal shields in front and their steel swords high and marched down the main street, tight grouped blocks of them. The streets were wide, groups marched eight-square formation, grim faced and determined. They slaughtered indiscriminately as they marched, elf and human. Bodies fell; some were meeting friends or simply taking a stroll, shopping, some sitting outside street cafes enjoying the spring air, others were simply fishermen bringing in a fresh catch from the sea, merchants carrying in fine goods, others taking their crafts to market. Not a soul was ready.

Hollyporth was civilised and peaceful, for Merrie's sake! No one expected this.

The wide, white streets ran crimson; blood mopped up by pale pink cherry blossom swept by the wind to the side of the road. Elvhen screams dissipated in the air.

The militia, for what it was worth, was called, taken out quickly by these men trained in the art of death. The militia was used to drunkards and occasional fights among sailors, not this, not warfare. No guardsman lived, no Temple Guard outlived this day, and the Temple of Merrie was taken and desecrated, her oaken statue dragged outside and burned in the town square for ashen-faced elves and their human friends to witness and to weep.

They took the port of Westlea also that day, useful and in both cases, so easy. Mer'edrynn was meant for humans only, for human males, strong in will and determination. *The rest had to go.*

The old ways of fertility and love were finished, for now was the time of death.

Chapter 1

Village of Haregroves, 19th day of Helios, Present day.

'Pop down to the river and get me some yellow flag will you, I'm running out of dye. Oh, and collect some toadflax on the way.' The order came from a dry voice belonging to a miserable-looking, middle aged herb dealer, or *quack* as Dane privately called him.

Dane looked up from his work table with pleasure. All morning he'd been dying to get out of the dank and airless store, just waiting for an excuse. Dane hated that so-called herbalist's shop, a musty smelling, dark hole of a place with few real medicines and a mean, mealy mouthed remedian who ran it. A herbalist's shop should smell clean and sharp with the fresh tang of healing herbs. This smelled of sour cough drops covered in dust, with a constant undercurrent of Ryebold's sweat. The man called himself a physician, *huh*! Dane had more healing in his little finger than Ryebold had in his entire store. And some of those potions were just wrong - useless or even downright dangerous. Still, the charlatan made a living off his sweetened juices and spectacularly coloured vials, no one seemed to notice.

If people recovered, it was thanks to the medicine, if they didn't, his excuse was that the Lady Merrie had chosen to take them at this time. They'd gone to her loving arms, were now with the ancestors.

Dane considered it was fortunate that he'd been around for the last few months to create some real potions. Ryebold didn't care one way or another, people could live or die as long as they paid him, but he had to admit more and more people were seeking out his store, thanks to Dane's knowledge. His brief reverie was interrupted by his master's insistent voice.

'Go on, hop to it, and hurry back quick, time's money, lad.'

'Miserable old sod,' thought Dane. *'I'll take whatever time's necessary.'* He needed the job to live, to pay his rent and buy food, but he hated being cooped up all day. He put the cork stopper back on the bottle he was preparing, stashed it out of the way before Ryebold meddled with it and left the store, glad to be in the open air.

It wasn't exactly fresh air.

The gritty, greasy smell of burnt and blackened bones invaded Dane's nostrils as he strode through the narrow street, his all too expressive face betrayed his feelings, his mouth curled up in distaste. Chicken bones or perhaps the remains of a hog roast, crackling and shattering on a hearth-fire? He hated that smell, too close to human, too many memories ... too close to the charred remains of his father ... the day the Adammites came to his island.

The young mage shook the disturbing image from his brain, too painful. There was no point dwelling on the past, despite how it had changed his life - nay - his world. He had work to do. The guy was a miserable sod, but the young man needed the work and it was easy for someone with Dane's knowledge.

It was warm, early summer, with little wind to freshen the air. Dane ran through the dusty village street, his nose still twitching; more smells of overused, old fat in blackened cooking pots, malodorous little children, un-swept pig sties and the stink of the cesspit assailing his nostrils. The burnt bone smell stuck with him though, couldn't get it out of his system. It had been a terrible end for his father.

He'd loved his dad, a charming man, a mage like himself, tallish and well built with cornflower blue eyes that laughed. Dane was glad he'd inherited his physique from his father and not his mother. But his golden hair was definitely from mum. Those same blue eyes temporarily turned misty. They'd been wonderful parents, full of fun and so much in love.

He turned down a small lane, slightly clearer and cleaner here, the two cottages on each side boasted gardens filled with fragrant summer flowers. He stopped to breathe in the heady clove aroma of some pink matthioli, stocks, broke off a stem and stuck it in the lapel of his cheap, calico tunic. That would smell better when he returned, a necessary nosegay.

He felt uncomfortable in these villages. Too much noise, the incessant *bang, bang, bang* of the blacksmith from dawn 'til dusk, the constant wailing of babies overheated by the summer sun, and the barking of hungry dogs snapping at each other as they scavenged for food. There was a saw mill here too, made a rare old racket.

His ears, like his nostrils, were assaulted twelve hours a day.

Still, his other senses enjoyed the place; the ale was good, the innkeeper's wife made a damn tasty pork pie, the pretty wenches were buxom and decidedly soft to touch.

Three out of five wasn't bad.

It was quite a prosperous village, Haregroves by name, just off the main highway between Draecastle to the north and Grimmpool, the main fishing port to the west. A good stopping off place for shoeing the horses, or an overnight stay. It boasted a small market, a wayside inn for better off folk, a damn good ale house and an annual fair.

He was hurrying down to the river when he caught sight of the large, brash notice tacked to the big oak in the centre of the village.

He stepped over to read, the brightly coloured words glaring at him.

Longshanks Circus!
Tonight for one night only!

Conjurers and fire-eaters!

> Juggling japes and exotic creatures!
> Drowman's magnificent dancing bear!
> Bold knife throwers' extraordinaire!
> Acrobats and Trampolines,
> The Bearded Lady behind the scenes!
> For an unforgettable display of delight
> Come to Longshanks Circus tonight!

'Ooh,' he thought, 'now that's worth seeing,' even if the rhythm of the rhyme was a bit iffy and there was an overabundance of exclamation. He loved a good circus, loved a good fair actually, watching all the tumblers and the jugglers. He came out on the highway ... surely he had enough time for a quick peep at the circus folk?

Oh, the life of the travelling players, whether circus, actors or troubadours. He envied them, their camaraderie, their itinerant life style, their creativity. *Must be fun*, he thought. He'd been travelling himself for the last five years, moving from village to village, barely making enough to live on. Always alone though, ever since his family died back on the Isle of Glasse.

It had been such a lovely place, so peaceful. And his mother - *now there was a beauty* - Llanetha, a dryadic priestess who, in what had to have been a fit of madness, married his mage father. She left the woodlands to live in their small manor. His father had to plant trees for her, especially rowans - he savoured the thought of her rowanberry jelly, the earliest of memories - and she brought small saplings with her, apple, cherry, plums, greengages. And naturally, in the centre of their garden, a sacred oak, mistletoe growing along some of the branches. Mum watched that one carefully, harvesting the mistletoe regularly, pruning back, taking care of her beloved tree.

Other women brought linen or crockery as a dowry - his mum brought trees and shrubs.

He shook his head, not good to think back, even now, too painful. *Those blasted Adammites ... mage haters all.*

Dane made his way to the highway, not far distant, passing a small wayside shrine to the Lady Merrie, oak-carved, her gentle hands stretched out in welcome, her naked body seeming vulnerable in the open air. He gave the statue a smile and bent his head reverentially, before blowing her a cheeky kiss. He remembered the old rhyme:

> *'Keep the Lady on your side,*
> *Love's sweet charms with you abide.'*

He believed in keeping the Lady happy. Truth be told he believed in keeping all ladies - or wenches - happy. They were always interested in what a mage could do with his hands ...

What he didn't know was that the Lady had plans for him, that She was about to take him by the hand, or in his case (as with most men) his ... er ... dangly bits, dig him out of his current, albeit pleasant rut and throw him into a totally unknown future. Ah, such is life.

He continued along the road, now whistling, his sorrow dissipating yet always within, understanding that like himself, the Lady Merrie was a Healer. He'd tried to forge a new life for himself from the ashes of the old one. Move onwards, move forwards, *'stop snivelling and get on with it,'* his mum would have said.

Ah now, there it was, out at the Old Field, the huge canvas tent had already been erected, big piebald horses with shaggy manes and baggage wagons everywhere and a couple of those funny little wooden huts on wheels that travellers like these seemed to live in. A number of dwarves were seen arguing in front of the entrance. *Oooh,* and a cage with a big brown bear in ... a real, live bear ... he'd only ever seen them as drawings in manuscripts before. He'd caught a glimpse of one once as he made his way through the dangers of Draconia, but he'd swiftly changed course. He crept over, dying to look in at the fierce creature. It seemed to be sleeping, or perhaps it was just bored into catatonia. He gave the bars a knock, hoping to wake the imprisoned beast, get a look at its sharp claws and teeth.

Frankly, it just looked sorry for itself. It longed for the wildwood.

'Oy, you, stop, keep away - it'll take your head off!' A swarthy giant of a man with a black beard and a mane of thick, black hair shouted gruffly over to him.

'Sorry, just curious ... ' Dane walked over to the big man. He must have been well over six and a half feet tall. Not that Dane was a small guy, there was strong Vikénar blood in his veins from his father's lineage, and years of handling a heavy mage staff had left a broad chest and shoulders.

'You must be Longshanks,' he began.

The big man shook his head morosely and pointed to the entrance. 'Nay, 'im wi't red beard.'

Dane looked ... looked again ... then realised he meant the three and a half foot dwarf with the face chiselled out of a granite mountainside.

'No matter,' he replied, stifling a laugh, 'only came over to have a look.'

'Aye well, look tonight after thee's paid.' The Carnie nodded to the field entrance. 'C'mon, out of it!' He was a surly character.

'*Aye well,*' Dane countered, 'I hope I get my money's worth then, you miserable sod.' He made to walk away.

The big man grabbed hold of his arm, pulling him back, his eyes even blacker, 'just watch what you say, mate ...' Clearly he was a man of short temper.

Dane merely smiled as his other hand discharged an *amberic* shock into the man's arm, blue lightning crackling from mage fingers. The black bearded giant jumped back, clutching his hand. *'Bloody 'ell!'* he swore.

'Just watch who you're manhandling,' countered Dane.

'You effing mages ... shouldn't be allowed ...' the big Carnie muttered as he went back to his tent, still clutching his arm.

Dane walked back to the village, still whistling cheerily, regardless of the sourpuss of a Carnie. He took a small path through the hawthorn wood down to the river. collecting toadflax as he walked, it liked the drier land. The yellow flag by the banks was bright and cheerful, ready for harvesting, but that river looked inviting on such a warm summer's day. He quickly kicked off his boots, rolled up his woollen leggings and waded in. It felt clear and cool and delightful. He wriggled his toes in the sand, then perched himself on a large stone by the bank, leaving his feet in the cold running water. The warm summer sun shone brightly on his face and he felt good: a temporary satisfaction of soul and body. He watched a heron on the other bank, it kept dipping its head in the water, searching for food. Curlews called overhead, and two swallows swooped in the blueness. It was pleasant here, calm, peaceful. A small silver fish began nibbling his toes making him realise he still needed to collect the plants. *Oh well ...* .

When he returned with armfuls of yellow flag and a bag of toadflax, Ryeman began grumbling.

'You've been a damn long time - what were you up to? Got a wench in the village or something?'

'Had to have been a bloody quick roll then,' Dane replied archly.

'Stop giving me bloody cheek ... if you want to keep your job, I'd learn to shut that gob of yours and do as I tell you.' Dane seriously pissed him off on a regular basis. 'Otherwise, you're sacked.'

'All right,' Dane went to pick up his mage staff in the corner, made as if to march out. He'd reached the door before Ryeman called him back.

'Where are you going? I didn't mean it, come back Dane!' Dane was more than useful, on several fronts.

'You know you need me, Ryeman. You know as much herbalism as the blacksmith, probably less. You know nothing about medicine and you have no healing skills. I'm expert in all of those, I've spent my life learning, from my mother's knee upwards, so stop threatening.

Anyway, I only stopped off to look at the circus - it looks great. Are you going tonight?' he smiled cheerily at his boss. 'It starts early though, you need to shut up shop around five.'

Ryeman shook his head. 'Nay, more money lost to that thing and they want me to spend my hard-earned cash on all that rot?' He'd have to close early anyway, everyone would be at the circus, waste of time staying open.

'Bah, humbug,' laughed Dane cheekily, 'you're a mean sod.' Nevertheless he got to work with the herbs, setting them to dry, sorting out the essential parts and working on vials he had prepared the previous day. He knew his preparations and potions would do some good, it was worth hanging around a while. And perhaps Ryeman might just learn a little from him ... although he doubted it.

Ryeman did indeed close his store by five o'clock and Dane hurried back to the tiny room he rented in the attic of the Rosins tavern, for a quick wash and change. He chose a white linen tunic and black woollen leggings, his good black boots suitable for a night out, not that he had much wardrobe choice. He had a mage cloak, but didn't wear a long mage gown, nor had his father, simple working clothes for them both. His great grandfather had started the new tradition; the bellicose Vikénar didn't really appreciate men in frocks, and you couldn't wander around up there without a massive sword or axe at your belt. They looked at you oddly, *something a bit iffy there* ... Mage staffs were carried at all times to show intent, and perhaps a little intimidation. His great grandfather moved to the Isle of Glasse where both his magehood and his manhood were accepted without question. Needless to say, there weren't too many mages left in Vikénar.

But however narrow-minded they were, they didn't indiscriminately slaughter mages as the Adammites did.

He decided to eat at the circus, there were always sideshows and stalls. He made sure to take his staff with him, a place like that attracted vagabonds and cut-purses. It saved a lot of bother, people here, as with the Vikénar, took one look at his black ash staff and stayed clear - he could obviously take care of himself, and no one liked the idea of fire up their backside.

The circus was buzzing with people, some nodded hello to him, he smiled back. The diminutive owner of the business now stood outside the tent flap, wearing a silver cloak and chanting the inevitable 'roll up, roll up,' to everyone, exclaiming the delights of the evening.

There was a goodly smell of roasting meat, Dane tucked in to several slices of wild boar and pork sausages, washed down with a weak and tasteless beer. His eyes were attracted to a stall selling apples dipped in caramelised beet sugar, but it was a bit sticky and after eating half of it he passed it on to a wandering child whose large, wistful eyes looked hungry. The boy ran off behind the tent to finish it before his benefactor could change his mind, or use it as an excuse to give him a quick swipe across the ear.

He joined the queue for the tent, paid his dues and found a bench with a good view to enjoy the evening. He didn't sit at the front, anyone at the front was a fool. They always got covered in water, vegetable peelings or sawdust, and he was wearing his best black leather jerkin over the tunic. He'd left his mage cloak back in his room, no need for it tonight, it was a warm evening.

Longshanks strutted in to welcome everyone and to introduce the acts, the crowd erupting with laughter as he introduced himself. The tent was already bright with oil lamps placed high on the interlocking poles of the structure, they would flare merrily as the sun went down, although that would be late tonight, so near to Lumentide.

There were three performing dogs, four performing dwarves with stilts, and a trampoline was brought out with a well-built young woman in a tight pink bodice who jumped and somersaulted.

That was one of the reasons Dane liked a good circus - the lasses wore next to nothing and left little to the imagination. He watched as her pert rump stuck up in the air for a few moments, before she turned over and jumped to the floor. *Very nice, dear ...* he applauded ... *very nice.* Dane was an unashamedly red-bloodied male.

Jesters in red and yellow motley came out next, sure enough the front rows were duly drenched and everyone laughed, including himself.

Nine dwarven acrobats wearing loose green tops and shorts came on next, accompanied by a lissom young female. He watched carefully, she was very good. Rather beautiful too, and very fetching in her white, one piece bodice and leggings. She was bare footed, sure footed, he watched eagerly as she cart wheeled and somersaulted, forwards and backwards. The dwarves too proved to be very athletic, making pyramids, the young woman thrown up to the very top of them. Dane thought she looked magnificent, her rich dark auburn hair flowing wildly around, a charming smile upon her face. There was appreciative applause.

The massive bear came on next, with his equally massive handler. It staggered around the ring kept on a chain. A dwarf played a jig on a flute and the bear was seen to step in time with the music. Or perhaps the music kept time with the bear? Dane looked carefully at the bear - he was sure it was drugged. He wondered how such a wild thing abided being kept in a cage all day?

... It probably felt like him.

Then it was the turn of the knife throwing act. To his surprise, the acrobatic young woman, now introduced as part of the 'Arne and Amber' team, walked into the ring. She still wore the white tight-fitting bodice but now a bright red leather jerkin was laced around her middle. Her beautiful eyes matched her name, deep amber eyes sparkled at the audience.

A table was brought to the centre of the room and a large circular board placed at the back, away from the crowd. The table seemed to be filled with knife belts, looked lethal. Dane held his breath, he didn't want her hurt. An older man, a dark, swarthy type, walked jauntily in, swaggering. He wore dark red leather trousers and the same red leather jerkin as the young woman, over a white linen shirt, his legs encased in those fancy boots from Sevillon with the big heels. He looked good and he knew it. He already had a row of daggers tucked in his belt. This must be 'Arne'.

He spent some minutes holding two daggers in his hands, twirling them, showing off, before casually throwing them at the board. They all hit the centre.

Round of applause.

The young woman began cart wheeling across the floor, back and forth, faster and faster. Every time her legs made a wide V shape in front of the board, he shot a dagger through them, landing in the bull. This went on for some time. Dane was sure she would get dizzy.

She retrieved the daggers and gave them to Arne, before being ordered to stand against the board, her arms and legs splayed. She arched an eyebrow at the crowd, as if to say, 'aye, aye, what's this?' Her smile was delicious, the crowd loved her.

Dane watched with heart in mouth ... *what if?* ...*what if?* He had his staff ready in case of mishaps.

One, after another after another dagger was thrown at her body. She barely blinked an eyelid and just looked amused. Her eyes twinkled. As she stood away, the daggers left a human, girlie shape behind her. The crowd applauded generously.

But what was now happening? The woman looked at the man, beckoned him slyly as if to kiss him, then pushed *him* against the knife board. She ran to the centre of the table, grabbed a knife belt and quickly fastened it around her tiny waist. Another second and daggers were in her hands, twirling and waving, except she somersaulted forwards several times, still holding them out before returning to the centre of the ring. There was an expectant roll of drums.

She smiled gleefully at the audience as she threw a dozen or so in rapid concurrence at the man splayed against the board. He stood with eyes widened in mock fear, but she was clearly as good as he.

When all were dispatched, Arne the knife thrower walked forward, leaving a man shape entwined around the woman shape on the board. She'd managed to throw in between his own daggers, not missed once. He took her hand, walked to the middle of the ring, they threw their arms up in the air and bowed.

The silent crowd erupted. Dane stood up applauding, the woman was magnificent. He blew her a kiss.

Arne and Amber walked off to thumping applause and stamping feet.

Everyone settled down for a few minutes respite, jugs of juice and small beer were brought around to be bought for a few pennies. Sticky blackcurrant sweets were offered to the children, these were actually free, but they smelled disgusting - that sickly sweet smell that always seems to be around unwashed children.

Then the bearded woman came on, a very large, ample bosomed lady, her shimmering cloak flowing around her. To their surprise she began to sing, accompanied by three dwarves on recorders, her voice was strong and sure, her range excellent. She sang a few of the more popular love songs of the day, and one rather difficult piece in a foreign language, possibly *Sevillain*. She was very good and the crowd were by now thoroughly happy and satisfied, another round of hearty applause was given.

More jesters and jugglers wandered on and the fire eater stood in the centre strutting his stuff.

Eventually they finished and the short-statured Longshanks took the floor. '*My Lords and Ladies*,' he began, then paused dramatically to peruse the audience carefully, before shaking his head in mock despair*, clearly not many lords and ladies here ...*

'. ... er, merchants, villeins, serfs, servants and children ... *village idi* ...' he stopped himself just in time, raised an eyebrow. The crowd caught his meaning and laughed ...*little bit edgy there, not nice to mock the afflicted.* 'We now present to you the act of the evening. Our major star will perform high rise feats of deadly danger and daring-do. I beg you, everyone, please be utterly quiet during the next few moments, we must not, under any circumstance disrupt her concentration.' He paused for effect. '*Her life may depend upon it ...*' adding another carefully contrived pause.

'I present you ... *Amber, Queen of the High Trapeze!*' He bent low then threw his arms dramatically up towards the top of the tent, gazing upwards.

There, high at the top of a rope ladder laughing down at them, was the beautiful young woman of earlier, waving and beaming at them all. She still wore the white leggings and bodice as before, the red leather jerkin and knife belt now discarded. Everyone gasped, including Dane. It was a long way up ...

... and a long way down with no safety net.

At the other side of the tent, high above them, her partner of earlier stood on a platform, holding a makeshift rope swing.

Amber too held a similar swing in front of her. There was a heart thumping drum roll as she took hold of the swing and gently rolled over into it. For some seconds she sat, beginning to swing to the rhythm of the drums, then gracefully she stood, took hold of the sides. She stretched and somersaulted and stood perfectly upside down on the swing, hands holding the side, then rolled over and down, her head hanging down, her hair, now in a ponytail waving at the audience. Again she swung, held on only by her legs wrapped over the swing, arms dangling. She pulled herself up, stood upright, swinging back and forth, back and forth.

The audience now saw that the swing on the other side was swinging in unison with hers, as Arne pushed it towards her she leapt surely across to the opposite swing. The crowd gasped and were hurriedly given an ominous *shh* by the ring master. She started twisting and turning over and over on the other swing while another member of the team shimmied up the rope ladder to collect the original rope swing and get its rhythm in time with hers. Again she swapped swings in mid air, a swirling pirouette between the swings. Several times she swapped swings, her pirouettes graceful and daring, seemingly oblivious to certain death below her if she fell.

Dane held his breath, he was held in wonder of her, she was marvellous. *Please don't fall ...*

Then came the climax of the evening, she seemed to spin faster and faster and suddenly she let go of the ropes she was holding, spinning ever upwards and over in mid air crouched like a ball, then a huge double somersault in a graceful arc, and came down grasping the ropes of the other swing, still turning over and over until her momentum slowed.

And not a thing beneath to catch her.

Eventually she came to a standstill and took one hand off the ropes, waving and laughing at everyone.

The whole crowd stood applauding. She was magnificent.

'What a woman!' thought Dane, *'what a glorious woman.'*

He didn't stay to watch any other acts after her performance. He grabbed his staff and dashed outside. He would meet this beauty tonight if he had to search the whole circus for her and stay up the entire night.

Dane was in love ... again. It occurred with regular monotony. But don't blame him, he was young and impressionable and full of life's fun. He ran through the falling darkness around the back of the tent, the Carnie's concealed entrance, saw her coming out, wrapping a small woollen cloak around her slender form.

He rushed to her side. 'Here, let me help you,' grabbing the cloak, pulling it to. 'Don't want to catch a cold in the chilly evening air after that.' It wasn't a particularly cold evening.

She stared at him.

'I'm a physician,' he explained, 'you're all toasty warm after your exertions, just the time to catch cold.' His piercing blue eyes smiled down at her. She was a tiny figure, small boned, lissom, lithe, svelte in fact. 'Watched you inside ... you were marvellous,' his voice breathy and eager.

'Well, er, *thank you,*' she replied. 'I need to get to my tent now and change, if you don't mind.'

Dane listened to her, ignoring her words as men often do, instead hearing the melodious sound of her voice. It was sweet and pleasant on his ear, honey rippling through nectar. 'Bet you're thirsty after all that exertion, why don't we go for a drink?' He didn't want to part so soon.

She paused, shaking her head, she got a lot of this after a show, men trying it on. 'I'm ... well ... it's late ...' she protested.

'Not so late, sun's barely set. C'mon, have a pint with me, you'll need something to relax you after that.' He wasn't giving up.

She looked at his eager face, decided it wasn't a bad face, kind eyes. Relented a little, the public were always after her when the performance was over, some even sent her flowers or sweetmeats. But his smile was kind too, and he was clearly a mage ... that staff.

'... um, well, OK, I still need to wash and change, but I could meet you at the ale tent later.'

He shook his head, 'you mean the stuff they serve here? It's pigswill, horrible stuff ... you want a *decent* pint.' He put on his most persuasive smile, 'no, the local alehouse serves a damn good pint, the landlord's from Erin,' as if that was explanation enough. He was determined to spend some time with her, he'd never seen anything like her. 'Good stuff - *puts hairs on your chest*.'

Amber stifled a laugh. 'Oh well, *put like that* ... just what a woman needs,' she commented wryly.

'You'll come then?' She heard the pleasure in his voice.

'Well, I have to let Longshanks know, he doesn't like me leaving the compound, but it's OK for an hour or so. I *could* do with a decent drink, it's thirsty work in the tent.' She watched the young man's eyes shine with delight.

Dane walked her to her tent, people were milling about now, the main tent emptying although a few hawkers were still plying their trade, people with children going home, young men and women wandering the stalls, grabbing food, drinking the overpriced, watered down ale, playing the rigged games of skill and chance in side-booths. 'I'm Dane,' he introduced himself.

She looked up, smiled. 'I'm Amber ...'

'I know .... I heard, I saw you ... you were magnificent - and so versatile - *wow*!' He couldn't praise her enough.

They reached her tent, she waved him away with one imperious hand. 'I need to wash and change, OK?'

Dane stood outside humming, waiting for her return. Eventually she came back out, not too long, bringing with her a pleasant smell of perfume, sweet and spicy, she smelled good.

'Mm-mm, that's nice,' he complimented her, 'I like that - let me see ... *clove, cinnamon, rose, violet and ... hmm, vanilla?*' he asked.

It was Amber's turn to be astonished. 'I'm not exactly sure,' she replied, 'how do you know?' The man intrigued her.

'I'm a herbalist as well, know every fragrance there is; need to know or I might put the wrong herb in a mixture if the light's bad. Don't want to kill anyone.' It was natural to him, been taught since a child by his mother.

Amber pointed out the black staff, 'you're a mage then?'

'Born and bred. Come from a long line of them.'

Amber smiled, intrigued now and nodded her head. 'Me too,' she replied. It had been a long time since she met a mage, they seemed to be a dying breed. This one looked livelier than most, they were usually book-worm types smelling of something dryly alchemical. He reminded her of home. A couple of drinks with him would be interesting, and she was certainly thirsty, the circus tent was too hot on a summer night.

They moved back towards the big tent, to the ringmaster. *'Hey Longshanks,'* the young woman shouted, 'going for a quick pint - thirsty now, just in the village. Won't be long.'

Longshanks ran over. He took out a pocket watch, looked at the time. 'One hour Amber, *no more*. We move on first thing, as you are aware and you need your beauty sleep.' It was clear he was in control, the young woman visibly stiffened. He turned to Dane, eyeing him up and down ... mostly *up*. 'Where are you taking her?'

'The Rosins, in the village, it's good beer there. I think she deserves one after all her efforts.'

'Bring her back soon then, *because* ...' he warned him, *'if you don't, I'll send my boys over* - OK? And ...' he added even more menacingly, 'watch out on the road - it's a typical Fae night.'

Dane nodded, then gave a quick salute, 'aye aye, sir, back within the hour.' *Fae night*, he thought to himself, *did he really still believe in those childhood tales?*

He grabbed Amber's hand, leading her to the village. When they were out of sight of the circus he spoke. 'Heavens, he keeps you on a leash, doesn't he?'

She laughed, 'I'm his prize performer. I'm worth a great deal of money to him.'

'Well, *I'm* going to have to work fast then, aren't I?' he quipped. 'One whole hour to down a pint or two, get to know you, sweet talk you, entice you up to my bedroom, make passionate love to you, then bring you back safely to your master.' He laughed, 'I think we need to walk a little quicker in that case ...'

Amber threw back her head and giggled, 'well, *you're* straight and to the point,' she replied.

They both quickened their pace.

The alehouse was getting full when they arrived, canny locals knew not to drink the circus rubbish. They made their way through solid but somewhat distressed tables and chairs to a quiet corner tucked away from the bar. It was growing darker now, small pewter and glass candle-lamps were lit, each table held a wavering glow, a few sconces lit the walls. Dane called over a maid, 'two pints of Gwyneth, 'Tilda,' waving a hand. The maid nodded, she liked Dane, went to the bar.

Amber unwrapped her cloak, Dane put his staff down against the wall.

'That's a nasty looking thing ...' she pointed out, 'you a necromancer or something?'

He shook his head, 'not actually mine, had a fight with the owner. He exploded mine. I pinched it off his dead body.'

'So you still beat him then, even without your staff? '

He nodded, 'yeah, he was a bastard, and he shouldn't have done that to my staff. *There's more ways of killing a cat* ... So I took his. It's pretty powerful, that's why I've kept hold of it, at least 'til I find something better. But I'm no necromancer, just plain old mage, a few healing powers and such.'

'I thought mages had to make their own staffs?'

Dane shook his head. 'No, we make wands, easy enough, but it takes a real craftsman to make a good staff. A mage charges the staff, according to his magic and some types of wood are better than others - like this one for necromancy as you said. I've yet to find my ideal staff.'

'Tilda brought the two beers, large earthenware mugs filled to the brim, thick creamy froth dripping down the sides. Dane looked at his with delight, pushed one over to Amber, 'there, drink that, just what you need.'

He picked up the beer-mug, toasted her. 'To you Amber, you're really something.' He took a deep drink, wiped a satisfied mouth, watched her. *'Well?* Good, isn't it?' The cornflower blue eyes beamed at her.

She had to admit, the rich dark beer with the thick creamy froth was damn good, damn strong too.

Dane watched her, looked her over. She'd changed from her skimpy outfit, now wore dark red leggings and a crisp cotton shirt with wide sleeves, looked like a man's, the sort they called a poet shirt A dark red leather jerkin was now laced tightly just under her bosom and she wore chestnut brown sturdy looking ankle boots on her feet. *Not exactly normal female attire.* But she suited it, or perhaps it suited her.

There was also a thick belt around her waist, bearing both short and long daggers.

'Coo,' he commented, 'wouldn't like to meet *you* down a dark alley,' pointing out her metal-ware.

'Never know who you're going to come across in these strange places,' she warned. She took a long gulp of the beer, finished it, shouted to "Tilda, 'can we have another two of these, they're great!' 'Tilda nodded, she'd been to the circus, had seen her, she too thought she was 'really something'. Soon came over with two more pints. Amber picked up her purse from her belt, made to pay.

Dane stopped her. 'Hey, no, my treat, you were marvellous, want to pay something back.'

'Tilda stopped them both, 'nay, *my* treat, you were wonderful miss, one of the best things I've ever seen. Those daggers and all that twirling! *Compliments of the house*!' She nudged Dane, laughed, 'trust *you* to get to her first.' He was known as a bit of a philanderer.

He looked over at 'Tilda in her barmaid's blouse. Normally his eyes were riveted on her, to put it mildly, *ample assets*. Couldn't help it, male hard-wired to such things. Tonight though, he glanced instead at the warm and sparkling female sitting across from him. She didn't wear low-cut clothing, her garb was more like a man's and the knife belt looked like she'd use it if necessary. There didn't seem to be a comparison, yet, she *glowed*.

They both thanked 'Tilda, carried on talking, Dane now grinning at Amber over the top of his beer mug. Like her, his eyes sparkled. He sat back, took an appreciative sip of the beer. 'So, where are you from?' he asked. 'Tell me about yourself.'

She put her head on one side, seemed to study him, '*you first* ...'

Dane looked surprised, women weren't usually curious about his past, preferred to talk about themselves, their sisters, their friends, the latest fashions and did he know there was a barn dance in Old Greendick's barn next Saturday? He appreciated her interest.

'Not much to tell, been on the road since I was eighteen, I'm twenty three. Spent my time doing odd jobs, gaining a little cash, moving on, you know, looking for fame and fortune.' He noticed she was watching him closely, bright open eyes looking into his. 'Do you know you have gold flecks in your beautiful eyes?' he asked.

She looked around, took a kerchief from her bag, wiped her eyes. 'Are they OK now?' she was quite sincere.

He shook his head laughing, 'I just meant they are beautiful, they shine, you're so full of life.'

She sat forward, ignoring the obvious flattery, '*you were saying*, tell me, I'm interested.' She actually looked like she was.

'Hmm, OK. For my sins I live here at the moment, work for a miserable quack in the village. At least his store of medicines has improved since I've been making them, as I said I'm a physician, with herbal as well as mage skills. I'm originally from the Isle of Glasse, nice quiet, peaceful place. *At least it was.*'

She looked up in surprise, she'd heard a little about the island's fateful history. 'Tell me ...' she questioned.

For a few moments he sat back in his chair, remembering that day, that *last* day ... .

*

'I'll be off then, mum,' he said, walking out of the small manor house with his fishing tackle in hand, grabbing a few apples and plums from the orchard. It was a beautiful morning, warm and sunny, a gentle wind in the air. Dane's mum looked pretty as usual, her tiny form always seemed to be wrapped in what looked like gossamer leaves, apple coloured today, floating in the breeze. She shimmied down from the tree she was tending, a few branches needed cutting or healing. 'What are you doing, mum?' He looked down at her, he was much taller than his mum. 'Don't hurt yourself, I could have done that for you.' He'd inherited his dryad mother's healing powers.

She just laughed. 'I've spent more time up trees than you've had breakfasts, my boy,' smiling up into his face. 'If you're going fishing, you'll need some lunch with you. Come back into the house for a moment.'

He followed her back into the big kitchen, aromatic with the smell of herbs and fresh bread. She began cutting a large loaf, spread butter and cheese generously. 'There's some for Alven too, and some currant cakes.' She piled them with the plums and apples into a leather bag, 'and here ...' she handed him a small bottle. 'Keep you warm out at sea - don't go too far today - it will be choppy further out, I'm telling you, I don't like the look of it.' He promised her they wouldn't, she knew weather-lore extremely well. He gave her a kiss for the food, looked at the bottle: 'Llanetha's Plum Brandy', home-made, *damn good stuff.* He gave her another kiss.

'Now that *will* keep us warm, mum, lovely.' Blessed woman thought of everything.

'What are you hoping for?' She meant the fish.

'Ah, a few mackerel will do, have them for tea tonight.'

'Mm mm, lovely, but you couldn't catch a nice bit of plaice or haddock for me could you? I find mackerel a bit strong flavoured.' Beautiful green eyes smiled into his.

'I'll tell you what mum, I'll send an order down with my line shall I?' he chuckled. 'I'll do my best.' He bent to kiss her again. She smelled of honeysuckle and sandalwood, always some sweet perfume on her. He picked up his staff from the corner. If the fish wouldn't bite, he'd cheat a little, shoot a bit of electrum down.

As he left the garden, his mum clambered back up the oak tree in the centre, but he saw his father come out of the house. For one moment he stopped, watching them, his dad wandered under the tree, his strong mage arms held out. Heard him say, 'Hey, Llanetha honey, come down, darling, come on, *the house is empty* .... jump ... I'll catch you!'

Dane turned away to go, smiling. He knew they always waited for their grown up son to leave for the day, wanted a bit of privacy. It was probably time he moved out, but he didn't really feel ready yet. He chuckled to himself, wondering if they knew about the couple of wenches in the village who kept a warm bed for him too?

He ran up the hill to meet his mate, Alven. 'Come on man, the gulls are calling. Have you got the cider? he shouted cheerily to him, as they wandered to the cove where they kept a small sail-boat.

*

Amber straightened up, 'haven't the Adammites taken it over? It's some kind of religious male monastery now isn't it?'

'Yeah, HQ for their military too. *Rotten bastards.*' He took a very large gulp of beer, wiped the sweet foam from his mouth. It was good beer but that froth got everywhere, he always ended up with a milky moustache. 'They overran my home, destroyed it. I wasn't there. I'd gone to see a friend up the hill, been fishing for the day. I saw them leaving when we came back - they were going over the island like locusts. Took everyone by surprise. They were on horseback and we were on foot. By the time we reached my parent's house they'd gone and it was too late. My father was a mage and my mother a dryad priestess, it couldn't have been easy, he was pretty powerful. The house was burning, I managed to get my mother outside, too late for my father, but he must have been dead before they torched the house. He was pretty good with ice magic - he was an *elementalist* - so it couldn't have burned otherwise.

My little mother had been raped and beaten, I mean, she was a dryad, for goodness' sake! She was tiny, delicate, they didn't give a damn. I did what I could for her, but she died that night, they'd really hurt her internally, beyond my abilities, at least at that time. The loss of my father too, I think it harmed her dryad soul, affected her mortally. I buried her under the one tree left standing - it's hard to burn down an oak - and I searched the ruins for whatever I could. I put my father's burnt remains beside her.'

He stopped for another swig of ale, then another. It was hard to talk like this, and he didn't really know why he was telling her. Nights out with wenches were usually just for a bit of fun and they told jokes and silly stories all evening until bed. But he carried on, she *had* asked. He saw she was watching him intently.

'There was little to find that wasn't burnt, but I had my staff with me and a good cloak, plus my fishing tackle. I spent the next couple of weeks hiding from the bastards, until I could get passage to the mainland. It was no good me trying to get revenge on them - there were too many, too well armed, it would have been suicide. I didn't see my mate again, I looked for him at the cove where we kept a small boat, but he and it had gone. I didn't blame him, Merrie only knows what he'd faced when he got home. This wasn't any kind of normal situation, it was life or death.

I spoke to a few people who were left alive on the island, we were all running, hiding, trying to get away. These Adammites, as we learnt they called themselves, hated us all. The island once was a haven for mages and one of the last true dryad forests in the whole of Mer'edrynn. They'd deliberately targeted us, a peaceful, quiet, nature loving people. Kind people - I can vouch for that. It was over before we knew what hit us and there was no possible way of retaliating.

All gone. Everywhere I went where they had been ... completely destroyed ... burnt bodies everywhere.

I suppose it's a lesson in war ... attack quickly while your enemy is unaware ... before the enemy even realises there's an enemy.'

That's about it really, a few of us stuck together and hunted until we found a boat, made for the coast of Draconia, been bumming around since then. No one did anything about the Adammites and they seem to have kept the island as their own. They've expanded somewhat, or so I'm told. I've heard of atrocities down in Elvinhaeme, true or not, I've no idea.'

'Any idea who they are?' Amber interrupted him.

'Just people,' he answered, shrugging his shoulders. 'People like you and me, but we don't want to go around murdering everyone.' He continued his tale. 'I went north, Draconia not exactly being a hospitable place, looking for a way to make a living, using what skills I have. I learnt elemental magic from my father and herbalism and medicine from my mother, the sum total of my education. Learnt a bit since, of course. I've been here a couple of years, working for the local so-called remedian, but he's crap. I have a little room upstairs here, pretty cheap.' He stopped and took a goodly drink, looked at her, 'go on, *your turn now* ...'

The tavern hummed around them, beginning to be filled with pipe-leaf smoke as people lit up. It was a warm evening, many bodies squashed together and the fire banked up well, roaring in the corner, a little stifling. A hearth-fire stayed in all year, bad luck to let the oak log die out. The tables were rough deal and the floor was covered in sawdust, but the atmosphere was friendly. A young man with a fiddle stood to play, his multicoloured scarf gave him a harlequin air.

Amber drained her mug, proffered it to Dane. 'Can we have more beer?' He nodded, *surely*. More was brought. She sighed and studied for a while.

Eventually, 'I'm truly sorry for what happened to your folks. But, *Holy Merrie*, that's like looking into a mirror, damn close to my own story. Actually, *both* my parents were mages. It happened, let's see, five years ago. I was sixteen, my sister Anaïs, fourteen. She too was a mage, I was the disappointing, normal one. Small village, much like this, not that far away either, just nearer Shirewood.

Big raid by the Alderfolk, you know, the wild people who live in the northern reaches of Shirewood, sort of cousins to the Bregantines. I think some of them are Outlaws too, or perhaps they accept outlaws into their society. They came every now and again to steal a few women, but I think they'd also had a bad winter. I remember how harsh it had been, so much snow. I think they were starving, but that's no excuse.

My parents were at the forefront of the defence, they worked truly hard, but, same as your parents, just too many Alderfolk. They have some mage powers too, brought a special *Aldervetch* with them, she was casting spells as quickly as my parents could dispel them. They managed to kill everyone in the village apart from young girls. My parents were the last to go down, they'd simply run out of *mana*, they had nothing left. They did their best to protect me and my sister, but we were eventually taken. The last thing I saw was my parents with about a dozen arrows each in them. The Alderfolk took everything of value from our homes and every young female in the village.'

'They sound as mindless as the Adammites. But, carry on, I'm interrupting you.' Dane watched her closely, she was clearly a kindred spirit.

She heaved a long sigh and drank hard. 'I don't wish to talk about the year I was with them, deep in the forest of Shirewood. After a month or two I managed to help my sister get away - I haven't seen her since - and they, *well*, they punished me for it. I still bear scars on my back and legs. I vowed to escape, managing one night in spring, some months later. I eventually found a good road and followed it, but believe me, I was starving, I'd no hunting skills at the time, although I can shoot a bow reasonably well now, plus dagger skills of course.' She stopped to briefly stare at Dane. 'Longshanks Circus came along one night and literally picked me up and took me off with them. They looked after me a while, they're not that bad as people go. But I'm now in hock to them, or so they say. The cost of feeding me, training me and looking after me when I had no skills ...' she explained. 'Now I'm trying to pay off that debt.' She looked down sadly, drained her glass. More ale was brought.

Dane took her hand. 'I'm truly sorry, I know where you're coming from. I too know how bad life can be on the road, and *I* can take care of myself. Why don't you just leave - you're certainly strong enough now?'

'No, can't face the open road by myself, not after last time - better 'the devil you know' and all that ...' she replied hastily. She looked around at the bustling alehouse. 'When does this place close, no one seems to be leaving?'

'It's a party night, your circus is in town. The landlord'll close when he runs out of ale.' He sat back on the hard wooden settle. 'So both your parents were mages, that's interesting. Don't you have any mage powers at all?'

She shook her head, 'no, not a mage bone in my body.'

Dane chuckled to himself, she'd walked into that one. *Now there was something he could remedy any time ...* She saw him laughing, raised her eyebrows, and her beautiful eyes twinkled as she realised what she'd said. She gave him the *'oh, you men!'* look.

He laughed back as their eyes met, sparkling. The inn was crowded now, getting too crowded, he could hardly hear her voice above the noise. 'We could go up to my room, it's quieter up there,' he offered.

She laughed, 'you're a cool one Dane, I'll say that for you. Some other time, I have to get back now I'm afraid.'

Yes, it had grown dark, he hadn't realised time had gone by so quickly. Her curfew was close and he didn't really like that Longshanks fellow. It seemed a shame to end the evening so soon, but he didn't want her in trouble because of him. 'That Longshanks seems a bit of a tyrant,' he suggested.

She nodded, Longshanks was quite a disciplinarian when he wanted to be. 'Yes, he'll will have a fit if I'm not back. He ... he can be quite stern.' She lowered her voice conspiratorially. 'Actually, I'd leave if I could, but I'm stuck with them, don't know where to go anyway,' she confided. 'Owe them too much, they'll send people after me, they've done it with others. They seem to be part of a large group of travellers, Rovers or Tsigani or something. Someday I'll pay my way out and will be able to leave without spending every day looking over my shoulder for dwarven hit men or Tsigani thugs.'

She sighed heavily. Whatever she felt inside, it certainly wasn't shown during her performances. She got up to go, kissed Dane on the cheek, added her beautiful smile. 'Thanks mage, been a pleasant evening, I like you, I truly do, but need to get back now. Come over to Grimmpool, watch our performance there, it's usually a long stay.' Amber eyes beamed down at him, her face held a radiance of its own.

'I'll walk you back ...' he didn't really want her to go, she was lovely, in every way. It was rare he met anyone who also had mage blood in them, there was a kinship there, he felt it. His mage senses always felt people's emotions, an inner skill. Sitting next to Amber was like bathing in sunshine.

'No, I'm fine, it's not far,' her voice firm, 'Don't worry, I can take care of myself.'

Dane looked at the well-equipped knife belt and believed her. She squeezed her way through the overcrowded bar. Men watched her admiringly, women weren't too sure, some cast disapproving looks at her, whether it was because of what she wore, or her itinerant lifestyle, is uncertain.

Dane felt empty when she'd gone, it had been too short a time with her. He wondered why he'd opened up so much, told her about his home island, his past? He'd obviously said too much, perhaps come on too strong, he should have been more light hearted, joked more. *Oh well, ships that pass in the night ...*

But it *had* been a good night, she was lovely ... and such sweet lips, 'kissable lips,' he decided, yet there hadn't been one decent kiss. Too late now. 'You messed it up, Dane,' he thought as he picked up his staff and made his way through the bar up to his small attic room. 'You met her, you had your chance, and now she's gone.'

He felt as if a light had been switched off.

He walked up narrow, winding stairs, past rooms with good solid doors where better off guests could stay, up yet more winding stairs that whispered with age, and along a dark stuffy corridor, opening a door at the end. Up a rickety set of steep steps he went, the attic floor, before stopping at a decidedly dilapidated door. He fiddled for a key, gave the door a slight kick as it stuck in the frame.

It was dark in the room, lit only by the bright moon outside. It was fresher in here than the stuffy bar, a little chilly now, and he closed the window he had left slightly open, it often smelled damp and musty otherwise. He sat on the bed and started to remove his boots when he heard a commotion outside.

'What the hell's that?' He went to the window, opened it a little, looked outside from his rooftop viewpoint.

'*Weird*,' he said to himself, 'there's a load of shouting outside, and something's burning in the distance. What the hell is all the screaming about?' He closed the window, curious now, and went back down to the bar to find out if anyone knew. In fact, everyone in the bar was talking about it, no one was leaving, more and more people were squeezing in by the moment. He soon understood what the commotion was for; the bear had escaped, had knocked over the lamps in the circus tent. The tent was on fire, several people had died, the flames huge and overpowering, rapidly spreading across the circus field. It seemed the bear was last seen making for the village and Drowman, his supposed keeper, was flat out, his breath reeking of usquebae. There were village archers out there now, along with some of the dwarves, trying to find the bear before he killed anyone else.

Dane had one thought ... *Amber!*

She was out there alone. What had happened to her, had she arrived back at the circus, was she still on her way, what about the bear? Dane needed no prompting. He ran back upstairs, grabbed his magic staff and dashed out via the quieter rear door of the inn, the bar too crowded to squeeze through.

He ran to the Old Field, took short cuts, hopping over hedges and fences, hoping to get there before her. The fiery remains of the circus were bright in the sky, it's oiled canvas tent quickly turning a small lamp fire to conflagration.

He stopped as he neared the Old Field, where was she? There was so much smoke, terrible flames, everything crackled as it burnt, the smell of burning overpowering, the air thick with the dreadful smell he hated, charred bodies, mixed with a linseed oil smell from the tent. Smoke ... far too much smoke. Everyone was shouting, a cacophony of voices.

He jumped over the dry-stone wall, ran towards dwarves hovering near the flames.

'Have you seen Amber?' The reply was negative. 'Anything I can help with?' seeing nothing but blackened bodies. They shook their heads, *get away*, they told him, *it's hopeless*.

He wandered anyway, trying to keep out of the smoke and the flames. Saw someone on the floor too close to the burning tent, pulled him to safety, checked him over and sent healing light into the smoke-filled lungs. Moved on to help another who was coughing, again cleared the lungs. Found a young woman sobbing, clutching some unidentifiable charred remains. He pulled her away from the fire, checked her over, soothed her burnt arms and hands. Someone was crying for help, still in the flames, he cooled the air magically as he began coughing himself, an air bubble around his head and body, he struggled his way to an unconscious dwarf trapped under a wooden beam. He lifted it with mage hands then dragged out the solid muscular body. The dwarf was fine, his iron lungs capable of combating the smoke, he woke and smiled wanly at Dane.

Dane moved on, sent magical ice from his staff over a fiery body, but no, useless, body too far gone. Looked around, too many dead bodies, blackened and charred, no help magical or otherwise was bringing them back. Still no Amber, where was she? How could you find anyone in this smoke?

He began to be very, very anxious.

He began coughing again, the smoke was so thick. He wondered how the dwarves could take it, but they were strong, their bodies probably matched Longshank's granite face. For a few moments he held another magic sphere around him, breathed easier, continued looking, but there was no one left that needed aid. The fire had consumed everything in its path. He saw a few dwarves and circus folk quickly moving horses and wagons down to the far end of the field away from the flames, desperately trying to salvage what they could. He helped carry some equipment down, asked about the young gymnast. None had seen Amber. He began to panic.

This shouldn't be, he had just met her and she was so full of life. He walked around the edge of the field, away from the smoke, he felt dizzy, took in deep gulps of air.

Eventually he found her, she'd seen the flames, wondered what it was, made her way to the Old Field, had to detour as she saw the bear wandering the lanes. She had collapsed in a corner of the field trying to get in to help, overcome by smoke.

He picked her up, carried her away until he found a quiet spot, the air fresher around them. Quickly he cleansed her lungs, cleared passageways. She woke, took a deep breath then made as if she would run back to the flaming field.

'I have to help,' she insisted.

'No good, love,' he explained, holding on to her. 'I've been in there. Nothing and no one left to help, I checked, the dwarves have shifted what they can and anything else has had it. You can't get close. Wait until tomorrow.'

For a few moments she stood watching the flames across the fields. 'That's my life just gone up in smoke,' shaking her head sorrowfully. 'And my friends ...' .

'But *you* still exist, that's what counts,' Dane replied. She nodded, *true*.

He began to lead her back to the village. 'C'mon, come away for now, that bear's still on the loose, you can come back to the inn until they find him. It's not safe out here for you, and besides, there's nothing you can do, it will die itself out by morning, once everything flammable has gone.' A few buckets of water from the river would do nothing, even his own skill of ice magic couldn't do anything against so big a fire. It would need a dozen elementalists and there were few mages these days. Besides, that's why they used the Old Field, the ancient dry-stone wall around it would stop the fire spreading.

Amber reluctantly followed Dane, she was shaking now, clearly in shock, the fire crackling behind them. They avoided the main street, too much commotion going on, the bear no doubt. Back through the rear of the inn, he led her up rickety stairs to the quietness of his room. Took her cloak from her, placing it over his own on the wooden peg behind the door.

'Stay here, you'll be safe, you can go back tomorrow when it's died down. I'll make a drink, that smoke was choking.' She nodded, anything, it didn't really matter, she felt stunned by it all. Life turned upside down - *again.*

He popped downstairs, got a jug of water, placed it on the small table. Went to a small shelf where he picked up a couple of mugs.

'Make yourself at home, such as it is.' His mage fingers spat a little fire to light the candle on the table, then heated the water jug to boiling in the same fashion.

Amber briefly smiled at the memory of a father who used to do just the same thing to light candles or fires, her mother's abilities quite different. She took off her weapon's belt and left it on the table, perching herself on the edge of the bed, there being no chairs. It was quite high, her legs swung at the bottom, not quite reaching the floor. Instead she kicked off her boots tucked her feet under her, trying to relax. Dane could see how tense she was. He knew exactly how it felt when people you loved and everything you owned had just gone up in flames. Shock didn't express it.

And this was the second time in her life it had happened.

'Would you like herbal tea?' We could do with something after that. You OK?'

She shrugged, *probably*, mages always had herbal stuff, you drank it, you smoked it, often pretty good. 'Why not?' she said, realising she was shaking.

He took down a jar from the small shelf, sniffed the contents, the herbs smelled clean and fresh. Dane took some dried leaves and a handful of crushed herbs, made a refreshing brew, added a few extras to the mix.

'Here, drink this, it'll ease your throat after that smoke, calm you down a little.' He poured himself a mug of the brew, took a deep drink, the room beginning to smell sweet and fresh from the aroma.

'Mm mm, *nice*,' she commented, taking in the heady scent, 'similar to something the dwarves drink sometimes.' Dane saw a tear form in her eye, watched as she sipped, she was still shaking. She took another long drink. 'Don't really know what I'm going to do now, damn mess out there ...' staring into space. Her eyes held a glazed look.

Dane was concerned, the herbs shouldn't take effect that quickly, besides, they were pretty mild. They were meant to calm her, not knock her out.

'Let me check you over, you're obviously in shock.' He wondered if she'd hurt herself when she collapsed, he'd only cleared the lungs?

She shrugged, life had just handed out another miserable blow to her. She tried, dammit, she tried. Every day she tried to keep afloat, to give more than she took, to live as the Lady Merrie asked. *To give of her best.* But it was hard and getting harder all the time. 'Whatever,' she replied.

He stood in front of her and closed his eyes for a moment, steadying himself, allowing his healing abilities to fully come to the fore before going magically inside her. He sent calming waves into her, relieved to note there was no more smoke damage.

What the hell ...? he thought as he began his more thorough search in her. He'd seen a few bruises on her arms, no doubt from the trapeze training, but he immediately understood there was more, much more than just a few bumps. He stood back, disturbed at what his mage senses had felt.

He lit a couple more candles, placed them by the bed, unfastened her shirt cuffs and rolled the sleeves back. There were marks of old bruises throughout. He went in deeper, scars inside and out, bruises on legs and body, spine not good either, stretched too far.

Up on that trapeze, she was probably in agony. He was confused.

'Was this what the Alderfolk did to you? Or, has it been since?' He'd been expecting a few old scars, perhaps some bumps and bruises from the trapeze practice, not this.

She nodded, 'Both really, the dwarves have their own system of teaching too, and Arne is a hard taskmaster - not so great, but it gets results. Let's call it the hard-knocks school of training. Longshanks wants us to perform beyond our capabilities. When I go back he and Arne will have it in for me, told you, I'm the prize performer and they'll both be frantic. Let's say that Arne isn't the most understanding guy in the world ... . Trapeze might be gone, but there's still dagger play and the tumbling routines with the dwarves. We'll just have to perform in the open air for a while.' She seemed quite matter-of-fact about it.

Dane looked at the lithe figure before him. A petite woman, one a man should be gentle with, but she seemed to have only known brutes. It was wrong, very wrong. Why hadn't she left before now? She was clearly strong enough and tough enough to look after herself now, so why accept this method of discipline? What kind of hold did they have on her? Did she take all this just to have a miserable job, a home of sorts? It wasn't worth it.

And she was ready to go back to a broken down circus for more beatings?

It was against everything he believed in, everything he had been taught. To do that to such a talented and beautiful young woman? To hurt her like that, and still she showed the world a face beaming with joy? What kind of resources were in her?

Something turned inside him ... something fundamental. This wasn't acceptable ... and besides, there nothing for her to go back to.

'You're not going back. These are serious scars, you've been hurt badly. I can tell some of these are recent. I don't care what you say, I don't want you to go back to those people. Anyway, there's no circus left.'

She rolled down the sleeves, 'it's OK mage, I know you mean well, you're being kind. Besides, they need me now more than ever, it would be unfair of me to leave. But I can look after myself.'

'Oh really?' Dane scoffed, 'Yet you allow them to beat you? Anyway, I'm not being kind, *professional opinion.* You shouldn't be treated like this. It's time you took stock, actually did take care of yourself.' He was angry at the circus, the Alderfolk and mostly at Amber for allowing this.

Amber studied him, sighed, 'not much I can do about it.' She needed the job, some protection on the road, towns and cities might be safe, but roads were damn dangerous. Anyway, there wasn't much chance of a decent job in a city for a knife-wielding female acrobat. She'd lived outside the normal world - whatever that meant - for too long.

Dane continued, 'besides, if you left yourself in my hands, I can rid you of not just the bruises but most of your scars and there's internal damage too. One or two scars are very deep and very old - you must have bled for days. I won't ask what they used on you, I take it that was the Alderfolk. But I can lessen them too.'

Amber gave a short laugh. 'Oh, what's the point, they'll only be back in a few weeks, especially now. Everyone will be short tempered after this. If you'll just heal the bruising, that would be of help.'

He rounded on her, *this wasn't right,* his mage hackles rising. She couldn't go on like this. He had to do something about it, preferably before someone went too far.

'Why do they beat you - and don't deny it - I can see they do.' he couldn't understand why she allowed it.

'It's just a way of teaching; hard, but it works. Better than Arne throwing a dagger in me, or me falling from the high trapeze. Besides, they're temperamental folk, and there's more of them than me. But it's been a home, of sorts, and I've also had a few friends.'

'Yeah, where were your friends when the beating started?'

Amber just shrugged. 'I suppose ... I suppose I feel it's all worth it when I'm up there on the trapeze and the audience is applauding.' Nevertheless, she knew it couldn't continue, Longshanks pushed them more and more, and she was beginning to wonder if she could keep it up?

He thought - very briefly - on his next move. She had to be persuaded somehow, she had to leave the circus, she needed healing and fast. Some of that damage would soon be permanent and her circus career would be over anyway. There was only one option if he was to help her - and he did wish to help her. Dane understood he sympathised with her but was also attracted to her in many ways. He had no ties here, nothing of any worth, no one would really miss him, and that job with the quack just about covered his rent and beer money. He hadn't really cared, it was just somewhere to stay and something to do. But this young woman touched him, she didn't deserve this.

He'd known her - what, a few hours? Despite the fire, they were damn good hours!

He certainly didn't want to lose her, he knew that when he ran through the village to the inferno that was once the big circus tent. He made up his mind with unambiguous finality, all his mage senses tingling ...

... and decided to take a chance - make a new start - if *she* would. If *he could persuade her* ...

Fate dangled on its hyper-elusive thread. He took a deep breath.

'Look, Amber, you have some wonderful skills, you're quite formidable with those daggers. You probably could make it on your own now. But there's no need to face the world alone.

Leave the bastards, leave them and ...,' he paused, '*come with me.*' The words came out unprompted, surprising himself, but he felt absolutely certain about what he was saying. 'I've no plans, nowhere special I'm going. But I guarantee, life on the road with me will be twenty times better than the life you have now.'

He was earnest, probably never been more so. He felt his heart beating heavily, his mage blood rising. She shook her head, surprised at his offer. 'Look, I believe you are in more danger by *staying* with them,' he told her. They would truly hurt her eventually, he was sure of it, she couldn't take much more.

She shook her head, it was absurd, '*no can do* mage, not letting you in for it.'

'I can take care of myself. So can you, I saw that tonight - *let them try*! You've grown since they picked you up, you've moved on. Why not do it properly? Now's your chance. We'd make quite a formidable pair,' he laughed at the thought. It was a good thought, he realised, *exciting.*

She laughed too. 'Nice thought, mage, but no.'

'*Why ... am I so repugnant to you?*' He was indignant now.

She smiled up into his face, warm eyes caressing him. 'You're not in the least, you're one of the nicest people I've ever met, and I think you look good too.' She gently touched his arm. 'It's just ... you'll get hurt. Believe me, they wouldn't give up, they'd hound me and probably break me ... you too, I told you, they're part of a large group. They all help each other. I would have broken their trust and I still owe them money. They won't forgive that,' her bright eyes pleading with him. 'They're good enough people, can be kind hearted, but they're rough and ready and they have long memories. They instinctively lash out, it's just their way.' She was trying to make excuses for the inexcusable.

Dane watched her expressive face, heard the concern in her soft voice, realised he didn't want her to leave - not for the danger he believed she was in - but simply for herself. He looked down into meltingly beautiful amber eyes, darkened now by dim candlelight, watched her 'kissable lips' as he put it, speak kindly to him. Put his head down, took hers in his hands, gently kissed her. She didn't pull away. It was a sweet kiss, turning into a passionate one as she responded to him. She had just placed her hands on his shoulders and he was feverishly kissing her neck when they heard more screaming and shouting from outside. He wondered what was happening now?

Amber hurried over to the window. Poked her head out, couldn't quite see everything, so opened it further and climbed out on to the roof. Sure-footedly she crept down to a better viewpoint, watched a while then came back. There was a hysterical giggle in her voice.

'I'm sorry to find it funny, but they're running all over your village after the bear. He and a line of dwarves are racing back and forth up the High street, first one way, then the next. It just needs some daft music playing along. They'll get him now, he's escaped before, although I think your villagers might get to him first, there are some archers out there too. He's pretty old and decrepit, been stuck in that cage for years, poor sod.'

She stood in thought, weighing and considering options, then seemed to make up her mind. Picked up the jug and poured herself another mug full, took a long drink before passing it to Dane. He accepted the brew from her, drank from the mug where her lips had pressed it. She seemed a little more composed than earlier.

'Strange really, just as I've met you. I have listened to what you said, it was very good of you. What a weird coincidence ...' Again she paused, wondering on events.

She sipped the brew, they passed it back and forth, a quiet companionship.

'I think I'll take it as a sign,' she finally decided, 'You're a kind man, Dane, you had no need to dash up to the circus to find me, yet you did. By rights I should be back in my own little tent now, I was tired when I finished my routine, I would have had a quick wash and turned in, but you came along .and we went to the village instead. I could have been burnt to death or killed by the bear. There's also not much circus left. With any luck,' she mused, '*they'll think I'm dead too in the fire.*' She looked at Dane, searching his face. 'No one saw me up there, it was too thick with smoke.

I don't actually want to carry on with the circus if I needn't. I think I like your idea, at least it's a new path to take. You don't seem a bad type, and as I said, I can't face the road by myself. It's - well - it's not good on the open road as a lone woman, believe me, I know. When all said and done, it's not good for *any* person alone on the roads.' For a moment she stopped, a final evaluation of possibilities, before concluding. 'I'll stay with you overnight if that's OK, I'm afraid I've nowhere else to go. As for tomorrow ... who knows?'

She stared him in the eye, she was taking a chance and she wanted an honest answer.

Dane responded quickly. 'You're welcome to stay as long as you wish. I don't like what's been happening to you. It makes all my mage hackles rise.'

Amber smiled briefly, taking note of the unambiguous honesty of his eyes, then went over to the little washstand, took a wash, rubbed her teeth with some minty mixture he'd left on the side. 'Mm mm, that's nice,' she commented, 'you're quite civilised aren't you? What's in this?'

'A little powdered oak bark and mint, mixed in a mineral solution, good for the teeth and gums, told you I was a herbalist. I make more stuff than just relaxing brews.'

She sat back on the bed, suddenly exhausted. 'I'm so tired; feel pretty much knocked out now. I like you Dane, I truly do, but I just really want to sleep, if that's OK?' She watched his eyes again, you could tell so much about a man from his eyes. Dane's blue eyes were kind, but they held a firmness in them also that she liked.

Dane nodded, she was clearly exhausted and obviously still in shock. The circus, at least as it stood, was over, *kaput*, no matter what she thought. He moved over so she could get in the bed, noting once more the scars. Got up and made sure the door was locked. Realised he was shaking slightly. Took down his jar of herbs and leafroll, not too much, wrapped and rolled them, the stuff was good for smoking too and right now he could do with something strong. Stood by the open window smoking a while, staring at her already sleeping form. Eventually he snuffed out the remains of the leafroll into a small tin on the table before blowing out all the candles, careful to make sure they were all out - another fire wouldn't be a good idea. He quickly undressed down to breeches, then climbed in the bed. He'd have slept on the floor, but there wasn't much floor to sleep on, not his size anyway.

She'd taken him at his word, she clearly trusted him. He wouldn't take advantage of her, vulnerable in her sleep. Trust was something that needed to be forged - and he knew he wanted to keep her trust.

For a few moments he mused on the evening, realising destiny had just taken him in hand and was building a new future for him - whatever it might be. As he'd said earlier, *weird* really.

He didn't know what to make of it, but if it held this beauty, sleeping now by his side, he was more than willing to take the chance.

Chapter 2

Much further south-west, at Westlea, Colonel Grey surveyed his troops with pride. Just a few weeks after the taking of Hollyporth, they had marched down to Westlea, another coastal town, taken it with the same ease.

They had performed well, nay, better than expected. They'd kept their discipline, adhered to the principles and remained staunch as they set about the sacking of Westlea. Not that there was much opposition, elves were pathetic creatures, ripe for the taking, his Master Von Adamm had said it would be so. At the rate they were going, Elvinhaeme would be theirs within months.

He wondered how they had kept their lands for so long? Clearly the human overlords of Westerling, Segantium or Mercantia were too soft. They surely could have taken Floriénne years ago. Probably tricky though, that Foraes Dair was difficult further in, and the inhabited region was well patrolled. One never knew where one was with the tricksy elves of Floriénne, a foppish set of elves, *should be put down*, but he knew them to be excellent archers and swordsmen.

Best way was probably to smoke them out, set fire to the forest, only trouble with that was it could take half the country with it and the wood was needed for ships, ballistae, trebuchets, carts and carriages and all the other paraphernalia of war. Oakleigh forest should be taken next, clear out those wood elves and the elder races, silly little dryads and naiads, fawns and the like. *Bloody parasites, using resources meant for humans, should have been destroyed centuries ago.*

In the meantime, settle in here, wait for more Adammites to arrive by boat, make the move on Belcast'el when the time was ripe, Von Adamm would know.

He took out his 'Commentaries and Considerations on the Management of Men' booklet, more of Mordecai Von Adamm's writings, given only to high ranking officers. By the Merrie - oh, no, we don't say that any more - by the Flame, he could write stirring stuff, got you in the stomach and the balls. Made such sense too. You didn't even need to read all of it, certain passages stood out, they were underlined for quick reference.

He stood ramrod straight in front of the assembled troops.

'You have done well, men. For the last few weeks you have performed excellently, according to both your training and to the overall plan, you kept your heads and acted as true Adammites. We have now taken the two most important ports in Elvinhaeme, allowing for uninterrupted entry for our own troops and staff from the Isle of Glasse. You have taken the next steps towards our ultimate goal, absolute control of Mer'edrynn and the complete annihilation of the lesser races, the parasites who have enjoyed the fruits of our world for far too long. Unfortunately we require the use of these underlings for some time, we require servants for our needs during these war years. Eventually our women will produce the necessary numbers, but that is in years to come. ' He briefly stopped talking, watching the eyes of the men in front of him, some looked proud, some anxious, a little unsure of what they had just achieved.

'You and I came from the great cities of Mer'edrynn, we are the pioneers, the forerunners of the Adammites, the sole and rightful owners of this beautiful land. Von Adamm teaches us the way ahead, he tells us to take it by any means possible, it belongs to you and to me, and the fruits thereof are rightly ours. We must continue to swell our numbers by steering men's hearts and minds to our cause, as well as ensuring our future growth. For every Adammite male who took part in the glorious victories at Hollyporth and here at Westlea, I will assign two human females for reproduction and as many elves as required for your personal use.

Always remember, we are the supreme species, the world belongs to *us*. *Glory be to Von Adamm!'*

The troops stood to attention, 'Glory be to Von Adamm!' they declared, most of them trying to keep the smirk off their faces. Two women each, eh? Bloody brilliant!

Colonel Grey returned to the quarters he had chosen for himself, a large suite of offices on the top floor of the Town Hall building. He'd already had a bed installed, just required a few more comforts for a long stay here, preferably including those females he spoke of to the troops. He realised he had never felt so powerful, he could put fear into anyone's heart now, one flick of his fingers and they were condemned to slavery, imprisonment or death. It was a heady feeling, left a rich taste in his mouth.

If all the elves were this soft, he could easily take the rest of Elvinhaeme, *by the Flame,* he could be rich, richer than he ever imagined. Von Adamm had been so right, those years in training on the Isle of Glasse had been worth it. Mer'edrynn was theirs for the taking.

Power, wealth and women - what more could he desire?

*

Village of Haregroves, 20th Helios.

Dane woke early, pondering on their situation. They were in a precarious position. If that bloody pint-sized Longshanks was still alive, he knew Amber had gone to the village with him. He'd be after them, both of them, as she said, she couldn't just walk away. He'd heard of the Rovers, they were a large dwarven clan, also allied with the Tsigani who wandered the waterways. If they got their clutches into you, they didn't give up, and they covered the entire country.

He lay next to Amber, staring out through the small window at the sky above. He had to protect her somehow, a masculine desire, ageless and eternal, in his blood. She lay sleeping comfortably next to him, her richly coloured hair spread across his pillow. She looked good, delicious in her sleep, soft and sweet.

He was *aching* to make love to her. But not a good idea, *no taking advantage*. She'd placed herself in his hands and it would be unfair. When she wanted him, well ... *then*.

He still found himself sending little wisps of magic over her spine, trying to redefine the scars, put a little strength inside the over-stretched tendons and muscles of her back. Given the right conditions, as opposed to constant abuse, she would soon heal.

It woke her. 'What are you doing?' she asked.

'Making a start on your back. Do you want me to stop?'

'Gosh, no, carry on, if that's what it is. It's not some kind of weird sex magic is it?'

He smiled, absurd, *although* ... 'No, of course not,' he quickly replied. 'If you turn over, I'll do a little fading of those scars on your stomach, then you'll see.'

She turned over to him, smiled, 'Hmm mm, *hello,*' her face bright. She looked up at the window, the blue sky. 'Nice morning ....' Suddenly she frowned, 'Hey, I flaked out last night - you didn't do anything did you?' Not that he wasn't attractive, he was, but fair's fair.

Dane shook his head. 'Of course not, born and bred a gentleman. You put your trust in me.' He looked down at her stomach, hovered his hands over, magic flew from him to her, making one of the lines just a little paler. He took a small line, reasonably new, easier to heal, concentrated, slowly repaired it until there was only pure skin left, just a pale mark. 'That little mark will disappear of its own accord, it's a bit like a pressure mark, but may take a day or two,' he explained.

Amber looked in amazement at her midriff. 'I can see the difference already, Dane. *Holy Merrie!* You really are good.' She felt good this morning, his healing was strong, muscles felt firm, not aching. The circus was over, she realised that, and her friends were probably gone.

Dane continued for a while, deep in thought. He knew his magic wasn't merely healing, but calming. She lay back on the bed, totally relaxed with him. He thought this was lovely, it felt right, her next to him, comfortable, he could do this for a long time. He'd love to get to know her truly. He needed to get her away from those Carnies.

Suddenly he had an idea and sat up. Went to the wash stand for a morning wash.

'Tell me, would you truly like to be rid of them, to move on with your life?' heating up the water with a quick burst of flame from his fingers as he spoke.

'I said so last night, I do. I quite like the life, but to be freer, to live my own way, well that would be something. And to not be browbeaten by them all - I mean, I give as good as I get, but they're many, and I'm one. It's hard to make a stand by myself, also - *painful*.'

She still sounded matter-of fact about it, regarding the pain as a reasonable trade off for skills.

'Well, I'm going to get dressed and get out early, get over to whatever's left of the circus, find out what the lie of the land is. I'll try and create a story for you, make out you went back and got caught in it all. Do you see? Give you a bit of space from them .'

He watched as she sleepily stretched. 'You mean, make out I'm dead? That's quite an idea. Hmm, it would be OK if Longshanks is dead too, he's the only one who knew I'd gone to the village. I'm sorry to say that, but, he could be ... difficult sometimes. Let's say he was a hard taskmaster, he could have spoken up for me many a time, yet he didn't. So ... why not? What should I do then, in the meantime?'

'Stay here, have a sleep. It's OK, no one comes up here. Just keep quiet and keep the door locked. Do you want some breakfast?' He could pop to the bakers, bring food back.

She was happy to sleep a while longer it seemed, it was probably for the best anyway, sleep was a good healer. He dressed and slipped out of the room. It was very early, not yet six a.m. The bar looked a mess, servants not cleaned up yet and the landlord wasn't around. He'd see him later, try to carry on establishing her story.

The sun was bright, a light morning sun in the month of Helios, it looked you in the eye, self-confident of its power over the day. The air was still smoky, became smokier as he reached the blackened remnants of the circus. The smell here wasn't good, back to *those* memories again. He looked around at the Carnies scurrying here and there, packing up what they could, trying to make the best of a tough blow.

He saw a dwarf, went up to talk.

'I'm sorry about what's happened, heard about it in the village. You had a good show. Did you kill that bear?'

The dwarf shook his head, 'no, *we* didn't but one of the village archers took it out. We ought to charge him, it was worth a fortune, but there's not much chance of an assize judge taking our part.'

Dane was somewhat shocked, people had been killed last night and he wanted monetary reparation for the wild beast who was responsible for most of the killing? What did he think happened when you kept something so wild locked up?

'Can't see that really happening, think you're stirring a hornet's nest there. But please tell me, it's the main reason I've come. That lovely little lass, what was she called ... Amber, is she OK?' He looked earnestly at the dwarf.

The dwarf merely shrugged, 'dunno, haven't seen her this morning. Anyway, she might have had to stay in town after the fire. We haven't grouped everyone together yet, although we are usually ready to move on by this time. Why do you want to know, what is she to you?'

'Just concerned that's all, saw your show, she was marvellous - star turn. Is Longshanks around?' He asked the question casually, obviously this person hadn't noticed she'd gone for a drink with him ... *good*. But Longshanks knew

'He's in his haemewagon, he's a bit upset, I wouldn't talk to him right now.'

Now that was a blow, Longshanks was still here. 'I'll go see him anyway, I'm sorry for all your losses. I was kind of hoping I might join you, but, not much chance now.' The dwarf pointed out the little cabin on wheels and warned him again - Longshanks temper wasn't too great at the best of times.

He knocked on the door to be rewarded with, 'piss off, whoever you are!'

'Sorry sir, just wanted to offer my condolences. I'm the guy that took Amber for a drink last night. She's a nice girl, just wanted to make sure she's OK. '

He heard an intake of breath and the dwarf hurriedly opened the door. A red beard popped around the door-frame followed by two grey eyes.

'Where is she? Have you seen her?' he was obviously worried.

Dane stood with his head down squeezing his eyes shut, looking worried. Then he looked up, his voice concerned, 'She's alright isn't she?' Anxious eyes pleaded with the dwarf.

'I thought she was with you, out of this mess. Thought she'd gone to your inn?'

'Yes sir, but she had a curfew remember? We had a drink or two then she got worried about the time.' He was earnest.

The dwarf blinked his eyes. *'What,* she came back?'

'Of course, sir, you'd stipulated. It seemed to me you act as her guardian, she made it quite clear she had to get back. I came up last night, but never found her, although ... there were quite a few burned bodies. Stayed to help a bit, being a mage. That's why I'm here this morning, been worried all night.' He kept his voice calm and reverential. Besides, it was true, she *had* returned.

The dwarf ran out of the little hut, made for Amber's tent, it was a blackened ruin. He searched through the remains but she obviously wasn't there.

'At least she wasn't in the tent. Haven't had a roll call yet, but I'm damn certain she's not here. She'd already be up and about helping, she's a kind lass, There are too many burnt bodies over there, under the remains of the big tent, we haven't exactly sorted them, although we know some are from the village. They are difficult to identify.'

'Oh , *then* ...' Dane looked horrified. 'I'm sorry ... terribly sorry. I wish she'd stayed longer with me, then maybe ... *maybe*,' he couldn't speak more. He took out a kerchief, blew his nose, gulped hard, gave a grimace. 'Doesn't look too good does it? Like I said, I searched last night, but all I could see were charred remains. Not very identifiable.' He made to turn away, 'I only met her last night, she ... she was a lovely lass. It's damn tragic.' He sniffed a little, blinked his eyes as if getting rid of tears, then shrugged and looked like he'd made up his mind. 'Are you holding a funeral at all?' he asked reverentially.

'We'll pile the bodies and the remains together and give them a decent burial. That's about all, I think I've probably lost a third of my crew - and that bloody bear trainer can sod off. I never want to see him again. That bastard has lost me Amber, best thing we had. If you want to come, there'll be a simple ceremony around noon.'

Dane nodded, he would come, as would probably most of the village.

He walked back to the village, quietly triumphant. Called at the bakers and bought a few pasties and buns. As he passed through the bar of the tavern, the landlord called to him. 'Nasty business last night. Did that lass get back safely?'

'The acrobat? Not sure. Just been up to the Old Field, there's a lot of burnt bodies and no-one's seen her.'

'Hope she's alright, she were grand.'

Dane nodded agreement and continued up the stairs. Quietly knocked on the door. Gave a cough to show it was him. Amber opened the door.

He slipped inside, proffered the bag of pasties, explained the situation. 'It's a damn mess. There's a funeral service for everyone later.'

She threw her arms around him. 'He thinks I'm dead?' This was excellent news but she was sorry for those who had lost their lives,. 'Did he say who else has died?'

'No, hadn't taken a roll-call.' She looked saddened, there were friends lost in the fire.

'So what now?'

'We could leave tonight once it's dark, go out the back door of the inn. At least get you away without them knowing, give you a bit of space from them.'

She considered this, relieved to be able to get away, move on with her life. There was time enough to mourn, but she had to admit they were nearly all itinerants, hard to get to know people who constantly moved on. *Who would mourn her,* she wondered?

She took the food, they ate at the table, it was kind of Dane. After quietly munching, she spoke, 'you sure about all this?'

Dane nodded, 'absolutely, if you are. What have we got to lose? I've no one, neither have you, unless you have some ties to anyone over there at the circus?' She hadn't. "So, let's give this a go, see where it leads us if you'd like.' He saw her smiling, she *did* like the idea. 'Is there anything you need, you lost everything. I could seek out stuff at the market for you?'

'Don't you think asking for female underwear might be a bit of a giveaway?' her eyes twinkled.

So did his. 'I could pretend it's for a girlfriend, a present.'

Her eyes rolled upwards. 'Oh dear me no, Merrie only knows what you'd come back with. It'll be red, satin and have important bits missing. No, if you bring me some fresh water, I'll wash what I'm wearing, dry them under your window. I'll wait until another town or village to get some basics.'

Dane agreed, then realised he needed to get to work. 'I'll pop in at dinnertime, bring you more food.' He fetched the necessary water, heated it with magic fingers, she stopped him before he went off, gave him a list of names.

'Let me know if any of those are gone, they were my friends.'

He understood.

Amber locked the door behind him, wondering what she was getting into? But then, as she had said the previous evening, the last five years weren't the greatest. He seemed nice enough, although appearances could be deceptive, but he seemed capable too. He certainly had cheek. Plus, he was healing her scars - really healing them and that ache in her back - absolutely wonderful!

She was still astounded that he hadn't touched her last night, he'd been very decent about it all. Hardly a kiss and yet he'd offered to make a go of it for a while. She might be taking a chance on him, but she appreciated everything he was doing. After all - what was there instead at the moment?

The fire and its resultant deaths left her stunned ... between the smoke and the shock she wasn't exactly thinking clearly, but ... she had to admit she liked the idea of the unknown life ahead of her. So - why not?

She took off her poet's shirt, underclothes and leggings, began to wash with the soapwort gel and water, determined to rid them of the smoke smell. They'd have to do for some time, at least until they found a town or a hawker. Perhaps she could adapt some of his? She peeked in his drawers for shirts or whatever, slipped on a tunic. Found shirts that also looked like they needed washing - *trust a bloke* - added them to the wash.

She wasn't particularly domesticated, but hygiene was always difficult out on the road, past experience warned her to start off well. Chores were boring, but necessary.

After washing, she had nothing to do so she perused the books on his small bookshelf. They had titles like: *'Blackwell's treatise on poisonous mushrooms and fungi'* or *'Existential uses for Derivatives of Crucifers',* or *'Cold extraction of oils from flowering herbs'*, or - and there were a few of these - *'Fanny's Adventures with Tom's Blade'* or *'Sir Randolph's Amorous Exploits'*. There was also *'The Joy of Pussy'*.

Hmm, she thought, *typical male*, peeking into the last one. It turned out to be a set of poems ... all about cats.

*

Dane hurried up to the Old Field just before noon, it had been cleared to a degree, but the burnt mess in the centre said everything. Dane saw that Arne fellow standing stiffly and grim faced. Longshanks was already speaking, quite a short speech for a dwarf, he obviously wished to get it over with. He thanked everyone for attending, he offered words of condolence for those who had lost loved ones from the village, he explained the Bear Keeper had been dismissed and he read a list of those of his own troop who were missing, presumed dead. The list included Amber, to Dane's relief, but only a couple of the names Amber had given him. He then spoke a few words of commitment, which he kept short, obviously not a religious man of any depth.

A large pit had been dug at the very end of the field and all the remains, for that is the best that could be said, were tipped into it. Everyone threw in a little soil, some said their own prayers for the dead and then two of the dwarves filled in the rest. Finally there was a prayer to Lady Merrie, the Mother Prayer. There were few actual Merrievian prayers, people prayed or meditated in their own way, or all joined in singing, but there was one prayer everyone knew.

Holy Merrie, Mother of all,
Care for us, your Children,
As we care for You.
Accept the love we bear ... for you, for each other, for our beautiful world.
For we are all One being, all part of Your glorious Creation.
May Your joy of Life and generosity of Spirit
be in everything we do and all that we become.
And so, as we wend our way to our final hour,
we can honestly say with peace in our hearts, 'we gave our best'.
So mote it be.

Longshanks gave everyone a few moments for quiet contemplation before ending the service. The villagers said they would bring stones, make a small cairn here. Longshanks agreed to give something towards a headstone.

Then it was over, life went on. Dane ran back to the village, picked up some bread, fruit and cheese at the market. Dashed back to his room, briefly told Amber. Gave her the names of the dead.

She nodded, saddened by the news. Nothing could be done about it now. Life was often short, agues, plagues or accident took their toll, but you had to move on regardless.

'I'm sorry Amber. Sometimes life is unfair.' He made to leave. 'Can't stay, already late back at the shop - he'll be having kittens if I don't get there soon.' Amber smiled briefly at the mention of kittens. 'Want to make today as normal as possible, I'll write out a note later, explaining I'm leaving, put it through his door before we go.' He sounded excited at the possibility of a new life. 'You sure about this?' watching as she nodded. He hurried away back to the dark and miserable quack's store.

For a few moments Amber let go, tears streaming down her cheeks. Life was not great in the circus, hadn't been happy, but still, she was sorry for her friends, sorry it was over. 'Get it together, girl,' she thought, 'you're alive aren't you, thanks to Dane? Let's give him a chance.' She felt tired again, still somewhat in shock, decided to sleep the afternoon away. It was warm up in the attic room and she would be awake all night.

Dane returned towards evening bearing more food, a knapsack for Amber, an empty water skin and a *skein* of small beer. She looked more refreshed. 'Don't know how long we'll be gone, or when we'll reach another settlement. I'm not the greatest hunter in the world, but I can shoot a few birds with my magic. How are your hunting skills?'

'I can shoot a bow but I haven't got one, just practised at the circus. I've no trapping skills at all.' She wished she'd practised more now. 'Good with daggers though ...' she laughed.

'Shit, babes in arms, aren't we? Still, I've managed in the past and I'll manage again. We won't starve, I assure you.'

He took parchment from a cupboard, reached for quill and ink and wrote a couple of identical notes:

'With apologies,

I'm afraid I have to leave immediately owing to unforeseen family troubles. Unfortunately this means it is unlikely I shall return. Sorry I am unable to explain this in person, but time is short and my family require my services.

Yours most sincerely, Dane Andarsson.

He added a short note to one. *'I have paid the rent to the end of the week, so you should not be out of pocket. Many thanks.'*

Amber read the notes. They impressed her, short and to the point, with well spaced clear writing, all spelled correctly, at least, she thought so. Not that many people could write well, or read for that matter, parchment wasn't exactly cheap. The notes were also polite and he didn't intend cheating anyone - he paid his dues. *Good signs.*

The notes had told her a fair bit about the mage. 'You must have had some decent schooling,' she told him.

'Only from my parents,' was the reply.

He popped downstairs to collect more beer, brought up a couple of pasties, they could keep the other produce for later. Around eight o'clock he took the note down to the herbal shop, stuck it through the door to be seen on the morrow. The other note he would leave on the table, with the door unlocked. They'd miss him by evening, he went every night for a pint, and worked two nights a week there for extra cash. That point worried him.

'I've got some coin,' he told Amber, 'we'll probably be OK for a couple of weeks, but I've no savings.'

Amber looked in the purse on her belt. 'I've some too, but not much. By the time board and lodging was taken out of my wage and a portion towards my 'debt', there wasn't much left. I had to pay for make-up and stuff, and the material for my outfits also.'

'He deliberately kept you short, didn't he?' Dane suggested. She nodded, knowing it was so, but it had been safety of a sort and she'd got to know the other Carnies. She'd valued their company. Now her friends were gone. No, there was nothing to go back to.

As she explained, 'time just went by and I got used to the situation.'

Dane agreed, he'd been here two long years, kept thinking about moving on, but hadn't. Tempus fugited pretty quickly.

'Ha! - same here,' he remarked. 'Actually, I'm glad you've come - I was obviously about to slip into a long, slow rut,' he smiled encouragingly at her. 'Anyway, I suggest you keep your cash for clothes and your feminine needs, you are obviously going with nothing. Women seem to need more than men.'

Amber appreciated the statement.

Dane collected what he considered necessary, offering a couple of smaller shirts to Amber, thanking her for washing his shirts, it was kind of her. He put his herbs in small pouches for convenience and only packed the treatise on poisonous mushrooms, *'for identification purposes as it was illustrated,'* explaining he knew the others back to front. She saw him also sneak *the Joy of Pussy* into his pack when he thought she wasn't looking. She was happy to see the roll of oilcloth he took from a chest - canvas with a layer of mixed beeswax and linseed oil, good as a waterproof base. Her tent had been a similar material.

They agreed to wait until after midnight. The days were long, it wouldn't be dark until after ten. However, the long days also meant light nights. If there was a clear sky and a moon, they could get along quickly.

Amber put one of the wool blankets from the bed into her knapsack, along with Dane's cast-off shirts and the empty water skin, strapped on her dagger belt and covered herself with her cloak. Dane added his few toiletries, soapwort and stuff, and a towel to her pack. His own pack contained his clothes, a couple of books, two spoons, two small bowls, the two tankards they had been using, a small whetstone and oil, a small tin kettle and the food. His apothecary's satchel contained herbs and potions, beeswax and a few cheesecloth squares to cut into bandages if necessary. He fastened the skein of beer to his pack and the roll of oilcloth was strapped over the top of the pack. He decided to wear his better black boots and leave behind the old worn ones he wore for work. He wore a cloak, carried his staff, and he also had a small skinning/paring knife strapped to his belt. He was leaving Haregroves with not much more than he'd brought two years previously.

It was pathetically little with which to start a new life.

Shortly after midnight the two sneaked away, deliberately moving south-east, in the opposite direction of Grimmpool and the Old Field, where the remains of Longshanks' Circus would lie forever.

Chapter 3

Helios - Feast of Lumentide.

Dawn came early at this time of year and the moon lit the night with silvery shadows. They travelled quickly. After skirting the village to keep out of sight, they returned to the high-road and made good time. They marched in silence for the most part, each within his or her own thoughts, wondering about the future.

Occasionally Dane would gently tap her shoulder, 'you OK? Want a rest or anything yet?' It was good he was concerned. But no, she was fine, felt a great deal better now, probably had more stamina than him anyway. He offered her the *skein* of beer every now and again.

They made some miles in good time before tiring. Dane looked for a likely place, preferably off the road. Childhood tales always told to stay off the roads on these bright Faenights. Dane thought it was garbage, stuff to scare children.

Nevertheless, they moved into the nearby forest, oaks, birches, the odd beech, as the moon began to fade, a chill now in the air. Time to take a rest. They'd heard a river nearby, perhaps a large stream.

Dane unrolled the oilcloth and took the small kettle and mugs out of his pack. Dane scouted round for a few twigs while Amber banked up some earth. He filled the kettle from the stream, placed it on top of the hastily built fire, lighting the fire with flames shooting from his fingers.

'Don't really need the fire for the kettle, but it's chilly in the early morn, thought you'd like it.'

Amber settled on the oilcloth, nodding, hugging her cloak around her. She decided he was a handy man to have around. To think he'd dashed up to the Old Field to save her?

Dane added dried tea leaves, mint and chamomile to the pot, a simple brew, waited for it to boil and infuse before pouring it into the tankards using a small strainer. 'Try that, should perk you up a little, sorry I've no honey.' Amber just smiled at him, both amused and delighted by his concern. His politeness and his manners, like the tea, were refreshing.

The pair sat quietly sipping tea, the silent, sleepy forest around them. The night was not yet dead, the morn had not begun, a world twixt dark and light. A time for reflection.

Amber studied the man sitting across from her, his features lit by the small fire, one knee up, his arm resting on it holding his tea, the other leg stretched out. He looked intent, a man studying his future. A broad forehead, wide intelligent blue eyes with crinkles between them as if he'd spent a lot of his early life thinking, and a long straight nose. His firm but sensuous mouth was currently turned down and looking serious. As she had seen last night, its edges were often turned up and smiling at her. There was a slight stubble now on his equally firm jaw. His shock of golden hair was now tied back in a black ribbon, combed back from his forehead, it had been loose before, shoulder length.

She liked the way he managed to look both serious and sensual.

Dane too had been thinking. 'Look, do you just want me to get you to a decent town, or are we on the edge of something between us? I mean, I don't want to force you to stay with me, but I did want to get you away from those people. So, before we move on, I'm asking you, I'd like to get it clear now, and to give you the opportunity to change your mind.'

'So, you're already sick of my company and want to rid yourself of me ... hmm, *great*,' she replied archly, mock pouting her lips.

Dane just laughed, 'no, I think you're the loveliest company I've ever had, but I want to know where I stand too.'

For answer she moved closer and pressed her lips against his. 'Does that answer you?' kissing him again.

He responded with passion, pulling her to him, his arms wrapped around her, a long, deep kiss. Last night was ... last night. But here was *now*. It was good ... very good. They were young, passionate and filled with life's joy. A newfound freedom, escape from possible death ... and a new day dawning.

What started as a kiss moved on. Soon they were pulling off clothes, exploring each other, feverish kisses and a tangled mass of arms and legs. A soft, sweet rocking and sighing until movement became frenetic and sighs became moans. An even sweeter joining as the two looked into each other's eyes sharing the final ecstatic moments of their coupling. And a quiet holding of each other, breathing in the fresh morning air of the forest, tender kisses, sweet words of love.

Finally, *'I think you answered my question,'* Dane replied with a satisfied smile. He took the blanket from the haversack, wrapped it and his cloak over them. For the next few hours they slept, tucked in each other's arms, until a Lumentide Day sun overheated them and they woke to brightness.

They bathed in the river, laughing like children as they happily splashed each other's bodies, made love again as the sun warmed them and enjoyed a breakfast of bread and cheese and more minty tea. Dane wouldn't let them move on until he had spent a little more time on her scars. She was overjoyed to see them disappear under his breath-like touch.

Then they set off on the road once more, wondering where it would lead?

*

They walked hand in hand, their newfound love leaving secret smiles playing across their faces. It was Lumentide, fourth week in *Helios,* the sun at its height, the longest day.

'It's strange that yesterday was Lumen's Eve.' Amber commented. 'I didn't even scatter rose petals, or put them under my pillow,' referring to the ancient custom of young women seeking to see their future husband in their dreams. 'Come to think of it, I didn't have a pillow either, I had your arm.'

He smiled cheerily at her, 'All the better then ... so did you dream about me?'

She shook her head, 'don't remember dreaming, just sleeping - but of course, I hadn't done the ritual had I?' she laughed. She suddenly stopped speaking and looked up in wonder. Pink, white and red rose petals were falling all around her, a shower of blossom. 'Hey, how did you do that?' she asked Dane, a vague memory stirring of illusions created by her mother when she was little.

He stood in front of her laughing. '*Elementary*, my dear Amber. It's what happens when there is a conjunction of an elemental mage and a dryad. You get *me*.' He gave a mock bow. 'Actually, I'm not very good at illusion magic, but I can conjure up a few simple images.'

She clapped her hands, 'well we certainly won't starve. We're a two person circus show, before we even start - although,' she hesitated, 'it might not be a good idea showing off our abilities. Longshanks might get to hear about us and put two and two together. *And if so ....*' she cast a warning glance at Dane.

' ... if so, he'll want his *property* back and send the Rovers after us. Not good, but I certainly think we can take them on - you aren't without skills yourself. Have you ever used those daggers to fight with?'

'I *have* actually, a couple of times when the circus has been ambushed on the road, or fights have broken out in a town. People think we are all just itching for a fight, so *yes*. I don't wish to fight, but if I have to, I will.' She looked a lot less tough than she spoke.

The rose petals disappeared as they reached the floor. 'Thank you, that was lovely. You're very *versatile,*' she commented.

Dane bent to kiss her again. He could do that a lot, he thought, kiss her and kiss her. So soft, so lovely. He didn't know if that was what she wanted, he knew so little about her. But he would find out, something to look forward to. He had a lot to look forward to, he realised.

Their kiss was suddenly punctuated by an arrow whistling through the air, just past Dane's ear.

(What - you thought they were going off into the Shimmering Sunset at the very beginning of the saga? Well, duh! Life's just not like that - so think on!)

Dane hurriedly looked around. Saw four horsemen encircling them. He smashed his staff on the ground and shot up a protective barrier immediately, a strange whirling opaque sphere that shimmered in the morning sun. It blinded the horsemen.

Dane saw they were Bregantines, ancient war-like tribes who lived in northern parts of Shirewood, perhaps the hills nearby, the Pendragons. Kin to the feral Alderfolk, their blood-shot eyes peered down at the pair. They were a terrifying sight, small branches were stuck to their heads using a bandanna, giving the impression of antlers, wild hair streaming behind. One actually wore a small pair of antlers tucked behind his ears. Their skin was covered in a mixture of mud and grease, a sort of war paint. It's dun colour complimented their rough hide cuirass' and canvas trousers tucked into fur ankle boots.

They were one of the reasons people rarely travelled the highways unless accompanied by militia or guards, or perhaps in a good coach-and-four. Others included outlaws and bandits, odd faery folk and wild beasts, a few invaders having a go over disputed borders and now those Adammite buggers.

Just as well to carry a sword or two.

Most of Mer'edrynn was civilised - truly. *Mostly.*

But currently four Bregantines were madly circling Amber and Dane, shouting a demented war cry of *'Yip, yip, yippee, yip yip!'* followed by the occasional 'Aieeeee!', long daggers drawn. They sounded like they were having fun.

But it wouldn't be fun for Dane and Amber. They were scalp-hunters who used the scalps to appease their old gods. Or possibly to bribe them - who knew? None spoke the common tongue Plaintongue, and their own language had been forgotten for centuries. They were a law unto themselves.

The protective circle wouldn't hold long, Amber took out her own long daggers, they resembled dirks, a determined look on her face. Dane watched the horsemen, looking for an advantage point. Four of them on horseback, against two on foot.

Dane took down the circle and aimed his staff at one of the horses hooves, a quick amberic flash. It hit the shoes of the horse, no lasting damage, but enough to startle. The horse reared madly, throwing off the rider. He quickly did the same with the other three horses, two more came off, one managed to stay on. Amber dashed to the first downed rider, and as quick as Dane's electrum flash, she raised one of her daggers and sliced the throat of the Bregantine. Blood gushed out, some of it on Amber as she jumped away. Dane was startled by her speed and her efficiency. She dashed back to his side, facing the others together, a pair. He turned to the rider still on the horse, shot another amberic flash, abruptly turning and hitting an oncoming Bregantine with the end of the staff. He changed now to a blazing fire magic, sweeping an arc across the three attackers making for him.

Screams were heard as flesh blistered. Amber stayed by his side, her daggers drawn, ready should they be within reach. Still they came, despite singed hair and smoking leather, determined to have their prey, high on adrenalin and the powerful rush of cruelty. The horses had run off, out of the way of the frightening flashes. One of the assailants went down with a blood-curdling scream, as a swift dagger was despatched by Amber. It went straight through his eye with an uncanny accuracy. Dane continued with massive blasts of flame from his staff, a horrible smell of burning flesh, something he detested. No doubt the recipient detested it more.

But one now had a long whip curling in the air, it came down around Dane's ankle, pulling him to the ground, knocking the staff out of his fingers. He found himself in a fierce tussle with a scorched savage, both fighting for their lives, the Bregantine hitting him hard in the chest, winding him. The Bregantine was laughing now, the joy of the fight upon him. Dane heaved himself up from the ground, rolling over trying to get on top, trying to get a hand free. But both hands were clasped by the Bregantine, Dane's nose wrinkled from his sour, stinking breath.

He wriggled his fingers free, shot electrum into the clasping fist, heard a yelp and pulled his hand back. That same hand now shot fire into the man's face, who stopped laughing, instead screamed and writhed and tried to get away, but Dane was steadily holding on now with his other hand, watching as he burnt the skin from his assailant's skull.

It was a horrible way to die.

At the same time, young Amber was screaming blue murder, as the fourth Bregantine threw himself on top of her, his knife aimed at her throat. The knife got closer and closer and Amber, panting heavily, tried to edge further and further away, trying to wriggle out of his grasp.

Dane grabbed his staff and swiped it right across the savages head, giving Amber just enough time to take her own dagger and thrust it in his side. He screamed as blood spurted from him, drenching Amber yet again. Dane hit the savages head once more with his ashen staff and shot fire from its end into the Bregantine. There was another nasty smell of burnt skin and bone.

Amber lay panting, slightly shaking. Dane quickly helped her up, his mage hands scanning her body. There were bumps and bruises, a few cuts. But Amber was quick and lithe, she had managed to scamper out of the way of most blows or thrusts. Dane was relieved.

If anything Dane looked the worst of the pair, and his chest was painful from the pummelling.

He didn't speak, just held her to him, kissed her lips. His heart was pounding, he had just found her, wasn't prepared to lose her. For a few moments they stayed hugging each other.

Then they looked around and took stock of the situation. Four dead Bregantine raiders lay around them.

Suddenly to Dane's surprise, Amber began laughing.

'Holy Merrie, Dane, look what we've just done, the two of us! I know those people, I know what their tribe can do - I've seen it in the past when I was with the Alderfolk - they're fierce warriors! Look at them, dead!' She threw her arms around him, kissed his lips hard, then stood back. 'Dane, you were *magnificent* - incredible - what a pair we make!' She stood laughing, slightly hysterical now the worst was over, shaking her head at it all.

Dane took her hands in his, held her at arm's length, his eyes scanning her face. 'No, *you* were magnificent - those blades, your speed, your reflexes, wow! Never seen anything like it!'

They stood holding each other, both shaking, both all too aware how close their deaths had been. 'We need to be more careful on the road, perhaps keep a little further in the forest, not so easy to dash upon us, go more slowly.' Dane spoke quietly but firmly. 'Let's get ourselves to the nearest town as soon as we can.' Civilised towns were definitely preferable to the open road.

They both stooped to loot the bodies, a few coins, some weapons, no point leaving anything for future scavengers. Besides, they needed cash, or something convertible to cash. Amber took one of the bows for herself, strapped on a quiver, collected as many arrows as she could find. Dane went to find the horses, but they had run into the forest, no doubt back to the tribe. It was a shame, they could have used them. Still, the swords could be sold and Amber always had use for an extra dagger or two.

They dragged the bodies off the highway, added twigs and bracken. Dane set the whole thing on fire. They left the bodies to burn, any remains would be eaten by wolves or other wildlife, pecked at by birds. They would soon be nothing but bones and a few bits of leather.

The two continued onwards in the direction, hopefully, of civilisation. Both kept their eyes and ears open, wary now of anything on the road, ready to dash off into the undergrowth if necessary. They stopped by a small stream for Amber to wash what blood she could off her clothes. The warm summer sun would soon dry her. Dane found cooling herbs for his bruised chest.

Both were extremely proud of their new partner. They were, it seemed, quite a formidable team.

They hurried along the road, cautious now. This new life 'on the road', was less easy than it sounded. Dane had forgotten how difficult it could be. But the road remained quiet.

A few miles further on and another stop for tea, as the initial adrenalin from the fight abated and weariness set in. But tea always perks up the blood and soon they were back on the trail, wherever it might lead. In fact, another couple of miles and they could hear music and cheering ahead of them ... of course ... it was Lumentide Day. Encouraged, they followed the sound, entering the village through a sweeping archway guarded by two bowmen.

A large bonfire was lit on what was obviously the village green. The young lads and lasses were clearly enjoying the summer festival. The females were all wearing garlands of red and yellow flowers and they had joined hands with the young men, merrily dancing around the crackling bonfire, the small village band happily playing flutes and fiddles. Flames shot upwards into the summer air. Bare-footed children wearing calico smocks with ribbons and flowers in their hair, were scampering and playing games of 'tig' or blind-man's buff. Elders stood nearby, clapping, and laughing, most holding large mugs of beer. A huge table stood next to the elder folk, spread richly with meat, pies and sweetmeats. It was quite a contrast to their earlier encounter. Everyone had a well-scrubbed look, all cleaned up in best clothes for a feast day.

They found they were welcomed by the locals. 'Come and join us,' they shouted, 'don't often have strangers at Lumentide, tha' can be't Oak King and Queen. Leave your packs under' table, they'll be fine.' Then, as they neared the Elders, 'You alright - you look like you been through a bit of trouble ...?' They explained their encounter with the Bregantines, the Elders either nodding sagely or shaking heads wisely. 'Aye, they're trouble those louts, bloody trouble. But ye'r here now.' Beers were quickly pressed into their hands with the words, 'help theesell's.' They were starving and took full advantage. Once more they were begged to take on the role of Oak King and Queen for the evening - strangers were always special.

It seemed that being Oak King and Queen meant standing in the middle while the revellers danced around them wildly. *'Clap thee 'ands,'* they were told - they did so. *'Tha can kiss 'er if tha' wants,'* was shouted. Dane did, and the crowd erupted with cheers. The young men and women laughed and continued dancing. *'Merrie, merrie, merrie, merrie,'* was chanted regularly. Sometimes the young men would run to the fire, collect smouldering sticks and wave them around in circles in the air, the wheel of life, the sign of the sun. Then they would all run around the fire and chant:

Sunlight, sunbright, sun's rays on us tonight.
Deep inside the forest fair, we shall make a merry pair,
Let the Fae ride in the sky, in the woods, they pass us by,
So lads and lasses, raise your glasses!

To Lumentide!

Everyone raised a glass and shouted, 'Happy Lumentide!' Then it would begin again, any excuse for another drink.

Dane surprised them all as they danced around them, by shooting out his hands and projecting bright stars and yellow sunflowers into the sky. They clapped at the spectacle, it was delightful.

Eventually, everyone seemed to have had enough dancing and they all made for the supper table. The older people all wanted kisses from Dane and Amber, part of their summer fun, and then more dancing began, in couples rather than in a group. They were both in heavy demand as the young people disappeared into the nearby woods and the older folk enjoyed a summer dance. Dane and Amber danced, drank and generally partied until midnight when the dancing finally stopped.

For a short time, Dane took out his staff and filled the velvety blue night with moons and more stars, flashes of pink and yellow radiance, there were cries of 'oooh' and 'ah'.

Finally, people began staggering off to their beds, again each offered hugs and kisses as they left.

Tha's been grand,' was the general opinion, or, from the older men, *'bet you want to get 'er off into 't woods now, don't tha'?* to Dane. Dane just smiled benignly at them all.

They both decided they might as well join the local young people mystically communing with nature in the murmuring woods, or as Dane said, 'let's finish off Lumentide properly ...' collecting the oilcloth roll from his pack. Amber collected the blanket.

They woke the next morning to a bright, sunny day. The table left on the village green still held a barrel bearing a few drops of ale, they drank thirstily. A couple of locals came to the green, collecting rubbish from the feasting and generally tidying up.

'It were good to have thee 'ere,' one said, 'extra luck for us for the season, ye strangers, and damn handsome ones too, not to mention the magic. Where be ye off to?'

They explained they were looking for the nearest town, the villagers gave directions and a bag of provisions, as payment. There was a largish village, Loxely, about ten miles south, a good road. They didn't feel they were in a hurry however, the day was bright and cheerful, a warm sun and little wind. They hung around awhile, helping to put things away, chatting casually to everyone. Dane even did a little healing of some of the elders.

It was an uneventful journey, only punctuated by Dane stopping to collect St John's Wort every now and again. 'Best time of year,' he explained, 'most beneficial properties.' She noticed he took only a certain amount from each batch he saw, left many untouched, it would easily re-grow.

Amber couldn't help watching him, she admired this new way of being. He lived as one with nature, revelling in it. The circus people were more like scavengers, they took anything they could, stealing if necessary. When they reached a town they bargained for the cheapest food and drink possible, rapacious in nature.

Dane seemed to offer himself wherever he went, people glad to see him. She wasn't aware that her own cheerful face and bright eyes made her just as welcome.

*

Merrievian Temple, Draecastle town.   Month of Firstfire (one month earlier)

Young Sister Alicia reflected on the day as she knelt on her prayer rug. It had been, as most days here, pleasant. A short prayer and blessings service first thing before a light breakfast, all the Sisters chattering and laughing. Then a couple of hours spent in the vegetable garden in the morning, helping Sister Artemisia with weeding and sowing leeks and beans. Music lessons followed, all priestesses to play some kind of instrument, music blessed by the Lady, beneficial to heart and soul. It was one of the reasons her family had sent her here, to learn the ritual music, she had quite a talent with a flute. She wasn't sure yet whether she would stay or go home at the end of the year. It was a lovely place, but she missed her family.

Later, there was prayer in the main Temple room and chatting to celebrants, often strangers, but all welcome. There were times set aside for healing, or meditation with Merrievian followers. Sometimes followers stayed for dinner. The sisters enjoyed having a few male guests around, good to have male company for once, and the occasional male staying over wasn't exactly frowned upon. No-one asked for celibacy as a way of life, it was just that these women preferred to devote their lives to the Temple rather than marriage. And of course, there were always feast days to enjoy. *Merrie* believed life should be as her name suggested.

Dinner had been a happy occasion too, mostly the Sisters and the High Priestess, but a few men were staying, overnight guests, and some of the Knight's Templar joined them at table. Rich red wine was passed around and the men told silly jokes, nothing vulgar, light hearted stuff. Manners and etiquette were important in the Temple.

It was just a typical day in a Temple of Merrie.

The banging and the screams began as she was kneeling just in front of the tiny shrine in her room. A quiet meditation to the Lady Merrie to end the day, her thoughts this day dwelling on the subject of kindness, as suggested by the High Priestess.

She stood hurriedly from the woollen rug and turned to the door as more screams were heard. She heard herself scream as it was thrown open and a large man in a black cloak and jet black uniform ran in, his sword waving menacingly at her. His eyes were filled with hate.

She watched him, confused at the interruption, the invasion of the sanctuary of her room.

'Bitch!' he shouted at her, 'damn little Merrievian whore!' She stood shocked, no idea what was happening. He grabbed the sleeve of her white robe and threw her across the bed, pulling it open, exposing her breasts. She struggled, could do little, she was no fighter, only a trainee priestess shocked into immobility. Saliva dripped down his chin as he bent and grabbed her breast, her eyes now wide with fear. He hit her as she tried to pull away, then hit her again, and again, and again, as if he couldn't stop. She screamed again, but the more she screamed, the more he hit her. She struggled, tried to push him away, tried to kick him. He was too strong, too powerful, his body huge and heavy over hers.

Eventually it became obvious that no one heard her screams, nor would anyone come to help her. Her face became swollen from his punches, blood pouring from her broken nose. Still she hoped he would go, this wasn't real, couldn't be happening. For a moment she looked dazedly into his eyes, but they were glazed with lust and hate. She lost all hope.

Her last thought was *'why ...?'*

With careless ease he slit her throat when he had finished, the blood pouring over his uniform. He took it as a sign of his initiation into the new cult, his adrenalin still high, his blood still up. He felt triumphant.

He joined the rest of the Adammite militia in the main temple room. They were laughing hysterically as they all spat on the statue of the Lady Merrie, and broke down all the pots and flowers in the hall. They piled the dead bodies of the Templar guards together in the centre. The Templar guards were experienced soldiers, but there were only ever a few on duty. After all, who would profane a Temple of Merrie?

'Dick-less creeps,' the Adammites shouted, 'bloody pimps, that's all you are ...' setting them alight.

High Priestess Serena stood helpless in the centre of the hall, her hands bound behind her, struggling between two black garbed soldiers, her head shaking from side to side at the senselessness, the mindless cruelty of it all.

They dragged her to the statue of Lady Merrie, held her head back, then, as she closed her eyes one final time, ritually slit her throat. Blood had to be shed, preferably all over the defaced altar.

Blood was shed throughout the Temple, an offering to their new male God of Death.

Then they set the place ablaze before leaving, purification through flame, another statement made to the weak, debauched world, *the Adammites were now in charge.*

*

By late afternoon, following a good road often patrolled by local guards, Dane and Amber had reached the outskirts of Loxely, somewhere in size between a large village and a small market town. It was a pretty enough place, a low bridge over a gently flowing river and then a row of whitewashed cottages with well-stocked gardens. Black and white timbered town houses filled the central square, and a market was in full swing. They quickly made for a market stall where they bought long drinks of sarsaparilla, quarters of roast chicken and some sticky looking buns.

They wondered if there was any work to be had, they needed coin and preferably somewhere to stay temporarily. They had no idea what would lie ahead, but decided to take it day by day, see what happened, go with the flow. Looking round, they found the village meeting hall with a notice board outside, a likely place to find jobs. A few notes were tacked to it.

'Anyone sees my cat Booby, send it back.'
'Reet gud peat fer sail goin cheep, Arrymans farm.'
'Woman wanted. Must be good cook and can take care of eight children. Wage, board and lodging. Might wed. Tom the Saddler.'
'Whoever keeps stealing my 'taties is in for it. I'm watching ye!'
'Loxely village Elders need capable team to escort a delivery south. Will pay well. See blacksmith.'

'*Aaah*,' they said simultaneously. Amber looked at Dane, 'well?'
'Well, why not?' was the reply.
They went to see the blacksmith, he was just shutting up shop for the evening. 'Too late, I'm doing no more tonight, barring emergencies, I've an important meeting to go to,' he told them. They explained why they had come. He looked them over, eyeing the mage warily, then seemed to make up his mind. 'Aye, good. Come and see, it's our priestess, she needs to go down to Manecaestr, to the Merrievian Temple, but we've no one to spare to take her, *not now*. We need someone we can trust - at least there's a woman with you.'

He led the way to a small chapel, bedecked with red pelargonium, red and yellow nemesia and godetias in big pots, summer sunshine colours. A shrine at the back held a statue of the Lady Merrie, surrounded by more flowers, and a large bowl of cherries and strawberries lay on the table in front of her, a gift, an offering. At the side was a small desk where a middle-aged woman wearing the long, pale grey gown of a priestess was writing. She looked up as they entered.

'My Lady, there's two here says they'll escort you to the temple. I'll leave them with you, then you can question them a bit. Shout if you need me.' He left them alone, but stood outside for a few moments, should she require help.

The priestess stood, examining them. 'What sort of experience do you have?' she asked.

Dane told her they'd seen off a group of Bregantian the previous day, left them for dead. He showed the swords as proof. The priestess nodded, inspecting them both carefully.

Amber answered honestly. 'To be truthful we've only just started out together, but if you come outside we'll show you what we're capable of. If we show you in here, we'll ruin the chapel.'

Once in the garden, she choose a wooden post some distance away. Threw her daggers one by one at it in rapid succession, a long line of daggers in a straight line down the post. 'I'm quite handy with those, I never miss.' She went to collect them.

Dane looked upwards. Mallards were flying overhead to their evening resting ground. He shot up his staff, blue amberic power blasting forth. Two fell at their feet. Dane picked them up, handed them to the Priestess.

'With my compliments, madam,' he offered.

She lifted an eyebrow. *'Fine,* you'll do. See you tomorrow, make an early breakfast then come here Do you have anywhere to stay tonight?'

Both shook their heads, hadn't yet been to the inn. She showed them the way, accompanying them, spoke with the innkeeper.

'Your board and lodging is now free for tonight, the village Council will pay.' She turned and left.

The landlord looked askance at Dane's mage staff, he wasn't happy having sorcerers in his inn, but if it was fine with their priestess, who was he to argue? He asked if they needed one, or two rooms; one would do. He took them upstairs, showed them a pleasant room, supper would be served until around nine thirty, nothing special, but good wholesome food.

They looked around the room, it was light and airy, simple but solid furniture and had a good, comfortable, clean looking bed.

'A real bed!' commented Amber, 'I could get used to this.'

Dane sat on the bed, patting the space next to him, beckoning her.

To his disappointment she shook her head. 'Come on, I need to get things from that market before they close.'

Reluctantly he followed her. The market was at that point when the stall holders are trying to put things away to go home for the evening, but nevertheless she was able to pick up a few essentials - an expensive bristle brush and a fine-toothed comb, (living as she had done, she knew the necessity of such a comb for head-lice) a small brush for her teeth, some ribbons, a tiny needlecraft set, a scarf or two, cheap calico underwear and a couple of linen over-shirts, along with a little bottle of lavender oil, useful in many ways. She also bought a long sleeveless embroidered tunic - a female surtout - to wear if the occasion demanded. A straw hat with a red ribbon completed her day's purchases, that midsummer sun was hot. Her purse was pretty much empty, but the few new possessions gave her a pleasantly feminine boost.

Dane too managed to find a herbal shop, bought a few necessary herbs and oils along with some cork-stoppered vials. Amber found some lambswool she could use, also bought muslin to cut and shape around it, could be washed and reused. *'Women stuff'*, she mysteriously explained to Dane. He nodded, understanding, he was primarily a physician after all. He also sold the swords, adding an extra bit of cash to their meagre purse. They returned to the inn.

Dane took off his cloak and divested himself of his pack and equipment. He pulled her to the bed. He was feverishly kissing her when there was a knock at the door.

With a muttered 'damn', he went to open it. The innkeeper's wife proffered a large jug of hot water. Politely he thanked her and deposited the jug on the small dresser next to a pretty, pottery washing bowl.

He was slightly disappointed when Amber took the soapwort gel and towel out of the bag and began to wash. 'I'd like to wash in hot water, Dane, it'll be cold otherwise.'

He decided to take advantage of the situation, stripped off and joined her. 'Come on, I'll wash your back,' he offered. 'But I can heat water any time you need it.'

She laughed at him. 'Dane, *I said you were a cool one.*' Nevertheless they spent some time carefully washing each other. He also bathed the bruises on his chest once more. For a few minutes he tended one or two of her scars.

Amber brushed her hair and put on the new red tunic over one of the linen blouses, wrapping a small slender scarf around her waist as a belt, tying her hair back with a red ribbon. Dane complimented her, she looked very feminine. 'Oooh, you look nice, all *girlified*,' he teased.

They enjoyed a pleasant dinner in a quiet room, just two other couples; the landlord reserved a small room for 'ladies to enjoy meals, rather than sitting with the raucous elements in the bar,' he explained. Amber was delighted, she was used to the hostile stares of women and the calls of 'hussy' as she walked in wearing her long jerkin and leggings.

'Make's a pleasant change,' she commented.

'You're better than all the women out there,' Dane protested. Amber just blushed and ate her dinner. They treated themselves to a flagon of red wine.

They laughed and chatted all evening, telling each other their life stories, about their likes and dislikes, their hopes and fears. The landlord had to ask them to move eventually, he wanted to close up for the night.

They moved upstairs where Dane carefully removed Amber's new clothes and carried on precisely where he had left off earlier that evening.

*

They met the priestess, Elandil by name, the following morning. To their surprise, and pleasure, it turned out she had a horse and small carriage, two fine horses in fact. They could make good time.

They took on extra water and she brought a large wicker basket with her, they were well supplied with provisions for the journey. It would probably take a couple of days, possibly three, all being well, by carriage. They would stop off at a convenient inns along the main route.

She confided in them as they rode.

'I need to tell you now, there's trouble ahead, especially for you, mage. The village elders have gathered what cash they have to send me to the Temple of Arboreal. They want me gone safely and need to stay to prepare and protect their homes. They held a special meeting last night to discuss plans.

There are rumours - quite solid ones - that King Kyneweth of Draecastle is allying with the Adammites. He is distancing himself from the old religion and Lady Merrie, taking on the mantle of this new Death cult, led by this Mordecai von Adamm I have no need to explain to you Dane, that people like you will be among the first to suffer, along with all Merrievian priestesses. There are terrible rumours of events at Draecastle, many of which I am sure are true.'

Dane responded with passion. 'You've no need to explain to me, I am from the isle of Glasse.' He told her about his parents.

She offered sympathy, but exclaimed further when he said his mother was a dryad, *'oh, how wonderful that must have been for you, a true dryad priestess*, and she left the woodlands for your father? And now gone because of these cursed men. There are few dryads here in the north, and that must have been one of the last dryad forests.' She was adamant, 'Dane, you must take care of your heritage, you need to leave the north at once.' She confided further, 'it's not just here, they're aiming for the south west too, they keep invading Elvinhaeme from their Isle of Glasse stronghold. They intend destroying every single elf left in existence, using them as sacrifices to their new god.'

She looked sadly at the pair of them. 'They wish to destroy the Sacred Temple and bring about a new existence ruled by Mordecai von Adamm, whoever he may be. These are angry and dissatisfied young men, all ready to kill, well armed and clearly well trained in the art of war - and more men join each day. It seems it is a cult centred wholly around men and male physical power. I do not understand why they relish death over life, but it appears they do. They delight in destruction for its own sake. As for people like you, Dane, I have already heard of mage and witch hunts, the burning on pyres.'

Dane nodded, that was exactly what happened on his home island. And now they were here, on the mainland, taking over bit by bit, turning good folk from the old gentle ways, the ways of the Mother and the Goddess, the seasons and the land. They seemed to relish death and destruction. 'I have to go north to Draecastle, try to help,' he stated immediately.

Elandil put out her hand to stop him, 'no, Dane, you are too valuable, you must get out of Segantium. You need to find those like you, return with an army of mages. We cannot fight this individually, only with strength. Go find the elves, join with them. Gather those loyal to our Lady Merrie. They seem to hate us, at least so I have been told, and they despise women. We must fight back - but with strength. And may the Blessings of the Mother go with you.'

They travelled the main roads through the countryside. Occasionally groups of beggars, mostly refugees running from Adammite incursions, assailed them. Elandil would throw some pennies, but they crowded the wagon, frightened the horses, Dane had to scatter them with fire magic. 'You shouldn't be too soft with them, my Lady, they take advantage, you must take care.' She knew it was so, but her kind heart would not let them pass such poor people without giving aid.

Later, as the road grew lonely, a pack of wolves came growling at them. Amber stood in the centre of the open carriage sending her arrows at them and Dane scattered them with electrum. They howled and yelped in pain and ran off. Dane looked at Amber, their eyes smiling at each other, appreciative of the support each gave. ... *Yes, they worked well together - a good team.* But it was odd, it was full summer, wolves were rarely hungry at this time of year, the forests were full of wildlife, normally unlikely to attack humans on the roads. Something was upsetting the delicate balance of their natural existence.

Besides, there was something odd looking about the wolves.

The rest of the journey to Manecaestr was in fact uneventful, until they reached the city gates. Already refugees were coming in from the coast, seeking safety inside the walls of the city. There was talk everywhere of this new drive by the Adammites. It seemed to take forever to get through the pushing crowds, listening to the Guards shouting, 'One by one now, we can't take all of you.' Only when they finally neared the gates was it seen they carried a High Priestess with them and they were allowed through.

Even so, a certain type, those who did not sit well with the existing system, thieves and vagabonds, drifters, beggars, were heard to mutter words of slander against the priestess. The name 'Von Adamm' was heard more than once.

Dane was relieved when they entered the strong walls of the sacred Temple of Arboreal. Two straight and tall Templar Knights in full chain-mail stood guard in front of the Temple, each bearing a great-sword in front of him, their white and red surtouts clearly showing their allegiance to Lady Merrie.

They both bowed to the Lady Elandil, made way to let them pass.

Dane left Amber for her to see Elandil through to the Inner Sanctum, a place sacred to women, a quiet place, one men rarely trod. It wasn't that a man couldn't go there, it just wasn't good manners to do so, unless requested. Instead he went into the main Temple Hall.

It smelled beautiful, summer flowers were everywhere and a green-clothed elf played a flute gently in a corner. The elf looked as gentle as the music, but Dane knew looks could be deceiving where elves were concerned. A fountain also played softly in the centre of the Hall. He moved quickly through the small congregation and over to the large oak-carved statue of Lady Merrie at the end of the aisle. She was almost naked, wearing only a gossamer cloak and garlands of fresh flowers. She smiled gently down at them all, her hands raised in welcome. But on her head was a wreath of holly, for she gave her blood so that the oak king could live. The young berries were yet green, but by the winter solstice, they would be blood red.

Dane bowed on one knee before her, made obeisance to the gentle goddess. He gave up a small prayer, something he felt he needed to do. He was on a strange path now, not sure how it would go. He felt a little lost, a tad overwhelmed, but understood this was a new twist on the thread of his life. The shadowed strands of the past were racing into his future.

'Help me, my Lady, help me to keep to your wise ways in these trying times. I know not what you want of me, but I do know my life is changing rapidly. Give me the strength, my Lady, to love you, and to keep your love in my heart, always. Help me, with the love you bear for all beings, to look after this new love in my life, that she may not be hurt or taken by these cursed people as my family were. Help me strive to do that which is right and follow the path of life and light. I offer my powers in your service as I have done my whole life, and shall always do. *So mote it be.*'

He spent some time in contemplation, the juxtaposition of music and the fountain both pleasing to the ear and relaxing. He wasn't sure if Lady Merrie existed as a Goddess or not - for what exactly was a Goddess? - but he was sure that her *essence* existed. It existed inside people, Her followers. Whenever he saw kindness, generosity, fertility, understanding, love or joy, She was there, part of all the good moments of his life, the cornucopia of being. Her Feast Days followed the seasons, the rising and falling of the year, the times of working and the times of sleeping, the renewal and rebirth of life. Each new child born was a joy to the Mother.

The Lady Merrie held a great inner beauty, the wellness of life, of living. She - or perhaps her teachings - gave him the strength to counter and live through the bad moments as well as the good ...

Life is all about balance.

Amber meanwhile accompanied Elandil to the Inner Sanctum, where they found the High Priestess Illumini, the leader of the Temple of Arboreal. Elandil gave her the news, the Lady Illumini nodding her head, she'd already heard some of it.

'We live in very troubled times, we must hold on and be strong. Unfortunately we of the Temple have few combative powers, we rely on others. We cannot fight these people, we need help.'

The Lady Elandil explained about Dane, his parentage, a mage and a dryad. When Amber told her that she too came from two mages, both priestesses were emphatic - *they must go now* - leave the north and get to safety. They were targets, undeservedly so. Go south, get to Mercantia or Westerling, find more of their own kind, safety in numbers.

'*Run*, the pair of you. We will give you lodging here tonight, also gold in return for your kind help bringing Elandil here to us. We will give you what we can, to send you on your journey. And may Lady Merrie be with you.' The High Priestess was adamant, they were a valuable asset in the coming fight.

Amber met Dane in the Temple Hall, told him what they had said. He nodded, 'I've already made my vows, I need no more prompting. It's kind of them to give us lodging.'

They spent another comfortable night in a soft bed and were woken early by the Lady Elandil.

'Come, break your fast and be away. If you go down to the stables, there are two horses saddled and ready for you. There is a little extra gold here for their upkeep. Also, here is a small package, if you could take this south with you, to the main Temple at Orlandium, it would be appreciated. It doesn't matter when it arrives, as long as it is kept safe.' They both looked at her, at the small sealed box, wondering what they were carrying? 'You will see when you arrive. Thank you once more.' She kissed both of them, said her goodbyes.

Both tucked into a hearty breakfast, then picked up their belongings and went to the stables. Two good horses with strong saddles and roomy saddlebags were waiting for them.

The pair left the Temple and made their way south.

*

They made good time with the horses and thanks to the extra gold, were able to stop off at inns for a night's rest. Orlandium was a long way south, it would still take weeks. They also discovered that the Adammite cult were gaining ground in many places, it's ideals of human male domination and death suddenly in favour. It washed around like a wave of fashion, yet so much more deadly. Dane's mage staff began to be looked upon with suspicion.

They reached Mortia,, the capital city of Mercantia, around ten days later. The ride fairly uneventful, the main road, the Long Ride, well patrolled by troops both north and south of the land border. This road was the central artery of Mer'edrynn, merchants and goods passed continually, protection was essential.

The city of Mortia was, as it sounded, a dour and forbidding city, tall grey buildings, dark alleyways, although the people they passed seemed cheery. They found a small inn, the Long Drop, where they stabled the horses along with some of the heavier baggage. It was afternoon and they decided to wander the city a little, find the market, Amber still needed some things. The city was wealthy, merchants did well here supplying the immediate area, as well as being the central point for north and south Mer'edrynn. The grey stone was relieved by fountains here and there, some pure marble. The people looked well dressed, although a little dull, browns and greys seemed to be in fashion, or perhaps just cheap to produce. There were several markets and a selection of fine shops - too expensive for Amber, but she enjoyed looking at the displays in the windows. Everything looked busy. Lord Black Morus, the Chieftain of Mortia looked after the city well.

It seemed that the Adammites actually had a large chapel of their own here and could be seen - and heard - chanting and shouting in one of the market squares, appropriately named 'Yamper's Yakkings', a yampy being a local phrase for a daft bugger. There was a huge bonfire blazing and black-robed men wore hoods embroidered with Blazing Sun symbols, a flaming red sun on a black background set inside a red square. Inside the red sun was a small black air symbol, a triangle with a line across it, adding fuel to the flames no doubt. It looked powerful and menacing. This black and red sign was also emblazoned on their chests and long sleeves, a startling contrast to the dull black robes. The men were all chanting as if in a dream or a drugged stupor. It sounded dreary, but compelling. They were certainly in earnest and the small crowd watched curiously.

When they had been in the Isle of Glasse, the militia merely wore plain armour, this Blazing Sun thing was a new addition, the Sun of Adamm. Clearly their Chieftain now claimed a deity as part of his army, or perhaps he merely identified with the masculine power of the sun?

Follow the true God, believe in the Son of Fire,' a tall, heavily robed man exclaimed, sounding excited at the prospect, 'cast off your sins ye followers of Merrie, follow the Blazing Sun. The Sun of Adamm sees everything, he sees into your heart, ye blackguards, he sees your evil ways - *only through purification can* ...' The robed man stopped chanting, catching sight of Dane and Amber.

'*Oh ye foul fiend*, son of *Abaddon*, ye should be cast into the flames!' he shouted at Dane, seeing his staff. 'Death to all mages!' Dane remained calm. He wondered why they took fire as their symbol of hatred, it was just an element like any other? He used it often. Why transpose it into a death symbol? Without the sun, there would be no life, it was a case of balance, as well as respect for the power of fire. He wondered too, were they saying Sun or Son? Or did they just mean both?

'Why, what have I done to offend you?' He stared him in the eye, then held the gaze of the others.

'Beware,' they shrieked to everyone, 'he gives us the Evil Eye.' No doubt everything he did would be interpreted as evil. The Adammites glared back, although some hid inside their hoods as if to ward off his magic.

'Look, I'm just passing through here with my lady, minding our own business. I don't know who you are, and I've no truck with you, *so if you don't mind* ...' He made to pass on, not wanting to start a scene, there were too many of them. He really wanted revenge on them all, the memory of their butchering of his parents strong. But that could not be today, he and Amber were too much at a disadvantage.

The Adammites obviously did mind. 'He born of the realms of sin must be cast out and purified,' they shouted, 'and the harlot with him. Only the flames will heal.' It was getting annoying now, they were obviously chanting from their sacred book of Von Adamm quotes, all clichés and solecisms. Whoever this von Adamm was, he was into ominous catchphrases, the followers reeked of self-importance. Then three of the cultists took out long swords, brandished them menacingly, the on-looking crowd now a little anxious. *'We must cast the evil of magic from this land!.'*

Quotes, chants, whatever, their voices held all the anger and hatred of the bigot.

Dane looked astounded at them. 'There's nothing inherently evil in magic,' he exclaimed. 'You're the devils who go around attacking and killing. You murdered my parents!' He shot a brief look at Amber. 'Leave us be, we're in a public square, we have a right to be here.'

But the Adammites seemed to be enraged, would not listen to reason. Dane wondered if they had taken some sort of drug, or perhaps they were high on the chanting? Whatever it was, they were dangerous, and becoming more dangerous with every moment. Dane and the woman wearing a young man's garb were the enemy and rightful prey.

'Let's get out of here,' he told Amber, 'there's too many of them.'

Amber nodded, *safest thing to do.*

But it was too late. They'd shouted and chanted for hours on end, were high on hatred and were just waiting for an excuse. Dane and Amber were perfect.

'Nay, no mage shall live!' they shouted, clearly from the von Adamm tome of antisocial behaviour, making for Dane, waving their swords high in the air. They meant it too, their eyes were filled with hatred. Dane grabbed his staff, Amber took out her short-swords, they didn't want this. Now the other cultists were revealing swords or daggers, five more, all aiming for the pair, someone at last to vent their spleen upon. Dane wondered what had caused such disgust of mages? Why should they have to fight for their lives for being simply what they were?

And there were eight against two.

Dane sighed sorrowfully, fight was inevitable, he didn't want this for Amber.

'Stop now, or I *will* use my magic against you,' he shouted. They ignored him, He pointed his staff at the group, 'I'm warning you, don't come any closer, we mean no harm here, let us pass.' But the group came onwards, they heard nothing, they wanted a sacrifice, they needed to show their power over the mage - and that indecently dressed female with him, the whore needed punishing.

Dane lifted his staff, fierce flames shot out, four Adammites found they had burning hair and cloaks. This was indeed the magic they feared and hated. In turn, Amber lashed out with her short swords, shimmying out of the way of their swords, managing a slice or two here and there. She was beginning to think she had been better off with the circus.

'Aah! Death to all mages!' one shouted at them, as Dane cast fire once more, pure elemental mage fire, now pointing it at their robes. *'Take the harlot, teach her the way!'* another screamed. It was probably another von Adamm sound-bite. Simple, emotive and easily understood.

It was also unfortunately all too real, too close and too dangerous. This was the moment they waited for, and they were eager to kill. There was hate on their faces and death in their eyes.

A huge sword was thrust towards Dane's face, he shot amberic jolts into it, was satisfied to hear a scream. As the sword dropped from the cultist's shocked hand, Amber efficiently came in with a quick slice, and a thrust into his groin. He doubled up in pain. But three more were now after Dane and the four that had been burnt by Dane's fire were recovering, having damped out the flames, filled with the desire for revenge.

Four men surrounded Amber, swords aimed at her and lustful grins on their faces. Out came her knives, one thrown straight into the heart of one, he went down in front of her. The other three screamed hatred and tried to grab her. She glanced quickly at the overhanging branch of a tree, hauled herself up and over, twirling as she did on her trapeze high above the circus. She managed to kick two of them in the face as she came around, twirled around again and kicked out ... but this time straight into the arms of two more ready and waiting cultists. She tried to kick them off and climb higher, but they had firm hold of her feet and ankles. The two she had laid out were also now back on their feet, nasty sneers on their faces, arms ready to grab her.

Four cultists pulled her down off the tree branch, tightened their hold and began dragging her along the street with them, spitting and shouting at her, one now holding his sword to her neck. She kicked and swore, managed to get a hand free, tore at one with her dagger before being grabbed again. She was rewarded with a backhanded slap across her cheek.

The crowd watched open mouthed, but did nothing, scared of both sides, scared of wild mage flashfire, scared of the long swords. Amber now looked like a crazy woman, shouting and swearing at the cultists. 'Let go, you bastards, leave me alone you damn cowards!' The cultists laughed, told her what they intended doing to her when they got her to the headquarters.

Dane was too having trouble, he was still shooting fire at the two attacking him, one screaming in agony, the others shouting *'devil's magic, kill the mage!'* two swords aiming at him, damn close, too damn close. He jumped back as a sword thrust at his throat, seeing what they were doing to Amber in the corner of his eye. Three men now, she'd got one down, bless her, on one small female, pulling her along. *He had to get to Amber.* But the other two were on him.

Amber was struggling, shouting, kicking out and trying to wriggle from their grasp. Dane shot a massive electrum bolt at the two closest to him, hitting out with his staff at their heads. He was trying to move around them, reach Amber, they were taking her - who knew where? And when they got her to their chapel, what would they do to her?

It was hopeless, he couldn't reach her. Dane cried out, 'Amber, get away, get away ...' flames shooting from his fingers, trying to aim for the three Adammites brutally pulling her along, ignoring the two trying to kill him.

She was screaming now, fully in their grip, being marched to wherever they held their headquarters. No one helped, the crowd watched silently with morbid curiosity; mesmerised by the scene; the cultists just laughed. They would enjoy the woman later before sending her to the Inquisitorial Assembly for interrogation. Amber struggled but was held fast, outnumbered. One kicked her, knocking her to the ground, then she was dragged by her arms and her hair, her screams piercing the air.

And still the crowd watched on.

Dane couldn't get to her, the other two were on him, attempting to knock his staff away, trying to capture or kill him too. He realised his mana couldn't hold much more magic, like stamina it was being depleted. He rolled over and managed to grab his staff, using it as a fighting club for a few moments, gain his magic back. But they had huge swords, he didn't want it chopping in two.

The two cultists fighting Dane managed to push him to the floor, one on top of him, knees holding down his arms, trying to slice through his neck with the sword. Dane managed to hit one with his staff, but the second cultist kicked the staff from him. 'Kill him!' he shouted triumphantly.

The uppermost cultist held up his sword in triumph, grinning with delight. Dane watched helplessly as the sword came down towards his throat ...

Chapter 4

The Court of Floriénne, 1st Firstfire - Feast of Beltane

The competition was going well, as he knew it would. Just a couple of rounds to go before he took the title. Tamlyn threw the last knife of the round into the board, another bull. He chuckled to himself ... *too easy*. That guy who'd come down from the north for the competition, what was his name ... Arne? Yes, he was good, he'd probably face him in the final, at least he hoped so, a worthy opponent.

The crowd cheered as he collected the daggers from the board. Tamlyn was always a favourite of the nobles and entourage of the Court of the Grand Dûchesse Elanriel in Floriénne. He was a favourite generally; a beautiful elf, of the broad-chested, slim-hipped variety, his prowess with the daggers and the sword left his arms well muscled. Fair of face too, with deep, dark green eyes and lashes too long for any male, often used to good effect. But it was his smile they loved, cheeky and cheery at the same time.

He smiled now as his friend Denath'lin sneaked up behind him, flicking one of his pointy elfin ears, putting his arm around his shoulder. Tamlyn flinched, looked into his friend's eyes, *'Hai! Sel malia!'* he protested in the purest Elvhen tongue, although there was a laugh in his voice. 'Leave my ear alone!' Elvhen was a strange mix of languages and Tamlyn, like many knights of the Inner Court was fluent in Mer'edrynn Plaintongue as well as Sevillain and Chev'allién.

'Brilliant as usual, Tammy,' he said, ignoring him. 'Watch out for that *eormynn* though, he's good.'

'Ha, esil méchan, I look forward to meeting him.' They settled on the bench to watch the next round, comfortable in each other's company. They'd known each other for years, brought up at

Court together. 'What about later, coming to the feast? I'm on duty, but there's little to do apart from mingle and look good - best uniform on, hey?' It was the Beltane festival, the Court of Floriénne was overcrowded with people.

'Yes, me too, we're supposed to keep visiting dignitaries happy. Have you seen the beauties from the Elvinhaeme Court?' His friend grinned lasciviously.

'Those two with flowing blonde hair and the long white dresses, cut low around the bosom? Oh yes, I think we can *do our duty very well* there ...' he laughed and clapped Denath'lin on the back. 'We're supposed to keep good relations with Elvinhaeme, aren't we? I can't make up my mind between them though, so how about a foursome?' The elves of Floriénne enjoyed a somewhat uninhibited lifestyle, especially the Court.

'OK, but only if you win, Tammy - I'll make it your prize.' He stopped as Tamlyn's name was called. 'Go for it, my brother.'

Tamlyn looked down and chuckled as he stepped up to the line. 'Better win then, ha!' he laughed, and threw his next three daggers, all as expected into the bull. He could do this blindfold. He made it to the final against this newcomer from the north, Arne.

The older man strutted to the line with his daggers. Dark and swarthy, obviously of Sevillon extraction, he was flamboyantly dressed in tight fitting black leggings and short ankle boots with very high Sevillon heels, a brilliant red shirt and a leather jerkin. But his whole demeanour was courtly, Tamlyn thought he fitted perfectly here, the Court enjoyed a little swagger, he bet the Dûchesse admired him.

They both threw three daggers perfectly. Then another three. Then it became boring as they made a third attempt at beating each other, to no avail. He watched as Arne turned to him, a bright light in his eyes.

'I hate to either lose or have to share a win - how about a little swordplay between us? I take it you fence as well as throw a dagger?' There was a definite Sevillon accent there, mixed with northern cadence.

Tamlyn rose to the challenge. 'Sabres?'

The Sevillain nodded, and added, 'let's make it a good play for them, I like an audience, and how about a little side wager?'

Tamlyn was happy. 'But, just remember we fight to the death here, we don't count touches or other such rot. We don't do fence-play - we are soldiers of the Realm. *We are taught to kill.* So be warned! You will have seen some of the sword-fighting - yield when it becomes too much.' The Sevillain merely sneered. They went to the adjudicator, explained their wishes. He too was happy, it added to the show, and he wouldn't need to find an extra silver cup. He stood in the centre of the arena and introduced them both.

They stood opposite each other, then bowed, sabres at their sides.

'En guarde!' the Sevillain shouted, but then he twirled his sword in the air and did some kind of pirouette, showing off. Tamlyn smirked and looked at the crowd with a grin on his face, he raised an eyebrow at the man's antics. The crowd laughed with him. Elves never made a show of sword fighting - it was too serious. Floriénne itself might be peaceful, but the Foraes Dair was not an easy place to live, sword skills were honed to perfection for sheer safety.

'Pret allez!' returned Tamlyn and moved in, feinting to the man's left, then a quick cut under the man's feet, laughing as he jumped. If the guy was so light in his feet, he'd use them. He cut back again, the Sevillain jumped again, but this time came down with a side swipe towards Tamlyn's sabre. Tamlyn parried it perfectly, then thrust up and in, almost to the man's chest, allowing him to jump back. Another thrust, then a parry as the swordsman cut back at him, but he followed with a moulinet, small circular movements around the man's sword point, showing off, teasing. He passed back himself, stepping away, before he could give him an opportunity to get the better hand.

Indeed, as the man stepped forward Tamlyn dodged sideways, then turned and neatly struck at the Sevillain's neck. Perhaps the man didn't understand he had been trained to kill, not play, but he struck blood, it gushed out over the fine shirt. He hadn't cut deeply, but it was messy. The Sevillain was wild, he held up his hand to the adjudicator, who shook his head. *Sword fighting, not sword play*. This was Floriénne, not Chev'alierre. We fight to the death here ...

Eormynn always mistakenly thought the pretty elves were as sweet as their looks ...

The man was a showman, but he was fighting a trained officer of the Royal Court, the Dûchesse required the best of fighters at Court as her protectors. Tamlyn was among them.

He took advantage of the man's temporary confusion and went in for the kill, using his pommel to knock the man's sword out of a momentarily weakened hand and then hooked his right foot behind the man's left, neatly catching him off balance. 'Unfair!' the Sevillain shouted as he fell.

No, it wasn't fair, but it did the trick. Tamlyn got down on one knee and pointed the sword at his neck again. 'Yield?' he asked.

Arne's eyes widened. 'I yield,' he cried, then looked up in disgust, 'You don't play to rules.'

Tamlyn's eyes blazed back at him. 'I warned you, we don't *play* with swords here, we *kill*. There are no rules when it is a matter of life or death. I have been taught to kill, just accept you are lucky to be alive.' He pulled back his sword, walked away. He hadn't entered a fencing competition, he'd entered a dagger throwing contest. Now the man was whining.

He walked to the table where he picked up the trophy, to everyone's delight, the applause thunderous. The 'tricksy elves of Floriénne' or so they were often called, had found Tamlyn's swordplay amusing. And in any case, Tamlyn was a favourite of all. But he felt in his pocket and passed a couple of coins to the Sevillain.

'I keep the trophy, you may have the cash, since it is worth more to you. I hope it compensates you for the loss of a shirt.'

He walked away, hearing a muttered, 'it is not the shirt, young elf, merely pride. One day I will pay you back.'

The elderly Dûchesse called Tamlyn over to her, she peeked out from behind a large ornate fan ... it was a hot day ... 'Tamlyn, you were naughty ... but delicious as usual.' She beamed at him.

Tamlyn gave her his best Court bow. 'My Gracious Elanr'iel, which would you prefer? That I should obey all the delicate rules of fencing while you are being mercilessly attacked by an enemy, or that I should cut him down before he strikes?' He fluttered his lashes at the Dûchesse, who held out her hand.

'You may kiss it, you scoundrel, then go and be nice with all the guests, especially the Elvinhaeme ones - we need to keep good relations with them.' The Dûchesse expected her well-mannered Knights to double up as ambassadors. 'But always keep your eyes and ears open, my dear Tamlyn, you never know do you?'

He bowed again and kissed the back of her hand. She watched him go, *he was so like his father*, she thought ... a man she had greatly admired in the past ... in more ways than one.

Tamlyn took the trophy to his chamber in the palace, a quick wash and brush up, then went back to the public rooms and joined his friend. 'How about doing that mingling thing?' he grinned. He and Denath'lin set off to find alcohol, food and the two 'delicious ladies' from the Elvinhaeme Court.

They passed a very pleasant evening. They performed their Court duty exceedingly well ...

The loud shrieking woke him up early the following morning. He looked across the bed, wondering momentarily where he was, ah, yes, his friend's bed and the two females between them. Now ... *that* had been a good night

But the shrieking continued. He climbed out of bed, grabbed a pair of cotton breeches - he was currently naked - and his sword, then dashed out, closely followed by Denath'lin. Out in the corridor he followed the general pulse of people, most of whom, like him, were in various stages of undress. Admiring stares from several women followed him as he ran through the throng.

He eventually arrived at the place known as the Vaults, where it was clear there was a commotion, and quickly understood the situation.

The most prized possession, the Longsword of D'rendiél, had been taken from its sealed glass case - a case that *couldn't be opened because it was magically sealed* - and indeed hadn't been opened for hundreds of years. It had once belonged to their greatest fighter, the Elven lord Diras Rendiél who had led them across ancient seas to Mer'edrynn, it's lineage disappearing back into the depths of time.

The sword held the power of the Elven peoples, or so it was said, and was never to be taken from its resting place. It was to be kept safe *in perpetuis* - forever. Without it, the elves would suffer disaster, death or slavery, or so it was foretold.

Throughout the ages, two specially selected mages from the most trustworthy Elven families were given the secret signs and sigils to open the two magic seals of the large glass case. They did not know each other, the secrets passed from father to son only; they would only have come together if word had gone out throughout the land that the Sword was needed - that disaster had come to Mer'edrynn. It also required the Royal Keymaster to unlock the final lock of the case with his key - visible only once the magic seals had been released - kept, naturally, under further lock and key in his own strongbox in the Royal Key Chamber. And the key to the Key Chamber was kept by the Dûchesse herself.

And the case was kept in the deepest Vault of the Royal Vaults, protected by the most loyal of Floriénne guards. Only the last Royal Guard held the keys to the small vault, protected as he was by many other guards before him. It had sufficed for hundreds of years.

But the guard had been knocked out at some point, had only recently regained consciousness, having been found by his fellow guards. The other guards knew, or professed to know nothing about the incident. They informed the Captain of the Guard. He informed the handmaiden of the Dûchesse who was still asleep and not to be disturbed. The handmaiden had seen, screamed and was now standing by the door in shock. She wasn't happy down here at the best of times, her duty to follow her Dûchesse, but this was unbelievable.

Tamlyn inspected the case. The case looked intact, the beautiful, but faded purple velvet on which the sword should lie, still bore the imprint of centuries. But the longsword had gone. He looked around the Vault itself, knowing he was wasting his time. Nothing, of course. It was his unhappy duty to inform the Dûchesse, the handmaiden shaking her head, declaring that she did not dare.

He quickly dressed and explained the situation to a wide-eyed and disbelieving Dûchesse, who, after inspecting the Vault herself, had the whole Court and everyone in it searched immediately. Word soon got out and the Court began to panic, distress on everyone's faces. The Dûchesse took the whole burden upon herself, she had failed in her responsibility, she had failed her people.

She was livid.

At noon that day, after a morning of fruitless searching, she called her Courtiers together.

'This is a disaster,' she expostulated. 'The Longsword of D'rendiél is precious beyond belief. You are all aware of the legends - *without this sword, we elves are doomed* - it must be returned at all cost. The thief must be found and heavily punished.' Briefly she stopped to cast her eye over the Court, 'Where were my guards, where were my Knights, last night? Were you all drunk or something? Those guards of the Vault will be punished for their lack of care, their total disregard of duty.

How did anyone get in and how did they open the case? Call the Mages for me, bring them here, have they conspired against us? Bring the Royal Keymaster here and have him questioned - I *will* get to the bottom of this - by one means or another. I have no intention ...' she shouted at the Court, 'of being known through history as the woman who lost the Sword and brought down the elven peoples!

Until that sword is found there will be no more feasting, no more Feast Days, we are all in mourning!' Again her eye swivelled maliciously over the Court.

'But - *you* - you are *all* partly to blame for this theft, not merely the Vault guards, it should not have happened! Someone has allowed this conspiracy, someone knows something! And something must be done about it – quickly!' She paused to take breath, gather her thoughts, remain fully in control.

'I have therefore decided that the Inner Knights of this Court, my most trusted servants, must go out into the world immediately and seek whoever has stolen the Sword. I want this thief or thieves apprehended and brought to justice, indeed I am anxious to question them and discover how it was removed without our knowledge. However, you also have the full authority of this Court to execute them if necessary.

You will go in groups of four, to the four corners of Mer'edrynn. I will provide you with fine horses and as much gold as is required for your journey and your needs. You will not return here until you have the Sword, *you are exiled*, do you hear me?' She was almost shrieking now in her despair. 'That is my wish and my order. *Sheer, damn incompetence* ! All knights here are equally to blame, as are the guards.'

She stopped, looked down, shook her head sadly, she was after all, in charge. '... *As am I*. So, I do not order you to do this thing, since you will be banished from Court as punishment until it is found. Instead I ask for volunteers, those whose hearts are true to our elven realm.' Her ashen grey face and anxious eyes perused her warriors.

Tamlyn put himself forward immediately. The loss of their greatest treasure was an ill omen for Floriénne, his own exile meant nothing in comparison with his duty to his people. His friend Denath'lin also stepped forward, as did some of his other friends and acquaintances. Four groups for the four quarters of Mer'edrynn. His group, including Denath'lin, drew the Foraes Dair, the great forest of Oak which stretched along the eastern side of the country all the way to the north, Shirewood in Plaintongue. They were off within the hour.

For some days they worked together, but the Foraes Dair is a a difficult place to travel, once out of Floriénne it becomes wildwood. They decided to split and follow vague rumours each going their own way after the thief, meet up at various points where they pooled scanty information. It was a more than a matter of honour that he be found. If the legend was true, the whole realm was in danger.

*

The city of Mortia, Mercantia, month of Shearing.

The Blazing Sun cultist grinned triumphantly at Dane, as he raised his sword to thrust deep in his throat. Dane struggled to keep away from the blade, throwing a brief blast of electrum magic at the cultist's back with his fingers, all he could manage.

Meanwhile, Amber desperately pulled, wriggling, squirming, trying to shake off her attackers. Like the cultist on top of Dane, they were merciless, driven perhaps by drugs, or by mindless frenzy. The crowd watched meekly, mesmerised into immobility by the ferocity of the attackers.

They could hear the cries of the pair under attack yet did nothing but stare.

Suddenly, two sharp daggers shot through the air in quick succession, one into the eye of the robed male on top of Dane and one through the heart of one of Amber's attackers.

Amber took advantage of the momentary confusion, lashed out with her feet as she jumped up and took down a cultist with a kick into his face, then whipped out her own daggers from her belt. Quickly she thrust one into the heart of one, before leaping out of the clutches of a third. He merely looked surprised at her, as a flaxen haired elf suddenly dashed across the square with lightning speed and slashed across his throat with a gleaming sabre.

Dane pulled himself out from under the dead body of the cultist and made for the last robed figure, hotfooting it down an alleyway. He picked up his staff and shot terrible streams of fire into him; the burning body fell screaming as he died.

'Don't mess with mages!' he screamed at the crowd. 'We've never harmed *you*!' The crowd looked alarmed, began to disperse. City Guards were coming to see what the commotion was about.

Amber quickly retrieved her short swords. She left the small daggers, no time to collect them.

Dane and Amber found their arms being pulled along by the young elf. 'Quickly, I think we need to leave,' he told them. His voice held the slightest of Elvhen accents, but his diction was crisp and clear, his Plaintongue as pure as his native language.

They nodded, it was so, eight dead bodies took a deal of answering and the crowd could happily fill in the blanks.

They followed the lithe elf down narrow alleyways bearing dour names such as Blood Alley, or Whipping Lane, until they came to a small ale house with an equally dark title - 'The Nightmare', a picture of a black horse swinging above. 'Let's go in here, it will be quieter ...' he offered. Two cheery eyes, the colour of rich green fern - the shade of grass at dusk when it gives off an unexpected luminous glow - beamed at them both. A bright smile accompanied the words, silver buttons and buckles shining on his long close fitting, black leather doublet and leggings. They seemed soft and supple, with neither hauberk or cuirass for protection, an armour born of peaceful times, not war, clearly more for style than defence. His sturdy boots and gauntlets too, were tight fitting black leather, yet they did not seem dour, merely official somehow, with more bright silver buttons and buckles. A sabre hung in an elaborately engraved silver scabbard at his side. He had collected back his small daggers, they seemed to be in various pockets, belts and holders around his person.

They piled into the small ale-house. He led them to a table by a window, 'we can watch here, in case any guards come after you.' His voice was gentle, pleasing on the ear.

Both Dane and Amber began to thank him, he'd helped save their lives.

He waved away their thanks, 'no thanks necessary, all in a day's work. If not you, it would have been me, I've seen this before. I'm sure you would have helped me.' He made a little bow, a short click of well-heeled boots. 'Allow me to introduce myself,' the same charming smile, 'I am Knight Captain Tamlyn Taenghelin, of the Court of the Grande Dûchesse Elanriel in

Floriénne. I am most happy to make your acquaintance.' Another smile, another bow of the head.

'Well, Knight Captain Taenghelin, we are *more* than happy to greet you,' replied Dane, 'I think you just saved our bacon.'

'We weren't doing *too* badly,' reminded Amber, 'we took some down, I wasn't giving in ...'

The elf looked at her, seemingly taking her in for the first time. 'I am sorry, I do not know your name,' he cocked his head to one side, 'you were most courageous, and your backwards roll around that branch was amazing, but you were a little outnumbered, I fear.'

'There *were* more than I cared for ...' she admitted. 'I'm Amber.'

The elf's long-lashed eyes flashed at her, 'such a beautiful name, and matching your beautiful eyes ...' he told her, quite sincere in his flattery. Amber stood a little mesmerised by him, he was that kind of elf. Tamlyn took her hand and kissed the back of it, again a metallic click of his boots as the short silver spurs made contact.

There came a cough, Dane interrupted him, 'would you like a drink, I think we could all do with one?'

The elf nodded, that would be good. 'Perhaps a glass of mead or a cognac?'

Dane went to the bar and returned with three beers. 'They do ale or genièvre, nothing else. It's not the most salubrious bar in the world.'

The Knight Captain lifted his glass. 'Vint'ii, vest'ii, vit'ii!' he toasted. The other two looked blankly at him. 'To wine, feasting and life!' he explained, then tried the beer. 'This is quite good, so no complaints. Tell me, does this sort of thing happen often to you?' He seemed unperturbed by the attack.

Dane shrugged. 'My parents died as a result of the Adammite invasion of the Isle of Glasse. I thought I had left these people there. But it seems they are now venturing into the rest of Mer'edrynn, and somehow have become a religious cult. Amber is a target because she doesn't look like their idea of a submissive female and I'm a natural target because I am a mage.'

The elf nodded, agreeing, briefly appraising Amber, clearly liking what he saw, he flashed another charming smile before he spoke, somewhat sadly. '... And I am a target simply because I am an elf - *not good*. Are you finding this in all cities?'

They both shook their heads, no, this was the first, although they believed Draecastle was now allied to them. The elf continued sadly, 'and now we have this Blazing Sun sect also allied to, or part of, Mordecai Von Adamm's not-so-merry men. *Definitely not good*.' He gave a despondent sigh, 'we live in changing times. Everything is disintegrating, dwindling. I have only been out of the F*oraes Dair* for a short time, but what I have seen in these few weeks is disturbing.' He pushed back a lock of flaxen hair that had fallen out of an elven braid, behind his small pointed ears.

Amber questioned him, 'I'm sorry, F*oraes Dair*? I'm not sure what that is?'

'Ah, of course not, you have no Elvhen, it means oaken forest, and truly, I rarely leave it. You call it Shirewood, but it is all of the forest from Floriénne to the top most corner of Segantium, the border with Picantés. Once it was the land of elves, now we are reduced to two small areas, Floriénne and Elvinhaeme. Still, there are many of us roaming the wildwood.' He sipped his beer, seemingly enjoying it.

'So you are a wood elf then?' asked Amber.

'You could call me that,' he replied, 'I am of the Sylvanii, the tree people, or perhaps more correctly in your tongue, the people of the woods.'

Amber was intrigued by the small brooch he wore towards the shoulder of his leather armour, a golden oak leaf with an acorn attached to it. He explained it was a symbol of his Order, the Oaken Knights of Floriénne - *the Dair Chev'al.*

Dane butted in, 'with respect, and please understand, we are extremely glad you are here, but tell me, if you are normally in Shirewood, why *are* you here in Mercantia?'

The bright eyed elf studied him carefully, and as with the High Priestess back in the village of Loxely, he obviously decided he liked what he saw. Something about Dane made you trust him, Amber had found it so also, or she never would have accepted his offer to leave together. Dane's eyes were guileless, kind.

'Hmm, to be truthful, I am following a lead. I am looking for someone, and I do not even know his name, nor what he looks like, although I do know he must be an elf. But I also know this ... once seen, no one will forget him.' He paused and the two looked querulously at him. He responded by raising an eyebrow. 'You obviously have neither seen nor heard of him. Very well ... *I am chasing a thief.* He has stolen something very precious, something that belongs to the Court of Elanr'iel, or more particularly the Elven Crown. It has lain for centuries in a glass case in the deepest Vault of the ancient Hall of the Elven Kings, the Dairhalle, or Hall of Oak. The oak is our sacred tree,' he explained.

Dane nodded, 'I understand the holy nature of the oak, my mother was a dryad.'

The elf acknowledged him, 'then we are distant cousins, my friend? There are not too many dryads around these days.' He studied him thoughtfully, ' ... but you are rather large for a dryad, are you not?'

Dane laughed, 'half Vikénar.'

The elf's eyes twinkled. '*Aah*... But I digress, the glass case was securely protected and well guarded, yet this elf stole our greatest treasure.'

He stopped to look at them as if to ask himself should he continue? He obviously made up his mind to do so.

'We do not wish to speak of this outside our land, but we do need to find him and retrieve it. It is the *Longsword of D'rendiél*, our most precious relic. It belonged to our greatest warrior, Diras Rendiél who, a thousand years ago, led elves from the darkness into the light. He protected us from the invasion of a hundred thousand warriors, the Serencii. There are rumours that the sword goes even further back, across the continents, across the sea, back to Trius, to Hecrates.' He paused for another drink. 'But that is just legend, it is immaterial. The sword on the other hand is very valuable and belongs to our people. This elf, this *bastedo*, took it out of our most hidden vaults, our most protected vaults, from inside a case that cannot normally be opened. No one saw him, no one heard him, yet the proof is there - it is gone. Not one elf among us, no Floriénne, would take it - without it, we elves are doomed. At least, so goes the tale.

But an elf from outside - an elf from the *foraes dair* itself, or even from Elvinhaeme, *well* ... So here I am, chasing through the country after a ghost.' He sat back upon the wooden settle, threw up his hands in exasperation.

The two were now interested, 'Just why did you say we could not mistake him if we had seen him?' asked Dane.

'It is not him, nor how he looks, but the sword itself cannot be mistaken. If he uses it, or tries to sell it, we would know. It is an extremely beautiful sword, the pommel alone is made of pure emerald, the grip and the crescent shaped guard are of burnished gold, it holds a dark red hue, no doubt to strengthen the gold. At the top of the blade below the grip, is a strange oval indentation, it sparkles. The blade is an unknown, ancient metal, harder than steel, is covered in silver and there are magickal runes etched into it. Put simply, *it shines*, it bears a light no other sword has known. We think it was given by a god to Hecrates, or perhaps Diras Rendiél, or perhaps any fearsome fighter in between. There are so many legends, too many to count.

We do not even know how he got it out of the glass case - he certainly didn't smash it. It has no normal lock, only magic symbols, unopenable except by two mages who hold the secret signs to display the special lock, and the warden who holds the sacred Key - three people in other words, none of whom live within the Court or its environs. No one has touched that blade for centuries - *it is forbidden*.' He shook his head in wonder.

'How do you know it was a male elf, not say a female, and why do you not know who went near it?' Amber asked, curiously.

The elf sighed deeply, 'it was a feast day, back at Beltane, many elves had come to Floriénne for the festivities and the Court was filled with strangers. We do not steal from each other, *we are not*

Eormynn, humans, at least, we do not steal normally. There was much rejoicing, dancing and singing. It was a good day, I was there. It was my duty to see to guests, to keep things moving smoothly, and yes, to be ready in case of any trouble - you know what alcohol does to people. I actually spent some time in the competitions, as you can see I am fairly good with daggers. I came up in the finals against a coxcomb of a man, a Sevillain I think, Arne, his name.' He stopped as he heard Amber give a gasp.

'Arne? Dark hair, poet shirts and leather trousers?' Tamlyn nodded, yes that was the guy. 'He was my partner at the circus - we did a knife throwing act - he was brilliant. You beat him then?'

'We were very evenly matched, we had a little wager on a sword fight, but he didn't like the way I played.'

'I remember, he'd been away, we were on the road between Mortia and Manecaestr. So that's why he was in such a mood?' *Respect due ...* she thought to herself, *this elf knows what he's doing.*

'It is a truly small world is it not?' He smiled warmly at Amber, his melting green eyes and big lashes complimented the smile. 'I take it you have left this circus?' Amber nodded - *long story.* 'Then I look forward to hearing it. But I digress. Back to Floriénne, *for now* - perhaps later you can tell me about yourselves?' His smile was infectious and his curiosity genuine.. '*The loss of our most precious relic.* There were guards on duty in the Halls and in the Vaults, always in the Vaults, *especially* there.

Women never go into the Vaults, never, they are superstitious. *The thing is ...*' he paused, trying to explain fully, 'all the relics down there belong to Elven male warriors and are symbols of death, of battle. Our women are bearers of life, they think if they touch these objects, or go near them they will not bear children, or they will lose a child. It is an old superstition, but ... who knows? If that is the way they feel, then it may be so. Belief is strong magic.' He sat forward, smiling at Amber. 'I see by your weapons, you have no such superstition as the women of Floriénne. I like that - you can certainly take care of yourself. You are a good fighter - I saw. Our women bear no weapons, but then, no male elf would dare strike them, at least, not in Floriénne.'

Amber acknowledged his respect.

'No one realised until the following morn - such a cry went up, one I have never heard in my life before. We all rushed to see, or rather we didn't see, for nought was there. The Longsword of D'rendiél was gone.' He placed his hands together in an arch, his forefingers tapping his mouth, then sighed deeply. 'I am part of the team who are out searching for it. *I have orders to never return until it is found.*'

Dane was thoughtful, he drank quietly for some time before speaking. 'Just how powerful is this sword again?'

'As I said, in the hands of a fine warrior, unstoppable. The legend is, that our elven hero, Diras Rendiél, held back an invasion of a hundred thousand warriors with it. True or not, the sword is invincible.'

Dane stared into space, deep in thought, realising there was something fateful about all this. The hairs on the back of his neck were pricking, something stirred in his mage blood. He felt as he had the first night with Amber, that he was touching some strange destiny. Then he looked up.

'You do realise this comes at an odd time, a time of strife? We've been relatively *peaceful* for centuries here, at least ...' Two pairs of eyes looked incredulously into his, ' ... no, hear me out. We've had raids from across the water, petty raids, mostly, the Chev'alierres prefer trading, and the Sevillain merely wish to fish in our waters because they over-fish their own. We haven't been at war with each other, Segantium, Mercantia or Westerling, for a long, long time, we've been fairly settled. Yes, there are always raids, but these are usually by outlaws, Bregantii, Alderfolk, the old people of Shirewood. Yet there are also many peaceful areas in the ancient woodlands. Those north of our realms, the Vikénar, Picantés etc., occasionally raid, but we have excellent forces and fortresses along these borders, and even they like to trade when they can.' He sat straight, his eyes full of a gleaming light. 'Some even come to settle, like my great, great Grandfather.

No, we have had nothing truly threatening for centuries until these Adammites; they are a brand new force, a new type of people. They've come upon us without our realising it. They took my island before we could take breath - and there weren't even that many of them then. Now they have clearly grown and are moving to the mainland - and, as we saw today, they wish to destroy our way of life, or at least, to disturb the flow of our existence.' He held up his hand to the Knight Captain. *'You, sir -* may I call you Tamlyn, or is that disrespectful?' The elf nodded, it was fine. 'Well, Tamlyn, *you and I,* humans, mages, elves, dryads, naiads, dwarves, all the old people, we live together in relative harmony, have done for centuries. We hold a certain respect for each other, we are all Merrievians, sons and daughters of the Mother. We trade, sometimes we intermarry as my father did, although it is rare. Sometimes there are disputes, arguments, misunderstandings. But we do not wish to destroy *whole races* of people. These Adammites, these people of the so-called Blazing Sun, wish to destroy all people like us, bring in their own way of life. Or perhaps I should say - their own way of Death.

I repeat, Tamlyn, your sword has gone missing at an important time in our history. We need to know what this means.' He sat back, finished his drink.

Both the Knight Captain and Amber nodded solemnly, realising the truth of his words. Before either could speak, Dane spoke again, 'I think I'd like to help you in this search, if you don't mind. I'm not sure about Amber, I cannot speak for her, although I hope she also will help, she has fine skills.' He looked across at her, his eyes asking a question, but she didn't respond, she too seemed deep in thought. 'My life has changed dramatically the last few weeks, I'm not sure what is happening, I only know I'm doing the right thing.

I believe we are well met, my friend.' He could feel shivers running down his spine.

Amber herself now spoke. 'I've been quiet, because all the time you have been speaking, both of you, I have been feeling strange, difficult to put into words, but as if I am on the edge of something. I felt it the night we met, Dane, when I stood on the rooftop of the inn, looking down at all the commotion. It's why I agreed to stay with you. I feel that same thing now, so ... yes, Dane, I totally agree with what you are saying.' She raised her amber eyes towards the flaxen haired elf. 'We have a parcel to take to the Lady Merrie Temple in Orlandium, but I believe it can wait, they said there was no immediate hurry. So, I too will help, if you will accept me.'

The elf looked surprised, his eyes widened. 'I appreciate what you are both saying, very much so, but I think it is wise to tell you the reason I am here today in the city. Four days ago I was meant to meet three of my fellow Knight's Captain, seekers of the Sword. We had agreed on a date and a meeting point, here in the city of Mortia. None have turned up, and each day I have gone to the rendezvous and waited. Today I realised I am wasting my time and so tomorrow I leave, back on the trail, I think back into the *Foraes Dair,* Shirewood.

I can tell you, I *would* be glad of your company, because I fear what has happened to the other knights. They are all well trained warriors, yet they have neither arrived here nor have sent word. Yes, I should like *you*, whom I have seen today fighting this evil force so well and so bravely, to join me in this quest. I only ask that you be aware of the dangers.'

He looked earnestly upon them. He didn't bother with his *pretty please*, best Court social smile, this was far beyond such foolery.

It was thus agreed upon.

*

He took them later carefully through the streets to his own inn, The Black Night, a very plush affair with velvet seating, hangings and waitresses, where he treated them to an excellent dinner with good wine. They all seemed to get on well, Amber knew many circus tales and jokes, and Tamlyn was full of funny stories about the Floriénne court. As the wine took hold, people in the inn began to look askance at their raucous laughter. He was, as are all elves, pleasing of face, with high cheekbones, slanting down to a narrow but rounded chin, a typical full-bridged elven nose, large deep set eyes, and sensual lips. Above all, he looked gentle, yet it was clear he was a warrior, and quite a formidable one. So much is the typical incongruity of elves.

They both complimented him on his swordsmanship.

He shrugged his shoulders and quietly confided, 'aah, it is only if necessary. I prefer to stay out of combat if possible. I do not think of myself as a fighter, *a knight ... yes*, but there are better methods than aggression.' Now the smile came into play, his merry eyes twinkled. He would use his formidable powers of persuasion any day rather than the sword.

Amber and Dane agreed wholeheartedly before taking their leave of him. They also agreed to meet at his inn on the morrow. Tamlyn bowed politely to Dane and took Amber's hand and kissed it again as they left. He never forgot social protocol nor the chance to kiss a lady, and he did indeed consider most women as 'ladies', his upbringing made it so. He lingered long as his lips gently brushed the back of her hand.

Simultaneously they said, *'I like him ...'* as they were walking back to their own smaller and cheaper inn, then both laughed. 'I have to admit, he's quite charming ...' said Amber.

Dane stopped in the street, took hold of her hand, kissed it, giving a little click of his boot heels. *'I too can be charming,'* he told her in a mock elvhen accent. 'Come to my bed, madam, the night is yet young ...'

Amber accepted graciously.

Later, in the darkness, Dane spoke to her. 'You remember what Tamlyn said about the she-elves of Floriénne, about children and so forth?' He felt Amber nodding beside him. 'Well, I'm assuming you don't really want children yet, do you?'

Amber wondered why he was asking her? Men didn't usually think about such things, it was always up to the female in any sexual situation.

'It's just that, to be on the safe side, I'm happy to make up some potions for you, if you'd like.'

She took hold of his hand. 'That's a very nice thought, Dane, thank you, I would appreciate it. But what if ... you know ... the last few weeks?'

'No problem at all, my love, I've potions for every eventuality ...' he assured her.

Amber smiled into the night. Dane was indeed, a very, *very* handy man.

Chapter 5

They collected their horses and met Tamlyn early the following morn. His was a rather beautiful grey stallion, the excellent black saddle and reins studded with silver and steel. He sat proudly astride it, his light blonde hair shining in the morning sun, complimenting the gleaming buttons and buckles of his Court uniform and the well polished sword in its silver scabbard. A delightful smell of cedar, leather and lavender came from him. Dane guessed he played up to the *shining knight* image wholeheartedly.

But their two bays looked good on either side of his. They weren't without style themselves, and Amber looked well in her red leather jerkin over dark red leggings and white shirt. She threw a claret coloured cloak over all.

Dane's mage cloak shimmered in the morning sun. He too wore a white linen shirt with his black leather jerkin and black leggings and boots. But his boots were plainer, looked sturdier, as indeed they were. They might have been three young nobles out on an early hunt. Only when people looked closer and saw the bruises on Dane's face would they begin to question. Dane had spent time healing many of Amber's wounds inflicted by the Adammites, although there were still a few bruises on her arms and legs. Fresh air would be good for them in any case. He would ensure that by the morrow they would be gone.

They travelled eastwards towards Shirewood, not too many miles to the wildwood. As they rode, the Knight Captain suggested they leave their horses at one of the hostelries a few miles into the forest. 'There are several,' he pointed out, 'a good place to leave our horses before moving further in. The wood quickly becomes a tangle of forest, easier on foot. Our mounts will be safe, well looked after by *Sylvanii*.'

The roads to the east were clear, few folk this early travelling eastwards, those that were on the road, farmers and such, were travelling west to market. They bought some cherries off a young boy pushing a barrow load of tempting produce before him, they were sweet and delicious. Most farmers were taking barrows of potatoes and carrots, hot flavoursome radishes and juicy cucumbers, products of the season.

They entered the forest gradually. It didn't loom up on you en masse, it straggled out into the valleys and plains, a section here, an arm there, as if it would sneakily encroach on all land, little by little. It covered most of the land in any case, it gently undulated, rose and fell across Mer'edrynn. Deciduous on its lower reaches, it rose at certain points where pines and firs held sway, where foxes and wolves roamed, the occasional bear. Sometimes those hills grew craggy and mountainous, cold treacherous places. But other areas, soft dales and valleys, were warm and sheltered thanks to the wild hills protecting them from northern winds.

Teeming with wildlife, interspersed with brooks and rivers, lakes and ponds, food could be had, if time was taken to hunt or fish. It was impossible to know it all, impossible to know all of whom lived there, a haven for outlaws, the unwanted, the forbidden or forgotten peoples of Mer'edrynn. But also the indigenous home of the elven people; there would always be elves here, scattered, slowly dying out, but determined to keep to the wildwood. These quiet people shunned the main elven kingdoms, they liked their solitude among the deer and the rookeries. The sweet-solemn sound of an elven flute would often be heard as a wanderer traversed the greenwood, prompting him to stop and listen for a while, perhaps seek out the gentle musician.

On the road to Shirewood the three passed smallholdings, cottages with land set out in rows of fruits and vegetables, weathered faces bronzed from the sun working in their gardens. Some waved at them, the riders were a pleasant sight to break their monotonous day.

The Knight Captain stopped regularly to ask if they had seen an elf with a beautiful, shining sword. None had. But the old women would keep him talking awhile, enjoying the merry smile playing on his face, would remember his twinkling eyes.

The road began to narrow, the trees began to thicken as the day wore on. Several miles in, it was obvious that it would soon become impassable astride horses. Tamlyn took out a small map he carried, it held listings of elven hostelries prepared for him by the elders back in Floriénne. He took them south along a small lane, eventually arriving at a large stone building in a clearing. Welcoming tubs of flowers stood before its doors and trestle tables and benches sat outside for their leisure. Long window boxes held bright red geraniums and the shutters of the hostelry were painted pale green.

A group of laughing young men, fairly well dressed travellers, sat at one of the tables enjoying the hostel's ale. They all eyed Amber with interest as the three arrived, but another look at the well-armed elf and the sight of a mage's staff made sure they said nothing. The woman too, she looked dangerous herself, two long daggers at her belt ... .

A grey haired elf came out to greet them, to have their horses stabled, to offer overnight rooms and meals. It was as good a place as any to stay, perhaps to enjoy the remainder of the day's sun, relax, find out a little more about one's travelling companions.

They left the horses well tended by a young elven stable lad, whom the horses took to immediately. Two rooms were procured where they divested themselves of their cloaks and took a quick wash and brush up, before meeting outside to enjoy an ale in the sun. The forest smelled good here, rich fresh leaf smells, the resin of the greenwood. Bees hummed lazily among lavender, rooks cawed warning signals to blackbirds trespassing in their trees, and the boys at the other table laughed with all the bravado and innocence of youth out on a jaunt. A few hens and tame ducks wandered the beer-garden, searching for dropped crumbs and crusts. A rich smell of hops pervaded all, the owner was brewing today. His house speciality turned out to be light and refreshing, ideal for a hot day.

The three turned to each other and lifted their tankards in toast. *'Merrie's blessings!'* they cheered, smiling and squinting into the late afternoon sun. Amber wore her straw hat with the red ribbon, she looked charming and both men sat idly smiling at her, watching her appreciatively.

'So, how long have you two been together?' Tamlyn asked them.

Amber said it hadn't been long, explained about the circus, the fire, the possibility of leaving, making a new life.

'You took a chance then. Yet the pair of you look very comfortable together, like you have known each other a long time.' Amber just turned her head and smiled into Dane's eyes by way of reply. The young elf smirked and tossed his blonde braids.

A hearty meal was brought, smoked hams, beef and fish, fresh soft bread and butter, some cheeses, pickles and more of the delicious cherries. The three contentedly ate their fill. More of the refreshing ale was asked for.

Tamlyn went to ask the group of young men if they had seen anything, then to the innkeeper and his staff.

The boys had seen nothing, but the innkeeper was more forthcoming. 'Aye, a week ago, a tall elf with a shining sword stayed for a meal. You couldn't miss the sword, although he kept trying to hide it, covered in a leather cloth. I don't know about a fancy pommel, but it shone, even under all the cloth. Damn big affair too, probably unwieldy to use it. *Might be who you're after* ...'

'Any idea which way he went or where he was going? And what did he look like?'

The innkeeper wasn't sure, might have been northwards, definitely further into the forest. 'He were a tall elf, High elf stock I'd say. Let's see,' he considered, 'ash blonde hair, bright green eyes - very haughty looking, although he had a nice smile I remember, wide and generous, he liked my ale. But he sat by himself talking to no one, *arrogant sort*, or mebbe just shy, who knows? *Hmm* ... moss brown leathers, ankle boots and dark woollen hose. The cloak too, mossy brown, aye, the greenwood shone all over him.'

The Knight Captain thanked him, returned to their table. 'At last, we have some sort of description to go by.' He filled them in with the details. 'I think you bring me luck. This is the first positive news I have had, all the rest have been vague sightings, no detail.'

They decided to spend the rest of the day there, better to travel the forest by day rather than night, even though the nights were light. But the deeper into the forest, the darker the nights would become, and roots and branches lay in wait with uncanny accuracy to trip an unwary traveller.

And so the rest of evening was spent as they had the previous evening, a few beers, much talk, many jokes and tales. The three began to warm to each other, Amber and Dane both charmed by the charismatic young elf.

'I think he puts it about a bit ...' Dane told Amber later as they undressed for bed.

Her eyes queried him. 'What, more so than you?' she laughed, realising *exactly* how he had been before he met her.

'I mean, I think he's been around a lot ... let's say I bet he was very popular at Court ... *with both sexes.'* Amber's eyes widened. 'I think I'm going to have to watch myself - he doesn't seem to have much preference ... ' He put his arm around her. 'Now I'm strictly a *woman's* man, if you care for me to prove it?' leading her to the bed.

'Well', she replied, pulling down the sheets, 'I'm definitely a *man's* woman ....'

*

They left the hostelry and the horses at the stables just after the sun arose, making the earliest start possible. They took some supplies with them, enough for a few days, although food should be plentiful in the forest at this time of year, but hunting or fishing would take time out of their own hunt. The trees soon began to thicken. Amber and Dane understood why they'd had to leave the horses; they hadn't ventured this deep into Shirewood previously. There was a path, of sorts, and little indications of civilisation left by previous wanderers - small signs were placed, twigs broken and arranged into clear symbols 'this way', evidence of a passable section of wood, or crossed, meaning 'no way,' or crossed twice - 'danger this way'.

Both males now carried small axes, bought in Mortia at Tamlyn's recommendation, good for when the trees were too thick. Amber would use her daggers and knives to help. She was glad of thick leather gauntlets to push back nettles or thorns. Dane's staff was very handy, holding back prickly bushes, or beating down flora. As he said, he didn't wish to use elemental magic, he might just burn down the forest.

But it was handy later as they set camp, tea would soon be brewing and Amber and Tamlyn would pluck the birds or skin the rabbits he had killed with amberic magic. They all carried water skins, filled up in streams or rivers, and Tamlyn had brought a small tent, a sort of oilcloth, but very fine, silk woven by the elven women. The whole tent was lighter than their oilskin sheet, a pale dove colour also, only the elves could make something so delicate yet so sturdy.

It was handy in the rain too. He invited them in one night when they were getting soaked and trying to create a makeshift shelter from the oilskin and branches.

'Come in, squeeze in, we can shelter here, bring your blankets,' he told them. They were glad to get in out of the rain, although there wasn't much room. But it was fun squashed together as the rain pattered on the roof of the tent, good natured by-play and double-entendres as they settled down to sleep, jokes and puns.

Over the days, a friendship blossomed. Knight Captain Tamlyn Taenghelin, of the Court of the Grande Dûchesse Elanr'iel, began to truly warm to the two humans, the *eormynn*.

They helped each other too. When wolves strayed too near to their fire one night, all three worked steadily to fight them off, soon dispersing them. They discovered they worked well together, each offering his or her own skills.

The forest became difficult, new growth everywhere, it was early Shearing and life was rampant. So too were midges and ticks in the forest. Amber began itching, red spots appearing. Dane created a salve for her and offered an oil to rub themselves with, deterring flies and mites.

And then they discovered the body, or more correctly, what was left of it.

It had been an elf, most of the flesh was now eaten, but the putrescent body still wore the crawling remains of a black and silver uniform. Just below the shoulder, still attached, was a small golden oak leaf with an acorn. His death was definitely not because of robbery.

The great slash across his middle and the blade-thrust through his neck told them everything. There had been a fight, his sword lay beside him, yet held no blood. Whoever he had fought, he had not marked.

Tamlyn checked the pockets, came across one or two identifiable items. 'I think Falconis had a tinder box like this. Unfortunately, his head, *his face* ...' he turned away, sick to his stomach.

Amber and Dane helped him bury the dead knight. They found an oak tree and took acorns lying beneath, planting them on top of the burial mound. 'That is the best I can give him,' Tamlyn said, 'I will take his crest to the Dûchesse.' His elven skin, half a shade darker than average Mer'edrynn human, heritage of Sevillain or the southern slopes of Chev'alierre, looked pale.

They moved on, knowing now they were on the right track, unfortunately not knowing whether to go east, south or north. They tried north east for a safeish bet.

Two days later they were definitely on the track one way or another, as they discovered another body. This was a slightly fresher corpse, hung from a tree. Tamlyn gave a gasp of recognition, shaking his head at the waste of life. The rooks and crows had taken the eyes, nibbled at much, but the wolves hadn't eaten their fill yet. Again, there was a massive sword-thrust through his centre.

Amber and Dane helped Tamlyn cut him down. Tamlyn knew him, could easily identify him. He took his oakleaf crest to take home, to show the Dûchesse, to give to his family.

'He was Denath'lin, my friend. I was ... *close* to him. We trained together.' He turned away, closed his eyes. Amber put her arm around his shoulder, he simply nodded. They buried him, found a few stones for a burial mound, said a few prayers to the Lady Merrie. Tamlyn sang a sweet elven song about love and battle and honour. 'I will avenge you, my friend,' were his last words.

They moved northwards, or rather north east, knowing they were following their prey. Tamlyn was silent that night as they camped, his eyes searching the flames of the fire. His eyes were large and expressive, tonight they seemed larger, sadder, the light had gone out of them. They both went to his tent that night, an unspoken mutual thought. They lay at each side of him, held him close throughout the night. He was grateful for their comfort.

And the third body, a day later, this time*, well*... hacked to pieces. The head just about hung on to the body, but an arm was cloven from the shoulder. His sword lay close at hand, almost ceremonially placed there. The body had been killed but recently. His oak-leaf brooch had fallen, but they found it in the leaf mould.

'The last of my group, Allendris. At least I have his symbol.' Suddenly he grabbed his pack, took out the small axe, began to vehemently strike the nearest tree, over and over and over again, until it rang with the sound of the blade. Eventually, exhausted, he sat down.

'*I said* whoever wields that blade is unstoppable, didn't I?' He looked hopelessly at them. 'The question is, if or when we catch up with him, what are we going to do?'

'I think we find out why he wants the blade?' suggested Dane, '*and* - you may not wish to hear this - did he attack them, or did they attack him? It's a viable question,' as he saw Tamlyn looking at him confused. 'Is this murder or self defence? I personally need to know.'

'Each one has their blade, none are in the scabbard,' pointed out Amber. 'But none bear blood. So none got a hit on him. He killed them mercilessly, although, as you say, Dane, it might have been in defence. We simply don't know.'

'All that truly matters is that they are *dead,*' responded Tamlyn. 'My fellow Knights, all dead at the hands of this thief.' He felt in the pockets of the body, took out some gold. 'We need this, we keep it, even if I am stealing from my dead brother. Help me bury the last one. The question is ... *who will bury us?*'

So the last of his group were buried.

'You two leave, if you wish. This is not your problem,' he told Amber and Dane later. Both shook their heads, no way were they leaving him to face certain death. He shook their hands, thanking them wholeheartedly.

Tamlyn's face was grim as he moved onwards, now he held his hand forever on the sword at his side, ready to fight, ready to kill. Yet how could he take on a clearly able warrior with such a sword?

That night they took it in turns to keep watch, they could now take no chances. The following morning they ate a meagre breakfast; tea, cherries, some stale bread toasted on the fire they dipped in the tea.

Tamlyn's bright eyes had turned sad and dulled, their lustre gone. But he knew his duty and he was determined to find this foe. The forest thinned out slightly, easier going, they followed a beaten path. It seemed to be a main thoroughfare, worth using.

The following noontide, the sun glinting through the firs, light and shadows cast about them, the three trod carefully over pine-needles. They breathed in the rich, aromatic smell. There was little wind, in fact it was steamingly hot in the forest now.

They moved warily, every step taken with the knowledge they were nearing the thief. They began to talk in whispers, taking no chances. Suddenly Tamlyn stopped, held his hand out to warn the other two, made a gesture of silence and pointed through the trees. All three stared with cautious curiosity ....

He was waiting for them.

He stood casually with his back to a tree, one leg propped up against the trunk. The sword was pushed slightly in the ground before him, he held the hilt between two gauntleted hands, resting on the guard. It was fully unsheathed now. It shone like the sun, the emerald glowing, it was so bright it lit the elf's face. A strange humming could be heard, like metal vibrating, it seemed to come from the sword pointed in the ground.

He looked relaxed, but annoyed, his head turned downwards, ash blonde hair hanging loosely around his forehead, tucked behind elven ears, his lips turned down in disapproval. His dun coloured cloak, somewhat worn, flashed green here and there, fastened to his right shoulder by a gold, six pointed star, a sun burst. Dull green hose met chestnut brown boots. Barring the hair, he could disappear into the forest in a flash.

Tall and strong, his shoulders broad, above a slim, narrow-waisted elven body, he stood as if awaiting his fate, fearless, but maybe an impatience to get it over with. Then his head rose and he turned towards them.

All three took deep intakes of breath, stopped in their tracks by his casual stance, his singular self-assurance. This man, this elf, was *very, very dangerous.*

Tamlyn stood observing him, hatred in his eyes.

Dane looked curiously at this odd, self-possessed creature.

Amber watched him warily, then, as his face turned to her, took another sharp breath.

He did not look like the average cut-throat or thief, although truth be told - what does the average cut-throat or thief look like? But as Amber observed him, she realised he was nothing like she had imagined.

His eyes were the deepest emerald, as bright as the pommel of the sword, set amidst thick brown lashes. They were intense, sincere ... and a little proud. His eyebrows, slightly darker than his hair, slanted a little upwards, elven fashion, towards a broad forehead. He had pale fine skin, his high cheekbones spoke of nobility. She saw a slender nose with a high elven bridge. A generous mouth was set above a strong chin, the jaw tapering, as with all elves. *'Firm and fair,'* his face told the world.

Those emerald eyes glanced briefly at her. *She* was not the enemy. He turned their burning gaze instead upon the Knight Captain.

'So, yet another to dispatch to an early grave ...' The voice was deep, melodious, his words in Plaintongue. It sounded like his natural tongue, he was definitely not from Floriénne. 'Tell me why you keep trying, you are aware of that which I carry? Or are you merely a fool?' He spoke haughtily and there was a formal tone to his words.

Dane and Amber remained quiet, this was up to Tamlyn. Tamlyn hesitated, his sword ready to strike, *yet* ... his three brothers-in-arms were all dead at the hands of this elf. Would he die as ignominiously as they? Perhaps a swift dagger ...? Yet, no, there was no honour in such, not for this. He would play it gently ... for now. He moved into the small clearing with the utmost caution and carefully replied.

'No fool ... we followed the trail of my *dead* brothers.' Tamlyn eyed him up and down, looking for a possible weak spot. The elf was glowering at him, ready to fight, to kill yet again. Tamlyn *was* no fool as he said. 'It seems that combat is out of the question, although as you have noticed, there are three of us here, and one is a mage. And the other ...' before the elf could speak, '... is a female with formidable fighting prowess, do not underestimate her.' He turned to briefly smile at Amber, before resuming, anger and sorrow barely held in check. There were questions to be answered, a certain protocol to follow, and in any case, he had no intention of throwing his life away. 'No, what I wish to know, is *why* you have stolen the *sword of D'rendiél*, and I should dearly like to discover just *how* you stole it.'

The elf smiled then, a full smile, a generous smile that lit up his face, one of triumph. The cool green eyes turned warm.

'You have *some* sense then, you are clearly aware the advantage is mine. But I did not steal the sword, *I reclaimed it.* The sword belongs to me.' It was simple statement, simply spoken, but with certitude. 'and as for how I recovered it, I walked in and picked it up.'

The Knight Captain shot back his head, his mouth open. 'What do you mean?'

'Are you stupid as well as a fool, or merely hard of hearing?' the tall elf replied. He picked up the sword with one hand and flashed it in the air, waving it around in alternating semicircles before holding it high. He spoke slowly and clearly as if to a dim-witted child. 'I repeat, for your benefit - *this sword is mine.*' His eyes briefly glanced at the sword held high in the air, he gave a satisfied smile. His pale hair and forehead shone in the light of the sword.

'No, I mean *how* did you steal it? It was in our deepest Vault, guarded beyond all else.' Tamlyn had to know.

The elf gave a frustrated sigh. 'You clearly do *not* listen. I walked in, I simply mingled with the rest. I went to your vaults, *I have some skill,* I was not seen. I opened the case and took it with me. *It is mine by right,*' he assured him, or tried to.

Tamlyn shook his head, nonplussed. 'I am listening, most decidedly so. But the case was sealed, could not be opened, has not been so for many centuries. It is locked and double warded, magically. So, how did *you* open it?'

'I put out my hand and opened the glass top, no problem. I came with various keys and glass cutters in case they were necessary, although I did not expect to use them, they were back-up only. The case opened easily at my touch. I closed it before I left ...' he added unnecessarily.

Tamlyn stared at him, incredulous. No one could open that case, it was seamless. Even the lock, if indeed there was really a lock, could only be seen once the two mages had unlocked the wards. He had no idea what to make of this, it wasn't what he expected. He thought it had been stolen for profit, or perhaps ill-will against Floriénne.

Dane was watching, there was something odd here. He had never seen anyone so completely self-possessed, so calm in the face of the danger. Three of them, versus one, but the elf didn't bat an eyelid. 'Just *who* are you?' he asked. *'What is your name?'* He knew as a mage, there was much in a name, his dryad mother had taught him so. Names held power.

The elf turned to him, studied him up and down. *'You* could not pronounce my name, I even find it difficult myself,' he laughed. 'But a shortened version, one comprehensible to you would be, hmm, *let me see* ... ' he spoke with care so as to clearly enunciate each syllable:

'*Nim'randuel - Soleus D'rendiél - Gilsylien - Estaran'elvian.*' He spoke in pure Elvhen. 'A brief translation into Plaintongue would be, 'He who is the White Shield and wields the Sword of Light which shines like the Heavens, is the true King of the Elves.' Something of a mouthful, but still easier than the full version.'

Tamlyn was studying him closely, his heart now pounding angrily in his chest - this creature who spoke so calmly had killed his fellow knights. 'True King of the Elves'? If you are that which you say you are, why did you not come to claim your throne - do it honestly?'

The elf made a strange snorting sound. 'And what would your Dûchesse have said? *'Welcome my king, here is the crown, here is the sword of your destiny, take my throne while I make obeisance to you?'* He threw back his head and laughed at the absurdity. 'Ridiculous! No, in any case, I do not want your Floriénne crown. Besides, it is merely a name, I know not why it was bestowed upon me. But the sword *does* belong to me, or rather, my family.' His eyes challenged the elf and turned to the others. 'So, are you also come to take this from me? You may try, *I will give you quick deaths*, I can offer you that at least.'

He lifted the shining sword, it was clearly humming a whining, warning note.

Again Tamlyn spoke, he had no wish to die as his brothers had, he chose his words carefully. 'So, if the sword is yours as you say, what do you intend to do with it?' He was more than curious, *King of the Elves*? There was no king of the elven realms.

Two bright eyes looked upon him. '*Why*, for now I take this home with me. Tomorrow, who knows? I was told it was mine, and so I have claimed it. Although ...' he admitted, 'I would have preferred a less clandestine way.'

Amber finally spoke. She had watched throughout, watched him wield the sword, watched it shine upon him, heard the odd wailing sound. 'You said, the sword of your destiny ... what do you mean?'

The deep-eyed elf turned to her, gazed softly on her awhile. 'Hmm, I do not know, that was merely a saying - beyond collecting it, I had not thought. It seems to me that there will come a time when this sword is needed, but as to when, I have no idea. Tomorrow comes soon enough.'

'I think the time is *now*, Sir, not tomorrow.' She spoke quietly, but determinedly, it was irrelevant to her where the sword had come from. The point was that it was in his hands. 'We have need of warriors. Have you heard of the Adammites, led by Mordecai von Adamm?'

The sword quietened and the elf nodded, 'I have heard a little. What I have heard, I do not like.' Amber saw him watching her, his eyes neither staring nor questioning, if anything they seemed to *caress* her. '*Why*?' he asked, breaking the momentary spell.

'We were attacked by these people, in Mortia, just days ago. You bear a mighty sword, a legend in its own right, at least so I am told. If you can truly wield it, we have need of you against this cult. They are strong and merciless and it seems they wish to kill all mages, elves and ... well ... *people like me*.' She looked down, a little embarrassed about the last words.

He laughed heartily once more. It was rich and round and deep. 'People like you? ... what exactly does that mean?'

'I don't fit in with their narrow viewpoints about femininity.'

'*Oh well then*, if it is to save a damsel in distress, then I *must* come out of my exile and protect, must I not?' He was teasing her.

'What exile?' asked Tamlyn. His curiosity was peaked, his beliefs suspended. He knew not what to think.

'I do not truly know, only that which my family have told me. I am the last of my line and have spent these years learning and training.' He stopped, briefly looked at the sword, held it out towards Tamlyn, 'But tell me ... I am sorry, you did not give me your own name ... ' he paused.

'I am Knight Captain Tamlyn Taenghelin,' he bowed deeply. Tamlyn was both wary, and confused. This was not the cut-throat or thief he had imagined. He thought the thief had stolen it to covet it, or sell it, or worked for someone, a mercenary. This elf was none of those things and claimed to own it. Strange times, strange days. But the thief continued speaking.

'Then, *Knight Captain Tamlyn Taenghelin*, can you please tell me where is the stone that should reside here?' He pointed out the oval indentation at the top of the blade. Tamlyn shook his head, he'd never heard of such a thing. The thief continued, 'I can assure you, there ought to be a large opal there, pure, lucid, yet with a pearlescent glow - so it has been described to me. And I can also assure you, this blade is not at its full power until that opal is set within.'

Tamlyn scratched the back of his head, he was puzzled. The elf knew far more about the sword than he did. He was inclined to believe the elf, yet his fellow Knights had been slaughtered by him. He certainly didn't wish to fight, he valued his own skin too dearly, it could only be a losing battle.

'I nothing of any opal. But, I do wish to know something. Did you attack my brothers or did *they* attack you? If you value your honour, you will give me the truth.' Tamlyn stared him in the eye.

'My answer to you is simple. *Did I attack you?*' Tamlyn shook his head. '*Well then ...*' he shrugged.

This time Tamlyn nodded, accepting the truth. He mourned for the loss of his friend, he knew that a moment's rashness instead of a moment's thought, had brought about his end. Somehow he had to explain this to the Dûchesse. Somehow he had to get that sword home.

'So who are you and where are you from?' Tamlyn needed much more information.

The elf laughed, shook his head, '*I have already told you my name.* It came as a surprise to me too. My kin are from Elvinhaeme, although my parents died when I was ten. I was sent to live with my uncle in the northern part of Shirewood. I therefore belong to both the North and the South. There I learnt the art of Knight-craft and swordsmanship. But I was never given my own sword, I merely borrowed from my uncle's armoury. My uncle said I must earn my sword. Three months ago he died, there were no offspring, I was his closest family. On his death bed he told me that my rightful name is ...' he paused, gave a slightly embarrassed cough, ' ... *as I have said* ... and if I wished my sword I should go and collect it as it belongs to my family. This I have done. It was clearly a challenge, and one I could not resist. Since then I have been followed, hounded and attacked. At least *you* gave me the grace to speak.' He looked at the three of them, 'I speak the truth, that is all I have to say.' His stubborn stare belied argument.

Dane chuckled, 'So, do you actually have a name we can all pronounce? I mean, what do your mates call you?'

Two emerald eyes bore into him. *'I don't do mates .'*

'Oh, well, I'll just say *'hey you'* then,' Dane retorted.

A sigh, then - 'Throughout my life my given name has been Estrién, until my uncle named me otherwise.'

'Hmm, *he who shines,*' commented Tamlyn, 'very fitting. And do you believe you are the rightful King of the Elves?'

Again the tall elf laughed. 'I have no idea. Can't say I wish to be, either. But I do know this sword is mine. From the moment my uncle spoke of it, I was sure and certain.' He picked up the sword, made as if to go, 'so, if you prefer not to attack me - which would be wise - I shall be moving on. I should like to get some miles in before nightfall.' He turned to leave.

All three stopped him. 'You can't just *go*!'

'I assure you I can.' He moved off, hotly followed by three anxious and curious people.

'Don't you think you need to pay something back?' shouted Amber. 'You've killed three people for that sword!'

He turned, shook his head. 'I defended myself, no more. Now I must go.'

'So why do you think you've got the bloody thing? And why *now?*' asked Dane. 'You need to do something with it, something with a purpose. You can't just nick a legendary sword, then bugger off *home*!'

The elf stopped momentarily. 'True, but I have no idea as yet what to do with it. Nor is it yet complete. I'm sure something will turn up.'

All three looked each other, then at him. '*We've* turned up,' they replied simultaneously.

He studied them. *'So you have.'*

Amber walked over to him. 'Do you *need* to return to your home?'

'Not particularly, there is no one there. I could go back to Elvinhaeme I suppose,' he mused.

'Why not come with us? We need people like you, your sword, your abilities, against these Adammites and their new religion, this Blazing Sun thing. You should have seen - and heard them - in Mortia, it was sickening. We are only alive now thanks to Tamlyn's help.' She paused to consider her next words, it was important to get this right. 'Do you *want* the Elven race to be slaughtered?' Amber was determined, something deep newly awakening in her. 'Do you want a land without mages or magic, forests without dryads and rivers without naiads? Do you wish to see an end to all the Elder Races?

Do you want a land without the breath of life, where death reigns supreme?'

She spoke passionately, not merely to him, but to all three males, surprised at her own emotion. There was a momentary silence as they considered her words.

'Do you think it will go that far?' Estrién asked her.

'It already has,' was the reply.

Dane was busy collecting firewood, making a pot of tea. 'Let's sit down, talk this through, as long as you are not going to run me through with that thing. At least discuss this with us. ... Tamlyn ... what do you think?'

Tamlyn studied the bright haired elf carefully, then slowly nodded, *'I will talk,'* he said, cautiously, 'as long as he did not cold bloodedly murder my colleagues.'

The elf stood straight, 'I do not lie,' he protested, his voice deep and firm with conviction.

Amber took his arm, almost backed away as a frisson of energy seemed to flow from his skin, then spoke softly. 'Please, Estrién, come and sit and take tea with us. Let us talk and see what happens?'

Tamlyn too sat down. 'I cannot return to Floriénne without the sword, yet I am really not prepared to take it from you, at least as yet. I'm not stupid, I realise fight is futile. Your words also ring true, you know more than we of Floriénne about this. Also ... ' he conceded ruefully, 'it looks right in your hand ... it befits you.'

Tamlyn preferred words to warfare any day, If he could persuade this elf to go back with him, plus a completed sword, he would have done his duty. He didn't wish to be exiled forever. As to whether the elf kept the sword or it was returned to the vault ... only time would tell. He considered the matter before continuing speaking to Estrién.

'What if we help you look for this opal stone that sits at the top of the blade? We can work together for a while. There is something fateful about all this.' Tamlyn had to rethink everything, the elf was not what he had imagined.

The tall elf thought carefully, drank his tea slowly, then eventually spoke. 'If you help me, I will help you, I can offer you that. But ...' he spoke pointedly to Tamlyn, 'you saw what happened to your friends when they attacked me, do not attempt the same, or your fate will match theirs.'

Tamlyn nodded agreement. He *was* no fool. He had vowed revenge, yet he already understood nothing was quite that simple.

It was generally agreed upon, they would seek out the opalstone and take it from there.

*

The summer nights were short and the moon was just past full. However much Amber snuggled up to Dane, the ground was hard and sleeping difficult. She lay awake watching the stars, then glanced across at Estrién curled up in his cloak. Unlike her, the men seemed to have no trouble sleeping roughly, outside.

The Longsword of D'rendiél lay on the ground shining with lunar luminescence, it's fair light attracting her. She wondered about the runes on the blade, conjecturing on their meaning? Curiosity overcame sense. Slowly she crawled out of Dane's arms. She needed a better look at the sword.

She crept across to where the sword lay, by the side of the sleeping Estrién. She bent her head trying to decipher unfamiliar signs and sigils, wondering what they meant? It was a truly beautiful sword - and yes, now she looked, it did seem incomplete. Suddenly a gauntleted hand shot out, grabbed the hilt of the sword.

'What is it you do, woman?' Estrién glared angrily at her from his sleeping position.

'I'm sorry, I was just curious - the sword shines in the moonlight. I just wanted to see the runes.'

'Frailty thy name is woman!' he quoted, 'truly, woman is weak and impatient. And always so curious ... . could you not wait until the morn?'

'No, the moon shone on the blade, it intrigued me.' She sat by his side, his words irking her.

He spoke vehemently. 'Then you should beware, woman! Do not creep up on me like a thief in the night. You saw what I did to those others, your female form is merely easier to slice in two.'

But even as he spoke, Amber had swiftly taken out one of her daggers and now pointed it at his throat. She did not need his anger for so little.

'And beware whom you insult, elf, I have skills of my own!' bending down to him. *'It may not be as easy as you think ...'*

The elf raised an eyebrow. The female had been quicker than he anticipated, he wasn't used to aggression from a woman. He lay his head back on the ground. 'Then we seem to be at a stalemate, as my blade is waiting to slice into your side.'

Amber retrieved her dagger, stood up, left him. Dane and Tamlyn were stirring, wondering at the commotion? 'Amber, you OK love?' came Dane's voice.

'I'm fine, Dane, just fine,' she returned to their makeshift bed.

Estrién called over. 'Could you *not* have waited 'til morning?' He sounded exasperated.

'And would you have let me look?' she replied.

He thought briefly, then, *'no, probably not.'*

Amber felt she had made her point.

*

As they began their journey back through the forest the following morning, Amber walked next to Estrién.

'I'm sorry about last night,' she apologised. 'I was just curious. I had no wish to disturb you.'

The elf just shrugged.

'But tell me,' she continued. 'why do you wear your gauntlets when you sleep? It seems strange.'

The elf shot an annoyed glance at her. 'it is in case I am rudely awakened and must grasp my sword ... *as last night* ... The blade is extremely sharp and I should like to keep my fingers. Now, can we get on, or have you more questions, woman?'

'I do have a name you know, it's Amber.' She was as annoyed as he.

He gave a sardonic laugh. 'Amber, *yes* ... electrum. Sharp and shocking. Is that what you like to do, Amber ... shock people? Is that why you wear red - a warning signal?'

Amber hadn't really thought about it, she just liked the colour. She shook her head.

Anyway,' he continued. 'You forget your *middle* name - *Curiosity!* Your parents should have named you Pandora.' He moved off, helped the others to hack back some thorny growth.

Amber took a deep breath, calming herself. She refused to be riled by him.

She caught up with them a few moments later, angry at herself, angry at the elf. She'd apologised, it didn't need all that hoo-ha. This was a bad start. Tamlyn had fitted easily into the group, his agreeable nature and his manners probably meant he would do so anywhere.

Unfortunately Estrién, or whatever he called himself, was of a completely different temperament.

They continued through the forest. Occasionally Dane would stoop to gather some medicinal herb. He had leisure to look now that they were not hurrying after the sword thief. Tamlyn spent time talking quietly with Estrién, trying to get more information about how he had stolen the sword. Despite the continuous declarations of, 'I did not steal it!' little was forthcoming.

As the morning wore on they heard the scrabbling sounds of something running on all fours, an animal of some kind. It was coming their way, clearly pursuing them. Perhaps it followed their scent, perhaps it was just going the same way they were.

All took out their weapons, should it attack. Within seconds it crashed its way through the bushes towards them. There was a sharp crack of twigs and branches and a large brown bear suddenly appeared in their midst.

For a moment it stopped, rearing upwards on its two hind legs, its eyes searched the four travellers. Were they a handy prey? Were they worth eating?

Amber and Tamlyn held daggers and short swords, it was too close for bowshot. Dane held up his staff ready to shoot fire at the animal, perhaps stun it with an electrum bolt.

But Estrién held up a hand. 'Quiet, all of you,' he commanded, 'be still, be peaceful. This bear is not hungry, there is much wildlife in the forest right now. He seeks passage through here, that is all.' He spoke with conviction.

He lifted up a hand to the bear. Speaking softly, but firmly, 'be calm, we will not harm you. Be gone, make your way ... *go*.'

The bear stopped in its tracks, unsure of itself. Estrién waved his hand, strange sigils, esoteric signs, still speaking calmly, looking the bear in the eye. 'Go, Bruno, take your path. Be at peace, my friend, go with blessings.'

For one moment the bear looked him in the eye, then lumbered onwards into the forest, away south, perhaps to its lair.

Three pairs of eyes looked astonished at Estrién. 'How did you do that?' asked Dane. 'it ... *listened* to you.'

Estrién merely shrugged. 'I know this forest, at least, some of it and its inhabitants. Sometimes I ... commune with them, the beasts. It is but a simple trick.'

Tamlyn nodded, 'many elves have some degree of empathy with animals. But I think there is more than just that - you have a gift there, Estrién.'

Amber watched, but said nothing. He might have empathy with bears or other animals, but clearly human females were outside of his ken.

They travelled further, making their way back towards the hostelry where they had stabled their horses, still some days hence. A small clearing was found towards evening and they decided to make camp. Amber went with Tamlyn to find food, their supplies now low, while Dane started a fire, Estrién gathered more twigs, dead branches, then also went in search of food.

Amber and Tamlyn returned with a couple of rabbits, her bow put to good use. Dane quickly skinned the rabbits and chopped them, not a great deal of meat on a rabbit, but they would do. He skewered them across two short poles, they would need turning occasionally. Estrién returned with hazelnuts which he left close to the fire for roasting, and wild sorrel, pleasant to chew. Amber dug up some pignuts, wrapped leaves around and roasted them too, in the fire embers. It wasn't a great meal, but they didn't starve, although they would be glad to get to the inn for some well-cooked food.

Amber considered that if they were to spend so much time on the road, in forests, away from civilisation, then they must prepare more. Dane and she had made do with the small kettle, but that was no use for four. A cooking pot, however small, would be a good investment even if only for a broth, many herbs could be placed in, both vegetable and medicinal, It was fine if they had horses, but on foot more difficult, cooking pots being bulky. Still, a full stomach was preferable.

The quiet campfire meal gave them the opportunity to talk about themselves, their earlier lives, Estrién listened as they explained how they had met, how Tamlyn had saved the day against this new cult, the Adammites. He spoke about his own upbringing, a bachelor uncle who gave him houseroom after the death of his parents.

'It was influenza, one winter, a bad winter. My parents were quite old, had been so when I was born, I was a late arrival. They did not survive, nor did many in the village. Uncle Reinolde was kind enough, I moved from Elvinhaeme to live in his house much further north in the *foraes dair,'* he too knew the forest by its elven name. 'There were just the two of us and two elderly female servants who saw to our needs. Sometimes we had company, a few friends. I had a visiting tutor and a sword master, plus my uncle taught me much. He knew some sage craft, beast lore, various things. He had no one else to pass it to, so he gave it to me.

That was my life, somewhat sheltered among the woodlands, until he died - a lung condition he'd had for a long time. I had been expecting it. But I was not expecting what he told me on his deathbed, my somewhat long and complicated Elvhen name, that my parents and family had been in exile for hundreds of years, that I was the last of my line. He said it was time we 'returned', whatever that means, and he told me of my sword. Exactly why we have been in exile, I have no idea, or whether we ever ruled the Elven lands - we may not even have come from here, perhaps from across the water. Frankly, I neither know nor care - those ancestors are too far back - indeed, Tamlyn, who knows, we may be distant cousins? You and I probably have a common ancestor between us somewhere.

But the sword - I knew with absolute certainty when he told me. And now that I hold it, it is right - it is mine. No one will take this from me.

I have thought on what you said, about these Blazing Sun people, these people who bring death to our lands, I need to get down to Elvinhaeme if they are being invaded, I must help, if I can.' He spoke to the fire, but actually to all of them, they nodded at his words. That seemed to be the first place to begin, down in the westernmost part of the country, to go and help thrust them out. Gather as many elves together as possible as a fighting force, work against these people.

First however, they needed to travel from the centre of the northlands, make the long trek south to Elvinhaeme, and to try to find the stone for his sword.

'One thing I can tell you, Estrién, it is not in Floriénne,' stated Tamlyn. 'It would be with the relics, or if not in the sword, in a crown or something. No one has ever spoken at Court of such a stone, no one knows anything about it. The indentation just looked natural, ornamental, no one even considered anything was missing, not that we saw it much, it was kept too deep in the Vaults. We certainly do not possess your stone.'

'Then I shall use the sword as I can, until we find it,' Estrién responded. 'No doubt there will be some lore in Elvinhaeme about it. I remember fine libraries in the fair cities there. We lived close to a good city, Belcast'el, my father went regularly. We can look there for information.'

'And the university libraries in Mortia and Orlandium, if we are travelling south,' suggested Amber. They all agreed, investigate the ancient lore, seek for clues as to its existence and its whereabouts.

Amber sat thoughtful at the edge of the fire. There was something she vaguely remembered as a child, something her mother used to read to her, a poem. She tried to put it together.

'Um, guys, I don't know if this is anything to do with it, but my mother used to tell me a rhyme about an Elfenstone. I don't know if it's your stone Estrién, but well - it goes like this.' She thought in the deepest recesses of her memory, it had been a long time ago.

The Elfenstone

Twas lost in battle ages gone,
The shining sword it lay upon,
Gave echoes of its beauteous light,
The Elfenstone casts back the Night

Pearlescent waves of milky hue,
Iridescent rainbows true,
pale yet lustrous - fae'ry-made
It sits within the flashing blade.

When ship to shore doth come to reign,
And riders black make all aflame,
The Elfenstone will rise again,
And make its stand for elves and men.

Does it make any sense Estrién? It sounds like your Opalstone doesn't it?' Amber sat back, pleased she had remembered the poem from so long ago.

Estrién raised both eyebrows this time, she had surprised him. 'You may have something there, Amber. It may be the very stone. But it does not tell us where to look, although ... it does seem to be the right time to retrieve it - *riders black, invaders on our shores* - yes, it may be.'

'Then we at least have a name for it - *the Elfenstone*, somewhere to start looking,' suggested Tamlyn. 'And it proves we do not have it - that humans knew of this and created legends and stories.'

Dane said nothing, but listened to all of them, his mage senses tingling. Since the moment he had seen Amber, he knew fate had taken him in hand, now he believed it with certainty. Events lay ahead of him, he knew not what, some good, some bad. He would have to face all, whatever the cost, with bravery and fortitude.

It was a warm night, and he was close to their fire, but he still shivered. *'You will gain and you will lose, Dane,'* he told himself, *'you will lose and you will gain ...'* He had no idea what that meant, but he knew it to be true.

He looked at Amber, his new love. She sat by the fire, her cheeks rosy with warmth, her chestnut hair glowing, her eyes shining ... *and he shivered once more.*

*

Dane was glad to get back to the hostelry, to something a little resembling civilisation. He hadn't been happy in the Wildwood. He ought to be, considering his dryadic heritage, but it was *too* wild, too untamed. His mother came from managed woods, she showed them to him, they were beautiful with flowers and fruit trees and comfortable homes, usually in the trees themselves. But where they had just been was nature run riot.

They sat outside again in the hostelry garden, a warm night, replete with a good meal, simple fare but tasty and plenty of it. Wine goblets were filled and yet another flagon of wine stood waiting on the table. They were all laughing, Tamlyn was full of tales of life at Court.

' ... and then Tirania came in shouting, *'I want my maidenhead back, help me find it, where did you put it?'* as if I had just borrowed it from her! I had to leave her in her friend's hands, let her explain.' The group laughed at him, he had been elucidating on his sexual exploits all evening. His sex-drive seemed to lead him into a deal of trouble.

In the past, Dane would have joined in, but now he felt embarrassed in front of Amber, he didn't wish to hurt her. He'd had more than his fair share of women in his bed. They all seemed to pale out of existence now she was by his side.

It was late, he looked across at her, held out his hand, speaking softly. 'C'mon Amber, I think it's bedtime, no?'

Amber nodded, smiling cheerily at everyone. 'Thank you for a lovely evening, it's been good fun.' She took his hand, the pair left.

Tamlyn turned to Estrién. *'Now, there's a beauty.* You haven't seen her in combat yet, have you, Estrién?' The elf shook his head. 'Oh, I tell you, she is *superb*, she surely raises a man's blood. Dane is a very lucky man. What wouldn't I give to be with her tonight?' He spoke lustily, then drank back his wine.

He was quite surprised to see the other elf scowling at him.

*

Dane held her close, kissed her lips, a final kiss before they parted. They'd seemed to be in the wildwood forever, too many people around. *Mind you*, he thought, *that dirty sod Tamlyn would have joined in if he could ...* he'd made enough innuendo when there were just the three of them. Putting out to *him* too, that elf didn't give a damn, as long as it was sex.

At last he and Amber were alone. She'd been able to enjoy a bath earlier, wash her hair after the days in the forest. She smelled beautiful, freesias and mimosa, a light summer smell. She liked to wear perfumes according to the season, she'd told him. And she definitely liked amber in her perfumes. He must find some for her, make something up, if only perhaps to burn it as incense.

He turned to the warm and satisfied woman at his side, caressing her skin.

'Can I fall in love with you, Amber?' he asked. He felt her nod, she wriggled a little next to him, he'd pleased her. He rose up and kissed her cheek, held her close. 'Goodnight, my sweet love.'

'Goodnight, my love,' was the sleepy reply.

He woke her in the night for more, finally falling asleep exhausted across her.

*

The horses were in excellent condition. The hostelry had a small paddock attached to it, any horses stabled for more than a day were given access. The young stable lad loved horses, understood them, took great care of those left in his charge. The problem was they had three horses between four of them.

Estrién said he was quite happy to walk, he would meet them in Mortia in a couple of days' time. They all disagreed with that one, once found, he wasn't going missing again.

'Amber is the lightest, and I am lighter than you two,' suggested Tamlyn. 'She can double up with me,' he grinned cheekily.

Amber had to admit it was so. She climbed up behind him. 'Hold on tight to me,' he suggested, 'don't want you falling off.' His bright elven eyes were triumphant as they moved out. Dane actually laughed, he was at peace with the world this morning.

Estrién carefully laid his sword flat along the side of the horse, wrapped in the leather cloth. He didn't want the horse harmed by it. He watched the pair on horseback as they rode away, shaking his head. He had no idea what to make of the woman. He found her exasperating, and if anything … a little frightening.

He wasn't really used to being around women, had lived a pretty sheltered life. He'd visited the local town a few times on business for his uncle, spent a little money there. But there had been no real relationships. Amber, as she had surmised, was something completely out of his ken.

He spoke gently to the horse, set off at a canter to join the others. There were, it seemed, things he must do, destiny awaited him. He'd started on the path the moment he went for the sword, he understood it was so. Whatever his future held, it had already begun.

So let's get on with it, he thought, never one to pussyfoot around.

Chapter 6

They arrived back in Mortia some hours later. The Blazing Sun set - the cult that is, not the dying sun - seemed to have disappeared, at least weren't visible in the streets. That was a relief. Tamlyn insisted on paying for temporary lodging and stabling. He had been given plenty of cash from the Court, it was to be used to find the sword, so why not the Opal stone, or Elfenstone, or whatever its name was? He thought if he ever returned he would be given more. Nevertheless it was not an inexhaustible supply.

'Would you consider coming back to Floriénne with me, later?' he asked Estrién. 'When we find the stone, I mean - we will explain about your right to the sword - and if we take it complete, then clearly we have added to the sword.'

Estrién stared at him, nonplussed. 'You mean return to Floriénne and be either imprisoned or executed? Do you forget I have killed three of your knights?'

'If anyone was going to kill you, it would have been me, or at least, I bear the right to do so on behalf of my people - and my friend Den'athlin.'

Estrién grunted, 'ha! You could try - though at least you have some sense. But, I thank you for your faith in me, Tamlyn, truly. You know, I have quite grown to like you - it would be a shame to have to slay you.'

'I'll take note ...' the young elf replied.

'I'm sorry about your friends, Tamlyn, but none of your knights gave me leave to speak.' Estrién continued, 'each one came at me sword in hand. I have been taught by an excellent swordmaster, and like yourself, I was taught to kill, not wound or maim. This blade is lethal, they stood no chance against me.'

Tamlyn duly took note again.

They also would require another horse for Estrién when they left, again, the wealthy young Tamlyn said he would provide. 'But, hey, it's not my cash, it belongs to Floriénne.'

'But you are of a noble house, aren't you, Tamlyn?' asked Amber.

Tamlyn nodded, 'Well, my father is a Lord, I therefore bear the title of Knight as hereditary, and thus why I am Knight Captain at Court. But many knights are from 'common' folk, to use an old phrase, having proved their worth to my land. They have therefore proved themselves. I have my title as due my birth, and although I have worked for my Dûchesse, I feel I have yet to fully come into the title. This quest with you Estrién, is worthy. I may not be able to return the precious relic to my people, but some day I shall display to them the rightful owner of it, and a completed sword. It is enough.'

'Why are you so sure I am the rightful owner?' Estrién was curious.

'Very simple. If you were merely a thief, you would be dead by now, one of us would have killed you, even with your incredible sword. I am not without skills Estrién, believe me, and I am more than capable of sneaking up on you in the middle of the night and cutting your throat. If I thought it necessary, I would do that. But, my heart tells me it is so, and I can express it no better than that. I also somehow do not think the sword would perform for anyone other than its' master.' Tamlyn added a fetching grin as he spoke, he truly didn't want hostility from a guy holding a sword with a four foot blade.

'Hmm, well this sword needs some sort of a scabbard and some way of carrying it ...' Estrién went off to find a saddlers or an armourer. It was too long to wear at his side and would need to be carried on his back somehow. Holding it permanently in his hand was not an option.

They agreed to meet later at the inn, the Double-Crossed Keys, for dinner.

The rest went to university libraries and bookshops in pursuit of knowledge, thankful the Blazing Sun brigade hadn't yet started book-burning.

Later, as Amber, Dane and Tamlyn walked along Kilmore Lane back to the inn after a fruitless afternoon, they were approached by heavily armed guards. Their surtouts were jet black bearing a silver coat of arms - four death's heads set amidst two crossed swords, repeated on the large shields they bore, it didn't look exactly welcoming. There was a general murmuring of *'uh oh,'* and hands went ready to their weapons.

'Are you the three who killed those Blazing Sun preachers just over a week ago?' It was a big man, heavy set with an even heavier looking sword.

They looked each other in the eye. How to answer that one with impunity?

Amber spoke on their behalf. 'I was actually set upon in the street by a group of thugs, sir, I'm not sure if that is what you mean.'

'If they had red sun symbols on a black robe, that *is* what I mean,' said the Sergeant at Arms, eyeing them up. *Yes, they were definitely in trouble.* They tried to look innocent, but they matched the descriptions.

'We've been trying to find you. You are to accompany us to Doom Castle. The Lord Black Morus wants to see you. That's *Evil* Lord Black to you, to give him his full title. And I said the Castle, not the dungeons. Don't worry, it's nowhere near as bad as it sounds. Everything around here has depressing names, but we're actually a fairly cheerful folk. It all goes back to some miserable bugger who founded the city and his equally miserable family.'

There were four well armed guards and none as yet seemed imposed to cast shackles upon them, so they followed the Sergeant, wondering what was in store? As they walked, they passed inns and alehouses with names like 'The Black Death' or 'the Devil's Brew', both of which, they were informed, referred to a strong ale. They passed the Hangman's Noose tavern on

Gibbet Lane, but the Sergeant explained that was just a joke. The lane had once been a chicken market and was actually Giblets Lane, but the sign-painter was illiterate. The tavern, 'named for just a bit of fun,' actually was a 'very nice place to take the ladies,' he told them. They peeked inside as they passed, noting the hearty fire blazing and the shining horse brasses over the fireplace. The Hangman's Noose tavern looked quite cheerful.

The Mortians obviously enjoyed a little dark humour.

Doom Castle looked as it said however, a dark forbidding affair approached by a long drawbridge over a black rushing river. It was a classic four-square castle, with four square towers, the stone now dark with age. But there were cheerful pennants flying, a couple of trimmed bushes in tubs at the entrance and children were playing in the courtyard. One came running over, flapping her doll at the Sergeant. Another kicked a ball to him, he kicked it back.

Two large entrance doors in the blackest oak appeared, death's head skulls grinning over the lintel. It could only be called creepy. Two coats of arms with more death's heads were emblazoned on the doors. Two guards stood by the doors, black and silver armour, heavy swords at their side, carrying heavy shields bearing the crossed swords and grinning skulls.

A sign on the lintel read, 'Tread carefully, we reserve the right to behead traitors, murderers and thieves.'

It wasn't exactly welcoming.

Inside was a Great Hall, but it was completely different. It was high and long and black-and white timbered. Enormous black iron candelabra from time immemorial hung from the ceiling. There were two huge fires blazing merrily at each end, a gigantic dog sat dozing in front of one. A large painting of an extremely ugly man with a beautiful wife and surrounded by six laughing children had pride of place. They all looked happy. On the other hand, there were many pictures of dour faced ancestors, all wearing black from top to toe.

A large, oak dining table bearing several bowls of fruit and more enormous candelabra filled half the room. Toys were on odd chairs and one wall was lined with bookcases, brimming with books, parchments and ancient-looking tomes. Books were open on colourful rugs that scattered the floor, and a child's wooden tricycle sat riderless in a corner where a young boy was jumping around on a hobby horse, neighing and braying for all he was worth.

Through the cacophony was a sound of music playing, a virginal. The extremely ugly man of the painting sat at the virginal, wearing nothing but long pantaloons, no top, no boots, happily pounding away. He stopped as he saw them enter, smiling broadly. He stood up from the stool, beaming at them.

'Sorry you've been dragged here, but I'm glad we found you.' He looked down, realising he was wearing hardly anything. 'Aah, just been working out - exercising, I was cooling off a little. I do this martial art thing - chop boards with the side of my hand and stuff, sit cross-legged for ages, do high kicks, stand upside down and so on. It's supposed to do me good, or so Violet says. Personally, I'd rather go hunting or have a shag. *Still* ... ' he laughed out loud at himself.

He left the virginal, walked over, quite unembarrassed about his state of undress.

'Need to go get dressed. Very happy to see you. You did me a good turn. *Sergeant!* he turned to the Sergeant at Arms, 'thank you, you may leave now.' He smiled at the newcomers, 'help yourselves to drinks, OK? ' He stopped, there was a shout, '*Grimwold - we need drinks!*'

An elven servant hurried out of what was probably the kitchen. He took an exasperated look at Lord Black Morus (Evil Lord Black).

'OK, OK, stop me from cooking, just to get you your alcohol fix,' he sounded peeved. 'I've got two geese, and several partridge I'm preparing, along with gooseberry sauce and roasted root vegetables. *And* pudding for twelve or more. *And* soup for starters, for the little ones. But, fine, I'll stop to pour drinks.' He grumbled but went to a large sideboard cupboard, looking at the three, 'We've probably anything you could name in here, keep it well stocked. What's your poison?'

'A glass of brandy would be good, if that's OK?' asked Tamlyn, hopefully, taking full advantage. Court type situations were where he felt most at home.

'Twelve, twenty or twenty five year old? There's older, but its somewhere at the back of the cupboard, it'll probably never get drunk.'

Tamlyn joined him at the *very* large cupboard, studying the bottles. He pointed one out, then saw the range of single malt usquebae.

'Ooh, I could begin at the left and make my way eastwards,' he commented.

Lord Morus (Evil Lord Black) returned fully clothed, black from top to toe naturally, and joined them at the drinks cabinet. 'I'll have a GlenRite 'Ard,' he said, 'before Violet sees me.' He looked cheerily at the three. 'and put plenty in.'

Grimwold poured drinks. Everyone it seemed was joining in the GlenRite 'Ard.

'Water?' he asked everyone.

'No, we're on a diet,' was the united response.

There was a clink of glasses and a general, 'Merrie's blessings' or 'bottoms up' from everyone, followed by a few gasps as it hit the back of the throat.

At least they weren't currently being tortured or put into the dungeon. Perhaps Lord Black Morus (Evil Lord Black) didn't actually intend to imprison them?

'You've done me a good service,' he confided in them. 'I hate those Blazing Sun, black-cloaked buggers. If anyone's wearing black around here, it's me and my family, no bugger else.' He stopped and laughed. 'Not particularly keen on their dogma either!' He stopped to drink the GlenRite 'Ard. Gasped a little then croaked, 'hmm, quite good. She'll have me on lettuce leaves later if she knows I've been drinking this.'

She entered at that very moment. 'Yes, and you can just pour me one of those, Grimwold, before you disappear …' *She* was a raven haired, half-elf beauty in her thirties, with eyes that matched her name and a good natured smile playing her lips. 'I'm only trying to look after you, dear, keep you young and *virile* …' She looked tenderly at her husband, a man clearly at least ten years her senior. Tamlyn eyed her appraisingly, she had a good figure, a pleasing face, wondering *if* … but she spoke again. 'We've been trying to find you. To *thank you* that is. Those Blazing Sunners are awful people, but *we* have to tread warily. We believe in this freedom of speech thing you see - you know, *I may not believe in what you say, but I'll fight to the death for your right to say it*. Thank you *so* much for removing them, we'd have looked like upper class bastards oppressing the masses if *we* did it.'

Dane suddenly burst out laughing. She was wonderful. 'They actually attacked us. We did nothing to enrage them, other than I carry a staff, and Amber's an athlete, she doesn't exactly dress like other young women …'

'I've noticed,' purred Lord Black Morus (Evil Lord Black) 'mighty fine woman …' Violet *looked* at him. 'Sorry love,' he replied, repentant. 'Tell me though, why are you back here? I mean, not often people revisit the scene of the crime, eager to get away usually.'

The three explained the situation, giving him the full story of the sword, the stone and the elf, plus the full résumé of the attack.

Lady Violet nodded, 'Exactly as I suspected, but we have to play fair, only right. We've rid the town of the rest, everyone told us what happened and we've been able to send in the town guard, driven them out. You did us a good turn.'

Lord Black (Evil Lord Black) continued. 'I like the sound of this chap, this Estrién. Takes what he wants, goes for it without fear, good man. Why not join us for dinner, if you don't mind the noise of six youngsters and a few friends, and er … their friends? Oh, *just come*. About six … bring Estrién … we'll talk.' And he wandered off, perhaps to continue standing upside down in a vain effort to preserve his youth to please his wife.

'Can't guarantee the food,' his wife told them, 'depends on Grimwold's temperament - I mean, it could be delicious, or, well, it could be a bad day. But, there's plenty of wine,' she smiled. '... This legend thing, I'm good at stuff like that, got several degrees, well ... philosophy, physics, and literature. I might be useful, might help you, know a few people at the college. Sounds interesting, up my street and stuff.' She broke off, her mind now elsewhere, she waved them off and ambled to another part of the Hall where she picked up a stray book, sat down, studying it with relish.

They had clearly been dismissed.

They walked back to The Double-Crossed Keys where they were staying, all silent. Estrién had arrived, he showed them the excellent scabbard and strapping he and the armourer had devised. The large sword now hung slant-ways on his back, the huge emerald covered by leather. The straps would pull out and unfasten if he tugged with his left hand on them, while taking out the sword over his shoulder with his right. It looked complicated, but it worked.

They explained to Estrién about being taken to Doom Castle and Evil Lord Black and a door with death's heads and a half naked guy playing a virginal and some really excellent whiskey and protecting the freedom of speech *and* ... Estrién just looked confused.

Suddenly they were laughing. It ought to be ridiculous, but somehow it wasn't. They'd found an ally, one that was clearly a lunatic, but equally one with power in the city. They asked the landlord about him.

'Evil Lord Black ? Aye, decent chap, lovely wife. Mass of kids - and I'm not just talking about the legal heirs of his body. He were quite a roué earlier in his life. In fact, at that time, there were no virgins left in Mortia - he'd been through the lot. Every male had to put up with second hand goods.'

He stopped suddenly, seeing Amber bristling, 'Sorry ma'am, *experienced women*, I should have rightly said. Except, they were all Evil Lord Black's cast-offs. He were after a wife, see. Then came young Violet Goodearth; now she's from a large family, and her mother's an elf. She's a clever 'un alright, *blue stocking*, and a rare beauty. He were running after her with his tail between his legs.

Aye, but she kept 'im at arm's length. '*Wed me afore ye bed me,*' she told him. Wedding took place in just a few weeks.' He looked up, laughing. 'mind you, there's six children now, and a few miscarriages in between. *She's not kept 'im at arm's length since ...*' he chuckled. 'But he's never looked at any one else since he wed her - mind you I don't think he'd dare!' He dried the large tankard he was holding with a big white towel, then absent-mindedly wiped it across the oaken top of the bar. '*Now, what can I get you?*'

The four ordered beers, decided to try the local brew, 'Virgin's Tears', named in honour of Evil Lord Black. They took a little time enjoying the atmosphere in the bar, some people playing table skittles in the corner, joking good-naturedly, a man and his wife toasting each other with goblets of wine, a group sitting comfortably by the fire, talking business, something about hectares of oats and the current price of barley, negotiating a good deal. The bar smelled of well tended cask ales, expensive pipeleaf and apple logs on the fire, plus a clean smell of lavender beeswax polish. It smelled good.

They sat comfortably on oak settles, copper topped tables in front of them. For once, they felt relaxed, one of those hiatus moments experienced between hell and high water.

'I think I'll go wash, and change into that frock for dinner, look a little more respectable,' suggested Amber. The others nodded and also went to wash and spruce up.

*

They arrived at Doom Castle, slightly smarter and cleaner, just after six. It was noisy. Half a dozen youths stood around the virginal, what had to be Lord Black's son, he was so like him, a good-natured smile lighting up his rather homely features, playing the instrument. A couple of other youths had lutes, one played cymbals and one played a large recorder type instrument. One sang tunelessly, occasionally shaking a tambourine. It didn't sound too good.

They were greeted by Lady Violet, a small child in her arms. 'Sorry, he's a bit fractious, doesn't want to go to bed yet. Let me introduce you to the twins ...' here two little girls crept out from behind her skirt. One had red hair, the other the fairest blonde. They looked nothing like each other at all, nor like either of their dark haired parents. 'Scarlet and Guinevere,' she proudly announced. 'This one's Helios,' pointing to the toddler, 'over there is Malachite and Ebonius. Hmm ...' she looked around. 'not sure where Azurus is, he's probably painting.'

Lord Black also stood by the fire. He waved at them, but was surrounded by two enormous dogs and three friends, all talking at him.

The noise from the group around the virginal seemed to increase, a raucous and somewhat inaccurate rendering of a popular tune. Tamlyn wandered over. The youths stopped playing, wondering who the newcomer was?

'Hello,' he said, 'I like your lute, it reminds me of the one I left behind at the Court at Floriénne. I don't suppose I could have a go could I?' He gently removed one of the lutes from a spotty faced youth.

He sat on a stool and began to play. Now the lute began to sing, he played well and it was a gentle melody, delightful to ears after the strident sound of the boys. Everyone stopped talking, even the young child took his thumb out of his mouth and lay his head on his mother's breast, peace coming over him.

There was an appreciative clapping when Tamlyn finished and a desire for more. He was happy to oblige. A maidservant came in and offered drinks, while Tamlyn played another tune, then the surly cook/retainer walked through.

'Dinner is served. The soup is chicken broth. Don't let it go cold,' and he laid a large tureen on the table. For a moment he stayed, watching Tamlyn. 'Very nice,' he was heard to mutter before he descended to his kitchen. *Praise indeed.* Everyone moved to eat.

It was a large table, it had to be, there were currently seventeen people around it, albeit some were small people. Lady Violet ladled soup into bowls and passed it round. It was very tasty, Grimwold could cook, it must be one of his good days.

The talk quickly turned to Blazing Sun, Mordecai von Adamm and Estrién's sword. He'd hung it by the entrance, as were everyone's weapons. Even in the scabbard it could be seen shining. They were all intrigued.

'The question is,' began Lady Violet, 'when and where was it last used, because that is the key is it not?' referring to the loss of the stone.

Tamlyn nodded, 'to my knowledge it was hundreds of years ago, protecting our people from Sevillon invaders.'

Estrién repeated the rhyme that Amber had told him. 'So the battle it speaks of must have been against the Sevillon invaders then,' he replied. 'I hope *they* don't have the stone. Certainly my family did not. Nor do I know why it was in Floriénne and not with my people.'

Again Tamlyn spoke, 'if whoever wielded it died in battle, and that battle was in the woods of Floriénne, it may have been scavenged, looted from his body. Perhaps there was no one left to give it to, perhaps your ancestor left a son, or a bastard son elsewhere.' It sounded reasonable.

One of the guests spoke up now. 'I'm from the university here, and I'm an expert in ancient runes. That is why Lady Violet particularly invited me here tonight. If you don't mind, after dinner, I could examine the sword for you, try to decipher the runes?'

Everyone looked hopefully at Estrién. He nodded, he too wished to know their meaning.

And so they enjoyed the rest of dinner, the goose was excellent and they all praised Grimwold, who nodded in his surly fashion. The children and the youths disappeared as time went on, to bed or to their rooms, the older boys took a few ales with them and moved off to the billiard room. The university professor went to study the sword. Estrién held it out for him. They took it to the fire to get a good light. Estrién noticed the sword always seemed to gleam strangely in firelight, or if it caught the sun or moon - not a natural gleam, but unearthly.

'Hmm, let me see,' Professor Crowley studied it carefully. '.... *Sulis Estrién nim lumien* ...' he pronounced, finally.

There was a general gasp, one of the words was Estrién's own name.

The professor thought carefully. 'Runes can mean different things, and each of these has its own magic. But I think it says, 'The bright star shines with white light'. Or, I cannot be sure of this, 'the white star shines with bright light.' Truly it could have both meanings, it is ambiguous. But the words are: *'of the sun and the star is the white luminescence.'* All the words have some astral or shining meaning - or both, and it refers to a shining light but not heat - a radiance. I cannot tell you anything further.'

Estrién simply picked up his sword and raised the shining blade in the air. 'I told you this was my sword, yes?' his voice triumphant. 'You call it the *Sword of D'rendiél* do you not, because it belonged to Diras Rendiél? But I think it is the Sword of Light, NimEstrién is its name, White Star.'

He picked up the scabbard and placed White Star upon his back. The green emerald shone in the firelight, an eerie luminescence. His hair and face took on the cold green glow, rendering him almost ghost like. 'I'm ready to fight those bastard Adammites whenever you want,' he laughed.

Everyone nodded. If he could fight as well as he looked, the Adammites didn't stand a chance.

The evening broke and the party returned to the inn.

*

Amber dreamed that night, a clear and lucid dream. She was wandering slowly through an oakwood at midnight. The moon was high, its cool white beams rippling around her. There were deep shadows in the woods and darkened paths led to uncertain places. She kept to the main path, shivering at the thought of where those other tracks led. A windless night, yet still there was a rustling of leaves. She heard the sounds of scurrying in the undergrowth and an owl hooted in the distance, its call long and eerie under the forest canopy in the pale moonlight.

She wore a flowing gown of white lace and silk, with long pointed sleeves, tied with a soft girdle. She had no head-covering but her hair was plaited, wound around her head, a long red ribbon waved down her back. Her feet were bare as she crushed leaves underfoot. There was something out of time about her, about everything.

Time is, time was and time still to be.

She felt serene, wandering, looking, seeking, humming a pleasant tune as she moved gracefully through the forest. She checked each tree as she passed.

As a large tree loomed in front of her, she nodded to herself, this was what she sought. A huge oak, with a small hole in the bole of the tree. With a satisfied smile she placed her hand inside and felt for that which was within. It lay on a pile of velvet, and she clasped it in her palm.

As she opened her palm, the moon shone directly on her hand.

There lay the most beautiful opal, creamy pearlescent, rippling moonbeams, waves of transcendent light, radiating a rainbow of delicate colours. But there was more, for *she* was in this stone, warm flecks of amber blazed, fiery like the sun, dazzling in the moonlight. A fire opal of perfect hues.

She felt a touch on her shoulder and turned to see the brilliant emerald eyes of Estrién smiling at her. Triumphantly she held out the stone, handed it to him. He beamed with pleasure.

He bent down and gently pressed his lips to hers, the stone clutched in his hand ...

... Amber woke, still feeling his kiss. She touched her lips where his had been, her eyes startled. For a few moments she could hear her heart beating, then she calmed herself.

That kiss had been magickal, transcending the physical, like nothing she had known.

She slept little the rest of the night, the memory of that simple kiss kept sleep at bay.

*

They spent a further two days in fruitless research in the libraries of the city. Lord Black had sent word to help, several people were researching, even his family came to help. There were odd items about the sword, mostly explaining how many people it had killed, it's combative prowess, but nothing about the stone.

Amber said nothing about her dream, didn't wish to say, and in fact kept out of Estrién's way. He wondered what he had done to offend her, then put it down to 'woman stuff', time of the month or something'.

All believed they needed to reach Orlandium, the great city south. It was a large city, capital of the kingdom of Westerling, run by a sound government and ruled over by King Alexis, a noble and fair king of good grace and even better temper. There were universities, ancient colleges and even more ancient temples with their own esoteric libraries. Knowledge of the stone must be somewhere.

Lord Black decided to give a dance for them before they left, invited friends and a band. Amber wore her red surtout again, it was the only feminine garb she possessed. The enormous table was pushed against the wall, groaning with Grimwold's delicacies. He actually stood at the side looking on with pleasure, joined in with the dancing occasionally. He'd been part of the family forever. In fact if he traced it back, he'd probably find that Lord Black's great, great grandfather and his were one and the same. The kitchen was his domain, where he reigned supreme, as the Hall was Lord Black's.

Violet, of course, ran everything. Her word was final.

Amber danced with just about everyone, Dane generously stood clapping if he wasn't dancing with her, but then he was in demand with the females too. Lord Black monopolised her, he was resplendent in a white silk shirt and black velvet doublet over black leggings and shiny boots. Tamlyn also danced several dances with Amber, laughing and joking, and then moved on to various other females. They didn't see him again that night, last seen bearing two giggling ladies, one on each arm, out of the main door.

Towards the end of the evening, Estrién came over. He had danced a time or two with Lady Violet, but mostly he stood watching, his eyes intent on Amber. Often he stood holding drink in hand, watching her curiously. He now stood formally in front of her.

'Would you ...?' he hesitated, speaking with his usual formality, but with a gentle cadence. 'Would you care to dance with me, Amber?' He seemed strangely unsure of himself. Amber smiled, but she remembered the dream she had of him, and she too hesitated before offering her hand.

Once more she felt a strange shock as he took her hand in his. They both felt it, and for one second glanced awkwardly into each other's eyes. Then he led her to the floor to join with the others, the moment swept away as they twirled and wove to the music.

They spoke not, he watched her silently as they danced, his deep green eyes fixed on her. Then he bowed formally and led her back to Dane waiting at the side. Without a word, he placed her hand in Dane's and walked away. She saw him move to the big table and help himself to a large glass of red wine. He drank it in one gulp, politely wished Lord and Lady Black goodnight, then left the Hall.

Dane looked down at her, kissed her. There had been nothing to see, and yet he saw it, and what he saw, he didn't like. He took Amber's hand for the last dance, sweeping her round and round, lifting her in the air, laughing, trying to cover for a pain that suddenly hit his heart.

When he took her back to their bedroom at the inn, he undressed her slowly, but his lovemaking was urgent with need. '*I love you, I love you Amber,*' Dane told her, '*my heart is yours ...*'

Amber remained silent, but held him close and kissed him. Her own heart was too full for her to speak.

Chapter 7

They left the following morning, Estrién now astride a chestnut stallion. His blonde hair gleamed in the sunlight, flying in the air as the wind caught him. The sword shone by his side, strapped on the horse.

They made good time the first day and encamped overnight. The second day they had to ride through a steep-sided narrow valley. The horses seemed uncomfortable through the vale, they had to dismount and gently lead them through. Estrién went to each horse, laying his hands on them, talking softly. As the pass became narrower, a group of men, green-clad outlaws, ruffians, accosted them.

'No passage here ...' one shouted. At least it wasn't a troll.

Dane moved to the front to face him. 'Why not, this is no private road? Is there a problem?'

'Not for us, for you maybe. We run the gap now. No passage.' The man was stubborn.

'We need to go through this way, it's many miles around if we don't,' persisted Dane.

'Then it costs you ...'

Dane was waiting for that one. 'So how much does passage cost then?'

'Your gold and your horses ...' the ruffian grinned maliciously.

Dane raised both eyebrows and glanced at his fellows, *we have a joker.* 'Are you effing kidding me?' he asked him. He saw hands twitching with knives and swords.

'No, not at all. There are at least ten of us, four of you - your money and your horses - if you wish to live.' He sneered at Anders as more bandits came into view, brandishing ugly weapons and even uglier scowls. They meant what they said.

Tamlyn quickly looked at Amber and smirked, they both nodded.

Two knives suddenly shot out, one into a bandit's throat, one bandit's scream faded as the second went through his eye.

'Eight, I think, now,' announced Amber.

With snarls and screams the group of bandits made straight for them, waving swords and nasty looking knives.

Dane shot fire through one hand as he picked up his staff, Amber and Tamlyn went in with sabre and short swords ...

... and Estrién ran into the centre of them clutching White Star. He swung it round in a deadly arc, two heads flying in the first circle he drew. Then he came again, sideways at the group, his sword swinging up and down in a great figure of eight, first one side then the other. Limbs went this time, blood crimsoning the air and soaking the ground, cries and screams and startled, horrified faces as bodies collapsed on the rocky floor. The sword flared in the sunlight as flesh was hewn.

Through it all, a vibrant hum could be heard from the sword itself, a sound of time passing, perhaps the sound of life passing.

It was over in moments, his speed and reflexes remarkable. Estrién stood amidst the dead bodies, hardly breathing, merely looking stern.

'I suggest we search these people, take what we can,' his voice emotionless. He walked away, bent down on the grass and wiped his sword. 'It stinks with their blood,' he complained, the sword now quiet.

The others briefly looked at each other with startled eyes, before doing as he suggested. Estrién was indeed a formidable warrior, and a merciless one at that. Tamlyn realised how quickly his friends must have met their death, and how close he could have been to an equally swift demise. The three efficiently looted the bandits, taking some coin and weapons. The bodies were left in a heap as Dane and Amber had done with the Bregantian warriors. Dane flashed fire magic over them, left a burning pyre.

They reached a town some miles south where they sold most of the weapons and various trinkets. Dane had found a small ring on one of them, silver with a tiger's eye stone. It reminded him of Amber. He washed it and presented it to her. 'I don't suppose you'd like this would you? I mean, I know it came off a dead body, but - it looks like your eyes.'

She took it, tried it on her middle finger, it fitted well. 'Why not Dane? It's lovely - and I'm not squeamish. Thank you.' She kissed him. He smiled with pleasure.

They put up at the local inn, it seemed the next town was a fair distance. Hot baths were offered, good to rid themselves of blood and clean their gear. Then they drowned the memory of the day with red wine, the drink of fellowship and bonding. They toasted Estrién, he had been amazing; also, a little terrifying.

But he just shrugged. 'I have been taught well and I have an excellent sword, no more than that.' But they could see he was pleased that the sword fulfilled its purpose.

*

They enjoyed being on the road together. Villages came and went, sometimes they put up at an inn, paid for by Tamlyn, although Estrién paid his share, mostly they camped out. They followed the main highway, the Long Ride, a road that started at Orlandium in the south and wended it's way via Mortia to Manecaestr and eventually to Draecastle in the north. There were plenty of stopping off points.

There was also plenty of shelter in the woods by the road, handy for hunting game; wood-pigeon, hare, rabbits as well as an abundance of berries and fruit. They lived well off the land, Dane was particularly useful when birds flew overhead and he shot up an amberic bolt. Evenings were spent convivially around a camp fire, laughing and joking, all told stories about their lives. Tamlyn's initial hostility began to slowly ebb as he learned more of the sword-bearer. He came to understand

Estrién was not the sort to rush in recklessly, to kill without need, or purpose. But when he did fight, it was, like all elves, quick, efficient and to the death.

Sometimes as they sat quietly around the fire, Amber would see Estrién looking at her oddly, as if he didn't quite know what to make of her. She didn't like to ask, she wasn't sure what he'd say. He'd done it again this night, staring at her, making her feel uncomfortable. She tried to ignore him.

'So, what happened then, Tamlyn?' she asked, listening to yet another tale of the Floriénne Court.

'Why ... I stayed inside the wardrobe until he had finished and fallen asleep. Then I crept out - very carefully, I may tell you! He had locked their bedroom door and kept the key, I'm sure he knew I was there. I had to climb out of the window - it was quite a long drop I assure you - I couldn't look down, but I made it safely to the next room. His wife and I met in the stables from then on, much easier. Stank a little, but the hay loft was comfortable ...' He gave a rueful grin.

Most of Tamlyn's life seemed to have been spent extricating himself from sexual misdeeds.

They settled down for sleep, but hadn't slept very long when Amber, always a light sleeper, heard a snuffling, followed by a howl. *What the ...?* She carefully took her daggers out of her belt and nudged Dane. He was awake in seconds.

She realised it was wolves howling, perhaps attracted by the rich smell of meat from their fire. As she looked up she could see at least a dozen pairs of cunning, eager eyes stalking the camp. They circled the tents and the fire, they looked large and fierce in the moonlight, teeth bared, fangs dripping. Their fur bristled and shone with an unearthly glow. They looked ... angry and hungry. For a few moments no-one moved.

Then Dane jumped up and grabbed his staff, a great mass of fire shooting in all directions. Yelps and howls were heard as they backed away, before they jumped once more into the circle to attack.

Estrién calmly picked up his sword and waved a figure of eight around them, the silver blade swiftly taking bloody heads off two of them.

Tamlyn crawled out of his tent, looking sleepy, but soon realised the problem. He quickly grabbed his daggers and sword, joined Amber.

Tamlyn and Amber threw daggers and went in with swords, careful to keep out of the way of Dane's fire. Amber took a branch set aside for firewood and thrust it into the fire before threatening the wolves with it. Tamlyn decided to do the same and they stood back to back waving the firebrands at the pack. Amber threw more daggers at two of the wolves, they yelped and died, the rest of the pack howling before charging in, baying feral wolves with bared fangs. Amber thrust her torch into the mouth of one of the wolves, lashed out with her dagger, another leapt at her, blood spouted from its throat.

The four grouped up, guarding each other's backs while they slashed and cut at the wolves.

Estrién sent the rest packing, cutting down several at once, his sword swinging wildly at them, whining in the night. The few that were left ran deep into the woods.

He stood confused, shaking his head. 'There's something wrong here,' he finally stated. 'They were no ordinary wolves. They shouldn't need to attack, not right now, they weren't hungry.' He went over to where the remains of one lay, just away from the fire. He studied it then looked up, shocked. 'Guys, come and look ... quickly, it's turning as it dies.' The three ran over, it was clearly seen that this so-called wolf was turning back into a human. 'They weren't all wolves ... ' looking at the remains, '... at least two were werewolves.'

He looked up at the full moon in the sky. 'Something is happening to our land,' he stated. 'We haven't seen anything like these for centuries. What's bringing this about?'

Dane knew exactly what it was. He felt it through his skin, his affinity to the life force of Mer'edrynn. 'These bloody Adammites. I've been feeling it for years, ever since they destroyed my home, but it's getting stronger. They're upsetting the balance, they're changing the natural forces, they're adding too much sun power, or malefic force or death worship, *whatever*. Everything's turning out of kilter.'

Estrién fully agreed with him. 'True, you can't go killing our indigenous races, like naiads or dryads, or murdering priestesses, without a reaction taking place. It leaves a vacuum and nature always fills a vacuum. What was once whole and healthy is turning sour and evil.'

Dane stared unhappily as he studied the creature. 'Hence werewolves, poor damn buggers bitten by a feral wolf, possibly poisoned by *them*, who unwillingly turn into wolves themselves on nights like these.' Mage light shone down upon a savage not-quite-human face.

They gathered the carcasses together, two now definitely in human form, and burnt them. They didn't stay to sleep but gathered the horses from where they had strayed into the forest and moved on.

Something was surely wrong with their world.

*

The following morning they continued making their way through the forest, a bridal path taken as a short cut. It wasn't part of Shirewood, merely woodland, mostly deciduous, oak and elm, some chestnut and hazel, quite thick in places, but nevertheless a shorter route than the Long Ride around its perimeter. They spoke anxiously of the problems now facing Mer'edrynn.

'it isn't merely physical, it's a spiritual unravelling of our world. That mad creature,' referring to Mordecai Von Adamm, 'is destroying the natural order,' stated Estrién. The others agreed, understood. 'He's misaligning the weave, disturbing the structure. It's as if he's sending waves of badness through our land. That bear of yours, Amber, the one in the circus you told me about, how long had he been with the circus?'

Yes, he was right. 'Years,' she agreed, 'and although he had escaped a couple of times, he'd never attacked people as he must have done that night.'

Estrién nodded, another symbol of the land's imbalance since this death cult had grown.

'Shouldn't have kept him in a cage anyway,' muttered Dane. 'Must have slowly gone mad.'

They followed the path, all deep in thought. The sudden appearance of werewolves had worried them, none had ever heard of werewolves within their lifetime, or their parents or grandparents for that matter. Things were crawling out of the woodwork.

For some time they continued, Estrién leading, Tamlyn bringing up the rear.

Estrién's sword was fairly visible at his side, although the emerald pommel was covered with leather, but it still shone. He had managed to move well ahead of the others, the woods being difficult to traverse on horseback, single file necessary. He heard voices ahead of him, horses hooves, perhaps in a small clearing.

'You - stop, who are you? What is that sword you carry?' The words were in Plaintongue, but the accent was Elvhen.

Suddenly Estrién found himself surrounded by four belligerent horsemen. Every one drew their swords, all pointed at him.

'Oh no, not again,' he thought, noting the black and shining silver uniforms, the small gold oak leaf with the acorn on their lapels. He held up a hand to parley, he even spoke politely. 'I have no wish to harm any of you, although I carry the means to destroy all of you. Please put down your swords - believe me, it is in your best interest.' He drew in his horse, waited patiently for the others to catch up.

The four elven horsemen stopped in their tracks, all peering at the sword next to him. 'You have that which we seek, and we intend to take both it and you back to Floriénne to face charges. Give up that sword immediately or you will die, thief.' They lifted their swords once more, ready to charge.

Floriénne elves took no prisoners.

'I am no thief!' he shouted, exasperated, he'd been through this five times now. He truly wanted no more killing of innocent, but rash beings.

Four horsemen closed in on Estrién, four swords held out towards his neck.

Estrién felt for the sword at his side, drawing White Star from its scabbard on the horse, it's eerie light beginning to shine. 'I will give you one chance to parley,' he shouted.

There were sniggers of laughter from the horsemen. 'Four of us and one of you,' one shouted, 'That is clearly the sword of D'rendiél which you stole as a thief in the night. I suggest you give up the struggle immediately, come back to Floriénne quietly and face the consequences. ...or perhaps you prefer death here?' The four elven horsemen laughed to each other, this would be good sport and a prize to boot to take home.

Estrién merely sighed at the thought of more unnecessary slaughter. He raised the sword ready to strike.

The others finally caught up to Estrién. 'Stop!' shouted Tamlyn urgently. 'Stop, it's me, Tamlyn, stop, I tell you! If you value your lives, for Merrie's sake stop!'

The four horsemen raised surprised faces to the newcomer. 'Tamlyn, what do you do here?' asked one, Knight Captain Kielan Penlachl'en.

'Kielan, lay down your arms, listen to me. He took the sword, but he is not what you imagine.' He dropped quickly off his horse, walked over to the elf. 'Come, get down, come and talk, this is truly serious. Would I lie to you?' He turned to his own group, explaining, 'these are another of the four groups who left to seek the sword. *Well, my friends, you have found it*,' turning back to the horsemen, *'but there is much to explain ...'*

Estrién and the others all climbed from their horses, stood in the small clearing, waiting. He still held White Star in his hand, ready to defend himself, his new friends if necessary. Eventually Tamlyn persuaded the now curious elves to join them.

Amber and Dane prepared a small fire, made tea. It seemed appropriate, they could be some time with this. They believed it best to let Tamlyn explain, elf to elf.

Tamlyn told the knights the sorry story of his colleagues, their friends, making them understand *they* had attacked Estrién, not the other way round, just as the group now wished to do. 'I found them, dead, but with their swords placed near, ceremoniously. I was very wary when I met Estrién, and I tell you, we have seen this sword in action - you do not wish to be on the receiving end of it. He did not attack me, he waited and let me talk, he explained his reasons carefully. Yes, he admits taking the sword, believing it to be his own. He says this is his family's sword from centuries back. Yet, he also tells me the sword is not yet complete.' And he continued with the tale of the Elfenstone, the Opalstone. The elves were wary, but wanted to hear more. He explained to them about meeting Amber and Dane, how they had agreed to accompany him on his quest, and how the four had now grouped up together to find this Opalstone.

Estrién stood with sword in hand; it looked like an extension of him, as if he and the sword were one being. It seemed to hum slightly as he held it, almost as if it breathed with him. Eventually he joined them around the small fire, explained himself, his odd name, his reasons.

The Floriénne elves were wary, they wanted him bound, Tamlyn disagreed. 'I believed as you did, I too wished him dead, but I have come to think otherwise. He is more honourable than you suppose, give him a chance.'

Tamlyn explained he *was* the rightful owner, at least, believed himself to be so. 'He just took it straight out of the case, no problems ...' continued Tamlyn. 'If you saw him use it, you would understand - when a man's sword belongs to him, it is *his*, and his alone. NimEstrién is his. *Rightfully his*. Even his name is carved in runes on the sword.'

The elves slowly began to understand, won over by the considerably persuasive Tamlyn. 'I feel this in my blood, it is so, and he is the true and rightful owner. We have not lost a sword but gained a swordsman, a fine warrior, a leader.' Estrién raised an eyebrow at that as Tamlyn explained. 'These are troubled times, this new group, the Adammites is far more dangerous than anything we have seen and they have come to destroy us. We need the sword to be used against them and we need a warrior capable of using it. Estrién is that warrior, i have seen so.'

The elves considered the disturbing news, they too had seen problems in the cities. They spent time questioning Estrién, eventually, like Tamlyn, they seemed relatively satisfied but still wary.

'Good,' asserted Estrién, 'at least no blood shall be shed this day. I assure you, I have no wish to kill your people, but I will always defend myself and *my* people,' briefly glancing at his new friends.

They stayed overnight in the clearing, Dane and Amber prepared a meal for all, whilst the elves continued talking, wisely keeping their own counsel. Estrién and Tamlyn explained about their quest for the stone. The other elves accepted this, but like Tamlyn, asked if he would return to Floriénne once it was found? Eventually he agreed, but only if they prepared the way, ensuring none would attempt to take it from him - for that could prove a bad day for Floriénne.

'This sword killed a hundred thousand once, or so I am told, and from the feel of it in my hands, it could easily do the same again. You would not wish for such bloodshed would you? Nor would I wish to have to use it in such a way ...' he looked menacingly at them, the sword shining and humming. The elves wondered at the hum, never having heard it before. It dawned on them that he and it belonged together, the sword knew its master.

They hastily assured him they would put his case fully, they would accept his word, persuaded by Tamlyn, as long as he was honourable enough to return.

'A thief holds no honour,' Kielan asserted.

'I was honour bound to my Uncle's dying wish,' he replied stiffly. 'I will come to face the Dûchesse, but not before I have been to Elvinhaeme, and I suggest once you have explained all to the Court, that you also join us there. We have need of you, I believe there are attacks by the Adammites on our people. You know that Elvinhaeme is not like Floriénne, the elves there are more gentle, there are few warriors among them. Elvinhaeme is a land of farmers, craftsmen and poets, not fighters. They will need our help.'

The four said they would think on this overnight. For the rest of the evening, once a good meal was in their stomachs and a few goblets of wine had been passed around, like Tamlyn, they joked and laughed about the pleasures of the Floriénne Court. Kielan paired up with Tamlyn for the night, joining him in his tent, as Dane smirked and said, 'I told you so,' to Amber. 'Gets around does our Tamlyn ...'

But all she cared about was cuddling up close to her own warm lover.

The following morning it was agreed the Knights would go back to the Floriénne Court and assure the Dûchesse that the Longsword of D'rendiél was not lost, it was, at least according to Estrién, in the hands of its '*rightful owner*' and he was repairing it or so he said. Tamlyn would be with him at all times to keep an eye on the precious relic and the thief.

He, this elf with the oddly portentous name, had arrived at an auspicious time for them all and they would be joining him to help the elves of Elvinhaeme against the Adammites. The elf would come, once the sword was complete..

He had given his word.

Estrién, Tamlyn and the others waved them off, all heaving sighs of relief.

Chapter 8

It was their own fault, they realised that. Wandering a lonely path, trying to make their way to Orlandium, or in any case, eventually to Elvinhaeme for Estrién to try to help his people. He was truly worried, rumour was becoming fact and he knew his people were not fighters. His own upbringing in Elvinhaeme had been gentle, the teaching wide and varied including music and poetry through to philosophy and science. His uncle in the north on the other hand taught him more practical skills as well as swordsmanship. He was fully aware that the gentle folk of Elvinhaeme wouldn't stand a chance against an armed invader.

But for now there were miles to cover and a possible arduous journey to undertake. It's difficult to be serious all of the time however hard life becomes, and this night the young friends were in the mood for some fun to lighten the load.

They rode until evening, then reached a crossroads on a wide open plain and couldn't make up their minds which way to go. It was late, they encamped at a suitable spot some yards distant. It was a very naive thing to do, they should have realised, but some lessons can only be learned the hard way. Wild youth often makes mistakes which wise age regrets.

They'd been laughing all day, singing daft or bawdy rhymes as they rode. Amber knew quite a few from her circus days, she taught the others new ones. They were merry even before they camped and they carried on during the evening, determined to make a night of it. Dane had flashed his amberic bolts up at passing wildfowl a time or two; wild duck and wood pigeon aplenty for dinner. So they made camp, drinking too much, smoking Dane's powerful leafroll, lying on the ground smiling stupidly at the moon.

It had been a good evening, and the four were too drunk to be wary. They lay in somnolent stupor, silly smiles on their faces, snoring into the summer night. But they had camped at a crossroads. *A crossroads.* A place were miscreants were hung, where demons gathered, where spirits rode and where ghosts collected, at least, so the stories went.

And it was the end of Shearings, the seventh month, when nights were still bright, like Helios, the White nights, just weeks after Midsummer's Day. *The nights when the Hunt rode.*

Now who believed in them, these days? Certainly not *our* feckless crew. Perhaps not feckless, but they were certainly naive. And in any case, they didn't believe the legends ... they were just that ... legends, stories. *Weren't they?* They were far too modern to believe in, or even remember, their children's tales. All those warnings by silly, superstitious old folks. In any case, they were proud of their newfound friendship, a team clearly powerful in many ways, possibly invincible, or so they thought. Ah, *the arrogance of youth* ...

The Fae people, riding merrily and perilously through a silver shadowed sky, wild hair streaming, laughing, screaming, were seeking their prey. The Fae, who came from who knew where? But they certainly came from the deep dark places; eyes used to darkness that could not see in normal daylight. And so they roamed the earth on nights such as these, daylight to *their* eyes, looking for the young and beautiful to take home, to steal and have as their own. To take them to their dim, domed and doomed caverns.

For most could no longer breed, and many were old, even if they did not look so. They sought babies, children, and lovers. Elven children were preferable as they were of mostly elven stock themselves, but there was human and other, stranger, blood intermingled with their own. Blood that weakened as the years passed, too many years. The young they would take as their own kin, bring them up in their dark halls. The bright youths and young men and women they would have as lovers, young blood quickening their slowly coagulating life forces. And thus these bright youths would die, as the Fae people slowly imbibed the life stream from them, or perhaps they too would become like them, mere hulks of what they once were.

They looked fine enough, gossamer cloaks flying, silver clad with golden crowns or helms, silver swords shining in the night. White horses they rode, pure white, like mist along the ground. One pulled a chariot, a woven silver basket to contain their night's catch.

No, the young never slept at a crossroads, or anywhere along an open road on light summer nights. Even on Midsummer, the young laughed and made love and slept in the greenwood, where these beings couldn't reach, for they would not leave their steeds, only for brief moments to capture their prey.

And here four young beings lay happily inebriated, sprawled out on the ground at a crossroads, on a bright summer night. They might as well have put a sign up - *hey come and get us* - a direct line to the Otherworld, the underworld.

The Fae were high in the sky revelling in their Faeride when they spotted them. They laughed and shook their heads at each other at the folly of these young folk. They flew down to look at them - four fair faces, four fine young people; three strong young men, two of them elves. The young men all had blonde locks, strong firm bodies, *good specimens*. Yes, they would be delightful.

A pale rider, strands of ragged silver hair streaming as he rode, stared down at the red haired beauty through cold blue eyes, and felt the bloodlust rise within. It had been some years since he felt heat such as this. *He had to have her.*

'Fair maiden of lustrous locks,

I look on thee with ancient eyes, revelling in thy splendour.

My loins do ache in reverence to thy charms and my blood doth stir to see thy form.

Thou will warm my bed and please my heart and I will devour thee.

And then thy blood will cease and thy looks will fade for I will have feasted on thee.

I will live through thee, for I shall take thy soul.'

'*Es tu, lorien, beainne laniré, lumien ar'amé.*' He muttered, the breath catching in his throat.

He sighed deeply, satisfied with the find. He nodded to his fellow riders. All took out of their pouches the Fae dust. No, not fairy dust from children's tales, but Fae dust, a deep hypnotic sleeping powder made from dried fungus, found deep in the bowels of their damp and dark realm.

They threw it into the air above the already sleeping bodies. It hit the dew in the atmosphere and changed, becoming a thick blanket of choking fog, surrounding Amber and the young men. As they breathed it in, their slumber deepened, becoming almost comatose.

Again the elder Fae rider nodded, and two younger ones with the chariot flew down, grasped each body and threw it into the huge silver basket, throwing in too, the few items they possessed. Any identity must be erased, no one must know they had gone. Unwary wanderers left their homes, their families, but never reached their destinations and there must be nothing left to say they had been taken. The Fae wanted people to disappear without a trace.

They flew off into the night sky again, the riders smugly satisfied with their haul.

They were legend, only legend, mere tales to scare the children. Weren't they?

*

Amber woke to find herself on a soft bed, rich hangings around, everything soft and velvety plush. She was very thirsty, stood to look for something to drink. Discovered she was naked, where were her clothes? But there was a jug on a table and a goblet. She approached it warily, smelled it, it smelled like water. Only when she had drunk her fill did she realise it had an odd taste. It made her feel strangely light headed.

Then the door opened and the silver haired leader of the Fae came in, wearing his long gossamer gown. Ice-glazed eyes pierced her. Truthfully, being naked didn't bother her - until now that is, until his lecherous eyes slid lazily along her skin, focussed on her nakedness. He asked her name, she replied *Amber*, asked where she was?

His reply made her go cold. 'You are here in the Fae realm. There is no way back. Your friends are dead and you now belong to me. You are here forever until I release you to death. Please me and you will live some time. Anger me and you die.' There were no other introductions, no pleasantries, she didn't even know his name.

He stood close to her, his cold, sharp-nailed hands pawing her, moving up and down her body. He knew she didn't want him, he would bully her into acceptance.

Amber shivered and moved away, he followed, backing her against a wall. He forced his mouth upon hers. Amber struggled, tried to wriggle out of his grasp, tried to push him away. He was tremendously strong, far stronger than any human she had known. He stroked her body with his icy hands, her breasts, her loins. She could hear him panting, he began to push himself against her.

Amber kneed him hard between the legs. It shocked him, knocked him back. But it made him angry.

The next thing she knew he had pulled her to the bed, thrown her down upon it, was kissing and pawing her and at the same time hitting her, again and again. She gave what she could, she struggled and kicked. It merely annoyed him.

'You will obey me you bitch, you will learn to obey ...' He threw Fae dust in her face.

She slumped back against the bed, stunned by the dust. She watched through a haze of fae drug as he took her, again and again. It was an odd sensation, but as he took her, she felt colder and colder, as if her blood heat passed to him. Eventually she passed out.

Twice more he came to her bed, twice more he forced her, but she was determined he would pay for his pleasure. Before he threw the Fae dust at her the next time she kicked and bit and scratched. She grabbed a hand and pulled back his fingers until he screamed, with satisfaction she heard a crack. He beat her again, threw more dust into her face, this time it knocked her out cold.

When she woke again she was tied to the bed. And then the others arrived ....

She never gave in. Once the drug began to wear off, she shouted and screamed in their ears and whenever any male was in range she bit them. She would not go without a fight, and she would not easily be taken by these animals. They would bear the scars of their lust.

And so they grew weary of her, took her down into damp and ancient caves where they laughingly tied her to a tall wooden stake in the centre of the cavern. She heard snuffling sounds and a strong animal stench made her gag as they opened a large grill at the side.

'We have no further use for you,' they told her as they left her to her fate.

*

They awoke simultaneously to blinding headaches and a cold floor. The light was dim rather than dark, the light of twilight, dull but not too dark, as was all this realm. They looked across at each other, seeing bodies naked save for breeches. They had no idea where they were or why they were here. Perhaps they had been taken to prison - drunk and disorderly, yet they had been miles from anywhere?

It dawned on them all at the same time. They shouted with one voice, *'Amber!'*

All three stood quickly, each moaning as he clutched an aching head, made worse by Fae dust. They looked around, discovering they were in some sort of cave, a prison of sorts, a barred door across the entrance.

And no Amber.

Neither had they weapons, packs or horses. Nothing.

'Where is she, where are we?' they said.

They crowded the bars, looking out into a grassy area, dark and dull like the end of winter. A hill could be seen across from them, but no buildings, what were probably caves, some with solid looking doors built into mounds that looked like barrows. There was neither sun nor moon, just the greyest of grey skies, a silver mist in the distance. No one could be seen, and what vegetation they saw, struggled to grow. There seemed to be a constant drizzle.

They turned back to their cell, or room, or whatever it was supposed to be. There was a table, plain but perfectly made, to one side of the bars. A large silver flagon stood with three silver goblets.

Dane stooped down, dipped a finger, tasted it, tested it with mage senses. 'It's OK guys, it's water, plain water.' He poured himself a goblet, drank it back. It was refreshing if nothing else. The others followed suit.

'Wherever we are,' said Estrién, 'I've never seen a prison of this nature before ... a primitive cave, but it bears a solid, well made door.' He felt ill, terrible, like the worst hangover he'd ever had. He noticed his hands were trembling slightly.

'Damn!' complained Tamlyn. 'If I had my doublet on, I would have lock picks inside it. In my *pants* ... nothing ... !' He suddenly grinned broadly, realising what he'd said. '*Well*,' he coughed slightly '*not exactly nothing* ... unfortunately, that will not help us at this moment!' The others smiled, a light moment in this darkness.

Estrién was shocked. 'Lock picks? What need do you have of those?' he asked Tamlyn.

'Ah, you'd be surprised,' came the reply. 'Always useful. But sadly no help right now.'

'Well, it's not stopping me,' declared Dane, 'It would be quicker with my staff, but let's see?' He tried throwing fire at the lock on the barred door, heating it to red hot, then a blast of ice, making the lock expand, then shrink. He did this a few times, trying to make it brittle, then shot a mass of amberic energy at it.

Eventually they heard a satisfied click and the door opened on its hinges.

'*Open sesame*!' he quoted. 'Come on guys, let's find out where we are, and what's happened to Amber.' All three crept out. There was no one at all to be seen.

Briefly they shouted, '*Amber!*', but there was no reaction, no answer. Nothing stirred at all, only a ground mist meandered around their ankles.

It was no lighter outside the cave than in it. Nor, as they looked around, did the light change, signifying time had gone by. It neither darkened nor turned to day. It stayed merely, nearly, dark.

It was also chilly. They could have done with their cloaks, when all they wore were breeches. But Estrién was now shaking more, couldn't stop. He began to feel sick, his head pounding. 'Holy Merrie, Dane, what was in your leafroll? I feel terrible.'

Dane protested, it was no stronger than usual.

They moved further afield, trying to find what was beyond the hill, but Estrién got to the point where he just sat down, shaking. Everything was spinning and he was almost blinded by the headache. 'Stop, stop, just wait a while guys,' he begged. Dane came over, threw mage hands over him, couldn't find what was ailing him.

'It's just a hangover, Estrién, *get over it* ...' he told him, shooting a little magelight into him.

Temporarily Estrién felt better ... for a few moments, that is. But with every step he grew worse. He felt he might be better back at the cave, it was darker there. He turned and retraced his steps, realising with each step backwards he felt a little clearer. *Something was strange.*

To begin with, he'd never had a headache in his life. Nor had he any particular ailments, in fact his mother had praised him for being so strong as a child. When the influenza came to their village, nearly everyone came down with it. Estrién had no symptoms whatsoever. He'd never even had a common cold. Apart from one or two stomach upsets when he was young, from something bad he had eaten, or more recently, too much alcohol, he didn't ever remember being ill.

So, why did he feel like this?

He reached the cave, slightly less crushing headache now. The others were running back, asking what he was doing? He just shook his head, he didn't rightly know. He walked past the cave, in the opposite direction, yes, something was easing.

Why?

He tested the theory, walked away again, in the first direction they had been following, grew worse. *This was ridiculous!*

And yet as he retraced his steps, the pain and the shivering grew less. He explained this to his two friends. They agreed on three things.

1) *It was weird.*

2) To follow whatever path made him feel better.

And 3) See where it led.

This they did. It was better anyway than blindly following your nose in an unknown land.

Slowly he began to ease, little by little, but the tremors, the sickness, the pain remained, merely became bearable. At one point they grew worse. He retraced his steps, took another direction, grew worse again. Came back to where a door led into the hill. There was absolutely no one around.

'Guys, we have to get in there, somehow.'

Dane did his magic stuff again with fire and ice and electrum bolts. Eventually the door opened and they stepped into what appeared to be a stone walled entrance hall, an ante chamber. There was nothing here except a low, long table and a delicate looking chair, a candle burning in a tall wooden candleholder. They passed through to the door beyond.

A long stone corridor, with corridors and rooms off. What seemed a maze of rooms and tunnels led inwards and downwards. They were lit poorly with occasional torches on the walls, the corridors etched into the hillside, the floor rough-hewn stone.

It was chillier in here than outside.

'Mountain people? Outlaws, Bregantines, Alderfolk?' asked Tamlyn.

Estrién shook his head. 'nor wood folk, Sylvanii, they would not dwell here. Outlaws possibly.'

They opened a door, saw a wood panelled room with a desk and chairs, elaborately carved, *elven style*, as Tamlyn put it. When they saw the painting on the wall, they knew. It was of wild horsemen flying in the sky, cloaks billowing behind, the eyes of the horsemen glowing.

They knew little of these people, but they knew enough. 'The Fae!' they cried, realising what had happened. Childhood tales were full of these people, and pictures that kept young minds awake at night. *Along with warnings* ...

It was the worst possible scenario. They now knew where they were, or at least who had taken them, *that damn crossroads, what fools they'd been!*. Unfortunately they had no idea if they were in their own world or somewhere else entirely. All they knew were tales and legends.

And none good ... cautionary tales for young minds.

Estrién shook his head, 'let's just go on, I *need* to go on.'

They followed him as he twisted and turned down passageways. 'With each step I feel better, revived, almost renewed. We are not far now.'

They arrived at a large door, locked yet again. Dane did his fiery/icy/electrum thing, it opened. It was pitch dark, Dane took a torch from the corridor, peered in. It appeared to be an enormous room, a huge ancient hall full of mounds of baggage. Unlit torches hugged the walls, Dane lit several with fiery fingers. It smelled musty, some of the things in here had been around for ... centuries? Evidence of those kidnapped by the Fae, many, many, years of victims. So ... it must all be true, all those stories, those legends.

'*Oh f**k!*' Dane was heard to mutter. A short, sharp expletive always cleared his mind.

Estrién made straight for it. A tall pile of bags and baggage, weapons, staves, clothing, all thrown together and left for eternity. Some were moth eaten and ragged, stiff with age, some still in good repair. All their own goods, that is their clothes, their personal baggage and their weapons lay here, the most recent collection.

The Fae didn't give a damn, everything in an unholy mess, thrown in and discarded, kept only as proof of their power, a few souvenirs. *Correction* - hundreds, if not thousands of souvenirs. Evidence of lives taken and destroyed, hidden from the seekers ... none must know. It was all here, mouldering through time.

Estrién saw a glow in one of the heaps, tore everything apart, almost in a daze. With a feverish look in his eye he pulled out his sword, White Star - the priceless weapon had been casually thrown among the rest as if worthless. Triumphantly he raised it above his head, noting that his sickness was gone, his voice now strong,

'Hear this ... *by the might of Herne the Hunter and the blessing of the Lady, this sword is mine and shall never leave my side again!*'

Briefly the sword shone bright, a slight humming sound echoed his words.

He turned to Tamlyn and Dane, both surprised at his outburst. 'This, my brothers, this is what weakened me - I was separated from White Star! Never again. Now I understand! I and this sword are one, I tell you, *One!*' He spoke with conviction. 'We were weak, my brothers, we erred, but we shall not err again! From now on we take care, we must grow from this, we must learn.'

He gathered his clothes, dressed. Kept his sword in his hand, he would need it this day. 'We are young and we were fools, but we will grow,' he told them. He found his pack, began looking for anything that might be of use, found Amber's pack, held it up, waving it at the others. '*Hers*, by the Lady!'

Dane found her clothes, so she too would be half naked somewhere ... *no wait*, there was a halter and pants here ... *what the hell ...?* He showed them to the others, his eyes blazing. Both shook their heads, what did he expect from these beings? Those stories, even the childhood tales were unkind, held fears not yet understood by young minds. They, as adults, began to truly fear them.

Estrién patted him on the shoulder. 'We will find her, my friend, we shall make them pay if they have hurt her.' Dane nodded, glad to have Estrién by his side.

Tamlyn found swords and various daggers, he placed them all on his belt and around his person, and took a fine sabre for his own use. It was well balanced, even better than his own. The two dirks in his belt were for Amber when they found her. They quickly dressed, searching for their own goods left haphazard among the mouldering piles, gathered what they could.

With care, they found everything they believed to belong to Amber.

Dane looked for his staff, then saw there were numerous ones scattered around. He studied them for a while, some looked quite good, he'd never really cared for the black ash one. Then, *'Oh yes!'* he exclaimed, walking over to a dark corner. He picked up a beautiful oaken staff with a glorious carving of Lady Merrie on the end, *'oh yes ...'* he repeated, getting the feel of it, trying a little magic through it. It would take time, it felt strange in his hand, it was so old. Yet it was perfect, the staff he had always wished for, and truly symbolic with the Lady on the end, he trusted her goodness, her splendour ... and it was made of oak - his mother's tree.

Sometime, long ago, a mage had carried this precious staff, had been taken by the Fae hunt, had left it long forgotten. Dane threw it from hand to hand, testing, like Tamlyn, its weight, it's balance. Perfect, absolutely perfect. It would take him a little time to bring it to full power, but it was far more powerful than the black ash. It was *his* power, life and health and fertility and grace. Everything elemental and whole, of the woods and the forests and the earth. He felt the age of the oak tree that this had come from, heard the birds singing in the treetop and small animals scurrying back and forth. He smelled the leaves on the branches, felt the roots deep underground, tasted the water that nourished them. He had never felt a staff so fully.

And among it all he heard a sound, a strange sound of singing stone amidst a flash of lightning.

He looked up, saw Estrién smiling at him, he nodded and acknowledged him; they were one, he and the staff, Estrién and the sword. Brothers in arms, brothers in battle, brothers in peace. He felt a pure kinship as his eyes met Estrién's. Both men laughed, the elf and the human ... the half-human.

Estrién walked out of the door. *'Now for Amber,'* he stated, a fiercely determined look in his eyes. The others followed him.

They moved onwards, through dimly lit corridors and passages, but the light of Estrién's sword and the mage light on the end of Dane's staff gave plenty to see by.

'Any ideas?' Estrién asked them. Tamlyn suggested simply following the largest passageway as it turned downwards.

'I feel we are going deeper and deeper into the earth,' he stated, 'the main path leads somewhere, perhaps to the Fae themselves - for where are they? Why are they not in the rest of this place? What are they doing? I tell you, be wary, my friends, I believe they await us.' The others nodded sagely, trod softly, all senses alert.

Down and down, deeper and deeper into the chilled halls of the dead, the *Fae* ... alive, yet not alive. Beings who lived off vibrant youth, sucking out their essence until they were young no more. *No* – not blood, something less physical and a little more esoteric ... the spark of life itself.

And so finally they came to a huge double door covered in runes. It had no handle, no visible lock, and would not open. It was old, of ancient wood, ebony perhaps, time had rendered it black. It stood there immoveable and impassable. No doubt a password was needed to unlock the runes, some ancient elven word of passage. None however could read the runes, and they certainly looked like nothing on Estrién's sword.

No doubt in another world, on another day, an older and wiser mage would have understood and the doors would have opened to his spoken command.

But not this day.

This was not another world and in any case, Dane didn't give a damn.

'Time I tried this out,' he said, handling the oaken staff with relish. 'Let's see ...' He studied the big arched door for a time, or rather, feeling magically; heightened mage senses seeking weakness. Then he nodded, yes ...*yes*. The door might be strong, and the lock magickal, but it was only as good as its hinges and the doorway it rested in.

He stood back. 'Keep clear ...' he told his friends, concentrating.

He shot a massive amberic blast at the hinges, followed by a blast of flame at the centre, between the doors. It creaked and whined a little but nothing happened. He didn't care, he had its measure now.

'For Amber!' he shouted as he shot one more huge electrum blast. It was bigger than he thought, the staff immensely powerful. He reeled back a little, gazing in awe at the oak staff. 'Wow!' he commented, realising he'd have to learn to use this staff wisely.

It tore the doors off their hinges and they fell clattering to the floor, leaving a great gaping hole. Dane laughed to himself. He knew he couldn't have done it with the old staff, *but this one* ... his full magic was here in this stave of oak.

They saw them all watching, even before they walked through, but still they went. If they were to find Amber, this was the only way, they knew it, were sure of it.

They walked in to a great Hall with a large circular open space in the middle, tiered seating rising against the curved walls. They were surrounded by Fae on all sides, all of them observing them closely as they entered. Some flew towards them, using their own wings, softly laughing in their faces, before fleeing away.

Dane held his staff firm, Estrién held his sword aloft, Tamlyn kept one hand on his sabre, one on a dagger.

'Where is she?' Dane shouted, 'where is Amber, what have you bastards done with her?' His anger was clear.

The Fae said nothing. They would wait until these young bucks were rendered docile enough and then take them as lovers, pass them around, use them. It had worked for centuries, they had patience to wait.

'Thou hast passed the first test, mage, we have plenty more for ye.' The voice of the silver haired leader, the one who looked down at Amber and craved her. 'One by one ye shall be defeated and we shall enjoy all of thee.'

'What have you done with Amber?' this time it was Estrién who shouted.

'Be silent elf! Do not raise your voice here, in this place.' A small woman walked forward, as old as the silver haired leader. A golden circlet wove around her head as thus a snake coils around its prey. She wore a long gown of grey, delicate patterns of silver and gold thread intertwined around the flowing dress. The garb was simple and fine, delicate, gossamer thin, but her nails were long and sharp, they had plucked the gossamer in places, shreds of fine thread trailed behind her. 'I know your sword, elf, I have seen it of old. Beware how you use it here, do not force us to finish thee off quicker than need be. There is much life in you for us to enjoy.'

She continued speaking, her ancient eyes shrewd and sharp. '*Mage*, you have passed your first test, you came through doors that could not be opened, yet you opened them. That is good, you may rest a while and watch.'

Dane shook his head, they could go to hell. *Perhaps they were already there.*

'You, *elf*, with the sabre, let us see thy abilities, let us watch ye as ye die. A brave death would please us, entertain us all.' The elder Fae leader beckoned to a younger Fae, a warrior, possibly one like himself, taken by the Fae some time previously, now drained and poisoned. The young Fae stepped forward eagerly, he still had the blood lust for battle..

'Fight!' they were commanded.

Both Dane and Estrién went to help, Tamlyn waved them away. 'Nay, it seems this is my fight, then so be it. Wait my brothers, we shall have them all yet.'

The Fae laughed - ah, a good one, a feisty one, he would be fun to watch ... and better fun to enjoy if he lived. Each looked on him with sensual delight, male and female Fae, he was beautiful - yes, they could all enjoy that one.

He turned to his foe; quick as lightning he threw a dagger at the warrior, it was cast aside by the Fae's own sword. Tamlyn stood to face him, threw another dagger at his left side, to see it cast away yet again. Tamlyn nodded, understanding this would not be easy, he must learn the weaknesses of this foe. He went in with the sword, a quick cut and thrust, matched evenly by the Fae warrior. They lunged and parried for some time, getting the measure of each other, a short sharp dance around the hall, the clang of swords as they clashed.

Dane and Estrién watched helplessly, held back by the Fae, cold hands on arms rigid with anger.

The young Fae was arrogant, he had performed this task many times now, his sharpened sword was excellent and he had the support of the Fae around him. As one of the Fae played a mournful tune upon an ancient pipe, he danced nimbly with the sword and waited for his moment to slip in and kill this new, young pretender. They waltzed and pranced and sliced and thrust their way around the Hall, a well matched couple. Yet, this was a dance of death, not life, as pure a perversion as the Fae world itself. Eventually he saw the elf was tiring, *now*, now he could make his kill, another notch to his belt, his roll call of the dead.

But as the young Fae moved in to thrust his sword at Tamlyn, the lithe elf parried and feinted and threw yet another dagger straight into his eye. Tamlyn kept plenty tucked around his uniform for just such eventualities. The Fae's own momentum ensured the dagger went through his skull and into his brain. He collapsed on to the floor.

'Did you mark him for death?' Tamlyn shouted at the Fae, 'was that why you chose him? Do you think I am without skill?' He stood defiantly in the middle of the floor, his sword still in his hand.

The Fae leader simply nodded his head. This new young elf had performed well, he still lived. The fight had been amusing, especially the little twist at the end. Tamlyn was allowed to stand by Dane's side. They both stood seething, held back by silvery hands.

He turned instead to Estrién, showed him an open door to an outer passageway. 'We are plagued by cave bears, they annoy us. *Kill them* and we may let ye go.' He had no such intention, but he considered the elf would not know that.

'Where is Amber?' Estrién's shout betrayed an anger barely controlled.

The Fae motioned to the doorway - 'down there of course. If thou seekest the female, then save her ...' The Fae looked smugly at him, eyes triumphant in their cold cruelty.

Estrién raged inside, but would not let it show. 'I will go.'

Dane pushed the hands away, ran over, wouldn't let him go alone, but was pulled back by the Fae leader's magical force. 'If he dies down there, thou may go, but not before ...' A dozen Fae warriors suddenly stood between him and the door.

Tamlyn too hurried to Estrién's side, ready to take them on, but more warriors appeared.

'Do not fear, my friends,' Estrién stated, 'Instead, *remember me?*' as he passed through the doorway and into the winding rock-hewn passages.

Soon he could smell the lair of the bears. He quietly stepped down the walkways, the smell getting stronger, becoming overpowering, a raw animal smell. It wasn't long before he came upon a large cave.

There must have been a dozen of them. padding around and around a long wooden stake in the centre. It reached to the ceiling, clearly used for sacrifice of unwanted or troublesome guests. He gazed upwards at Amber, her body naked, hands bound with silken ropes in front of her, clinging on for grim life at the top of the pole, her legs wrapped around the structure.

Under any other circumstances it would have looked supremely sexy. Under these circumstances she rendered a pitiful figure, Estrién saw the fear on her bruised face, she had been beaten, much of her skin swollen and bruised. He also saw remnants of dried blood down the inside of her legs ... it was clear to him what had happened to her.

Every now and again a bear would rear on its hind legs and try to reach her. With widened eyes, she clung desperately to the stake.

Estrién's heart went out to her. These fiends had brought her here to die, to be torn apart in the most savage way possible.

'Stop!' shouted Estrién, not to Amber, but to the bears. They turned to the newcomer, wondering what to make of him? He placed his sword back over his shoulder, holding out his hands. He could smell their hunger, taste it. 'Oh you poor bastards,' he said, 'you ill-treated creatures.' He looked up at Amber. 'They have deliberately starved these animals, kept them as pets to use against their prey.' He turned back to the bears, stared each one in the eye, calming each one. His hands made strange signs in the air as he had done the day in the forest. One by one the bears sat down on their hind legs mesmerised by Estrién's own elven magic.

He looked up at Amber, 'Will you trust me Amber? Will you let me help you down? They will not hurt you, I promise.' He walked over to her, held out his hand. She nodded, what else was there to do anyway? She allowed herself to slide down into Estrién's waiting arms. He tore her bonds apart with the small dagger he kept on his belt, then handed it to her. 'There, I suspect you feel better with that in your hand.'

He carefully undid his cloak, not wishing to startle the bears, wrapped it around her. 'A little warmer, huh?' trying not to look at her naked body. He smiled kindly. 'They think they sent me to my death, but I have an idea, one they cannot suspect. I only hope Dane and Tamlyn understood me when I entered the lair.'

He turned back to the bears, keeping hold of Amber's hand, leading her with him, 'come, my friends, you are hungry no? *Let me take you to a feast.*'

He led Amber away, carefully holding her hand. He hadn't time to register the *frisson* that happened every time he touched her. The bears followed, spellbound by his voice, his own innate beast magic. Slowly, carefully, they took the passageways back to the Hall of the Fae. Occasionally he would turn back to the bears, raise his hands in strange signs, look them in the eye, calm them. As they neared the Great Hall he took his sword from his back in readiness, pulling Amber to one side, squashing themselves against a curved hollow in the walls.

'Now, my friends, *enjoy!*' he shouted as the bears rushed through the opening.

Screams and shouts could be heard. Pandemonium reigned. The Fae had no such magic as the elf

Dane and Tamlyn were waiting. They had quietly edged to the back of the hall, back towards the main doors, the blasted doors, ready to run. They understood his meaning, remembering the day in the forest when Estrién quietened the bear. There was a short but exceedingly fierce blast of flame at the Fae from Dane. Estrién let White Star loose with a wide sweeping arc, taking out several Fae as they rushed through the group. A blast of white light from Dane's staff blinded the Fae long enough for the four to make for the broken doors and dash through the opening. Then they ran and ran and ran back towards the entrance door of the huge cave dwelling, hearing screams fading in the distance. Some followed, but Dane constantly threw heavy blasts of amberic magic at them, delighted by the sheer raw power of his new staff. Every door they reached, Dane shot ice magic to solidify it, or blast it at angle to hinder them or stop them. As they reached the outer rooms, they gathered furniture together and Dane set the whole alight, making passage impossible, the fire quickly taking hold.

The main outer door he left intact, but he wedged it hopelessly in the doorway.

They found themselves back near the cave where they had been imprisoned, hills and the barrow-like structures all around them. The air was chill with wisps of morning mist, yet this mist would never dissipate, for here was no sun to warm the ground.

Dane handed Amber her clothes, boots. She returned the cloak to Estrién and quickly put them on, Tamlyn and Estrién politely averting their eyes. Once dressed, Tamlyn passed her the dirks and daggers.

'Thank you for coming for me, they were vile ... *repulsive*.' She looked up at Dane. 'I need your help Dane, not now, later. I ... *they* ... oh just let's get away!' She began running up the hill, no idea where she was going as long as it was far, far, away from here ...

... far, far away from these soulless bastards. She was crying inside, but determined not to show it, she would be strong. Her friends had been strong, so would she. Run, Amber run, anywhere, just away from here. Get away, far away, with these three kind men who had come for her, risked their lives to save her.

Her soul shivered at the memories of the last days.

They continued running, a hill far ahead looked like a landmark, it was at least a place to make for, before the Fae killed the bears as they surely would, and followed them.

But when they reached the top of the hill, all they could see was lonely moors for miles and miles.

Nevertheless they continued running, often looking back to see if they were being followed, but no one appeared. Either the bears had eaten their fill, which seemed unlikely considering the sheer raw power of the Fae, or the fire had kept the Fae from leaving. There would of course be other exits, but none knew where. Whatever, they were obviously busy for now. Running seemed to be the only option, dashing across rough heather clad moors under dirty grey skies towards nothingness.

Eventually a dim grey light was seen in the distance, a fae light, a fey light. They ran towards it, the only object on the horizon. It grew as they neared, a swirling, whirling mass of cloud filled light. Oval shaped, it hovered over the heather, a possible exit? Was this how the Fae came through to their world? They stopped, looking at each other.

Was it the way home? Would it lead them to their normal world?

'Oh come on, boys, I'm trying it. I'm not staying in this blasted realm one more moment. Death would be better than what I've just been through,' and Amber stepped through.

The others quickly followed her, *the lady had spoken*. They each stepped through the iridescent grey fog: a short but ice cold journey. The air grew colder and colder with each step, time too seemed to have stopped or, more correctly, elongated, eked out, time-yet-no-time. The cold-blooded Fae would not feel it, but to a hot-blooded young human or elf it felt like icy daggers and needles in the face and against their bodies. It became harder and harder to walk, breath difficult to take, steam rising from their mouths, turning to ice as it drifted away. The fog too, harder, more solid with each step, as if the other world was pushing this world in, squashing the very mass of the exit, driving it away from the everyday existence.

Each wondered if they had enough breath to last?

But they could see a clearer, cleaner light and slowly, gasping and grasping towards normality, they forced themselves through the thick and deadened air.

One by one they stepped out of the Fae passage, each gulping the pure air of a just-awakening Mer'edrynn day into their lungs.

They found themselves on another moor, but this time under a morning fresh sky, the heather now purple and white around them. The air smelled good, clean, summer-warm. When they looked back, there was nothing to be seen, the passage one way only, or perhaps it collapsed after their passing. Who knew?

Now they ran again, towards familiar looking hills, a forest in the distance.

They were back in their own realm, free of Fae, possibly not many miles from the damn crossroads they had camped at. They eventually took their bearings at the top of a lush green hill, found their way back to their camp.

The tent and ground sheets were still there, empty wineskins, the product of their misspent evening lying cast aside. They picked them up, they would do as water skins now. They found some useful items, pewter goblets, plates, a towel. Carefully they packed what they could.

But the horses were gone.

They would have to walk, at least to another town, perhaps get passage on a coach. They didn't think they could afford another four horses, not of that calibre, the beautiful pure bred stallions. Tamlyn's cash was running out, their own stocks meagre, at the most it would be four weary old nags.

They set off along the south fork of the crossroads. They would spend no more bright summer nights out in the open, at least not without one on watch. It would be inns, lodgings or a forest canopy for them from then on - as it should have been.

They found a village some miles hence, it had a small inn. Gladly they entered and asked for a couple of rooms, Tamlyn and Estrién happy to share. All wanted hot baths, much to the innkeeper's horror - four baths at once? All that hot water! He set to, stoking the fires.

But mainly, Amber wanted to wash away the Fae.

Dane found her weeping in the small wooden bath. He placed his arms around her.

'Tell me love, it's OK, I need to know, to help,' he spoke softly to her.

She looked up at him, her amber eyes red rimmed. 'You already know, it's obvious.' She washed her face thoroughly, began to scrub her body. 'I was drugged. That blasted old guy, he came first, not for long though, I fought the bastard, cracked his dirty fingers, before he passed me on. Then I was drugged again. I woke up tied to a bed. They came one after another and took me. I knew who they were, I could tell they were the Fae. What else is there to say? When I began screaming and cursing them, they got annoyed. When I bit every little shit who mounted me, they stopped. Dragged me naked to the bear pit and tied me to the pole. There was a grill they opened and the bears came in. I shimmied up the pole and hung on, and on, and on. Eventually Estrién arrived, calmed the bears with that incredible power he has, helped me down. I couldn't have lasted much longer.'

Dane helped wash her, took a towel and gently dried her, checking her body; bad bruising around her loins, some tearing. At some point they had also beaten her from the looks of the bruises over the rest of her body. He sent healing magic into her. He guided her to the bed.

'Get some sleep love, I need a few things, rest now.'

He left the room, knocked and entered the other room. Two pairs of worried elven eyes sought his.

'Is Amber OK?' asked Tamlyn, already aware..

Dane shook his head. 'Multiple rape, beating, bruising and tearing, infection and even pregnancy for all I know. I thought those people were supposed to be unable to have children, but seeing Amber, I'm not so sure now. Plus they threw her to the bears ... *hey*, they must have hated her, she was tied up, but she still bit them and she broke the old git's finger!' The others smiled, yes, she was something of a wildcat. 'I'm off to get some herbs, medicines, if I can find what I need. I carry a potion to rid her of a child, if there is one, I can't truly tell yet, but I'm not wasting time finding out, just bring on her blood-flow early. I'd like some strong herbs against any infection.'

He left them to seek out the potions he needed.

The elves looked at each other. This was the worst possible scenario for her.

'We need to be extra kind to Amber for some time ...' suggested Tamlyn. Estrién just shook his head sadly. He had seen her pathetically clinging to the wooden stake, the staunch set of her mouth yet coupled with a look of wild-eyed horror; he cried inside for her.

Outside Dane looked for a herbalist's. His mind was spinning and he was blazingly angry at himself.

'I guarantee, life on the road with me will be twenty times better than what you've got,' he had told her that first night. *Had promised her.* And what had he led her into? She would have been better off staying with bloody Longshanks. He realised too, that this probably wasn't the first time. She had spoken the same way about the Alderfolk, when she was young ... and who knew what went on in the circus?

He vowed to himself he would change her life, make it good for her and that from that moment she would only know the touch of love.

*

Amber woke a few hours later, an evening sun gently shining through the window, it's peaceful glow blushing the walls. For a few moments she forgot where she was, what had happened and then it all flooded back.

That bastard, that old Fae guy, the one with the straggling silver hair and the dry crackling fingers .... She shivered momentarily, remembering ...

The abuse; the panting, huffing, stink filled breath of her rapists. Then the beatings and being dragged to that cave ... the pole, the bears, the fear. She'd never shimmied up a tree as quickly as she climbed up that pole.

And hung on, limbs wearying, arms aching, wondering how much time left before she fell?

And then, Estrién came, so softly, so kindly. She didn't know he could be like that, he'd always seemed so stern.

She shook herself, *'c'mon Amber, put those shitheads aside* ... she'd done it before, she could do it again .... effing male savages! If she'd had a knife ... she laughed to herself ... there wouldn't have been a whole male left down in those bloody dust caves. One day she would revenge herself, perhaps she and her three new friends? They were good men, she thought, and Dane was wonderful. So different to most of the bloody twats she'd come across before. Yes ... fine men, fine friends.

Briefly she wiped a tear from her eye. Not a tear for the pain and misery she had been in, but a tear of warm gratitude for three young warriors who had come to find her.

She decided to get up, get dressed, go downstairs, shake off the beasts. She didn't hurt so much now, thanks to Dane's healing magic. Wow, that magic of his! The boys were probably in the bar - yes, *go and get royally pissed.*

They were surprised to see her. All three rose formally as she entered the bar, their backs straight, three pairs of male eyes curiously watched her as she made her way towards them. Dane moved across for her to take the seat next to him. Tamlyn shouted for another goblet and poured wine for her. He offered it like a sacrifice, bending his head humbly.

'The wine of friendship, Amber. I hope your rest has helped a little.' It was clear they were all concerned for her.

Dane fiddled in his bag under the table, brought out a small bottle. 'Get that drunk, and I've made up a balm for you. Also, tonight, later, a potion I'd like you to have.'

She turned her amber eyes to him. 'And do I get some of that soft healing magic of yours again, too?'

He chuckled, 'as much as you need or want, my love. I'll have you well in no time.' He lifted his goblet in toast; she acknowledged him with a smile. Then she looked gratefully across the table at Estrién.

'What can I say, Estrién, I cannot thank you enough? I couldn't have held on much more, you saved my life.'

He gazed astonished at her. 'No thanks necessary at all, that creature also sent me to my death. *Or so he thought.* I ... I was just happy to be able to help you.' He picked up his wine, looking a little embarrassed, took refuge in the drink.

None it seemed had eaten, Amber said she needed food. They were all surprised, thought she was probably going to be 'delicate' for some time. Amber ordered prime steaks all round and tucked heartily into hers when it arrived. All three men watched her eating, amazed at the resilience of the woman. She was far tougher than she looked. Their respect for her grew

Chapter 9

She spoke to Estrién the following day as they were making their way southwards, 'That trick - no, that's a bad word for it - that skill you have, with the animals - that's incredible. I watched you with the bears, I've never seen anything like it - and I lived in a circus! What wouldn't Longshanks have given for someone like you!'

Estrién smiled quietly, 'just something I picked up. But I think it's innate in me, as my uncle taught me the various signs and sigils, but he didn't seem to have the full ability I have. He was good with horses and dogs though.'

'Well, you saved my life ... all our lives ... we owe you.'

He turned to her. 'You owe me nothing, Amber, nothing at all. I'm happy to be with you all. I'd no idea what to do once I got my sword, I would have been drifting, or aimlessly sitting back at my uncle's manor, no more. I believe *we* have purpose, or we would not have come together.

Besides, I quite like my new friends. You're good people.' He walked off, slightly embarrassed about his speech, he wasn't used to opening up, letting people in, not been brought up that way. But these last days, he felt a close bond with them all.

Particularly Amber.

That thing that happened whenever she touched him ... her nearness ... she made his skin tingle and his mouth go dry. He felt like a fumbling fool when she was close.

He shook the hair from his face and held his head high, 'Come on, let's get a move on, put some miles in,' he called to the others, quickened his pace and marched onwards.

Tamlyn set up a bawdy marching song and they all joined in. It was something about four hard soldiers, three willing wenches, two hungry bulls and a cock that crowed in the morn. Or words to that effect. They sang with gusto.

They made good time, they were not too many miles from the border with Westerling, the roads were patrolled well here. But there were constant rumours about the Adammites and the Blazing Sun cult. Many of the rumours spoke of atrocities against mages, elves and women. They were slowly advancing across the mainland.

They made an overnight stay on the Mercantia side of the border, Amber was tired, didn't actually feel well.

'Probably all those horrible potions you gave me,' she stated.

She began losing blood that night, the potion certainly worked quickly, Dane helped, cleaned her up, stayed with her. It wasn't too bad, not like a full blown miscarriage, more like an all-at-once blood-flow, it may even have been merely that. It was just that she felt so ill. The other two supplied her with hot drinks, the odd brandy. Then she slept through most of the next day, although Dane thought that was probably due to shock.

But she looked brighter and cheerier the following day, She was grateful for their help, and their kindness. They even carried her pack the next couple of days to let her get her strength back.

They bought a cooking pot in one of the villages. Amber tried to make tasty stews or broths on open fires - she wanted to pay them back for their help. She enjoyed the idea of the 'cauldron of plenty' with her at the helm, discovered she enjoyed the whole cooking thing. Also, loved watching them eat appreciatively when it turned out well. Anders particularly appreciated the cook pot to brew potions and he was quite handy himself when it came to stews. 'I had to look after myself,' he stated, 'couldn't live off pasties all the time.' He showed Amber the herbs he used for flavour. The boys certainly enjoyed their food more and they looked out for herbs or tasty roots and leaves while they walked. It made quite a difference, especially if they had a flagon or two of wine with them. But they always camped in a forest, with the fire up all night and one stayed guard. Fae, bears, wolves or werewolves ... who knew what next?

The roads however were much easier to traverse here, well kept and well guarded. King Alexis looked after his kingdom, trade was its life blood, the roads must be kept passable at all costs. At the first large village they were able to get a coach to the capital, Orlandium.

Orlandium was actually an inland port, the river being so wide as to allow passage of smaller ships or great barges to the city from the coast. Often ships would discharge their cargo at Pennyport on the coast, (so called because there was a levy of at least one penny on every boat or ship that docked there, according to its size.) Great barges would be filled, taking all the goods up the River Ambrosia to Orlandium. The barge people, the Tsigani, made a fair amount in this trade.

They travelled in on a hot Herneset day, the eighth month, summer at its full heat. The pennants hanging over the city entrance hung limp, no wind at all, but they were brightly coloured, very regal, red with golden lions 'passant' and an eagle soaring above. The buildings were all a honey coloured stone, warm in the noontide light. They piled off the coach, glad to be out of the sticky, sweaty mass of bodies and took stock of their surroundings.

It was a large pleasant city, with wide clean streets and they had been taken straight into the market centre. Gaily coloured stalls lined the square, hawkers were shouting their wares, a good smell of baking, grilling and hot coffee assailed their nostrils.

They went straight to a stall for the luxurious drink, Amber loved the aroma. There were small tables surrounding the stall, they sat down. Coffee was an expensive drink, imported across the high seas, but it tasted delicious. They all decided it was a good start. This place was civilised.

'What do we do now guys?' Amber asked, slowly sipping the steaming drink. 'We need to stay for some time, it's a big place. But what about you, Estrién, do you want us to move down to Elvinhaeme immediately?'

He shook his head, 'no, I'll give it a few weeks here, as you say, much to discover in a place this size. If I don't find the information I seek here, it isn't likely elsewhere.'

They decided to look for some cheap accommodation, they had no idea how long they would be here. Inns were expensive and even Tamlyn's fund would run out. If they could rent a small lodging for a few weeks, it would be ideal.

Orlandium was central to Westerling and both Floriénne and Elvinhaeme. All roads led here, or so the old tales said. Three universities, several libraries and the biggest Lady Merrie temple in the northern kingdoms, the Temple of Oak, they called it, although there were several smaller temples dotted throughout the city for everyday reverence or meditation.

The square they were in held a large oak in its centre, in fact several of the large thoroughfares were tree lined, oaks, poplars, chestnuts, rowans, cherries. It was a bright, warm, leafy city, the afternoon sun dappled through the trees.

They asked the coffee stall vendor if he knew of accommodation, or places where they could arrange some? He pointed across the street to a bookshop, its door window filled with small notices, mostly student lodgings, or the tavern at the edge of the square may have something. The bookshop door had various notices of rooms or houses available to let, so they took note.

Tamlyn wanted a decent area, fewer drunks and cut-throats, better to rent a smaller but pleasanter property, he thought.

They all laughed at him, he was being picky - this wasn't the Floriénne Court. But he maintained he'd sleep easier that way, and anyway the local inns and taverns would be that much better than in a poorer area, and of course, no one wanted to rent somewhere down by the stinky docks.

'You're just fussy,' they told him.

'No, I'm *particular*, I have standards, and Amber shouldn't have to walk through drunks or prostitutes just to get home.' They all admitted he had a point there.

Eventually they found a small house in a reasonable looking area, a large sitting room with a range fire and a small scullery attached, two bedrooms above, one with two beds, one with a double. The furnishings were dull and unimaginative but solid.

They paid for a month, considering that was all the time they could take, needing to move on to Elvinhaeme as soon as possible. It was only when they'd unpacked their belongings and Dane's new staff lay against the wall next to the weapon's rack where the others had laid their own swords and daggers, that they took stock of what they were doing.

'It's kind of fun this, isn't it?' Tamlyn suddenly said, 'we've only known each other for a few weeks, and we're suddenly living together, well, sharing a place, at least.'

'We've been through a hell of a lot in that space of time,' replied Amber.

The others nodded sagely.

'And there's always safety in numbers,' Dane added, 'I've spent years on the road by myself, Haregroves was the longest stay. But always alone. This is good, especially with Amber.'

The other two males of the party nodded. It was *especially* good with Amber as part of the group.

'I don't know about you,' replied Estrién, 'but I'm enjoying being with you. I spent all my life with an ancient uncle and two old maidservants. It's good to have company my own age for once.'

'Let's go and find a good tavern and have a decent meal, I'll put my best frock on,' laughed Amber. 'Well, I'll put my only frock on.' It seemed a good idea for their first night.

They all helped bring buckets of water in from the small well out in the courtyard and Dane heated it with his magic fingers, each taking turns in the scullery to wash.

They found a good chophouse, just a couple of streets away, rich smells of steaks and lamb cutlets and fried potatoes as they entered.

'Told you, huh?' said a triumphant Tamlyn. 'Good area, *good living* ...' They all drank to that. He regaled them with tales of Court life all evening. Amber wondered where he got it all from, surely it couldn't all be true?

Later a small minstrel band set up and the crowd in the chophouse took to singing and dancing.

As usual they all drank too much and staggered back, singing. But the fresh air did them good and they weren't set upon by thugs or accosted by prostitutes. As far as drunks were concerned, they *were* the drunks.

As Estrién said when they entered the small house, 'It started out as a nice area, but we've just brought it down. Their house prices are sinking rapidly.'

Tamlyn had brought a wine bottle back with him. 'Tomorrow I go out and get stocked up, we make this place comfortable, hey?'

All agreed and toasted each other. 'To friendship,' they shouted, *'to friendship!'*

Dane took Amber's hand, led her upstairs. 'How are you feeling?' he asked.

'Recovering,' she replied.

He bent to kiss her. 'Tell me if it's too soon?' he asked. 'I'll stop, I'll even sleep downstairs if it makes you feel better. You went through hell.' He was concerned for her, didn't want to push, didn't wish to appear to her like those Fae.

She put her arms around his neck. 'Dane, you're beautiful. I've only been holding back in case I was infected with something. If you say I'm fine, then I am. Do you honestly think I could compare you to them?' She smiled up at him.

'Oh, you're fine, love, really. I just want you to know it's your choice. I want you to be comfortable, easy. Dammit woman, I want you to want me.'

Her amber eyes sparkled. *'I want you ...'* she said, 'I only ask that tonight, you be kind and gentle, go slow huh?'

Dane took her in his arms and softly kissed her, *'as gentle and slow as you like,'* leading her to the bed, as his mage hands shot soft, scintillating magic over her.

*

The four split up the following morning. Dane and Estrién went to find one of the colleges, Tamlyn and Amber went to the market; food and household items were needed, candles, wine, soapwort, a delivery of logs for the fire. Amber bought another gown, a soft turquoise shade, with blue and green embroidery, more underwear, a silk shawl for evening use, almost the last of her cash. She enjoyed her moments of femininity. Tamlyn too enjoyed the morning.

'I'm an elf, not a human male ...' he asserted, 'I like beautiful things. I like seeing you in pretty things too, Amber.' He found a necklace of blue and green beads on a stall, 'look, this will look good with your gown,' he said, buying it for her. 'Please accept this from me, I want ... well, like Dane I wish to make up for those Fae people.' He handed her the gift, looked hopefully into her eyes. 'it's nothing expensive, just pretty. Will you wear it?'

Amber took it from him, nodded, kissed his cheek. He was pleased, flashed her a brilliant smile. They wandered the market for a while, then sat enjoying coffees again at the coffee stall. Amber accompanied him to a shop selling musical instruments. 'I miss my lute,' he explained, 'should have brought one with me,' as he picked up various instruments and began strumming them. Eventually he was satisfied with the sound and chose one.

'I think we need to look at the local notice boards,' he suggested, 'we need work, cash to live off.' Amber agreed, but they also needed to help search the libraries for information about the opal. *'Aaah,'* he protested, 'I'm beginning to think we could spend our lives looking for that gem. It's stuck down some troll's cave somewhere, or a dragon's lair. I suggest we go dragon hunting, make our fortunes,' he added, then looked at Amber. 'You know, with the diversification of powers between us, we could easily become dragon hunters, adventurers.'

'So you don't care about the fact that the Adammites and the Blazing Sun people are trying to invade Elvinhaeme?' she asked.

'I certainly do,' was the reply, 'but we can't live off nothing - and what do we do when we reach there? Join the army or something, end up in barracks with a sergeant major shouting every morning? *No way!* I am Knight Captain in Floriénne, but it's not a paid position, more of a sinecure. I like our group, Amber, and I think we can do great things together. Hey - how many people have escaped the Fae? Not many I can tell you. No ... we *have* something, the four of us, as long as we work together.'

Amber had to admit, that was quite true.

He took her hand, kissed it. 'and you know something else, Amber? I like *you- very much indeed*.' He briefly looked her in the eye, then marched off, stood at a shop window, pretending to be interested in horticultural supplies.

Amber watched him, slightly shocked. She wondered what Dane would think about his remark? As for herself ... she didn't rightly know. She'd never been in such a situation before, they seemed to be living a different kind of lifestyle to other people. At the circus too, relationships had been casual, but Longshanks had watched over her, protected her to a degree.

Her life had changed enormously, and she realised any choices were for her alone to make.

*

They spent an evening at a small theatre, various acts on stage, humans, elves, dwarves. Tamlyn decided to take his lute, perhaps play for cash. He had a word with the proprietor and was told to come by the following day to play a few things for him. He returned ecstatic in the evening, had played all afternoon and was actually paid for doing so,

'Hey, I can make money,' he told them proudly. 'I've filled our coffers today, c'mon, let's go out and eat.' And so all the money he'd earned went on a night out. But there were gaming tables in the café, Amber looked on curiously at them. Various card games were being played as well as dice.

'Can you lend me some coin, Tamlyn? I'll give it back, I promise,' she indicated the card tables. Tamlyn raised an eyebrow. 'Just trust me, OK?' He gave her some gold.

'Hey, deal me in, folks,' she squeezed into a chair at a serious-looking group huddled around a large circular table. They all looked up, *ha, a nice little girlie to divest of her cash.* They welcomed her with open arms.

The three men watched on as the nice little girlie fleeced the unsuspecting gamblers of everything but their shirts. It was a fine night's haul. She'd lived with circus folk long enough to know all the tricks they were up to and they had certainly taught her well.

*

The other two spent their days in research and had found one of the universities, but no information. It was disturbing however to hear further reports about Adammite advances, particularly in Elvinhaeme itself.

It had been a fruitless day, although the boys brought beer and wine back with them. They enjoyed a pleasant meal cooked by Amber and Tamlyn treated them to an evening of his lute playing. It was a fine evening and they sat outside in the courtyard smoking Dane's leafroll, occasionally dancing to Tamlyn's merry tunes.

The neighbours weren't keen, they thought a group of noisy students had moved in. They were truly letting down the respectable neighbourhood.

Not that they gave a damn.

They were young and intended to enjoy themselves while they could. The storm would soon break. Amber danced mostly with Dane, Estrién sitting by the side, watching, smoking, his eyes upon her all evening. Finally he managed one dance with her, after he got up enough courage to ask, while Dane went to fetch more cold beers from the scullery. He smiled as he danced, looked briefly in her eyes.

He kissed her hand as the music ended. 'Thank you, Amber, that was lovely,' was all he said before bidding goodnight to them all, and he went off to bed.

'You're too much for him, Amber,' stated Tamlyn, after he had left. 'He's gone upstairs to have a little privacy before I go up,' grinning fiendishly. ' ... *know what I mean*, huh?' He took a generous drink from his beer mug, waved his hand up and down suggestively.

Amber stared at him, but Dane burst out laughing. 'Tam, *you're terrible* ... but I love your honesty.' They both looked at Amber, waiting for her reaction.

She turned a little pink, then swallowed some ale. *I've chosen this life*, she thought. She gave him the *'oh, you men!'* look, the one where a woman frowns but her eyes twinkle.

Both men laughed and raised their glasses in toast. They smoked a little more leafroll, Tamlyn telling dirty jokes for the rest of the evening. He hugged them both as they left for bed.

'That guy's incorrigible,' stated Dane later, when they were lying in bed together. 'You do realise he's been putting out to me all evening again, as well as you? At this rate, he'll end up in bed between us ...'

Amber burst out laughing, she'd realised it too. 'Neither of us is safe with him,' she finally admitted. 'so do we send him home, kick him out, or what?'

Dane scratched his head. 'I honestly don't know, Amber. I mean, I'm pretty easy going, and I know you're game for anything - *hey* don't take that as a slur,' as he saw her face. 'It's meant as a compliment. You're unique, my love, I've never met anyone like you. You are beautiful, charming, intelligent, extremely capable and you have one of the loveliest natures I've ever known. You're an incredible athlete and I've never seen a woman who can throw a knife or use a short-sword as you can. I'm hopelessly in love with you.' He turned to her, 'Oh, come here, why am I wasting time talking?' as he kissed her.

He blew out the candles next to their bed.

*

They settled themselves into a routine for the next few days, the three males would go off to the local university in the morning to seek out professors and ancient texts and find out any lore they could. Amber would go to the market early to get the freshest produce she could find, join them towards lunch time. She was enjoying being the cook of the household, getting fresh herbs and spices, experimenting, even if it turned out burnt or not exactly as she imagined, no one complained, they just drank more wine and laughed. The males of the household kept the place reasonably clean and washed the dishes for her. They all felt it was a good arrangement.

Besides, it was good experience. If at some point, way off in the distant future, she was in charge of a large household, neither servant or shopkeeper would be able to dupe her.

Estrién spent his time searching for any connection between the Sword and the Elfenstone. He was disconcerted to find none. He wandered the streets looking for antique bookshops, old second hand affairs, anything that might have some information. Antiquarians were usually full of esoteric knowledge.

What worried him however, was that he found he was beginning to be looked at warily. As he passed a market stall he heard murmurs of 'damn elves, why do they have to come here, why can't they stay in their own ing forest?'

He looked shocked at the man on the market stall. He'd never come across this before, not a direct insult. 'What's your problem?' he asked. 'Have I done anything to offend you?'

'Yes, you're a bloody elf, piss off out of here. Von Adamm's bloody right about you, clear off, you're not wanted.' As Estrién examined the stall he saw it was filled with small books, all bearing the red and black symbol of the Blazing Sun cult. The man was spreading sedition and dissension. Several people were perusing the stall, all ready and willing to accept the loud-mouthed man's words, watching Estrién with distaste, hate always being an easy thing to generate. Estrién wasn't carrying his sword, he had a bag of books on his shoulder and a small dagger in his belt, if anything he looked like one of the students. He wasn't hankering for a fight in the middle of a civilised community.

A community rapidly losing its veneer of civilisation.

Nevertheless Estrién spoke to them all, watching their eyes, their reactions as he spoke.

'I have no idea why you should dislike me, or my kind. We have never done anything at all against you.' He stood straight, his shoulders back, his fine hair waving in the breeze, his lips set. 'We live in harmony with the land and the forest. We trade with you, we sell you fine wine, mead, honey, herbs, fruit and flowers. We offer the most beautiful, carved furniture and goods, the finest bows and arrows. We give you song and story, why ... my friend Tamlyn plays his lute at a local theatre for your delight. We only offer kindness, courtesy and care to all - human, elf, whatever race, including all animals. We do not intrude on your lives. So why are you now hating us?'

He stared them all in the eye, but didn't stop. A small crowd was now gathering. *'I will tell you why.* Because someone out there wants to destroy this world of ours. He wants to set human against elf, elf against dwarf, *human against human.* We haven't fought each other for centuries, so why now? A certain person knows how to divide us all and thus conquer us, little by little, so he can take control.' The crowd were now silent as Estrién spoke with conviction.

'*He* is your enemy, not me, nor elves, or any of the old woodland folk. Mordecai von Adamm wishes to set us all against each other. He appeals only to your base senses, greed, selfishness, a delusion of power. I suggest you think on what is happening here, you think deeply about it. Take note of all that we may lose, and pray to the Lady that we keep all that is good. And remember, it may be *you* he wishes to destroy soon, merely because you do not fit in, you may be too old, too tall or too short. He might not like your flaming red hair or your bald head. Beware of such a narrow-minded man, you too will have to conform. Your world will get smaller and meaner with every day that he holds sway, so think, *think carefully.* He will kill the world you live in, leave you beaten and hungry.

We live in balance here, in harmony with nature, remember that. And above all, remember the loving and generous ways of the Lady Merrie to whom you should stay true.'

He walked away, hearing them discussing his speech. The crowd began to disperse, but it was the stall holder they frowned at, while nodding quietly to Estrién's simple words.

*

The following morning the four were passing one of the main notice boards of the city, one of the 'job boards', offering rewards for the return of items, needing help on their farm or with their business, or requiring the services of a creditable warrior to see off beasts on their property. A large notice caught their eyes.

Big Reward!

'Help! A damn big bastard is plaguing me camping in my back field. He has a big mace, but the soft buggers of City Guard won't do nothing unless he hits me. They say he'll get tired and move on eventually.. Any roads, I wanted him shifted - now!

Apply Jock McJack's farm, Piddling Lane, Owd Dodderers.

Directions to the said farm were given underneath.

'Hmm mm,' said Amber, 'Big Reward - worth looking into. We need cash.'

Tamlyn nodded, 'four of us, one of him. Are we interested?'

'*Amber's Intrepid Adventurers* to the rescue!' shouted Dane.

The others laughed and agreed, cash was cash, it looked like a quick, well-paid job. After a brief diversion to a bookshop for detailed maps of the city and its environs they went off to Jock McJack's farm.

They could hear the intruder long before they saw him. It hurt their ears, and probably Jock McJack's too. The offending trespasser was playing bagpipes – very badly, possibly deliberately so.

McJack greeted them. 'You come about the notice? Aye good,' staring them up and down. 'That bugger is out there all effing day with the bloody pipes and he canna play a bloody note.' As if to prove this he took out his own bagpipes and performed a reel upon them. It sounded quite good. 'Tek that, you swine,' he shouted at the now dancing figure in the field.

The four were caught in the middle of them. They marched to the encampment of the trespassing piper. It included a tent, a small fire, some scattered pots and pans, a sheepdog and two goats. And a big mace, a *very* big mace.

They put up their hands to parley. The wild-haired man picked up the mace.

'No bloody closer or ye'll get this on yer noggins.'

Amber called out, 'Sir, we wish only to talk - if possible, over all this noise ...'

'Aye, I'll speak, when that bugger stops ruining his pipes with such blather. This 'ere's my land and I'm staying on it, as sure as my name's Jack McJock.'

The four looked at each other, eyebrows were raised.

He continued. 'Aye, this is my land and I've deeds to prove it. Me uncle died recently, left me the farm. 'Im ...' pointing to Jock McJack - is trespassing on my land. It's in the will.' He held out a badly written copy of Jock Mcjock's Last will and Testament.

He continued playing a wailing tune through the bagpipes, eagerly watching Jock McJack's face.

The group perused it eagerly, although admittedly it was difficult to think. This had been Jock Mcjock's land until he died some months ago, never farmed by him, but owned through his wife's family. They had been childless, but he left the farm to ... and here the problem lay. It was written in bad longhand and could barely be read. It could say Jack McJock or Jock McJack - they were both cousins in any case, sons of Jock McJock's brother and sister, Jack and Jocelyn.

Jack McJock meanwhile picked up his bagpipes once more.

The air was filled with two sets of pipes, discordantly playing against the other, each trying to outdo the incomer. Sadly, neither played well, using the pipes instead as an act of war, a weapon. The Orcadians took their pipes into battle to scare the pants off the enemy, these two followed in their ancestors' footsteps. A tactical retreat at such times always seemed like a good idea.

'Stop!' Amber's Intrepid Adventurers shouted to both parties. There was a banshee-type wail as the two players trailed away. 'We need to talk ... it's the only way!

She beckoned Jock McJack over, pointed out the problem to him. 'It's probably his farm as much as yours.'

'I towd thee to get *rid* of that bugger,' he shouted, 'not give him the bloody farm!'

'The point is,' suggested Amber, 'do either of you have any farming experience at all?'

'A bit ...' answered Jock McJack.

'I've kept a few hens and goats,' replied the other one.

'Why not farm together then?' she suggested, 'you're obviously a long way from home.'

'Aye, we're from Orcadia, nay bad for some, but our parcels of land were shit, fit for naught but cattle. Uncle Jock died and we cam doon, I got here afore yon mucker and took me farm as is me due.' Jock McJack wasn't giving in.

'Yon can bugger off!' shouted Jack McJock to Jock McJack, now waving the mace again.

'Why don't we all have a nice cup of herbal tea?' suggested Dane, trying to calm things down. 'We could smoke some leafroll and quietly discuss this.'

Jock and Jack stopped shouting and stared at the newcomer in horror. He was obviously one of those hippy-dippy mage types. They stared at each other, *herbal bloody tea?* There was a joint snort of disgust.

Jock nodded to Jack. 'I'm not listening to yon great Jessie. Look ye ... I've got a wee bottle or two of the hard stuff in the farmhouse - I suppose we could talk. I need some help on the farm any-ways.'

The other raised a shrewd eyebrow. 'What sort o' usquebae?'

'GlenRite 'Ard?'

There was a brief raising of eyebrows followed by an even briefer nod. Jack McJock lay down his mace, gently picked up his bagpipes and lay them in the tent. With a grunt and a brief disgusted grimace at Dane, he followed his cousin across the fields.

The four young adventurers were forgotten.

Tamlyn was curious. He went over to the abandoned tent and brought out the bagpipes. He gave an experimental blow or two ... It sounded like a cartload of deranged hens high on Dane's leafroll.

'Nooooo!' the others screamed, running away and covering their ears. Tamlyn shrugged his shoulders and gave up. It took a special sort of person to get music from those pipes, and Tamlyn wasn't one of them. He'd stick to the lute.

They walked miserably back to the city, clearly Amber's Intrepid Adventurers would not be paid for this job and were finished before they had even begun.

Chapter 10

The days went by, lore-hunting interspersed with boozy nights out. Amber often saw Estrién watching her, studying her as if he didn't quite know what to do with her. Sometimes, as with the earlier evening, he would ask her to dance with him, holding her stiffly at arm's length, but staring deeply into her eyes. When he saw that she caught him watching, he would turn away, red-faced.

And of an evening he would read aloud elven poetry from books he had found, most of it about lost love or tales of elven heroes. Amber didn't know if he was trying to impress just her, or all of them.

Once he gave her a bunch of violets, explained they were being given away at the end of day's market. If he had been out in the city he would bring sweetmeats or cakes home, present them to Amber, 'they were for everyone,' he would say. But they were usually Amber's favourites.

In turn, Dane studied Estrién, noting the small tokens of affection with a growing fear ...

One morning Amber was sorting through her pack looking for some misplaced hose, when she came across the small parcel given to her by High Priestess Illumini in Manecaestr for the Temple of Oak. She'd completely forgotten about it. She mentioned it at the breakfast table.

'Aah, I forgot about that Amber, I'm glad you still have it.' Dane suddenly had a thought, 'they'll have their own archives there won't they? You can kill two birds with one stone.'

Amber nodded, 'Yes, I thought of that too, I'll ask the priestesses.'

To her surprise, Estrién asked if he could go with her. 'I'd like to spend a little time at Her shrine. I've never had time to mourn my uncle, I feel I've neglected my duty to him - he had no other kin. I ought to go and pay my respects and prayers.'

Amber was surprised, she hadn't realised he was religious.

'I'm not particularly, although I never say no to the feast days,' he laughed, 'but I think She has brought some good things into my life recently,' smiling at her, 'and I owe my uncle a few prayers. So, I'll come with you if that's OK?'

Amber nodded, it was fine.

It wasn't that far to the Temple of Oak. Each Temple of Merrie had it own dedication. It might be general as in Arboreal, back in Manecaestr, or it might be dedicated to a particular tree as this was. The oak of course was the finest tree in the land, nothing stronger or more hardy, with so many special powers of its own, Merrie's own tree.

There were several Templar Guards, all looking very splendid in their uniforms with shining swords at the ready. Each Temple had its own guards, with their own symbol on the surtout. The surtout was usually white with a large red cross, overlaid with the temple symbol. Here it was an oak tree image. Sometimes it was a cross within a tree, or a tree within a cross. Indeed, some temples merely had a symbolic leaf over the cross, an oak leaf, beech, birch etc., depending on their dedication.

Whatever the case, the tree or leaf represented life, love and fertility; growth. One symbol of life overlaying another; the four corners of the earth, the four elements, earth, air, fire and water, sometimes the whole within a circle, spirit. Sometimes the four points of the cross would have a further four points within it, representing the sun itself, if the temple was a sun temple, for where would life be without the warmth of the sun?

All of Merrie was about *life*, both masculine and feminine, in harmony and living it to the full. 'Go forth and be fruitful' was typically of the Lady Merrie.

In Segantium there were two special temples dedicated to a rose, one where the guards wore a unique red surtout with a white cross, overlaid by a red rose. The other was a normal surtout with a red cross overlaid by a white rose.. Only in these temples were there male priests, guardians of the Rose, great gardeners, devotees of Lady Merrie herself, her own Warriors.

In the Arborean temples Templar Guards were there to protect the priestesses from possible harm. There were to be no squabbles or fighting inside a Temple of Merrie, and sometimes, particularly on feast days, people arrived a little merrier than the priestesses would wish. The Templar Knights were mostly ceremonial positions, but they were all experienced soldiers given the privilege of temple duty. There weren't many attached to each temple so, as Elandil said at the Temple of Arboreal, they wouldn't exactly stop an invasion. But they kept the temples safe on a daily basis.

They saluted now as Amber and Estrién walked through the doors, part of the courtesy given to visitors and worshippers to the Temple. Estrién was asked to leave his sword in the weapons' deposit, no weapons were to be taken into the sanctuary of peace. He acceded, he knew the rules, was given a receipt for his sword. The assistant looked on it in wonder and carefully stored it in the weapons' receptacle.

It was a very large temple. A massive temple hall, with a huge ceiling and a large statue of Lady Merrie at the far end. Amazingly, an actual oak grew through the centre of the hall. It was kept trimmed so that it wouldn't overcrowd the Hall, but nevertheless its leafy canopy was a strange sight to behold. A circular wooden seat was placed around its large trunk, people could sit and meditate or pray here.

Incense was burning, a woody smell, adding to the rich smell of the tree.

Amber stood in front of the tree contemplating its beauty. She held her head in prayer and dedication for a few moments. She breathed in the heady smell of incense, mixed with the green-leaf smell of the tree. She felt good, *right,* at peace with herself.

There was a large circular seat around the tree trunk, Estrién sat down. 'This is beautiful,' he said, 'perfect for an elf, like me. You go and find the High Priestess, Amber, take your gift, or whatever they have sent. I am happy to stay here awhile. This reminds me of my uncle and my parent's homes, not that we grew trees inside ...' he added, laughing, 'I am content.'

She went in search of the High Priestess, explaining to a young priestess she had a gift from the Temple of Arboreal in Manecaestr. She nodded her head. 'I will take you to our High Priestess, I cannot open this myself.' The young woman took her through myriad passageways and corridors all twisting and turning, labyrinthine, the place was so large. Almost every corridor bore paintings of oak trees or symbolic images of oak, beautiful oaken pillars richly carved with leaves and acorns. It was almost a painted forest.

As Amber followed the young priestess she began to feel light-headed, the corridors twisted and turned, slightly dizzying, the large, rather overpowering paintings of trees on the walls beginning to mesmerise her. Once or twice she experienced an odd sensation, a sense of déjà vu.

Eventually she found herself in a large, oak panelled room, gaily bedecked with flowers and again, smelling of woody incense. It was bright and airy, the oak being light, not dark with age. An elderly woman with grey hair tied into a bun came across the room to her, smiling. She wore a simple white robe upon which a small green oak leaf was embroidered, and a golden circlet over her brow, also decorated with the same oak emblem. She looked serene.

'I am High Priestess Ceriisia. What can I do for you, my dear?' she asked. Amber explained about the gift, took out the parcel, handed the little package over. The priestess took it to her desk, unwrapped the parcel. Amber watched with increasing curiosity, her mind wandering, beginning to float. There was something strange happening, but she couldn't figure out what.

Inside was a small oaken box bearing a oak tree in full leaf on its lid. The carving looked like the tree in the centre of the temple, almost an exact copy. Amber felt a small shiver run up her spine, they were familiar, very familiar.

For a moment or two, Amber stood quietly in the room, transfixed by the box, the tree symbol.

'Do you know what lies in this box?' the Lady Ceriisia asked. Amber shook her head, but she looked oddly at the Priestess, something caressed the edge of her mind ... '*I do*,' the Lady Ceriisia continued, 'and although I am grateful for this finally returning here, I understand this could only have been brought at a time of great danger to our temple and to our lands. It is a precious treasure - did you know?'

Amber shook her head, she'd had no idea what she carried.

'I take it this was sent here because of the Adammite invasion, and the treaty with Draecastle?'

Amber nodded, the priestess continued. 'This signifies great trouble ahead. I hear they are invading Elvinhaeme, the elves are only just keeping them back. There is trouble too on our own borders. I am not sure that it is safe even here, and yet ... it is in its rightful place. Come let us take it and only uncover it in the temple hall.'

She led the way back to the main temple hall. Amber now felt a little faint, her skin tingling. There was a certain unreality happening around her. If she could just take control of her mind? The huge paintings of oaks in full leaf were dramatic and imposing, affecting her thoughts. She followed the priestess as she made her way through the crowd.

The priestess stood in front of the great oak tree. People gathered around to see what she was doing. Amber saw there was a hole in the tree, realised it was *exactly* .... she shook her head to clear it. Her dream ... this was like her dream?

She looked across at Estrién, he was intrigued, he came over to her. 'Are you OK? What's going on?'

'I feel odd, I don't know why.' He nodded, Amber wasn't the only one to feel strange, he'd felt it since the moment he entered the Temple. But it was a good feeling.

'I feel ... *right*,' he responded.

Amber looked curiously at Estrién. Estrién's elven eyes questioned hers. Something electric passed between them.

Amber wasn't sure where she was, time no longer held true. The temple seemed to sway, it changed around her. The light darkened and she heard an owl hoot. She shook herself, 'get it together,' she thought.

Estrién stepped close to her. 'Do you need some air, do you wish to get out of here?' He was concerned.

'No, I'm fine. We need to see this, Estrién.' She was breathing heavily, something was happening.

She watched the priestess, who displayed the box to the worshippers. 'See, I hold a precious gift here, a gift for the Goddess, one that has come from our temple in Manecaestr, one that actually belongs *here*.' Everyone crowded round.

The priestess opened the small oaken box. A pure light came from within.

Estrién stared at the box. Amber stared at the box. They stared at each other ... more electric waves passed between them, an esoteric ambience.

The priestess put her hand inside, grasped the contents, placed it within the hole on the tree. *'There,'* she spoke ceremoniously, 'I offer the Light of Gilsylien to the Goddess of the Oak tree and to our Lady Merrie. Let all live in its pure radiance and never in shadow.' She placed the gift inside the tree, light flowed out of the aperture. 'Later we will put it away safely, it is too precious to leave there,' she spoke softly to Amber.

Estrién stared open mouthed at Amber. Wide eyed, she pointed at the tree. Like Amber, he understood, all his senses alert, his skin tingling, his spine shivering.

Amber could feel her heart beating wildly now, she knew the truth. *This was the tree of her dreams.* The place was right, only the time setting was different, this was clear day, not night ... yet, she also understood she now lived in a world rapidly turning to night. With wonder she spoke to Estrién.

'Estrién, get your sword, dear,' her voice, low but urgent. He nodded, *yes, of course, it had to be*. Pale-skinned, Amber turned to the Priestess. 'My Lady, please let Estrién get his sword. It is so important ... *please.*'

The priestess frowned at her, but saw something was affecting the young woman. 'We cannot have weapons here in the Temple Hall,' she protested.

Estrién bowed before her. 'Please, my Lady, I am happy to be escorted by your Temple Knights. I give you my word of honour that I will bring no harm to this Temple. Quite the opposite in fact.' Like Amber, he had turned white, his lips firmly set. *'It is essential.'*

The priestess looked at the two pale faces, realised something was happening out of her control. They looked earnest, pleading. They looked ... they looked unearthly. She nodded, sent for two guards. After a brief discussion and further vows by Estrién, they went with him to fetch his sword.

Amber took off her boots. It was a silly gesture, but she remembered walking barefoot. She waited patiently for Estrién to return.

'We may be wrong ...' she began, looking at Estrién.

'No,' he shook his head, his eyes gazing softly at her, 'no Amber, you are not wrong. It explains such a lot to me.' He smiled with fondness at her.

Estrién took his sword carefully out of its scabbard, it looked beautiful, the emerald shining brilliantly. The guards admired the workmanship, but kept their hands on their own swords in readiness. Again, he assured everyone there was no danger, he would not use it against them. He held it down, the point on the floor, both hands on the hilt, to show he meant no harm. Everyone was silent, all were now aware something peculiar was happening.

The electricity was palpable to everyone.

Amber went to the bole of the tree and placed her hand inside. *Yes, as she had surmised.* There was a small ledge on which lay a dish lined with a velvet cover. It was there, as she expected. She clasped her hand around it, took it out. There was a gasp from the onlookers, what was she doing? The Temple Guards took out their swords - was she stealing this precious relic?

She turned to Estrién, she could already hear the sword humming, a slight whining sound, like it was singing. The sword lit Estrién's face. Those close by heard the strange sound, saw the change in the sword, wondered at the magic, for magic it must be.

Amber opened her hand, offering the precious gift to him. The opal took the gleam from the sword and shone like a thousand tiny lights in her palm, creamy white, with iridescent pinks and purples, yellow green and blue. *But the predominant colour sparkling within the pale stone was amber.*

Estrién just *looked*. He stared at her immobile for seconds, perhaps minutes. In time and out of time, no time, all time. Eternity within a moment. No one spoke. The High Priestess watched on, this was beyond her, she had no part in this ritual but she understood enough to remain silent. She held up her hand to the Temple guards to warn them to do nothing.

The sword sounded like it was crying, wailing for its mate. It was so loud that all who stood in that Temple heard it, wondered at it? Felt the thrill of it.

With a muttered, *'Amber, I accept your gift.'* Estrién took the Opalstone from her, bowed his head reverently. He stood staring at it for a while, both at the stone and at Amber. Then he carefully placed it in the hollow of the sword. It not only fitted perfectly, it gelled there. Estrién realised it could only have been prised out of it with great force, perhaps when its owner died, it could not have been otherwise. He could hear the sad, whining sound of the sword turn to a keen, high pitched singing.

The sword now blazed with light, Estrién was lit like a shining star in the Temple Hall. For a few more moments the sword sang, a strange melodious whine as the stone settled into place. Then it lay silent.

The whole Temple stood silent.

Estrién looked across at Amber, her eyes gazing softly into his. He walked over to her, bent his head. For one moment he pressed his lips gently to hers. An amberic shock passed between them. His head shot back and he looked startled at her.

Amber by name ... amber by nature ...

She stood, like the rest, silent. But her heart beat wildly and her body shook.

Then, triumphantly, he held the sword aloft. Its beauty lit the faces of those who beheld it that day. He spoke aloud the runes on the sword.

'Sulis Estrién nim lumien,' he quoted. 'I, 'Nim'randuel Soleus D'rendiél Gilsylien Estaran'elvian bear the Sword of D'rendiél - NimEstrién, the White Star, which has lain for centuries in the deep dark Vaults of the Elven people in Floriénne. It has lain quiet and somnolent, awaiting the return of its owner to bring it to the light of day and to receive the Light of the Opalstone. Nevermore shall it lie in dark halls, but shall bear witness to the coming fight against the darkness now looming over our lands. I wield NimEstrién on behalf our Lady Merrie and on behalf of Life itself.'

He bent down on one knee in front of the High Priestess, bowing his head and offered her his sword. She accepted it gracefully, understanding the importance of what was happening, and in solemn ritual, she touched first one shoulder, then his other shoulder with the blade of the sword. Something portent had happened in her world, something had turned and she must prepare.

'I, High Priestess Ceriisia, of the Merrievian High Temple of Oak, do this day pronounce you *Sir Estrién, Knight Commander of our Lady Merrie* and return this sword to your hand. May you never use it in anger, but with pure will and the love of the Lady in your heart.' She handed the sword to him with a ceremonious bow. 'Arise, Sir Estrién.'

He received it, bowed, then held it aloft once more so that all could see.

He looked across at Amber. Unlike the first time he saw her when his eyes looked on curiously and caressed her, now his eyes blazed, with surety they bore into her, shining and triumphant. And he smiled the lovely smile that lit up his face.

The priestess spoke to the crowd in the Temple. 'Today we have witnessed a great miracle, that which was lost is found and that which was separate is now One. The stone has arrived here at our holy temple in our time of need. We must make haste to prepare for the coming war. The Longsword of D'rendiél is our hope and our prayer.' She turned to Estrién, spoke quietly. 'The king of Westerling, King Alexis, will need to know of this, we will send word. He will probably contact you.'

Estrién nodded, explained where they could be found in the city. He replaced the sword in its scabbard over his back. He looked at Amber, gently offered his hand, 'come Amber, there is work to do.'

She took his hand and they left the Temple.

Once outside she spoke to him. 'Estrién ... *did you ... I* ...?' She gazed into his eyes. Everything felt unreal.

He stopped to look at her. 'I felt it too Amber. I have felt it since I met you. *It scares the life out of me.*' He spoke gently, confessing to her, 'I have no idea how to respond to you. I should have known you carried the opalstone, why was it not obvious to me?' He saw a seat by the fountain near the entrance to the Temple, he led her to it. He sat down, holding her hand in his. Only now could he explain to her, yet he was afraid.

'When the *Fae* took us, when I was separated from the sword, I felt terrible, like a part of me had been wrenched away. But it led me to you Amber, I wasn't just separated from the sword, I was also separated from you. When I came down into the bear pit and saw you, my heart wept for you, but I knew I was almost complete.

Today I have the Opalstone, *you* brought it, *you* gave it to me, and the sword is now whole. It seems as it should be.' He stopped briefly, he had to say this, although it pained him to do so, he was too unsure of her reaction. 'But *I* am still not whole, and never can be. *You and I* ...' His voice sounded on the edge of breaking.

He turned away from her, could say no more, instead watching the spray of the fountain, he couldn't look in her eyes. He stood, started to walk away. It couldn't be, it could never be.

He quickened his pace to put distance between them.

Quietly he spoke to himself. *'I can never be whole until you and I are One, Amber ... only when our two hearts beat as one, shall I be complete.'*

Amber started to follow the quickly disappearing figure through the streets back to their lodging. She hadn't heard Estrién's last remarks, but she didn't need to. She saw his face, felt the pressure of his palm against hers, felt the strange shock of him run through her.

Suddenly she started running, anywhere - it didn't matter - as long as it was away from him. She ran and ran, putting distance between them. Eventually she ran out of steam and stopped, panting, her hand against a wall steadying herself.

'Don't do this to me!' she thought. 'Dane is such a lovely man. And I know so little about you. You keep everything to yourself, you hide all those emotions that Dane wears on his sleeve. And Dane is so kind and loving, he's the nicest man I've ever met. I love him ... *I do.*'

But that kiss ... the touch of his lips on hers. He had done that in her dream, but it was a poor echo of the gentle kiss in the Temple. For a few moments her whole body was ablaze ... she hadn't even heard what he'd said as he held the sword aloft, she had been so much absorbed with his kiss.

Not even a kiss, just his lips pressed to hers. Sweet, gentle, soft. She could smell his elven skin, like the forest, woody and spicy, his essence lingered with her.

'Don't do this to me!' she thought once more, angry now and confused. She gathered herself together, took deep breaths. Decided to make her way to the university, find Dane and Tamlyn, tell them the news about the stone, no need for any more research.

Find sanctuary in Dane's loving arms.

She found them in the university library where they spent their mornings. Dane had his nose stuck in a book on dryad legends, he'd found it on the shelves, it was more interesting to him than the Opalstone.

She hurried over, explained the situation. 'So we've found it!' they cried. There were severe looks from everyone and a librarian told them all to hush. She pulled them outside.

'We were carrying it all along ... isn't it amazing?' she asked.

The two were astounded. 'We had it with us? That package, the High Priestess at the Temple of Arborean sent? But that's unbelievable!' Dane was incredulous.

'You carried it in your pack all the time, Amber?' Tamlyn shook his head. 'But, you know, it shows how we are fated together, we four. You would not have found Estrién if I had not found you ... and saved you from those dreadful cultists ... and Estrién would not have found his stone. This is truly mind blowing.' He took their arms in his, walked between them. 'But you know what? It feels right ... *so right*. Come on, let's get back to see him, have a look at this amazing stone.' He pulled the two along.

It wasn't far back to the small town house. They were surprised when they entered it to find it empty.

'He was ahead of me, I thought he'd be back by now.' She was a little upset, where had he gone?

Tamlyn went upstairs to take up some items he had bought earlier from the market. He looked around, there was something wrong. It slowly dawned on him that the room was looking sparse, items were missing - had they been burgled? Hmm, no, his stuff was intact ... it was all of Estrién's things.

Everything belonging to Estrién had gone.

He dashed downstairs, 'hey guys, all of Estrién's stuff is ...' He stopped, they were both reading a sheet of parchment. Amber looked white and Dane was shaking his head, incredulous.

'He's gone, Tamlyn, he's left us,' Amber looked about to cry. She held out the note, he took it,

'My dear friends,

It is with the deepest regret I find I have to leave you. I have come to understand I cannot stay with you, please do not ask why, nor follow me. My time with you has been wonderful, and I thank all of you for your gift of friendship.

The sword is now complete and I go to use it as it should be used, in this war of the dark against the light. I beg you not to follow me, it would cause distress all round - to all of us.

Please do not think ill of me for leaving you - I do this with your best interests at heart.

I remain,

Your friend, **Estrién**

'Amber, have you any idea why he should leave us?' Tamlyn couldn't understand. Amber shook her head, whatever had happened between her and Estrién was best left unsaid. There was nothing she could be ashamed of.

Nevertheless, she looked upstairs in the room he had shared with Tamlyn, just in case there was anything left of him. There was nothing. She went to the window, looked outside, but she was blindly looking at the view, merely staring as if he would turn the corner and walk back to them.

Dane walked into the room. 'Amber, come downstairs love, he's not coming back ...' he took her arm, guided her down the rickety steps.

Tamlyn was waiting for her. He saw her stricken face, put his arms around her. 'We all liked him, Amber, we were becoming close, perhaps too close. I found a kinship with him, both of us elves, he was something special. He just doesn't let people in, does he?' He thought a little while, 'or perhaps he just used us to get his sword and the stone?' sadly, he shook his head, 'yet somehow, I do not believe that.'

'So, do we go after him, or leave him be?' Dane felt it was appropriate to ask, if they were going, it would be now.

Amber thought carefully. She knew perfectly well why he left, he was putting distance between them. If only she hadn't run off, remained with him. Perhaps she could have persuaded him to stay with them? Who knew? That exchange of the most chaste of kisses had been too much - for both of them.

'Amber, I asked, what do you think?' it was Dane again, she'd forgotten.

She shook her head. 'No, Dane, he wanted to go, let him be. He's made up his mind.'

The three were dumbfounded. Dane made herbal tea for them all, some relaxing magical herbs, calming. Later Amber cooked a light meal for the three of them and Tamlyn played quiet tunes on his lute, sad and mournful. They went to bed earlier than usual, too depressed to stay up.

None slept well.

The following morning there was a knock on the door, it turned out to be a King's Messenger. They were all requested at the palace for ten a.m.

It seemed a waste of time going, but to refuse the King would have been ill mannered. In any case, they needed to explain what had happened.

King Alexis and his entire council sat waiting in the council chamber. He seemed a fine man, a fair smiling face, a firm brow, strong looking, as if he knew how to wield a sword.

He realised as soon as they entered there was something wrong. He stood, came towards them, shook hands. But he looked confused.

'I was told there was a tall elf with a marvellous sword.' He looked at Tamlyn, he wasn't a small elf, but could not be regarded as tall, nor did he carry a beautiful sword with an emerald pommel. 'I was rather interested to see this elf with the odd name.'

They all explained that had happened, he was no longer with them. 'I think he has gone straight to Elvinhaeme, he left us a letter explaining he was prepared to fight in the 'war of the dark against the light,' or so he had said,' explained Amber. They did not show him the letter, it was too personal.

'I'll get scouts out on the road, we need to know where he is, this is too important for him to toddle off by himself - and he cannot fight these Adammites alone.' The king looked them in the eye. 'They've been coming in through the Bay of Gulls, just south of the Whitecaps, it's a bit of a no man's land. Some go south and invade Elvinhaeme, some are coming east here and are making a bloody mess of everything they touch. The Temple of Merrie at Sunstones had been destroyed, the priestesses fled, but only because the Knights of the Temple held the Adammites off long enough for them to escape. The knights are all dead, or so I believe.' He looked sadly at them all.

'I've got more troops across there now, we didn't need them before - it's usually a peaceful place. Elves go occasionally to worship there and we have good relations with Elvinhaeme.' He smiled, proudly, 'Actually, *very* good relations, my wife comes from there, Queen Neria. We have a young daughter, Anna'laeth. She goes to see her elven grandparents every now and again.' He beamed at them with paternal pride.

They stood to go, it was clear there was little more to be said. But he stopped them. 'Look, how long are you staying here?'

None knew, they were only staying to look for the stone for Estrién. 'Then stay a few days longer, I'll see what I can find out. If he's on the way to Elvinhaeme, we'll soon know, but I'll send scouts south and east also. Stick around until I've got some information for you. I take it you wish to find your friend, or at least know what's happened to him?'

They all nodded, and so it was agreed they would remain in the city for a few more days.

It was Tamlyn who asked on their way back to their lodging. 'And if they find him, do we seek him out?'

Dane answered for them all. 'Of course we do. You know, *I* know, we're a team and we're a team of four, not three. As soon as he joined us it felt right, balanced. He feels like a brother to me, and I'm not letting him go off and do this by himself. He needs us with him, whether he knows it or not.'

The house felt empty when they returned. Amber remained silent, her feelings were too ambiguous, too dangerous to touch on. She asked if Dane would sleep separately that night, she needed to be alone. He nodded, dissatisfied, but went off to sleep in Estrién's bed in Tamlyn's room. She heard them talking long into the night, sleep not coming easily.

The King sent for them a few days later. It was late afternoon.

'We've found him, or at least we know where he is. I'm sorry to have to tell you he seems to have taken up with a band of renegade elves in the forests at the lower end of the Whitecap mountains, near the coast. Most of them are outlaws, expelled from Elvinhaeme for their crimes, they call themselves the Freowulven, the Freewolves.' He pointed to a large map on the table of the council chamber. 'Here, or thereabouts. They are probably quite easy to find, they raid regularly along the roads of north Elvinhaeme. I wonder what he's doing with them?'

Dane spoke on their behalf. 'Then we go find him, we'll find out why he's joined them.'

'I'd be careful,' said the king, 'their leader is pretty dangerous, and they have no love for humans at all. Remember, the reason they are outlaws is because of the crimes they have committed here or in Elvinhaeme – very serious crimes. They are murderers, traitors, cut-throats, all of whom ought to have been executed. But our law says they can be given the chance to live - as long as it is outside our society. In our towns and cities, they no longer exist, they are, to all intents and purposes, dead - 'less than a wolf's head', we say. This they have chosen. They ride into Westerling occasionally, raiding and thieving. Then they disappear back into the wilderness of the Whitecaps. If you are going after him, I'd take care.'

This was shocking news. To live as an outlaw meant exactly that, outside the laws of the land, no trading, no working, not even speech allowed between them and the lawful folk. And if they were recognised, they could be killed with impunity.

They went home, prepared everything to leave first thing on the morrow. Dane asked Amber one last time, he wanted to be sure.

'Amber, you do want us to find him, don't you?' he asked her, watching her face closely.

She nodded, she'd made up her mind. 'Yes, Dane, I do. But the question I ask is, are *you* sure you wish to do this? It may not be beneficial for *us* ...' She was trying to be honest with him, as well as herself.

He understood. He'd always understood, he was a mage with all that entailed, including feeling the emotions of others. He looked deep into his own heart, he had to ask her, he had to face this. 'Amber, tell me, would you love me any less, if we do find him?'

She smiled up at him, 'Of course not, you know I love you.' That much was true.

He touched her cheek with his hand, 'I'll always love you, Amber. *Always*. I'm not totally sure why he's run away, but I think I can guess. *You're just too lovable* ...'

He took her hand, led her to bed.

The following day they were off as soon as it was light, the road westwards to Elvinhaeme and the lower slopes of the Whitecaps, possibly even into Draconia.

They had no idea what they were walking into.

But they did know that Estrién was part of them and shouldn't have left them. They had become a team, and regardless of his personal feelings and hang ups, they wanted him back. Even if it did mean going in search of a band of renegade, murderous, elves and outlaws - *the Freowulven*.

Somewhere out in that wild land amidst thieves, murderers and cut-throats, was Estrién.

Or to be more precise, *'Nim'randuel Soleus D'rendiél Gilsylien Estaran'elvian' 'He who is the White Shield and wields the Sword of Light which shines like the Heavens is the true King of the Elves'* had disappeared into the wilderness carrying a priceless sword, the lifeblood of an elven nation.

The Adammite revolution had only just begun, the fair land of Mer'edrynn would be trampled upon, its people would be used, abused and slaughtered. Warriors such as Estrién were needed to fight against the coming storm.

He had to be found.

Part 2
En Quattro.
Our band prepares for war.

Chapter 1

Westerling, close to the Whitecap Mountains and Bay of Gulls. Month of Herneset.

Estrién stepped sharply down the street putting distance between himself and Amber.

A large part of him wished he hadn't kissed her. Not exactly a kiss, just a touch of her lips - still too much. The other part simply ached, he ached every time he looked at her, a heart swollen and fit to bursting. Estrién briefly turned around to see if she was following him, when he realised she was running in the opposite direction. *Running* ... she obviously couldn't get away from him fast enough. He should have said nothing, instead he said too much.

His throat caught and there was a sudden pain in his heart. *So, that was that then.* She couldn't stand to be in his presence ...

It made up his mind for him, there was no way he could stay now. He hurried back to their lodgings, grabbed his pack, odds and ends. But he felt it would be wrong to simply disappear, so he sat with quill, ink and vellum trying to explain, in so many words, why he had to go. He didn't wish to make it obvious, but he needed to say something. He owed them that much ...

It had been good. *Very good.* He'd found three good friends. It was just that ... one of them was ... he couldn't bear to bring the thought to fruition ... *too much.*

He left the note where they could find it and swiftly walked away.

He could march quickly and the roads were good. He found a coach was also heading west, jumped on it, took it as far as it would go. It crossed over a long narrow bridge above a steep valley, the view beautiful, if you had a head for heights, something he would have loved to share with Amber. It finally stopped at a coaching inn, had a good meal there, then moved on. The moon was up and he could put some miles in this night, besides, the sword shone brightly now, lit up the night if uncovered. *That sword*, what a beauty, and to think all that time she had the Opalstone in her pack ... amazing.

Amber ... he spoke the word softly, it was a name you whispered, preferably in the darkest recesses of the night as she lay by your side ... *Amber* ... he whispered again. Then he shook his mane of hair, blinked his eyes, *stop*, stop now. He concentrated on the path ahead.

Eventually he took himself off the road into the trees, lit a fire, wrapped himself up in his cloak and slept for a few hours. There were no disturbances, no rude awakenings and he woke starving, decided to go deeper into the forest to hunt.

He saw them before they saw him, his dun coloured leathers and dull green tunic blended into the forest greens, as he intended. Plus, he could walk softly, silently, as one with the forest. It was an innate skill which came in useful, certainly useful when he retrieved the sword. *His* sword, the family sword - what was it doing down Floriénne anyway?

He peeped carefully around the tree he was hiding against. There were, what, half a dozen of the ruffians? They looked pretty cut-throat; one, a tall dark haired elf, had an eye patch, he seemed to be the leader. He wondered why the leaders of these groups always had an eye patch, was it some sort of rite of passage?

He imagined the conversation: *'Look you lot, I'm going to be leader of this gang - right?'*

'Hey, hang on, where's your eye patch? You've two good eyes ... you can't be leader of a pack of brigands, it's not on.' The evil and invincible leader always wore an eye patch.

Mumbles and grumbles all round by rest of badass gang.

'Oh for Merrie's sake ... look, hand me that dagger, OK?' .... squiggle, squiggle, rumble, eeek, erk, plop .... 'Right - anyone care to challenge me now? Then pass me the bloody eye patch.'

Estrién stifled a laugh.

He remained by the tree, listening in to their actual conversation, watching them carefully. They wore a motley collection of clothing, various shades of forest green, knives and cutlasses hung about their bodies, bows and arrows on their backs. - well-armed all. It appeared they were discussing the day's hunt, their take from the last raid and bemoaning about the fact they couldn't use the cash anywhere to buy goods. That last remark proved they were as he guessed, outlaws.

Outlaws - *o*utside of the law. The law was simple. They were outcasts, rightly so for their crimes, totally outside of society. Should be dead, should have felt the hangman's noose, but didn't. Were given the choice as the law permitted, left society instead. Lived, but became *the dead ones*. No one could deal with them without suffering strong penalties, nor could they go into any town or village. No trade, no barter, no work. Their lives would be forfeit immediately, it was the right of any citizen to kill them on sight. They were *'less than wolves' heads'*, was the phrase. Pictures and likenesses were hung in sheriff's and bailiff's offices and outside town or village halls.

They had this wild forest, nothing more. But it was better than the hangman's noose or the axe.

Estrién heard the leader speak. 'Those Blazing Sun bastards took out Callen, I want revenge, he was a good lad, he didn't deserve that. They killed him for the plain and simple reason he was an elf. Yet another of our young folk gone - and two of our women last month. Those *Eormynn* bastards are getting closer and closer. I tell you, I'm not taking it. When we reach base I'm ordering a full raid on their camp at the coast there. It just sickens me that we have to do the work the lazy, good-for-nothing Elvinhaeme Guard should be doing.'

Another piped up, 'well, no one will thank us for it.'

'No,' replied their leader, gruffly, 'but if we don't make a stand against them soon, there will be too many for us to take out. They are arriving daily. We need to wreck their camp, show them it's unsafe for them here, give ourselves some breathing space. Shame the good-for-nothing Elvinhaeme militia into getting off their backsides. Or do you all want to have to move further up in the mountains? It gets effing cold in winter, not to mention those bloody dragons. Do you want our women dying?' He felt he'd made his point.

It was at this moment Estrién stepped out from his hiding place. They all looked startled and six cutlasses were drawn. Estrién held up his hands. 'Peace, please. I mean no harm - indeed, I may be able to help.'

The leader turned to him. 'I don't know who the hell you are, elf, but you do realise you are in deep shit don't you?' his thin, cruel lips snarled at Estrién.

'Oh, I don't think so,' Estrién replied calmly, taking out his sword, holding it out ready to fight. 'Would any of you care to take me on? I can take out several of you at once with White Star, merely with the first swipe.' The blade shone with iniquitous light, blinding the elves.

The leader put up his arm over his one good eye, 'hey, put that down, what the hell is it? We'll parley, I'm not stupid ... who *are* you?'

'I do believe I am *'Nim'randuel Soleus D'rendiél Gilsylien Estaran'elvian'*, or so I am told,' Estrién laughed, 'but I am also Knight Commander Estrién of the Temple of Merrie. What you see is the Sword of D'rendiél, also, NimEstrién, White Star. I heard what you had to say about the Adammites, and I am happy to be of service to you … for a fee of course.'

The Freowulven leader looked at him. 'Well, that's quite a mouthful. But it's also quite a sword. You wish to be of service to us? You don't look like an outcast. Are you aware who we are - we are Freowulven, *outlaws*, and you are breaking the law by merely talking to us?'

'I have no problems whatsoever with that. What I do want is an effective band of capable people who, like me, wish to remove the curse of Von Adamm and his Blazing Sun cult from this land, preferably before you, I and all the elves are destroyed by them.'

The leader nodded, 'they are landing on the coast close by our forests and we are regarded cheaply by them. We do not officially exist after all. Perhaps we are good sport for their young fighters, perhaps it is merely that we are elves. Whatever the case they come into the forest in heavily armed groups, prey upon the unwary. We've always had this forest, at least the lower slopes, as our own, they are picking out the younger ones one by one when they go hunting. Merrie knows, life is bad enough here, but to have to contend with them as well ... '

Estrién nodded, he understood. Whilst the forest was kind now during the warm months, it would be harsh in winter. These people couldn't barter, except perhaps with smugglers at the coast, may be deal with the odd hawker, no more.

'As I said, I offer my services. I am no outlaw, nor brigand. I merely wish to rout these people from our lands, for all our sakes.'

The elven leader, Jovan by name, had to admit, he could certainly use his help. 'We Freowulven have to help ourselves. We take what we can, when we can. Any aid is welcome.' But he warned him as they left the clearing. 'It is good you are an elf. If you were *Eormynn*, with or without that sword ... *I would have killed you.*'

Estrién followed them through the forest.

*

Like Estrién, Amber and the group took the coach to the west of Westerling. Their only idea was to continue west until they found a reasonable way into the forest, then travel northwards. None believed they needed to actively seek the Freowulven; as trespassers in the wildwood they would be sought out, probably attacked. But if Estrién was with those people, there was little choice.

It was already growing late when they stepped off the coach. They went straight to the coaching inn, asked about an elf with a beautiful shining sword. All were relieved to know he had been that way, but had only stayed for a meal.

It was something - they weren't on a wild goose chase. They ordered food and a couple of rooms for the night, no reason to go wandering about the roads or forest in the dark tonight. But it seemed they were forever on the trail of this elusive elf.

Amber remained quiet. She had no idea what would happen when they found him. She had committed herself to Dane, she had no wish to hurt him.

But you couldn't help who you loved. Torn between conscience - and sense - because she knew Dane was a good man in every way for her - versus the complete unknown with Estrién. If truth be told, she didn't wish to lose Dane, he was a good friend as well as a lover.

At almost twenty two, her birthday actually in a week's time, she considered she'd had enough experience with men to make up her own mind. There'd been various lovers in the circus, all casual. Dane was the first person for whom she truly felt love, both bonding and binding. And then suddenly it was happening again, only worse. She'd tried to hide it, from herself as much as from Dane and the others, but it was difficult. There is no hiding from your own heart.

Every time Estrién touched her - or even looked at her, when their eyes met and ... *the need in his eyes* ... probably echoed by her own. This was a terrible pain, one she hadn't known.

She'd let him go. She'd been a coward - or perhaps simply loyal to Dane when she ran away from Estrién's disappearing figure. But she knew she should have run *to* him, stopped him, taken his arm. *Never let him go.*

Some things in life should be ruled by mere instinct.

Her eye was distracted as a bird flew past the window, a large magpie. It landed on the slope of the hill just behind the inn. She watched as it walked up the hill looking for worms. Why couldn't her life be that simple?

She went to the wash stand, threw cold water over her face. Time to face the two downstairs in the public bar.

She spent the night trying to smile and be happy. It's amazing what a glass or two of wine can do.

The next few days were on the road, trying to find Estrién, or to find news of him. Those they came across were mostly elven travellers, peddlers, hawkers with their carts and farmers taking wares to market. Every one of them knew of the Freowulven, were terrified of them, but none knew about an elf with a shining sword.

There was only one thing to do - leave the road, go into the forest, and, if the rumours were anything to go by, wait until the Freowulven found them.

They wandered the forest with trepidation, stories about Freowulven not pleasant, often singing to themselves to keep up their spirits. Two nights they slept in the forest, expecting to be woken rudely with shouts and threats, or, taken prisoner as they had with the Fae.

It was strange, but when you *wanted* to be found, nothing happened ...

... until they walked into a clearing.

'Not one step further or you die, *eormynn!*' A lone elf stood before them, a hard-bitten, ruffianly archer whose drawn bow and arrow now pointed in their direction. A tall elf, he stood lean and muscular, the cedar green of his leggings and tunic matching the forest around him, his black hair tied back with a leather thong and his left eye covered with a black patch. He clearly wasn't a man to be trifled with. He saw Tamlyn behind the humans. 'Ah, and you too elf, don't hide behind *Eormynn*, it is not worthy of you.'

Tamlyn stood forward. He quietly spoke to Amber and Dane, 'There are archers in the trees, take care ...!' He turned to the elf, 'these eormynn are my friends. They are good people. We wish you no harm, we merely seek a friend of ours.'

The elf shook his head, 'no *eormynn* traverse this wood. Either they leave, or they die!'

Tamlyn persisted. 'We have no desire to stay, I can assure you, but we have heard our good friend is with you. He is called Estrién and he carries a wonderful shining sword.'

An eyebrow shot upwards, the elf looked surprised. 'Who is this elf to you, and why do you wish to contact him?'

'If you know him, perhaps you could pass him a message from us?' Tamlyn asked hopefully.

'Give your message, I will see if there is such an elf in this forest '

'Tell him ... tell him that we wish to see him, we miss him. Tell him that ... *Amber is here.*' Tamlyn looked across at Amber, she turned pink, embarrassed. Her eyes widened ... *he'd known*?

The surly elf nodded, then motioned to his men. Half a dozen dropped out of the trees. 'Take these back to the edge of the forest. Stay with them, don't let them out of your sight. Await my orders and if either of the two eormynn try anything, *kill them*.' He disappeared into the tangled trees.

They were escorted for a couple of miles towards the outer edge of the woods. They sat down awaiting the reply.

'You knew?' asked Amber of Tamlyn.

'Pretty obvious, Amber, we're not blind,' replied Tamlyn. 'We both know. Don't make a big fuss about it. What do you expect - you're very beautiful.' He looked her in the eye. She turned away, her face reddening. Tamlyn chuckled at her embarrassment.

But Dane looked away, into the forest, into his own heart, wondering if he could bear this pain?

*

A few nights earlier.

The band of elven renegades and outlaws crept through the night towards the coastal camp. Estrién kept his sword well sheathed, it shone far too much otherwise, would give the game away. He wondered if it was possible to tame it, communicate with it in some way, since it seemed to be tied to him? The sword hummed when he was emotional, he understood that, he'd found he could quieten it if he stayed calm. Perhaps he could do the same with the light? He had no idea, but it was worth a try, perhaps it would just take time and discipline. He had plenty of both.

A large boat lay at anchor by the jetty. More of these damn Blazing Sun people had come in this very day, they were all being hailed by their brethren. A large fire lit the scene, the smell of greasy pig or boar meat roasted on a spit earlier, pervaded the camp.

The black and red robed men stood or sat in a circle around the fire, all with hoods close over their heads. They were chanting and praying and saying something about their Lord God of Death, and the right of man, or perhaps the rite of man, and their superiority above all.

Estrién heard a scream to the edge of the camp, watched warily as two of the cultists dragged out an elven woman. It seemed she had to go on some sort of trial. Whatever it was, it consisted of stripping her of her clothes and tying her to a stake.

Religious cult or not, to Estrién this just looked like a group of men bullying and sexually assaulting a young female. *'Effing cowards,'* he thought.

The Freowulven looked quietly at each other - this was clearly the time to move in, she couldn't be left like that. Jovan nodded to Estrién ... *anytime you want.*

Estrién nodded, unsheathed White Star and threw himself into the centre of the cultists. White Star sang and shone, momentarily blinding them all. He always believed in the element of surprise, and put it to good use. The blade whirled in a huge circle, taking several out with its keen edge. The rest of the Freowulven group ran in behind him as he wielded the blade in a massive figure of infinity, up and round and down and up and round and down, infinite circles of death. At first, the blade hummed a discordant tune as he killed mercilessly. Estrién saw no point in sitting down, talking with these people, there was no place for a nice cup of herbal tea and a good chat - he understood they were unapproachable. There was only one solution to this disease of man - annihilate or *be* annihilated.

Estrién moved like a vengeful god as he tore into them with his blistering sword, gracefully, purposely and precisely. The Sword of D'rendiél fully lived up to its reputation, a shining, blinding eater of souls. He gritted his teeth and continued the circle of death. But his was not a blazing anger, his heart was cold, logical and merciless,. He counted each one as they fell, they were no longer people in his eyes. The sword bit silently.

Jovan and the elven Freowulven flashed their own cutlasses and brought more death. The cultists did not give in without a fight, but they had not seen true battle, nor had they had to live off their wits through hostile winters, friendless and disowned. The Freowulven proved to be strong warriors, Jovan at their head, his cutlasses fine-sharpened to kill without grace or pity.

As the last of the robed and hooded men lay dead around the fire, Jovan raised his hand for a halt to the carnage. The scene was a mass of blood, guts and severed limbs, the smell abominable. Jovan ordered that they be left like this - a warning to the next boat docking here.

Then Estrién went to the woman bound to the stake and cut her cord, but she screamed and ran, frightened of her new saviours. Cultists or Freowulven, she had no desire to remain with either. She ran naked into the night.

The Freowulven gazed in wonder at this new warrior. They had never seen the like, not in all their born days. He was a miracle, he brought a blade of death. They could only thank the Lady he had come to help them, and not to seek them out and destroy them. Even Jovan, their finest hunter and savage killer - with or without his left eye - was left breathless watching him.

When they returned to their camp Estrién was hailed as a great hero. The women of the camp came to congratulate and to reward their men, with wine and kisses and promises of more. The tale was told of the battle. Two elven beauties nodded to each other and wandered across to their new hero. *For the greatest of all was Estrién.* He did not complain.

He spent the next days running raids with them. Down along the coast, stopping any groups who arrived on the northern reaches of Elvinhaeme. He watched Jovan as he laid into the Blazing Sun cultists, a fierce anger in his eyes, a shout of satisfaction as another was slain. He guessed it wasn't merely because they were cultists, it was the fact they were human.

Estrién was startled at the vehemence of the Freowulven leader's loathing of humans, or *eormynn* as he said. He talked to him as they sat by the fire.

'I've never seen such hatred of humans - why?' They spoke Plaintongue, Estrién was fluent in elvhen, but strangely Jovan wasn't.

'I come from Westerling, born and bred there. So was my wife. Some drunken fools of eormynn, one a so-called nobleman, thought it was fun to attack and rape her as she returned from market one evening. She was having my child also. She fought them, but they were too many, she and the babe she carried died that night, they were drunken brutes. I didn't wait for the law to bring justice, I took it for myself. To be fair, they did not imprison me, merely cast me out, I was 'too dangerous' to stay in Westerling, which was probably true. From that moment I could not stand the sight of eormynn. I joined the Freowulven, I'm comfortable among folk who, like me, have blood on their hands. I have no desire to return to Westerling, although to be among elves is a different matter. It pains me never to walk the fair streets of Belcast'el or to wander the paths and forests of Elvinhaeme.'

'And women?'

The Freowulven leader just laughed. 'These 'waived' females, all fugitives from justice, thieves and murderers too, are friendly enough. They satisfy a basic need, *as you are already aware*. But nothing more than that, none of us truly wish to be here, we merely comfort each other.'

Estrién had to agree with him, they certainly did satisfy a basic need. They kept his nights warm.

But it didn't stop his heart aching.

Later, he went hunting with them, food was running short and too much time had been spent on the Adammite cultists. They didn't have larders to fall back on, nor had they markets to go to; what they caught they ate. Jovan was as good an archer as he was with the sword, up in the hills they tracked a stag. He explained that the women folk found berries and roots during the summer, but it wasn't filling enough for the men. One or two of the women joined in with hunting, skilled archers; wild birds, rabbit, hare, everything went into the pot.

The lower slopes of the woods were deciduous, he explained, but it became too open once the leaves were shed in autumn. In winter he would move further up the hills, perhaps a cave if they found one, there was one he used, although they usually had to clear out the bears first. He'd lost an eye that way. Wild deer and game were essential come winter, there was little else to eat. Fussiness or idealism wasn't an option. Starvation was always a possibility, and further up the slopes, dragons would swoop down. They got the deer first, there was often little left for the outlaws. Winter was a hungry time.

But here, on this slope of the hills, a youngish stag stood patiently, he was sniffing the air, taking a mouthful of sweet grass, or perhaps acorns. As Jovan aimed at it, the stag must have realised something was amiss. He suddenly ran off into the woods. Estrién and Jovan ran after him, Jovan determined to have him. He sent an arrow after the retreating deer, managed a shot in its rump. 'Come on, slow down you beauty,' he murmured. The deer stumbled but ran on. They tracked it for probably half a mile or so, then saw it had stopped to drink from a small stream, blood oozing down a hind leg.

'Oh, I have you now,' Jovan said with satisfaction, as he shot two arrows in quick succession. They both watched as the stag fell to the ground. Estrién nodded and patted Jovan on the back.

'Well done, we eat well tonight,' knowing how much it meant to these people.

It was so big it took four of them to carry it back between them. There was a great cheer in the camp as they walked in. It wasn't just meat, all parts of this fine beast would be used, skin, hooves and antlers included, every part necessary for survival. Before the feast Jovan gave a short prayer to the god of the forest, to Herne the Hunter, and a toast to the brave stag itself. Game such as this should be honoured. The two elven women served Estrién large platters of venison later, rough wine was drunk and the elves sang songs until late into the night.

And Estrién took the two women to his bed once more.

*

An hour later a runner came through. 'You are to be allowed into the forest,' he told Amber and the boys. 'But you must all be blindfolded, and your weapons removed - and that includes the mage's staff.'

They began to protest, but he had his orders. 'Do as we say or leave the forest, that is all.'

They begrudgingly accepted, if this was the only way to see Estrién. *'You ruin that staff and there'll be hell to pay,'* warned Dane.

They were bound and roped together, blindfolded, and taken through the forest, each led by a heavily-armed elf. Although they were a little rough with them, none were harmed. Eventually they arrived at a camp. Blindfolds and bonds were taken off them; blinking at the bright sunlight and rubbing of wrists was the order of the day for a while.

Estrién stood in the middle of the camp in front of a large fire, the Freowulven main base - a few tents and ramshackle huts, no more - watching their entrance. The fire blazed behind him, a halo effect. He looked sadly at them, shaking his head.

'Why did you come, why did you follow me? Did you not read my note?'

Dane answered. 'Yes, we read it, Estrién, we merely ignored it. You can't get rid of us that easily.'

'Leave me be, it is better so,' he was clearly annoyed. 'I had my reasons.'

Tamlyn shook his head, 'no, Estrién, not good enough. We all know the real reason you left us ...'

'You do *not* know why I left.' His voice was firm, but there was an edge of anger. He looked across at Amber. She said nothing.

Dane spoke again. 'Estrién, I understand, truly. I know why you ran away ...' All eyes were on Amber.

But the elf just snorted, 'Huh! It was not *me* who ran. Ask Amber, the first time I offer her the smallest part of my love, *she ran from me*. Don't worry Dane, you are in no danger. She is true to you.' His emerald eyes were blazing, the sword on his back shining fiercely. humming could be heard from White Star.

Dane turned to Amber. 'You ran, love?' He gave a slight laugh. 'You love me so much that you ran away from him?' He took Amber's hand, kissed it. *'Oh, Amber.* But you know, love, you forget I'm half dryad, as well as a mage. *I feel you.* I know you care for me ... but I also know ...' his eyes were downcast , '*well ...* .' He looked across at Estrién, 'you *are* a fool, you let her run and didn't go after her?" he asked him. But it was a rhetorical question, he expected no answer.

Two elven women now stood and joined Estrién, placing themselves one on each side, both put a possessive hand on his shoulder. One spoke quietly to him, he was seen to shake his head. He lay a hand over hers.

Tamlyn's eyes widened. 'Hey Estrién, that was quick work! Didn't know you had it in you.' His laugh was cut short.

Estrién stared fiercely at him, his voice sharp. 'You know little about me, we were together only a short time.'

'Time enough for us to care about you, and *that includes me.* Come on, Estrién, come back with us,' Tamlyn replied. 'Hey, and don't forget I cannot go back to Floriénne because of you!'

Dane suddenly shouted out, 'you forgot Amber quick enough though, didn't you?' It annoyed him to see Estrién being pawed by the two elven females, he knew it would hurt Amber. Dane had the ability to love kindly, not possessively.

Estrién just shook his head, ignoring their jibes.

The Freowulven elves watched on, not quite understanding the relationships. The atmosphere was charged, like the silence just before a thunderstorm, the Freowulven wondered what was going on?

Amber finally spoke. She'd said nothing, only stared curiously at Estrién. The females did not exist for her, only the elf standing defiantly between them.

'Why are you with these people, Estrién?' Her voice was sombre, held a warning edge to it. 'You know they are outlaws, outside our lives, our world, our legal systems. They aren't here because they stole a loaf of bread or some other petty crime. They are here because they committed murder, or High Treason and they've conveniently escaped the hangman's noose. Estrién, if you stay with them much longer, you too will be placed outside our laws. Do you want to live like this for the rest of your life, permanently on the run?

You will hide in shadows and creep in the light.' She spoke determinedly but softly, she had no wish to antagonise him.

He turned to her, his voice as sad as his eyes. 'Why did you come, Amber? I can get along perfectly well here. I have friends who will help in the fight against the Adammites, I have food, shelter and ...' he looked down at the two women next to him, 'women to warm my bed at night. Why should I leave? In any case, I don't expect to live long, but to use my remaining time to destroy this enemy of our world. I shall die happy in that at least.'

She looked him in the eye, his words were false, not like him at all. 'You surely do not mean that, Estrién?' He stared belligerently back at her. 'You are far more than that, you *must* know it. You cannot live as an outlaw, but in the world of free elves and men, fighting for *all* of us. Estrién, you have a future, but that future cannot come to pass if you stay here.

You are hiding, that is all, as are these people. They have to, they have no choice, *but you do*.'

They stared into each other's eyes for timeless moments, a battle of wills, a war of the sexes. Eventually he seemed to relent. He shrugged the two women off his shoulders, moved over to her, held out his hand, beckoning her.

'Come, walk with me a little way.' His action was kind, but his voice was harsh. He led her behind the huts, stood with his back to one, his leg bent with one foot against the wood. He folded his arms, deep green eyes blazing. 'Apart from the inspirational speechifying, tell me, why are you here?' His voice sounded cold, merely annoyed with her.

It hurt Amber, she would respond in kind. '*They*'ve already said. There's no need for me to repeat it,' Amber too was annoyed after seeing the two elven females pawing him. She would at least keep her dignity.

'Did you come here because *you* wanted to, or was it their idea?'

'Dane and Tamlyn wanted to find you, they want you to come back with us.' *He'd* left *her,* she would not openly admit she wanted him back. She stared past him, at the trees, the forest floor, anywhere but him.

He needed to see her face, why didn't she look at him? *She really didn't give a damn, did she*? '*They* want me to return and *you* just toddled after them, then?' He could hear his sword whimpering.

'No, that's not true,' she countered, her voice low. This was embarrassing. He'd clearly already made his choice.

'Then *why* did you come?'

'We're a team aren't we? Anyway, we were told you were with the Freowulven. We couldn't leave you with the outlaws,' her voice held steady.

'What, you sought me because of a social conscience?'

'Call it what you like ... I just think that what you are doing is wrong, it isn't for you.'

So, more moralising then. *'I* will be the judge of that, woman,' he replied. Harshly he asked, 'what right have *you* to make choices for *me*?'

'None, I suppose. I just don't want you losing your way.' Her reply sounded reasonable, but who wanted reason at this moment?

He studied her, she clearly only thought of him as a colleague, at the most a friend, that was no good. 'I choose my *own* way woman, my life is mine to choose, my path my own, no one makes decisions for me.'

'Then if my hopes and wishes do not concern you, I must go. We made an error following you.' How else could she respond when his own responses were so cold? *Dammit ... they hurt!*

He heard the sadness in her voice as she made to leave.

His heart lurched, there was so little time left. She would be gone, probably forever - his own fault. Did she care for him or what? He had to know, they had come this far, his friends, followed him into this danger - and among Freowulven, humans were truly in danger, more so than they realised perhaps. He couldn't just let her go.

He grabbed her arm, that same *frisson* as ever shooting between them.

She appeared startled but shook him off, turned away. 'Look, we'll go, *you don't need me.*'

Need her ...?

He touched her shoulder, turned her to him, saw the pain on her face, deep eyes hurting.

They echoed his own.

Now he spoke, his voice urgent, *'Amber, I need you as I need air to breathe ...'* He'd said it, said what was in his heart, whether she wanted to hear it or not.

So break it woman, and let it be done.

She gazed at him, her eyes startled, briefly closed them, biting her lip. Opened them once more to see his face, his beautiful elven face, a worried frown deep across his brow. Every emotion showed clear, none hidden from her.

A small sigh escaped, *'oh ...'* searching his eyes. She moved a little closer to him, lifted her face just a fraction. 'Estrién?' she softly whispered.

It was enough.

She heard a short intake of breath as he took her face in his hands. For a moment he gazed into her eyes, making sure, before he kissed her. His hands shook.

First, that same soft touch of his lips against hers, the electrum shock of him, then her lips parted as his tentative tongue probed her. Finally he took her mouth in his in a long, deep, lover's kiss. It was the kind of kiss that makes time stand still.

They stood as one, their eyes closed, their lips together, hungry mouths seeking each other. He clasped her hands in his, held her close, tight to his body. The sword on his back shone brightly and sang softly. Curiously intense currents, waves of light and heat flowed between them

Finally he stood back, swallowed hard, spoke gently, 'If *you* wish it, I will return with you.' His eyes sought hers for confirmation.

Amber touched his cheek with the tips of her fingers. 'I wish it more than anything in life,' her voice caressing him, knowing it as an absolute truth. She had no choice over where her heart led.

He kissed her once more, then nodded his head. 'So be it.' His own heart too full to speak more.

Silently, they walked around the hut, back to others crowding around the fire. For a few moments he and Dane stared at each other. Neither smiled, if anything, sorrow was in both their eyes.

He moved to one side, found his pack, then spoke to Jovan, the elven leader. 'I have appreciated the last days with you, and I am glad to been of use in the raids on the coast against the Adammites. I now go, although, I may need your services later, when I have organised a full resistance against these people. This war is against all of us, freeman or outlaw. Will you help?'

Jovan clasped his hand, 'I knew you would not stay. But we will help, call us when you need us. Meanwhile we will continue the raids against them.' They turned to go, 'stay one moment, Sir Estrién, we said we would pay for your aid.' He went off to one of the huts, brought back a small bag of gold. 'It is of little use to us, we have few places to spend it, that is your share. Thank you, and farewell.' The weapons and Dane's staff were handed back. 'You are free to go, he fully vouches for you.'

For a brief moment Estrién bowed his head to the two elven women with whom he had shared bed and body. They acknowledged him, then turned away.

Estrién led Amber by the hand, guiding them out of the forest, back to the main highway and to civilisation.

Chapter 2

They found a coaching inn further on the highway leading into Elvinhaeme. Tamlyn booked two rooms for the night. Estrién said nothing, had not spoken as they walked. But he had kept hold of Amber's hand as if she would run away. When they received the keys to the rooms, he held out his hand for Tamlyn's key.

'You are with Dane this night,' he announced.

Amber said nothing.

He hitched his pack over his back and took Amber up the stairs with him. They watched him go, watched Amber taken away by him. Tamlyn saw Dane's eyes as he watched, touched his shoulder. 'You are not alone my friend, I am with you. Let us go and get settled in, then come down and get extremely drunk, huh?'

Dane let himself be led away. Fighting for her was not an option, he knew she had made up her mind. *'You will gain and you will lose,'* he remembered from the night around the camp fire in the forest, a slight shiver running down his spine. He had always known. He had led her to him, he knew it was what she wanted, but she had no idea how much it had cost him.

Whatever she wanted, *this night* she wanted Estrién. Did it make him less of a man, he wondered, for giving her that? Or merely for giving in? Would she be true to her vow that, despite her feelings for Estrién, she loved him no less? Because, he knew, this was love not mere sex, a depth beyond.

And yet, all his mage senses told him this was right. He looked out at the deepening sky, *this night ... this night ...*

Upstairs, Estrién unlocked the door of their room. He stopped to look Amber in the eye. 'If you do not wish this, tell me now. When we go through that door, there is no turning back.' The words were simple and clichéd, repeated over countless years by many men to many women. The men watched their women with pleading eyes, hungry eyes, wolven eyes, waiting for her reply. Yet Estrién's eyes blazed with the light of his sword, Amber could hear a slight hum.

One last moment of choice.

She just smiled at him, walked through, her mind made up, knowing there *was* no going back. He followed her and locked the door, throwing his pack on the floor and unfastened White Star, carefully placing it against the wall. Amber unhooked the bow and quiver from her back, the knife belt she wore around her waist, hung them on the small weapons rack and placed her pack next to his.

The room was pleasantly warm, the summer sun just dying. A gay cover was thrown on the dark oak bed, matching the pretty green and yellow curtains, candles in brass candlesticks at the sides on small tables. An aged washstand with a pale cream jug and ewer stood in a corner near a dark table, with a chair and an oval wood framed mirror. It was just a wayside inn, nothing special.

But the atmosphere was electric with undercurrents.

He took her hand in his once more. They stood opposite each other, seeking each other's eyes, drinking each other in.

'I love you,' was all he said, slowly undressing her.

She nodded, gentle fingers began unfastening his tunic.

Softly he kissed her neck, the tender skin of her throat, the shock of his lips ran through her; she gasped. He carried on, kissing, gently biting, he wanted all of her. They stood together, hands clasped, their embrace tight, their breath whispering in each other's ear. White Star hummed in the corner.

When they finally stood naked, he stepped away to look at her, shaking his head at her beauty. She mesmerised him. 'I love you,' he repeated.

'I love you,' she softly replied.

He held her close again. Kissed her neck, her shoulders, he sucked her skin into his mouth, turning it red, he would bruise her with his love, his need. He didn't care if everyone saw. Amber was his and he would display that to the world.

Yet gently he tugged her to the bed, pulling her to him, his hands roaming down her arms, the touch of velvet, the touch of love. With one finger he stroked her breast, he heard her breath catch, he bent to kiss. He could smell the heady smell of life in her, her sweet perfume. He licked her skin, breathing her in. He lifted his head to take her mouth in his again, hands roaming, feeling, finding all the hidden spots, the soft and delicious parts of her.

Estrién had thought his first time with Amber would be rushed, if there would ever be a first time, that it would be over before he had barely begun to explore her. He thought there would be frenzy and groans and screams as they tore at each other. ... *If.*

But he found it wasn't like that, he was in control, he was patient, he had no desire for it to be over soon He was strong and sure, fully at ease with her, wanting to please her, to pleasure her, his own pleasure somehow unessential. He watched her, listened to her, smelled and tasted her, his hands and lips roaming her body with a slow and delicate sensuality ...

... while his heart beat a rhythm of fire and velvet.

Eventually he rose over her, knowing it was time. He watched her arch her back, heard her gasp. The shock, that electrum bolt, as his body and hers melded together, his sword now singing in the corner. As the evening light dimmed he had no need to light candles, the sword sparkled with their love.

There were no words, only sounds, moaning, sighing, as their rhythm rose and fell. Sometimes he closed his eyes, sometimes he opened them to watch her, to find her beautiful amber eyes gazing into his own emerald ones.

He pulsated with her essence, there should be no ending, never, ever, it should last all night, the two of them, this deep, deep rocking and swaying, this fathomless sharing of love and desire.

But he could feel his elven blood soaring, the rhythm quickening, the heat rising. His slow movements changed, her need matching his He clasped her palms, entwining his fingers around hers, pushing them across the pillow, his pace urgent now, his head shaking from side to side, his breath catching. He arched his back, thrusting deeply, groaning out loud ... so little time left.

With absolute satisfaction he cried out her name, shaking uncontrollably, deep inside her, fulfilling those weeks of need, the pain at leaving her. He heard her cry match his, her body shaking. He heard the sword sing a high keening note.

He had no idea how long it carried on. For an eternity he was lost in the pleasure of her body, until the heat subsided and he lay quietly over her. He only knew he fell asleep in her and it was dark when they awoke.

He held her clasped in loving arms, her breasts against his own, her breath on his skin.

'Now I am complete,' he whispered to her, 'now I am whole.' He felt her nod and kiss his cheek, his forehead. She kissed his mouth, her soft lips on his, her kisses now urgent. His own need rose again and matched hers.

And once more the sword began to sing and shine in that deep velvet night.

*

Some hours earlier.

Downstairs, Dane was trying to put a brave face on it. He drank back his third large goblet of wine. They didn't eat, neither hungry.

'Why are *you* not eating?' he asked Tamlyn.

'I love her too,' was the honest reply, as he poured more wine. 'Come on, man, give us some of that leafroll of yours, and make it strong.'

'*I thought so* - damn the woman ...' Dane piled the herbs heavily. They shared the roll, toasting each other, commiserating at the meanness of life, the fickleness of females.

Tamlyn drew the smoke in to his lungs, then coughed. '*Man, this is lethal stuff!* Just how many years are you taking off my life with this?'

'Fewer years than if I sit here all night, thinking about what he's doing to Amber. It's killing me.'

'I thought you were OK about this? You said so.'

Dane shook his head, he slurred his words a little, that leafroll mix was strong. 'No, I said I *understood*. Not the same thing. I love her, I want her, but *he* has her... it's shit.' He poured more wine down his throat. Went to the bar, came back with a flask of usquebae. 'We need something stronger.' He poured two out. They toasted each other again, refilled the goblet.

For some time the leafroll was passed back and forth, each deep in their own thoughts.

'How long have you loved her?' Dane eventually asked Tamlyn, he was curious. Tamlyn just shrugged.

'Long enough to be jealous of you both. *Aaah, nix virandem* ...' he added dismissively. Tamlyn nevertheless glanced hopefully around the bar checking for available females. There weren't any, it was disappointing. Then he chuckled to himself as he gazed across the table at Dane, his long-lashed elven eyes gleaming with mischief. '*Do you never wish to experiment?*' he asked quietly. Dane looked back at him, nonplussed.

'What do you mean?'

'Come on, man, you're half dryad. Don't you wish to discover that other side of you, the dryad half, the tree sprite, brother of Pan and all that?' Shameless eyes twinkled at Dane.

'Never thought about it, but yes, thank you for reminding me. My dryad half only seems to come out with my healing abilities and my natural affinity for growing things. It's probably in much of what I do, but I don't usually think about it. I mean, I'm not tied to a tree or anything.'

'Shall I tie you to one and see what happens?' Tamlyn laughed, staring him in the eye, challenging him.

He stubbed out the leafroll and picked up the flask of Usquebae, beckoning him. 'Come on, Dane, let's take this upstairs, we can finish it there. I think you and I ought to spend a little time together.'

Dane looked querulously at him, only to find the elf grinning at him. 'Tamlyn, what are you suggesting?' His mage senses already told him, but he wanted confirmation.

Tamlyn just laughed. 'Dane, I'm saying there's plenty of ways to have a good time - and I know *all* of them ... ' He put on his most persuasive, charming smile, whispering 'Come ... *grasp the night, seize the moment.*' He stood up, made for the door, '*well* - you coming?' His eyes were pure mischief.

Dane raised his eyebrows, but followed. He didn't see any reason to stay miserably by himself in the bar.

On the way up the stairs to their room, Dane felt a shiver as Tamlyn's nails travelled down his spine. His eyes looked startled for a moment, then he laughed.

'You know I'm effing desperate, don't you?' he asked Tamlyn.

'Oh yes,' was the reply, *'and I'm taking full advantage of it,'* unlocking the door to their room.

Inside he poured a goblet of usquebae and handed it to Dane. 'You may need this,' he said with a lascivious grin. 'You know, Dane, I can assure you, you will be just as satisfied after a night with me, as you would be with Amber. I have no inhibitions whatsoever.'

'I've always said I'm a woman's man, not a man's man ...' Dane began.

'But I'm no man, Dane, I'm an elf. Try it and see, you may find me quite pleasing.' Tamlyn's sultry olive-green elven eyes with the ridiculously long lashes, gazed sensuously into his. They gleamed with pure pleasure.

Dane thought of his woman along the corridor with the other elf. Considered his situation. He finished the usquebae and set the goblet down on the night stand, as he felt Tamlyn's hand caress his shoulder.

'Oh drat it,' he thought, *'there's a first time for everything ...'*

*

There was a small dining room where guests could have breakfast or dinner in the inn. Estrién and Amber were already eating breakfast when Dane and Tamlyn came down.

She looked radiant. She rose, put her hand in Dane's, looked into his eyes. He noticed a large love bite she was unsuccessfully hiding with a silk scarf. He raised an eyebrow at Estrién, who gave him the ghost of a smile. Amber took his face in her hands, kissed him on the lips. He nodded, accepting she wasn't pushing him away.

As she stood back, she saw the bite mark on his own neck. She pointed her finger at him, her eyes querying. He'd forgotten Tamlyn doing that, he fingered his neck, pulled up his collar, like Amber, trying hopelessly to cover it.

Tamlyn burst out laughing.

'You look like you had a good night yourselves?' Estrién asked them. He didn't seem unduly surprised.

Dane too started laughing. 'We surely did,' he replied. Tamlyn blew him a kiss.

Amber's mouth dropped open. 'Are we talking about what I think we're talking about?'

Estrién took her hand. 'I think we are,' he replied. 'I was always told to beware of the somewhat uninhibited elves from the Court of Floriénne, let's say they look both ways.'

Tamlyn looked sweetly into her eyes. *'Aaah, the pleasures of love ... .* You're not jealous Amber, are you? You look like your night was good too. Anyway, there is always room in my bed for one more ... '

Amber's mouth dropped open again, as she watched three males grin and two shake their heads at Tamlyn's cheek.

Suddenly all four were laughing. The landlord wondered what the joke was as he brought them their breakfast.

*

Later, when they were out on the road, while Tamlyn was making fun of Amber and she was laughing at his antics and jokes, Estrién spoke to Dane.

'Thank you for coming for me. I know what it has cost you, my brother. You knew how I felt for Amber did you not - you told me as much?' He stared him in the eye, there was to be no holding back. He hated dishonesty and hiding his feelings for her had been difficult.

Dane managed a mumbled, 'I knew.'

'Yet, you came.' A statement, not a question.

'I owed it to Amber. I knew what you meant to each other. Even if it means losing part of her.'

'Then you truly are a fine man. I do not think I could have done that. I am proud to call you brother, as indeed we surely are now.' They walked along the road in silence for some time, Estrién trying to put his thoughts into the right words. 'Dane, I have no wish to fully take her from you, and I don't think she wishes that either.'

Dane just shook his head, this was ridiculous. 'Whatever I've said on a rational basis, because I care for *her* feelings, it isn't exactly how *I* feel, and frankly I could beat you to a pulp.' But then he gave a brief snort. 'Look, that damned elf over there - the oversexed one - kept me up half the night. I'm, how can I put this? ... *calmer* this morning than I would have been, OK?' He saw by Estrién's smile that he understood. 'But I am also saying, take care what *you* say - I'm on the edge.' He moved away from the elf. 'And don't forget Estrién, I can kill you from a distance, far, far away from the length of your sword. *Just don't push it ...*'

Estrién caught up with him, ignoring the last jibe, he was curious. 'I can't make up my mind. Are you embarrassed or happy about what happened between you and Tamlyn last night?'

He heard Dane sigh and rub his neck. 'Look, I don't know. He's been seducing both Amber and me ever since he joined us. Last night he caught me at a bad time .... thanks to you. I'd say wait until he turns those big elven eyes on you ... and see how you stand up to it.'

Estrién grinned slyly. *'Who's to say he hasn't already?'* was the reply.

Dane stopped walking and stared at him, '*that blessed elf surely gets around*! So what do we do with him?' he laughed.

'Keep him away from Amber - he's after her, and she has enough to cope with the pair of us.'

'If you think I'm luring him to my bed to allow you to sleep with Amber, you've another think coming, mate!'

Estrién merely smiled and quietly spoke. 'I don't mean that Dane, I'm thinking of Amber, not us. It's a lot for her to cope with, she's trying to come to terms with an unusual situation.' He stopped to look him in the eye. 'If you love her as I do - and I'm pretty certain you do - you'll want to protect her - and right now that means protecting her from that oversexed elf! '

'Hell's bells!' came the cry down the road, the elf himself, the oversexed one, was staring at a notice tacked to a roadside tree, 'By the Merrie, guys, come and see this!'

Amber stood rigid, reading the notice, her face pink and her lips set in anger. 'Dane, Estrién, read this!'

Notice to all people of Mordecia
(previously Elvinhaeme)

By the Right ordained by Mordecai Von Adamm,
the following Rules to be Obeyed at all times.

For the preservation and promotion of **Mankind,** *all Elves, mages, dwarves, half-castes and any non-human lesser races as well as human females henceforth forfeit all legal rights and will be dispossessed of all land and property.*

All **must** *leave Adammite lands* **immediately** *or pay the penalty of* **servitude or death.**

Religion:

Sons of the Blazing Sun

There is only one Male Deity, and only male priests of the **Blazing Sun.**

*The cult of Merrie is **banned outright** in all Mordecai lands. All Temples of Merrie to be dissolved, Feast Days disallowed.*

Only Worship Days ordained by the Blazing Sun are permitted.

Those who do not convert to be sent to work camps or purified by flame.

Behaviour:

Marriage to be arranged as per Mordecai code, strictly non-interracial. We, the superior being, expect absolute obedience, seemly behaviour and decorum, and that the female be modestly and plainly attired. Women are not allowed in the streets unless appropriately accompanied.

No public drinking or smoking by either sex, inns and taverns to be licensed under Adammite regulations. Dancing and public displays of affection are banned henceforth.

Penalties for above include birching, imprisonment, stocks, cat or ducking chair.

*All **acts of magic** are hereby banned. Penalty:* **death**.

***Mordecai von Adamm** is **Absolute Ruler** and his is the* **Word.**

Long Live Mordecai von Adamm!

Four hands shot out, Estrién's was the first to grab the notice. His face was ashen as he tore it to shreds and scattered the pieces into the wind.

'By the Lady Merrie, this shall not come to pass!' he swore. The others stood open mouthed, Dane shot his staff in the air and electrum bolts poured out of it. Amber placed her hands on her hips, breathing heavily. Tamlyn just shook his head back and forth.

Amber suddenly went to each male, kissed them all on the mouth, to Tamlyn's surprise.

'That's the first of their so-called rules I shall break,' her voice defiant. 'Here and now I give my word to the Lady Merrie, that if it is within my ability I shall protect all Her priestesses and all who worship at Her shrine.' She blazed with anger, took a deep breath to steady herself. 'I will uphold each and every one of Her Feast Days, and enjoy them to the full. As for all that 'behaviour' crap, I'll bloody well wear any effing clothes I like, smoke and drink when or if I wish - it's my blessed body, not theirs - and if I want to dance and sing in the streets, I certainly shall. And I'll marry the man: elf, human, mage or bloody dwarf I love, and not whom I'm told to marry. *If I choose to marry that is* ...' She looked all males in the eye, challenging them. 'And if any of you think I'm obeying *your lordships* just because you are males, you've another thought coming.'

She took out her two short-swords, waved them menacingly under their faces. 'I intend to use these to personally remove the regenerative organs of every effing Adammite I come across, so let's get effing moving ...'

She turned her back on them and sharply marched off down the road.

Three wide-eyed males watched her go, then looked at each other. There was a collective sigh.

'*Oh, I love her like that*,' said Dane appreciatively, the others nodding in agreement. 'What a woman! Mind you, I wouldn't want to be on the wrong side of her ...' he continued thoughtfully. The two elves looked at each other and shook their heads simultaneously, no, not good.

'*But she is wonderful*,' Dane concluded, both elves now nodding sagely again in unison. There was another collective sigh of appreciation.

The three males quickened their pace to catch up with the furious woman ahead of them.

*

In a dark corner of the world *Someone* moved through the forest. His path disturbed the life forces there, squirrels and rabbits ran, birds fled and even the trees sighed and shifted sideways to allow him quicker passage. He caught the resonance of Amber's anger and it rankled within.

'Don't spoil my work, bitch,' he thought.

Chapter 3

It wasn't a large village, just a dozen pretty houses and an outlying farm or two. There was a village store which also seemed to be the village meeting house, hanging baskets of red and yellow begonias and trailing, lobelia adorned its walls and tubs of Livingstone daisies were all raising their little pink and white heads to the sun. It had a small tea garden outside for passing trade, roses, lavender and goldenrod were out in full force. It was a typical elven village, every house had a garden filled with flowers, fruit trees and well tended vegetable patches.

There was another Adammite notice tacked to the tree in the centre of the village. Two male elves were also hanging from the tree, their dead eyes stared sightlessly.

Two of the comfortable homes were now blackened ruins.

They heard weeping coming from the small store, where they found a dozen elves, all in shock. The Adammites had been through two days previously and had randomly torched the homes *as a warning*, they were told. Equally the two young elves were chosen in the same random fashion. They were all told to leave, get out of what was now *Mordecia*, or suffer the same fate.

'We're a peaceful people, as you well know,' one elf said to them. 'I don't understand why they are doing this, we're no harm to them. We live in harmony with nature, we protect the countryside, we have nothing against any other races, we trade and have a good friendship with Westerling and certainly King

Alexis. I don't understand.' His ashen face stared in horror at the newcomers.

'*I do,*' spoke Amber, 'they are evil, cruel, selfish men who are too weak to take their place in normal society. They are swaggering cowards who come to an undefended village like this, knowing you have no militia or fighters and bully you into submission. They are starting with the quiet places of our world, the peaceful places, because they can take you easily and you won't fight back.' She looked determinedly at them.

'Well, you *are* going to fight back. You are going to get yourselves armed and the next time you are going to fight for your land.' She walked over to the tree, pulled the notice off, tore it in pieces. 'now, get these people down and give them a decent burial or whatever, according to your rites.'

Estrién, anger barely held in check, held his sword high in the air. The emerald shone fiercely and the blade blazed in the afternoon sun, the opalstone gleaming it's pearlescent power.

'I am Knight Commander Estrién of the Temple of Merrie. Amber has spoken on behalf of us all. By the Sword of D'rendiél I swear I shall not rest until until we obliterate this blight from our land.'

The open-mouthed elves of the village wondered who had come among them? Times had changed and they too had to change ... or die.

Dane and Tamlyn were already at the tree taking down the dead bodies, they carried them to the back of the store. They all went back out into the small tea garden, a place used to happy families enjoying a rest in the sun. There they held a meeting about the defensive possibilities of the village, arranging certain elves on watch at all times, a pooling of all weapons, including pitchforks, clubs and even garden spades. They arranged that every person who had any skill with a weapon to give lessons to everyone else. The sole mage in the village was to hone all battle skills he had. These were to be the home guard of their village and this was to happen in every village they went through.

They nominated runners, the young of the village, to get word to the next village in line. They decided that a system of beacons were to be built, high wooden structures that a youngster could climb quickly and light to warn the countryside.

They weren't far from the sea and decided to check the coastal towns along the western coast. Now the four began to realise what they were up against - the closer they got to the coast, the worse became the position of the elves. These raids on the small villages had only been that, outings for the Adammites to get a bit of experience or exercise, or even fun.

During the last years, since they first took the Isle of Glasse, the Adammites had been spreading and growing, honing their skills, acquiring the means by which to invade fully. Young men had arrived from across Mer'edrynn.

Mordecai von Adamm had trained an army.

Hollyporth and the fishing port of Westlea were indeed taken by them. The two large coastal towns, fishing vessels in the harbours, white buildings that shone in the sun, were overrun by them.

The once beautiful cherry trees had been cut down, the city now bare. They learned that the Adammites had marched in, a full army, all clad in their jet black uniform with the red and black sun on their breasts, and had cut down all the young men with their bows and arrows, broadswords and cutlasses before any could retaliate. Too late had the elven guard been called out, the Adammite militia was well trained, well disciplined and well armed. Those that Estrién and the Freowulven had come across the previous week were mostly Blazing Sun cultists, the fanatical devotees of the new Death cult, they had swords and training, but they were not the militia.

The Adammites took the small Guard buildings for their own and the town halls as their headquarters. They forced people to work for them, or leave, *or* ... there were pyres still burning to show what *'or'* meant. Many elves ran, trying to find safety in the smaller inland villages. The Temple of Merrie in both towns was burnt to the ground. There were stories of mass rape of the priestesses.

Amber and her three fighters skirted the ports, learned more from the refugees; each seemed to have a worse story than the last.

And as they went from village to village, they found the same had happened as the first, random elves slaughtered, random homes burnt to the ground. Estrién was in despair, they needed to raise an army from a group of peaceful beings who only wished to dance under the elm tree on a summer evening, or write poetry and song. They were farmers, gardeners, woodcrafters. The only time they quarrelled was when they disagreed with the prize-giving at the harvest vegetable show. They had neither the desire nor the inclination to fight.

As Estrién said, 'we have our work cut out.'

Dane sought out mages everywhere they went. There were few, and none of the elven mages had used their powers for fighting, content to use healing powers or sage craft. He held demonstrations and organised practices for them, he wanted them to work in tandem with the militia or home guard.

And the Adammite militia must have heard of them, because one evening as they moved towards yet another village near the coast, they were ambushed.

The Adammites laughed, the were looking forward to the slaughter of this unlikely-looking bunch. None could stop their might ...

But the four were ready now, were on alert at all times in case of such an eventuality. As a dozen Adammite fighters charged at them, Dane immediately put up his Circle of Protection, giving the others the few seconds required to draw weapons. He could hold it for a few moments only, but it sufficed. They stood *en quattro*, to give an Elvhen phrase, backs to each other in a circle and faced the onslaught. Amber and Tamlyn threw knives simultaneously taking out two, then drew short-swords and Tamlyn's sabre. Estrién was already circling his shining sword in the lethal figure of eight, or perhaps more correctly, an infinite figure of death, and Dane changed to fire magic with his oaken staff.

The Adammites were now experienced fighters, their swords flashed and came down on the four, trying to knock White Star out of Estrién's hand. But it was impossible, the sword belonged to him, would not easily be dislodged, it only took them closer to his blade.

Estrién was heard to shout wildly as he jumped in to the oncoming group of Adammite fighters. White Star flashed with horror as he decapitated the nearest two. *'Any more?'* he shouted, 'come on, come closer*, feel my blade ... it hungers ...'*

As Dane threw electrum magic at a soldier, Amber dashed in and finished him off, shimmying quickly sideways as he called to *watch out*, a swordsman was way too close to her. Tamlyn saw the danger and his sabre slashed mercilessly at the fighter, protecting her. Dane was back to fire magic now, it seemed fitting to him to set these people to the flame they swore by. He shouted and swore at them, his oaken staff concentrating the hatred that he felt for these people. *'and that's for my mother, you bastard,'* he called, as he rained down flames on another Adammite. The oaken staff felt marvellous in his hand, part of him, a third arm.

Two of the Adammite militia managed to run off, they knew they were beaten. Dane sent amberic magic after them. Amber and Tamlyn took out their bows, shot arrows into them. They heard cries, but saw no more as the pair ran into the cover of trees.

'Do we go after them, or what?' Amber asked. The others shook their heads.

'No point,' Tamlyn told her, 'let them run back and tell the others. We'll grow with their telling, they'll be too ashamed to admit twelve of them were beaten by four, so by the time they reach their headquarters, we'll all be giants with magic swords and a mighty mage who used Devil's magic.'

They looted the bodies for cash or valuables, a few swords - nothing was ever wasted. They were on a long and lonely path together, with little money. As they piled the bodies together, Dane set the lot on fire. 'A fitting end,' he said. 'Go to your Maker in the flames you wish on others.'

They finally arrived at the fair city of Belcast'el, the capital of Elvinhaeme. The city guard stood proudly upright as they entered the city walls. But the guards eyed them warily, although it was clear they could not be the enemy, and they did not look like refugees.

Whitewashed cottages gave way to honey coloured stone buildings and eventually the white walls of the city loomed. White pennants bearing the city symbol of a cherry tree in full bloom flew proudly. Like the two coastal towns, it was a vibrant city, lively market stalls lined the tree filled streets, blossom everywhere in tubs and planters. There were white-washed houses and buildings of white sparkling stone. In the sunlight, the city shone. Everything looked blessedly normal.

The elves loved marble statues and fountains, these filled the large open squares of the city. It was peaceful to sit on wooden or marble benches, smell the flowers and watch the spray of the fountains. The squares would get lively as elven players, troubadours or minstrels came to sing, or a group of acrobats tumbled, or perhaps a merry group of maidens dancing in a circle to a traditional elven song. Yet the squares were quiet, people milling in groups wondering what would come next?

It too had its own great library and university. The elves mostly studied medicine or land-husbandry, for they were great farmers and healers. Literature and music too were well-loved areas of study, elves and humans coming from across Mer'edrynn to learn their skill. The students roamed the squares and the parks, studying in the sunshine, carousing in the inns and alehouses of an evening, enjoying their youth. The universities were still full, parents had written to offspring to stay in the safety of the city. Their youthful callow faces were lined with worry.

These great cities of Mer'edrynn had thrived in the peace years, had traded with each other, had sent their young to study and mingle and wed, all the kingdoms bound by their unified reverence of the Lady Merrie and the great Circle of Life.

But the militia had grown weak and would now pay the price for that weakness. Only in the north, along the borders of

Caladin, Picantés and Vikénar, had they kept up the necessary armies. The south hadn't needed it. Further along the coast to the east, Fenland, they had maintained a good army, they were open to raiders from strange lands. And the south kept a coastguard against the impudent fishing vessels of Sevillon, or smugglers from Chev'alierre. But none had a navy which could repel the large fighting ships of the Adammites.

Worse, in the north, King Kyneweth of Draecastle had allied with Mordecai von Adamm, a king who had a large army of men.

Amber wondered what kind of man, a king in his own right, would ally with these people?

Obviously an ambitious one, one who had designs on the whole of Mer'edrynn.

Here in Belcast'el, refugees were beginning to pour in from throughout the Dûcdom. Some were coming to find relatives in the city, stay with them, some found hostelries, some were on the streets, cast out and penniless. Some were given room in the temples and public halls, frightened elves with shocked eyes, hopeless eyes, eyes that wondered what was happening to their gentle world? The priestesses offered warmth and soothing balms, elves would not deny their own. But food was essential, trade routes had to be kept open.

Estrién told the group that his home village was near here, that he used to come here as a boy with his father, although he did not remember it all that well. But he remembered the wide, white streets lined with cherry blossom, and the wonderful smell of a big autumn fair once, ripe peaches and plums, the taste of a toffee apple his father bought him, and the sweet tangy sarsaparilla, drunk at a market stall on that warm Harvesthaeme day.

Briefly they went to the market, Dane bartered for a good price for the swords, got a reasonable amount. They searched for lodgings, found a small inn tucked behind one of the squares, an old black and white timbered building, ivy growing profusely over the walls. Estrién asked for two rooms, paying with some of the gold he had been given by the Freowulven leader. Ill-gotten gold possibly, but none here would know that.

It was dark and cool inside, a rich smell of hops over everything. Their rooms were fresh though and the beds looked soft and inviting with multicoloured patchwork quilts and white linen pillowcases, pretty curtains at tiny windows that almost reached the floor. Amber and Estrién paired off in one, Tamlyn and Dane in the other. This was how it was, for now.

All wanted, nay needed, hot baths, having slept in the open for most of the nights previously. Tamlyn's tent and the oiled sheet had been put to good use, the four creating a makeshift home under canvas. They had piled in together, laughing at the cramped space, joking with each other. Amber lay somehow in the middle of them all, protected by them. They felt if anything happened in the night, if they were attacked, Amber should be protected, kept safe. It was a male thing, a male need to fulfil their duty. However, none imposed upon her, feeling the situation wrong and Amber herself was aware of this. They gave her the courtesy she desired.

Dane felt better in clean gear, wandered through to Amber's room, she was drying her hair with a large towel. He went over and kissed her, she smelled sweet from the bath. Estrién was outside in one of the public bathrooms, still bathing.

'Thought I'd catch you alone. We've never had a chance to talk, love, we've been so busy with these bastards the last couple of weeks.' He looked into her eyes. 'Amber, we do need to talk, I'm not giving you up as easily as that.'

She looked up at him, at this kind man, this mage, fair in face and character. She put up her hand to his cheek, 'Who says I want to give *you* up? I can't help what's happened between myself and Estrién, but I haven't stopped loving you. I told you, Dane, you are one of the loveliest men I have ever known.'

Estrién stepped through the door, wrapped in a towel, he looked fresh and clean . 'Wondered when you'd come to ask her ...' he stated.

'What do you mean?'

'You want Amber, of course you do. So do I. The thing is, I know for a fact that Amber doesn't wish to break your heart, or mine.' He looked across at her, she smiled back, slightly embarrassed, they'd talked long and deep about this. He stared Dane in the eye, 'look, let's go down and enjoy a decent meal for once, there's a pleasant beer-garden at the back. Let's go and see what the night brings hey? In case you hadn't noticed, there are four of us in this weird relationship of ours, don't forget Tamlyn.'

Dane had to agree, their group had become pretty tightly knit the last weeks. 'Yes, there *are* four of us, and if the Adammites catch us, they'll put us on four adjacent pyres and chant happily as we blaze. We're everything they hate.'

'Yes, aren't we?' replied Amber, unambiguous delight spreading across her face. 'For that reason alone we four need to stick together.'

There was a polite knock on the door and Tamlyn himself, the fourth one, appeared. He had washed and dressed, was now wearing fresh leggings bought that afternoon, his boots and a big white 'poet' shirt, over which was a soft doeskin jerkin. His hair was unbraided, it fell about his face and shoulders. He looked like a young troubadour.

'Am I interrupting anything?' throwing himself on Amber's bed, 'Aaah, this is comfortable,' lying back with his hands behind his head.

Dane repeated the fact they were probably the ultimate symbol of Merrie against the Adammites.

'Ah, so true. Four feisty, feckless, careless, rather beautiful young warriors, who flirt mercilessly with each other and live in each other's pockets. We drink too much, smoke some dreadful leafroll, we love dancing, singing and sex. ... *Aah, we are so bad* ...' Tamlyn grinned wickedly at all of them.

They burst into laughter, Tamlyn jumped up off the bed, and grabbed Amber's hand. 'and you fair maid are the best of us all.' He bent to kiss it. Amber shook her head at his antics.

'You're incorrigible,' she stated.

Dane and Tamlyn went down to secure a table outside and get drinks ready for them. Amber and Estrién carried on dressing. He suddenly spoke to her.

'I love you with all my heart, Amber, you know that. I know you love Dane, I'm fond of him too ... not in *that* way,' he hastily added, 'elves are one thing, men are another, not my scene.' He bent over to kiss her. 'I know you want us both, I've never denied that. I watched you with him, before, well, before *us*. I never asked to take you from him - as long as I know I have your love, Amber?'

She kissed his lips, her hands around his head, stroking his elven ears. They weren't large, they were neat and pointed, without lobes, as were Tamlyn's. She loved nibbling them. *'You know you have.* I'm beginning to learn that there is more to love than I thought,' she considered, kissing him fully ....

They arrived somewhat later for dinner than they had planned.

The others were basking in the setting evening sun in the garden of the inn. The stone walls of the garden emitted a sun-soaked warmth, and the wooden tables and benches too were filled with the warmth of the day. There was a heady smell of night scented stock in the air, and young birds just born that spring were doing their crazy dance around the garden from tree to tree, before being called to their nest.

The table already had two empty pewter tankards on it, two more were half empty. They'd been drinking the local cider. 'Hey, you took your time,' sniggered Tamlyn, 'Good way to start an evening!'

Amber reddened slightly, he was always embarrassing her. She'd have to get used to it. More cider was brought, all were thirsty from their hike that day. She wore the pale turquoise gown she had bought back in Orlandium and the beads Tamlyn had given her. Her freshly clean hair flowed over the dress, contrasting richly, shining in the evening light.

All three men looked approvingly at her.

'You look lovely, Amber,' Dane told her. She smiled and acknowledged him, kissed him on the cheek, he took her hand in his, kissed the back of it gently. The three males watched her as she sat down. She suggested getting food. They ordered venison pasties and a selection of meats of the day, bread and apples arrived too. More cider was brought in a huge jug. Everyone tucked in.

Amber sat taking stock, while the men of the party were absorbed in the important process of eating. So much had happened in the last two months. She had lived a peculiar life, she considered, nothing normal about it in any way, some of it tragic. Now she had taken up with three men - well - two elves and a mage of odd and possibly unique parentage. She herself was the product of two mages.

A strange lot, a motley crew. And pretty obvious that all three wanted her. It was quite a heady thought, although she had no idea what to do about it. Two were more than enough. But the companionship was fun.

'It will sort itself out,' she thought to herself. 'Things always do.'

She popped a piece of apple into her mouth then raised her head to the setting sun, it was going rapidly, leaving a pale indigo and orange light in the sky, an idyllic late summer evening. The air smelled sweet and warm as only it can in summer. There was a group of students, humans and elves, dressed in gay tunics, sitting at one of the tables, laughing and enjoying themselves, a little raucous. They looked happy and carefree. Like many, they were staying over the summer, too dangerous to travel.

Similarly another group of young folk, a mixed bunch of elven men and women sat chatting over a large flagon of wine, they looked more earnest, it was clear they were discussing the invasion.

She could hear laughter in the city, someone playing a flute and singing close by. One of the young birds, a small sparrow, set down on the table, picking up a few crumbs. It all looked so normal.

She thought of the Adammites and how they wanted to destroy this. She wanted to weep at the sheer inhuman cruelty of their desire. She quietly offered up a small prayer to the Lady Merrie, to help her in the fight against those who would destroy this fair land.

Tamlyn went off to get his lute, he thought he'd play awhile in the garden. Dane started doing odd things with tankards, lifting the empty ones in the air using magic, and creating a tall tower of tankards. Some of the students saw him, began clapping. He bowed, acknowledging them. Tamlyn returned with his lute, began playing. It was a lovely old elven song, and Estrién joined in with his rich voice. Some students also joined in.

Q'ell arêth illumini,
Q'ell daêth illucidae,
Q'ell ar'amé, dulci'aré,
Est ben Elvién

En decorum sanguinae,
En etheran draconae,
En el'andis, triumvantis
Est ben Elvién.

Lauralae unt salixae,
Bel rosea, menaedai,
En foraes de paradais
Est ben Elvién.

Estrién explained to her that it was a song about the beauty of being elven, of their race, of their world. He hoped she had enjoyed it. Tamlyn moved on to another song, watching her eyes. Dane looked softly at her and smiled, wriggling his fingers, throwing gentle magic like a summer breeze into her face.

It dawned on Amber that each male was performing for her, showing off. All watched her, waiting for her reaction to them. She beamed at all of them, her smile lighting up the evening.

Some of the young female elves now came and sat on the grass by Tamlyn. His eyes shone as he played, enjoying the adulation in their eyes. They carried on laughing and singing elven love songs.

Amber noticed a man sitting by the wall, alone, watching them. He looked with displeasure upon their gaiety, he frowned. A dull grey cloak lay at his side, as if he had just travelled here. He was human, not elf, dark haired and dark-browed, the remains of a sparse meal of bread and cheese and one meagre tankard in front of him. He seemed to study Amber, his eyes disapproving and probing, making her feel uncomfortable. He frowned at her.

Amber wasn't the only one to notice. Estrién stood and walked over to him.

'Do you have something against my lady?'

The man looked startled, 'I was just wondering what a human female is doing with two elves and a mage? It is a little unusual.' His voice was cultured, but stern.

'I do not believe it is any of your business, Sir, and I would appreciate if you kept such dark looks to yourself.'

The man eyed Estrién haughtily, 'I'll look as I please, elf, thou has naught to say to me.' A fine sabre was tucked into a scabbard on his belt. Estrién's sword lay upstairs in their room.

Dane stood up now, light beginning to spit and crackle from the end of mage fingers, fizzling ground-wards.

Amber held him back, then moved over quickly to Estrién. 'Dear, I'm fine, please don't start anything on such a lovely evening. We've had enough troubles the last few weeks, leave it be.'

'He knows not whom he crosses, Amber.' She dragged him away. The man finished his ale and left. But he took one last look at Amber as if to fix her face in his memory. She shivered.

It left her uncomfortable for the evening.

Dane covered her hand with his. 'Cheer up, love, he's gone. If you're unhappy about him, I can go and throw a bit of electrum at him, make him think twice about scowling at you ...'

She shook her head, many people had scowled at her over the years, one more meant little. But his eyes ... they were chilling. She took a long draught of the cider. 'I think I'll go upstairs to bed, if you don't mind, guys, it's been a long day.'

Three pairs of disappointed eyes followed her as she left. Tamlyn and Dane disappeared with the students for the night. Estrién joined her later, but she was fast asleep. He undressed and curled up next to her, hoping she would wake, he even kissed her, murmured in her ear, but either she was fast asleep, or ignoring him. He contented himself with wrapping his arms around her body, tucked spoon-like behind her, soon fell asleep holding her close to his heart.

*

They made their way the following morning to the Dûcal Hall, the residence of the Dûc de Luxonne, the elven leader of Elvinhaeme. It was of course, like the rest of Belcast'el, a beautiful white building, huge statues of elven archers gracing it's marble entrance, a large fountain playing in the courtyard. It was surrounded on all sides by perfectly kept gardens, flowers in overabundance, baskets and urns and beautiful vases, sweet smelling and luxuriant in their summer growth. Poplar trees stood to attention along the pathways to the palace itself, two olive trees grew before the main door, white painted, adorned with nymphs and grapevines. The palace was elegance personified.

On each side of the door stood equally elegant guards in pale silver chain-mail, over which lay a white surcoat with a cherry tree emblem embroidered on the left side, over their hearts. Their boots and gauntlets were also shining silver. Each carried a longsword and a shield bearing a star shining over a symbolised cherry tree.

One or two elven nobles traversed the courtyard.

Tamlyn spoke to one, 'I am Knight Captain Tamlyn Taenghelin, of the Court of Grande Dûchesse Elanr'iel in Floriénne. I bring with me Knight Commander Estrién of the Temple of Lady Merrie, we seek entrance and an audience with the Dûc de Luxonne.'

The noble merely laughed, 'so does everyone in Elvinhaeme at the moment, join the queues.'

Estrién stepped in, quietly saying, 'I think we have more to say to him than most as we come to offer ourselves in the war against the Adammites. I also carry the Sword of D'rendiél.' He uncovered the end of the scabbard on his back, allowing the emerald to shine. 'We are the group who has been travelling Elvinhaeme in the last weeks, mobilising and preparing the villages, which is more than he has done.'

The noble studied him for a few moments, then nodded, 'come with me, we have need of people like you.'

They followed him through the great engraved door to a cool white Grand Hall, completely circular, more fountains inset in small pools where golden fish swam and statues of gentle nymphs and virile satyrs hugged marble niches around the walls. Ferns and ivies trailed from urns. White candles in silver sconces adorned the marble walls and tall silver candelabra stood on the floor. A spectacular marble and glass dome was set in the ceiling, allowing in the sunlight. It was all, like it's name, quite grand.

On a dais ahead of them, sitting equally grandly upon his white marble throne, sat the Dûc de Luxonne. A golden circlet adorned his head, a white cloak embroidered with gold was tucked snugly around him. With all the marble in the room, it was a little chilly and the square fire pit near the throne was lit today.

The nobleman, Lord Agliétte, spoke quietly to the Dûc, who beckoned them over.

All bowed, then Estrién spoke, 'Your Grace, I am *Nim'randuel Soleus D'rendiél Gilsylien Estaran'elvian*, or if it please you, Knight Commander Estrién of the Temple of the Lady Merrie. My companions are the lady Amber Sageborn of Segantium, Knight Captain Tamlyn Taenghelin, of the Court of Grande Dûchesse Elanr'iel in Floriénne, and the mage Dane Andarsson, once of the Isle of Glasse.

We hope to offer aid in your war against the Adammites and their intrusion into Elvinhaeme, the invasion and consequent violation of our fair land.' He spoke as befitting the Court. He had not been brought up at Court as Tamlyn had, nevertheless he was aware of protocol.

The Dûc de Luxonne seemed startled as he rose from the elegant throne. He had stopped listening after Estrién had told him his name. 'What exactly do you mean by calling yourself *the King of the Elves*, no one bears that title.' He spoke softly, but his voice was commanding.

'Exactly as I say,' commented Estrién, 'My uncle gave me my full title on his deathbed, I see no reason to contradict him. But I have not come to claim any throne, merely to offer my help to your own.' He looked down at the silver slippers on the Dûc's feet. They seemed foppish and inappropriate considering that Belcast'el could be attacked at any moment. 'You do realise the Adammites are on the march, they could decide to take Belcast'el at any time? The rest of the country is in uproar, people are being murdered, homes are being burnt, temples desecrated. Your Grace, we need to raise an army.'

The Dûc sat back down and took a drink from the large silver goblet at his right hand. 'Hmm, so I am told. But they will not enter here, the city guard will protect the entrances.'

Dane spoke up, 'your Grace, we cannot sit in the city and wait for Elvinhaeme to fall, nor can we win a war by merely defending the capital city. We need to *wage* war on these people, eliminate them from this land.' He spoke urgently, the last two weeks had shown the extent of the invasion here.

The Dûc dismissed him with one hand. 'and how do I raise an army out of elves who have never borne arms? How do I tell the peace loving people here, that they must fight and kill?'

Amber now interjected with 'if you do not raise an army you will have no country left. They intend to kill all elves. Here ...' she rummaged in her bag, took out one of the notices left around the country by the Adammites, 'have you read this? It's what Mordecai von Adamm intends to do to us all. He has already started in the west and has taken Hollyporth and Westlea. He had even renamed Elvinhaeme, as if it no longer exists. Don't you care?' She handed him the notice. He studied it for a short time, handed it back.

'And just what can I do about it?' he retorted. 'Yes, he can probably walk in here any time he wants and he knows it. We have no real army to fight him with.'

Estrién closed his eyes for a moment, trying to steady himself. To give in, without even the semblance of a fight? This elf had lived in decadent luxury for too long. Slowly he took out White Star, brandished it in the air, it blazed in that white room with an incandescent light, casting an eerie sheen over everything. His face glowed under its dazzling light, temporarily blinding all in the room, as if he held a sun in his hand.

Yes, it was a dramatic gesture, but it wasn't merely a sword, it was a symbol.

'I carry the Sword of D'rendiél, NimEstrién, White Star and I wield it in honour of the Elven race and all races who fight this Bringer of Death. I have with me three fine warriors, one of whom is a mage. We intend to fight these invaders, even though we are but four. We need elves to rise with us. Now are you with me in this fight or do we go elsewhere and leave you to your fate?'

The Dûc sat back on his throne, perusing the marble floor for some time before he answered. 'I will do what I can. I promise nothing. We have few fighters here.' He took another large drink from the goblet. 'For over a hundred years we have not fought, we have had no need, only a few guards along the coast. We have kept only a small trained army, mostly ceremonial. We are weak and this von Adamm knows it, it is why he has chosen here to invade first on the mainland. Do you think I am unaware of our shortcomings? But it is all I can do to keep this city. If people wish to come here and we can keep trade routes open, I can help the refugees, even if we become chock full. But as to retaliation? ... *Impossible.*

Sir Estrién, come back in a year and a day's time and I may have a trained force for you. Alas, I fear we do not have a year and a day, and anything less would mean certain disaster. I repeat, all I can do is try to protect this city, no more.'

They were dismissed from his presence.

Once outside Amber fumed once more. 'He's too bloody lazy to even try. What are we supposed to do now? We can't fight this bastard by ourselves.'

Lord Agliétte, the nobleman who had gained them entrance, had followed them. 'Sirs, we have some knights, although not many. I can perhaps find fifty well trained knights for you, plus their esquires. I would suggest you try to raise what you can as an army, allow what we have to join yours.'

'And I suggest you use those knights to train others,' Estrién replied. 'We need archers and swordsmen in their hundreds, possibly thousands. You offer me fifty knights. And am I to lead this fight? Should it not be led by your own Dûc?'

Lord Agliétte shook his head sadly. 'I fear the Dûc de Luxonne is no warrior, nor is he any kind of strategist. The Court has wallowed in wine-filled ease and luxury for most of his life. He has sadly no idea of leadership. He knows this and it depresses him, he is not actually a bad man, merely a weak one - which depresses him further.' He looked to Estrién as if he would find an answer.

'Well, I need someone capable of raising and *leading* an army, someone experienced in the art of war. That cannot be me, neither was I brought up to war. This has come upon me and my friends as it comes to you.' Estrién turned to the group, 'come, we need to return to Orlandium, see if King Alexis has the means - or the desire - to help Elvinhaeme, for surely its own leader cares nought.'

He walked out of the palace disgusted.

But the Dûc de Luxonne sat on his throne in the marble hall of the palace after he had gone, and looked into his own heart. With intense sorrow and shame, he put his head in his hands, knowing he was incapable of saving his people, his land, from the Adammites.

Chapter 4

Another elf had listened as Estrién spoke in the Great Hall of the palace. He joined the group as they left, catching Estrién's arm. 'Excuse me, Sir, I couldn't help overhearing. I was in the Hall with you, I too requested an audience with the Dûc, but I see now it would have been useless.' He was a smallish elf, simply clothed in a green tunic, leggings and soft ankle boots. He carried a large bow over his shoulder. 'I cannot offer an army, but we may be able to help with archers.' He held out his hand to Estrién, 'I am Rowan Firethorne, and I hail from Oakleigh Forest. You probably know of it,' speaking to Estrién.

Estrién nodded, 'My father told me of the great woods and the woodelves who live there. I have never been there. You are close to Mab's Bay are you not?' They shook hands, the elf shook each hand in turn.

Tamlyn spoke, 'I know of you also, you are spoken of at the Court of Floriénne. You are fine craftsmen .'

The elf nodded, 'Good bows we make, fine straight arrows, also we craft wood in all its forms. Like you, we are extremely worried about this interloper in our world. We have archers, but few swordsmen, we need both. I was sent to ask for help, if the Dûc could spare us some knights. Obviously he cannot and I waste my time. But you intrigued me, Sir Estrién. That sword you wield is of legend. We need you, Elvinhaeme needs you. Probably by the time this Mordecai von Adamm is finished, all of Mer'edrynn will need you.

Look, will you return with me to Oakleigh, at least come and see us? We may be able to help you.' He watched them all hopefully.

Estrién quickly made up his mind. 'Yes, of course we will come. What say you, my friends?' They all nodded, it was the first positive news they'd had.

They trooped back to the inn, collected their packs and equipment and followed the elf out of the city.

They followed the highway leading to Westerling for some time before turning off the road and moving eastwards. It would, it seemed take another two days to get to the forest, but he had a friend en route who would put them up overnight, a woodcutter.

After a few miles along the road, Estrién turned to them. 'My home village is here, we could take a short detour. It would warm my heart to see the old place again.' But he could see as they approached that the 'old place' had been treated as had other villages, with several houses burned to a shell, including his parents' once pleasant home.

He stood silently for some moments in front of the remains, before speaking. 'I haven't lived here for, hmm, fifteen years, and I do not know who dwelled here afterwards. But it still pains me to see it so, and to consider the poor people who once lived here.'

It looked like it had been quite a large house. Amber clasped his arm, kissed him. 'I'm sorry, my love, this must be awful for you. At least your parents died naturally, not at the hand of these bastards. Tell me, had the house been in your family some time?'

'It belonged to several generations of my family until my parents died. Then it was sold and I do believe I was paid some money, but it went to my uncle for my keep. Not that he ever kept me short or anything, he was a generous man, and I, of course, his sole heir. If I ever get back to *Ravenscroft* in the Foraes Dair, I have a good home left to me.'

'Tell me about it,' asked Amber, she was curious, but she also wanted to turn his mind to happier times.

'It lies just east of the Bollands in an outcrop of Shirewood, is pleasantly sheltered from both east and west winds, and is a good sturdy stone house, in its own grounds. The town of

Thornsgate is just a few miles south west. The forest around is filled with game and it is fairly peaceful there, at least there are no Bregantine or Alderfolk. There are quite a few elven folk live close by, a small village, it is comfortable enough.'

'I'd like to see it some time,' she replied.

He stood by the blackened ruins of his childhood home, looked at Amber, took her hand. 'Why, Amber, I was hoping that at some point in the future, you would share it with me.'

There was a moment's stunned silence as everyone around took in what he was saying.

'Estrién?' Amber was startled. *'I ... well, I ...* ' she stopped, kissed him on the cheek instead. 'That's a lovely thought, Estrién.' There was no point in humming and aahing, life was too short, particularly in the shadow of a looming war. 'I'd certainly love to come to your home, it would be pleasant to know that, if this war is ever over, there is indeed a home to go to. I haven't had a real home since I was sixteen. But I have to ask, what about Dane, or Tamlyn?'

Estrién burst out laughing. 'You look after us all, don't you, my love?' He saw Amber blushing. 'Well, there's plenty of room there, and we could always build on - what say you guys?' It didn't seem the worst of ideas. Weirdly, it suddenly seemed fitting.

Dane and Tamlyn breathed a little easier. Dane particularly wasn't happy with the thought of her being taken away. 'We haven't known each other long, but we seem to be a team. I have no home to go to in any case, thanks to the Adammites. I think it would be fun,' he replied.

'Isn't it cold in the north?' asked Tamlyn. *It all depended on where you were, how sheltered the valley and so on,* Amber and Estrién explained. 'Then it sounds good to me.'

There were handshakes, kisses and hugs all round. Something to look forward to, *if ... if they all came out of this ...* .

'We're probably going to be wandering the country for months, but the next time we go up that way, we'll visit, I'll show you, OK?' There was a general sound of approval, it seemed good.

The elf from Oakleigh watched on, sussing out the relationships. 'Have you all just decided to live together?' They all nodded. 'That's good, *so very elvish*,' he stated. 'now, let's get moving. Once we reach Oakleigh I'll make sure you have some group quarters in that case. I was just wondering what the arrangements were going to be, you seem a very tight bunch.' He smiled at them all. They followed as he marched off.

It was a quiet crew that followed him, each absorbed in his own thoughts. Amber walked between Dane and Estrién, both had taken her hand. Dane occasionally squeezed hers, trying, without words, to express his pleasure at her. His brilliant blue eyes sparkled into hers every so often. Estrién too, tucked her hand in his, a contented smile on his face. Tamlyn left them and walked on ahead, talking to Rowan Firethorne.

After some miles they reached a turning and wandered into the forest. A couple of miles later he turned off again. 'My friend lives this way, he'll give us lodgings for the night. We could just make it to Oakleigh tonight, but it would be better to arrive during the day, besides, I haven't seen him for some time.'

The cottage was small and neat, a privet hedge surrounding the front garden, trimmed into a pleasing wavy shape, with blooming lavender shrubs growing along the garden path. Sweet-smelling honeysuckle covered a wooden porch, by the side of which sat a large pale blue rocking chair upon which sat an embroidered cushion. The front door too was painted pale blue, and blue and white check curtains were tied back at the small windows. A beautifully carved wooden fawn sat under a tree and a notice on the door in poker work said 'Home, sweet Home.'

Amber and the others looked at each other, some sweet but doddering old guy?

Rowan's friend turned out to be a huge, ancient satyr called Woodmoss. He had long elven ears, but there his resemblance to any elf stopped. He looked like a man mountain. He was colossal, with massive hands and a large head, which ended in a demi-pointed chin. His black hair was long and wild, he had an enormous straggly beard flowing over the hairiest chest Amber had ever seen. He wore leathern hose, and thick brown boots - whether he had feet or cloven hooves, no one knew. Equally his arms and hands were covered in thick black hair, and he was currently using them to drag a large tree trunk back to his cottage.

He greeted Rowan with delight. 'Ah, my old friend come to see me and you have brought friends with you. This is good, I have had little company recently. Come, come, take wine with me.' His voice was deep and jovial, and he ushered them all into his small cottage. 'you are on your way to Oakleigh then?' Rowan nodded, 'Ah, that is good, perhaps you could take this bag of platters for me.' Rowan opened the bag, took out exquisitely carved wooden plates, adorned with tiny flowers, fruits and leaves. Some had intricate abstract curving designs.

Amber thought they were beautiful, complimented him. He seemed pleased. He brought out a large flagon of wine, obviously one of his own, again, beautifully designed with delicate swirls. They all wondered how his massive hands could carve such delicate beauty? The table too held carved wooden candlesticks, he was a master of his work.

'I'm not much of a mixer,' he explained, 'I'm a big ugly satyr, I don't go well in polite elven society. The ladies and the children, you know - they find me a little frightening. But I like to spend my time in contemplation, and carving helps me. I also get paid for it, which is good.'

He was also a good host, the flagon was kept filled with wine, the table was quickly laid with bread, cheeses and fruits and later he took out his panpipes to regale them. Tamlyn joined in with his lute, the pair making sweet music into the night. Amber danced with Estrién and Dane to the merry music.

He gave them his bedroom to sleep in, he would sleep outside in the rocking chair, it was a fine evening. Amber and Estrién shared the bed, Dane and Tamlyn found cushions for the floor. They all slept well.

Before they left, they warned him of the Adammites, he knew of rumours. 'if they come here I will leave, join the elves in Oakleigh, they may need me. The house means little, but the forest and its people must be protected. I will help, you have my word.'

All thanked him and Woodmoss bristled with pleasure when Amber gave him a big hug and a kiss as they left, thanking him again for his hospitality. 'Come again, whenever, all friends of Rowan are friends of mine,' he replied.

Rowan led them through the woods towards his home. All manner of creatures began to appear. First it was simply the woodland animals, red squirrels, badgers, an occasional deer or fawn. A fox sniffed at them, waved away by Estrién. But as they neared the centre, the folk of the woods also began to show themselves.

The singing attracted them first, high in the trees, sprites and wood nymphs watching them as they neared. Dane looked up in wonder as he realised some of the trees held dryads. He called to them, greeting them with song as his mother had done. Soon they came down to meet him, seeing the half-dryad in him. The group were all greeted with pleasure as friends of his, offered sweet wine and honey cakes. They stayed for a short while, listening to the melodic speech and singing of the dryads.

Dane discovered that one or two were unwell, there was a sickening in the trees, the 'bad black-cloaked men' were bringing it, they'd passed through the forest, evil, shouting, swearing, relieving themselves against the trees. It was a human disease, they said, and were unable to cure it. The woodland folk had hidden high in the trees when they came through, but their filth was left behind.

Dane offered some of his magic, it was an infection caused by the diseased tree bark. He healed some of the dryads, then took his staff to the trees, held it to many of them, listened and felt the sap. He sent healing flames inside, just enough to burn the disease away, his oaken staff understanding the heart of the tree. It pleased the dryads and the wood nymphs, they sang and danced with pleasure.

He told them of his mother and how the Adammites had ended her life; they wept with him. They tried to cleanse him of pain, but a pain as deep as that does not easily go.

Two of the dryads decided to join them to the main hub of the forest, the central grove. Dane's face was filled with delight as they walked on either side of him. For a short time, he felt at peace. The forest was managed well, as was the one near his home, where his mother had taken him as a child and as a young man. Well beaten paths ran through, all trees were carefully tended, shrubs and flowers grew profusely. They pointed out the sickening ones as they walked. He spent time burning away the sickness. His staff of oak felt the pain of the tree, it also knew how to heal, guided by Dane. His staff was so old, it was older than the forest, it had control over all. A shudder of delight ran through the forest.

They saw small wooden houses on wheels dotted here and there, elaborately carved, elf families sitting outside enjoying the summer air. Eventually as summer turned to winter they would all gather together deep in the forest, huddled under great canvases, lashed together like one large umbrella. There they would stay until spring, only venturing out on bright days to go gathering or hunting, or perhaps sending their wares into towns and villages in exchange for food.

When they reached the central hub of the forest, the Great Grove, dotted with huge carven images of ancient gods and goddesses or woodland animals, the two dryads ran to the Elf Father to tell him of Dane's magic. He listened and came to Dane with open arms. An old elf, grey haired, almost two centuries old, bent a little, but with sharp eyes that knew and saw a person. He thanked him profusely. It was human disease that had brought this, it needed a human mage to heal it. It also needed the peculiar magic of a half dryad as Dane, to understand the trees fully.

The Elf Father wished to know the real reason they had come? Rowan Firethorne explained to him and the gathering group, of his unsuccessful mission to Belcast'el, and how he had met the four. He introduced them fully, Estrién's blade was examined with care and reverence. They all looked at Estrién in a new light.

They were led to a large carved table, with perhaps twenty seats around it. Great platters of food were brought, and wooden flagons of sweet wines. Amber wondered if Woodmoss the Satyr had carved them, but they looked slightly different. They spoke long about these interlopers who would end their world, spoke of their need to help, and to gain help.

As the night came on, tall elaborate candlesticks were placed, bearing beeswax candles, the elves took out their pipes and some rolled the leafroll beloved by Dane and Tamlyn.

Estrién now spoke, he had an idea. He understood how precious was the forest, he would not take from their warriors, but add to it. 'I am more than happy to offer you our help, Oakleigh is sacred, it must be preserved, it cannot be captured by these people. At the moment we cannot stay with you because we have to get to Orlandium and see if King Alexis will help raise an army. You have archers, but no swordsmen. I have a proposal you may not like, but these people are indeed good swordsmen, I can vouch for that. They are also used to living in a forest and will treat yours with respect.'

The shrewd old Elf Father listened, wondering what was coming? 'Tell us, let us prepare. We have little choice against these beings. They are not fully here yet, although some came, leaving their filth and disease in our trees. They did not attack us, there were too few of them, but next time, who knows? But we have heard of what has happened in the west. If there is help, we need to take it and be thankful.' He watched Estrién carefully.

'I talk of the Freowulven, the outlaws, who live northwards at the bottom of the Whitecap mountains.' Estrién watched as they gasped. These were elven outlaws, had committed unpardonable crimes against their own, murder or treason or rebellion. Mostly they were murderers. He continued. 'I only ask you to think on this. I know Jovan their leader. He is not as bad as people make out, although in some ways he is worse. Yet, that can be used. He was condemned to death following the murder of a nobleman, a human from Westerling. He swears that was in revenge, his wife was brutally raped and slaughtered, his unborn child kicked to death by drunken wretches as she made her way home from market. He associates all humans with this so-called nobleman and his entourage, spends his time attacking travellers along the main western highway. But he has no quarrel with elves. He has vowed to help me in my own quest to rid our world of these Blazing Sun bastards, we have already taken out a group of them. I am certain he will gladly help you. However you would have to agree to his band coming here, there can be no other way.'

The Elf Father stood, shook his head. 'It is against all our laws, as well as the laws of humans, to deal with outlaws, they are beyond our reach. Each of them should be dead, they are no more than wolves' heads, not worthy of speech. They are the forgotten ones, the undead, the not-here. They no longer exist in our world. How can we work with such beings?'

Estrién steadied himself, what was logical to him was outside of their ken. 'You need them. They have the ability to protect your lives from people who would destroy you. May I remind you they would destroy these woods also. The Adammites have no respect whatsoever for the forest, they have already caused disease in your trees, simple by walking through them, spewing their waste upon them. You know not your danger. Yet you refuse to parley with people who love the forest as you do, because a court once held them guilty of a crime.

How much worse are the crimes of these Adammites? Do you know there are elves burning on stakes in Hollyporth and Westlea? Dane has told you of his family, of how the Isle of Glasse was overrun by these people, the groves torched, the dryads and wood spirits of their sacred forest slaughtered. Don't you realise they will do that here? Do you wish to die?' He stared the Elf Father in the eye. 'You sir, are old, you have seen nearly two centuries of summers. But look around you, see the young elves, see the children ... do they not deserve long lives too?'

Amber wanted to speak, but realised he had said everything she would have said herself. He thought as she did, it was part of their nearness. He understood the things she believed in and felt so deeply. They had run from each other that day at the Temple of Oak, both of one mind, both too honourable to let it go further. She loved Dane, he was kind and gentle and he made her laugh. But Estrién and she were bound spirits.

The old Elf leader spoke again. 'You speak truly, but unpalatably, we must think on this. I will sit with the elders tonight and talk of this. If we can find another way we shall take it. Meanwhile, please accept the hospitality of our Grove.' He shook his head and turned away, mumbling *'Impossible'* to himself.

There was nothing else to do but wait until morning. Dane asked Estrién, 'do you think they will accept, you're asking them to allow cut-throats and felons into the forest?'

'Of course they will accept. Do you think I would have suggested it if there was another way? Do you think I went to those people casually to ask them for help? I find them as unacceptable as you do, despite what I said at the time, but strange times make strange bedfellows. No, he just prevaricates, he knows they will accept. He has already made up his mind, but it is preferable to pretend otherwise. He will spend the night guiding the other elves, although they will think they have come to an independent conclusion. It will take me just a few days to return with the Freowulven, it would take weeks if I went to Orlandium, or further north - and even then, they would send troops to protect the towns, not the old forest.

And in any case, who knows what is happening further north right now?'

They sat separately from the elven elders, a quiet corner. Tamlyn took out his lute, played for everyone, but there was no mood for singing or dancing that night. Towards the end of the evening he disappeared into a haemewagon with a bright eyed elven female. Dane sat by Amber, holding her hand, occasionally kissing it, his eyes longing for her. Estrién filled wine glasses, spoke little.

Eventually Rowan Firethorne joined them. 'There is a haemewagon available for you all, if you care. It is well appointed and comfortable. Come, let me show you.

The three followed him to the edge of the clearing where a small hut on large wheels lay waiting. It was similar to the one used by Longshanks and some of the wealthier circus folk, and also the Rovers, the travelling dwarven clan, but larger and more ornate.

Amber pointed this out and Rowan explained they, the elves of Oakleigh, made these haemewagons, had a good trade in them. They were beautifully carved and when they went inside, comfortable beds were laid out, small colourful linen blinds on wooden rollers were at the windows, cupboards were neatly stacked at the sides and a small washstand stood in a corner. He showed them that on the morrow they could stash the bedding away, convert the beds into a table, and two side seats. At the far end was a little iron stove, currently unlit, with a thin, tin pipe leading through the roof. It would be a tiny, but comfortable home.

They thanked him and made ready for bed. The three would share, as they shared the small tent. But sleep did not come easily to Dane, the room was stuffy in the summer heat, and during the night, he gently woke Amber.

'I need you Amber, you've kept me waiting for too long,' he whispered. He pulled her over to him, caressing her skin, kissing her bare shoulder. She turned her head to Estrién by her side, but he was fast asleep. Her arms went out to Dane, hot, sleepy bodies entwining, kissing, fondling.

In the dark of the night, in the heat of the summer, they turned to each other.

Dane was never very quiet in his lovemaking, he spoke his need out loud, he gasped and groaned and didn't give a damn who heard. So Estrién woke in the depth of the night to find two bodies rocking softly next to him, hearing Amber's sweet moans and Dane's more urgent cries. For some moments he lay quietly, listening, watching, wondering whether to be jealous or to feel hate? Then he turned over and saw Amber's eyes burning into his own. His response was immediate, all thought disappeared as he joined her, enjoyed her, loved her. When he at last lay quietly in her arms, he felt a gentle hand on his shoulder and two laughing eyes gazing into his. Two males smiled at each other before laying quietly next to Amber, side by side of her, tucking their arms around the woman they both loved, falling asleep with contented smiles on their faces.

Amber lay between them, watching the light slowly change as dawn arose. For some moments she wondered if she had done the right thing, then decided it was probably the best thing she had ever done. After all, would the Lady Merrie have turned a loved one away? She didn't think so. To be a Merrievian was to give your love, not keep it in convenient packages, tucked away and hidden. To be Merrievian was to acknowledge love and life.

... Something the Adammites could never understand.

She too slept peacefully.

Tamlyn entered the haemewagon early in the morning to gather his pack, finding them entwined on the bed. He started laughing, and woke them all.

'Ha! I wondered when it would happen - I knew you would return to him - he has pined for you.' Tamlyn beamed with pleasure. 'There's nothing like a hot summer night ... But you need to have a great deal of love and kindness, Amber, too many males are after you.' His seductive eyes gazed softly upon her, why should he not say this now? 'And I can assure you, I am one of them. One day, Amber ... *one day* ...' He blew her a kiss.

She sat up in bed, 'Stop teasing me, Tamlyn, you do it to embarrass me. Who knows, one day I might invite you to my bed? But I will do that when *I am ready* - and not before, so stop trying to seduce me.' Her eyes challenged him.

She saw Dane look approvingly at Estrién. She had taken charge of the situation, and they both appreciated that. Tamlyn merely raised his eyebrows, gave a low whistle.

'Well then, dearest Amber, *let me know when you need me.*' He took her hand, kissed the back of it with a little click of his boot heels. Then he turned to join the other elves outside and see if they had come to any conclusion of the night before. Breakfast too would be good.

Dane touched Amber on the arm, 'that was well said, dear. Whatever happens among our group surely ought to be up to you,' He saw Estrién nodding, 'You're really something, Amber, we're all glad we met you.'

Estrién kissed her mouth, 'I knew this would happen sometime, just not *when*. But we've moved on, haven't we? If you are happy, Amber, then, by the Lady Herself, so mote it be.'

*

It was as Estrién had surmised. The Elf Father came over as they finished their breakfast.

He nodded his head gravely. 'We have agreed to do as you say. We do need good swordsmen as well as archers. We need a fighting force. We will accept these ... *beings* ... here. But under one condition. They are not part of our world, they are still exiles. They may roam the woodland for game and food, as long as they protect our people. But they stay on our borders and do not associate with us. Should we be attacked, we may communicate with them then - it will be necessary. But until then we will not consort with them in any way.' He left, there was no more to be said.

Estrién accepted the situation, he had expected no more.

The two elves left Oakleigh to find the Freowulven. Dane was going to continue his healing of the remainder of the diseased trees, if he could, the ones at the other side of the forest, and Amber chose to stay a while. Tamlyn thought that Estrién might need a little help on the road, who knew what they would come across these days?

'We'd be a deal quicker with horses,' Tamlyn complained.

'Yes, we were fools that night,' Estrién agreed, referring to the Fae episode, 'we need to learn from our mistakes. Next time we get steeds, we look after them.'

'Yes, it was a shame, it was a really good night. I didn't think about the Fae, never seen them ride in my life. Thought they were just tales.' Tamlyn briefly paused before speaking with emotion, 'they hurt Amber. I should like to find them some day, pay them back.'

'Wouldn't we all! Maybe I could have done it that night, perhaps the bears got them, although I doubt it.'

'Ah, well, if we leave it long enough, perhaps the Adammites will take them out and do us a favour.' He stopped as he heard a sharp intake of breath from Estrién.

'Don't ever speak of those people to me unless it is to tell me they are dead. I will not rest until every Adammite in this land is hacked to pieces, preferably by my own sword.'

Tamlyn raised his eyebrows at this, then nodded agreement, before asking, 'any idea who this Mordecai von Adamm is, or is he just made up?' He wondered what kind of cowardly little dictator could wish to destroy their world?

'He's real, Tamlyn, he's real. And if I ever find him, my sword will tear him to bits.'

'It's just, you don't hear of him leading these people into battle. It's always, 'the Adammites did this, or were here or whatever'. No one actually says, 'Mordecai von Adamm was here and gave a speech, and was first in with his sword on a white charger', or other such shit.'

'Ah, I see what you mean. Does he exist or is he merely some sort of idea, a name to follow?' Estrién spoke with conviction, 'I'm pretty certain he exists, but he cowardly keeps a low profile. Personally I think he's a wizened little stick of a guy with no balls, a small prick and too much body odour.'

Tamlyn burst out laughing. 'Oh well done, Estrién, you've reduced him to m*úcheld*! Of course, if Amber gets there first, he really will have no balls.' He sighed. '*Ah, she is wonderful.*'

Estrién studied him. 'I know, *and Tamlyn,* I don't care how much you seduce me or Dane, keep off Amber, at least for now. *Listen* ... she has come a long way ... two men are already in love with her and she has just made up her mind to keep us both happy. Don't upset that, it's a delicate balance. She's human, not elf. We can accept things she finds difficult. This is a huge step forward for her ... into the unknown ... actually for all of us.'

'Aren't you jealous?' Tamlyn certainly was.

'Yes, *and no.* I've taken her from Dane, and he's a truly good man. He's also my friend. I feel I owe him.' Tamlyn heard a deep, deep sigh. 'Dammit Tamlyn, I want her to be happy. She and I are ... well ... we were meant to be together. We are one.'

Tamlyn stopped in the middle of the road, took his friend's hand, looked him in the eye, spoke earnestly. 'You are *soul mates*. You have found each other. Nothing can alter it, even if she loved a hundred other people. Now, I have a great capacity for love, but it never occurs to me to look for my soul mate. I am too independent, and I fall in love too easily. But I tell you, these weeks have been good, you three are enough for me, if you accept that.'

'I thought we already had ...'. He laughed gently at the elf.

'Aaah, it is enough, and yet, not quite enough. *One day ... one day.* But you are right, too much, too soon. I will not push her, even though I long for her. *But it doesn't stop me with you or Dane*, huh?' he laughed.

Estrién gave a wry smile. 'As Amber said, Tamlyn, *you are incorrigible*!'

*

Time past. Anno Merrie ?

His mother had to go out again, she said she would be back later. Not to worry, he would be fine.

The boy huddled in his little truckle bed, watching the moon shine through the holes in the raggy curtains. There was no other light, no candle or lamp. The moon cast frightening shadows on the walls, one looked like a witch with long clawed fingers. It was worse in winter, worse when the wind blew and the trees had no leaves, then skeletons were climbing through the windows at him, waving their bony hands and grinning mercilessly. Sometimes she didn't come home until dawn, she'd been out in the greenwood or the ale house with her men friends. He lay awake terrified until he fell into an exhausted sleep.

Sometimes she brought them home, he could hear them moaning and groaning in his mother's bed at the other side of the curtain. Once he got up, he thought his mother was in pain, but a naked man suddenly dashed out of his mother's bed and hit him. She told him never to look behind the curtain again or he'd have no food for a week. Knowing his mother he could believe that.

She just about fed him, clothed him, rarely spoke to him. He wasn't wanted, never had been. He asked about his father once, the boys in the village all had fathers.

'Your dad is the Greenwood dear, leave it at that. One day you'll understand, but I was just a young girl and a fool then. Now I'm a great deal wiser. Just how do you think I put food on your plate?'

He watched as she brushed her hair and put some sweet smelling oil on her wrists and neck, a little down her ample bosom, getting ready to leave, again.

It wasn't that she was unkind with him, she just wasn't ever there. Also, she never kissed him or hugged him, which was wrong considering how much she kissed and hugged those strange men. And anyway, her breath smelled of genièvre and ale.

As he grew up he came to understand what his mother was. *A whore*. He knew that because the village boys told him. They seemed to know more about his mother than he did. He fought them and got a thrashed body and a cut lip for his trouble. He wouldn't have minded but she just laughed, told him he was too young to act as knight protector, and anyway, they were right, she was a whore, never said otherwise. *And by the Lady Merrie*, she would continue, it was what she lived for.

'Dancing, drinking and having a good time - what else was there in life?' she asked him. He didn't know, but thought there ought to be something.

When he was fourteen, a stranger appeared in the village, no one knew where from. Clad all in black, but with a red fire sign embroidered on his shoulder and another etched into his hand, a cloud of darkness surrounded him. 'Ye are all sinners!' he snarled at the villagers, 'ye are destined for hell.' He spoke with absolute authority, and under his cloak, his eyes glowed red. The villagers wanted to ignore him, it was Beltane, they wished to enjoy the feast and the dancing. He frightened them, he was a terrifying presence, there was something demonic about him, like a black dog following him. The villagers ran into their homes and locked their doors.

But the youth was intrigued, talked to the hooded figure, didn't understand why he should be a sinner considering he'd done nothing with his life? He told him about his mother. The stranger sighed deeply, explained his mother was the root of all evil. He needed to cleanse himself, purge the evil out of him. There was only one way.

He took little persuading.

That night, whilst his inebriated mother lay enjoying herself behind the curtain with the blacksmith's older son, he set the house aflame. It was flimsy, a wooden structure, it went up quickly. He didn't even stop to find out if she died, he followed the black-cloaked figure into the forest. Later that night, a moon-dark night, as they camped, the stranger made a fire, put his knife into it until it glowed red hot.

Take off your tunic,' he said. The youth did as he was bidden. The hooded one took the knife out of the flames and used the point to burn a large fire symbol into the youth's chest. When he stopped screaming, the process was repeated with a smaller symbol at the top of his right arm.

'Now you are cleansed,' he told him. 'Now you are free. You will be my dark warrior, son of the Sun, cleanser of the world, you will herald a new Age. The Mother Goddess worshippers with their fertility rites and drunken orgies have overstayed their welcome. We will cleanse this polluted land of all the old filth, the degenerate races, their time has ended. We will purify this world through fire and bring in the new clean age, the age of Man. Death is the only thing assured in this life, power through death.'

The boy felt strong, the first surges of his manhood.

'You have been reborn this day, so I will rename you. You are the first of my children and so I name you *von Adamm*, but you are also the bringer of Death and so I name you *Mordecai*.' He threw a black cloak around him, 'Come, follow me, we have work to do.'

The young Mordecai von Adamm followed his new father deeper into the forest.

Chapter 5

Month of Harvesthaeme, present time

Amber stayed to help Dane finish healing the forest. Some of the diseased trees needed branches lopping and dead twigs removing. She shimmied up the trees with the dryads, helping with a small axe, hanging from branches, getting rid of the dry, crackling sticks. One old oak was enormous, she spent time climbing up. Dane wondered how to fix some of the top parts of the tree, although he'd seen to the roots. He was no climber, at least, not like Amber. He found a short branch of oak, whittled it down to a wand shape and charged it through his staff. He threw it up to her.

'*Point it just* ....' she moved the wand around, 'yes ... just there and hold on,' he concentrated as magic flew through the wand. 'Aaah, good ... now there ...' pointing. She shifted around the tree, high in the branches. 'This is good, there are parts up there difficult to get to. Now a bit further along ...' pointing to a branch way up and out.

Amber gritted her teeth and edged along the branch, holding cat-like to the bough. Finally she neared the place he wanted and pointed. Fiery magic flew into the stem. 'Right, now that bit below ...' he shouted. She looked down. Hmm, easier just to hang. She wrapped her legs over the branch and swung downwards, until she steadied and pointed at yet another branch. More magic flew. Eventually Dane seemed to think they'd done a 'really good job' ... it *was* the tallest tree in the forest and now was probably the healthiest.

The dryads congratulated her, they were used to climbing the trees, it was natural to them, and they all agreed they'd never seen a human so limber. They kept the trees well, but this infection had been outside of their knowledge, they were able only to keep the trees alive, but not to heal.

She jumped down. 'That was weird,' she told Dane, 'that wand, it buzzed in my hand, it was like I was doing the magic, but of course it was you – incredible!'

'Glad you liked it, er ... I can think of other things that might buzz in your hand?' he smirked, his eyes wide and mock-innocent. Amber did that *look* thing at him, the female one. 'Sorry love, couldn't resist,' he smirked again. 'Anyway, you did a great job, we make a good team, Amber.' He stooped to kiss her.

She realised they did make a good team, they worked well together. She knew she could have been content with Dane, if Estrién ... if Estrién hadn't showed up. She was so relaxed and comfortable with Dane, everything flowed easily and he made her laugh.

With Estrién everything was so much more intense, also there was a formality to him, a sense of high purpose that was part of Estrién himself. She thought it could be difficult to live up to, but she would try, and in any case had her own set of values. She knew however, she could no more walk away from Estrién than cut off her hand. ... *Or her heart.*

It was just a different kind of love, she decided, and she liked both kinds.

They walked back to the big clearing where the elves were gathering, congratulated on all sides by them. The trees were healing, it was a time for celebration. They had decided to enjoy a feast tonight in honour of Dane and his able assistant, Amber.

So out came the wines and the delicacies, the big tables were decked with flowers and the best beeswax candles, and the elves brought out their fiddles, lutes, lyres and flutes. They were all in high humour and full of fun. Amber put on her pale turquoise gown and beads and Dane his best linen shirt and black jerkin. The elves wore garlands of flowers and the Elf Father gave a speech congratulating Dane and thanking them both for their help. The dryads came to enjoy the feast and thank them both.

Then the dancing and merriment began, Dane and Amber led the first dance, but only the first. They were in big demand with the elves and Dane particularly with the dryads. When they all stopped to eat, the elves stood one by one to tell terrible elven jokes such as:

'Did I tell you the one about the elf with the rounded ear?
Aaah, but there's no point to it ...'
Or *'Why couldn't the oak tree walk away? ... because it had a corn on its foot ...'*
Or *'Did you hear about the elven nihilist who didn't be-leaf?.* (groans all round)
Or *'A human, an elf and a dwarf walked into a bar. The dwarf was OK though, it was too high for him.'* (with apologies)

And so on. And of course, they all giggled and shouted the traditional toast *'to your 'elf!'* (more groans)

Luckily, there was lots to drink, which probably made the elves worse, and more dancing. Eventually Dane led Amber away to the small haemewagon, he and she had a lot of 'catching up to do' or so he said. Whatever it was, it took until late the following morning, when both were seen to emerge with bright smiles on their faces.

*

Estrién explained the situation to the Freowulven leader, Jovan. 'You are needed there and you offered your help to me. It is surely preferable to being here in the wilds.'

'So we will have free movement in the forest in return for protection?' Jovan thought briefly, very briefly, this was an opportunity that would not come easily again. He agreed. 'As long as we can bring our women, the few children we have here, there aren't many.' There were fifty or so Freowulven warriors including five females, perhaps a dozen non-combatant women and a few children.

Estrién and Tamlyn stayed a couple of days while they made ready, then took the journey back to Oakleigh forest with them. They loaded up some carts with their few odds and ends, tents, bedding, cooking equipment. It wasn't much.

Estrién and Jovan left the main group close to the outskirts while they met the Elders. The Elf Father was waiting for them. 'Please do not come any further. It is preferable you live on the outskirts of the forest.' He aimed his words at Estrién rather than Jovan, still unable to accept that the Dead Ones were alive.

'But you accept us being here in Oakleigh forest?' Jovan was astounded.

'The threat of Adammites is far worse than you. I have told everyone you will protect both the elves and the forest. You need to work with our archers, work as a group, although few will talk with you. We will not feed you so you must make provision yourselves - there is much game now anyway. But no thieving, in fact cause no trouble of any sort. Keep your families away from the main hub. Have no contact with the elven or dryad families here. So what do you say?' He didn't really wish to talk to the Freowulven leader, but right now he had no choice.

'Oakleigh forest is a beautiful place, and some of my outlaws are from here. I will make sure we keep the peace, Merrie knows we will never be given another chance like this. But shouldn't this have come from the Dûc?' Jovan still couldn't believe what he was hearing.

Estrién tried to explain the situation. 'He has no jurisdiction in the forest, it's up to the Elf Father. I didn't even ask Dûc de Luxonne, it's too far out of his ken. The Oakleigh elves will not acknowledge you, but neither will they act against you.'

'So basically we are an unpaid militia, living on the edge of Oakleigh. It sounds fair enough though. It's a big place, we won't intrude.' Jovan stood with his arms folded, 'but I warn you, if any elven militia come here seeking us, we shall kill them as we would the Adammites - so do not betray us.' He stood staunch and dark in his cedar green leather doublet, black hose and a dark woollen cape. The swarthy features teamed with black hair and the eye patch produced a threatening figure under the fair trees of Oakleigh.

'Protect our forest and we have no reason to act against you.' The Elf Father left to return to the grove. He felt unclean, dealing with the Freowulven left a sour taste in his mouth.

Estrién shook Jovan's hand. 'It's the only solution. Elves must stick together now, the past is past, and unless we forgive that past there will be no future. There are too few elven warriors, we must take what we can. I can leave here, knowing that at least Oakleigh is in good hands - one worry off my mind. All I can say is, good luck to you, and please keep the peace.'

Estrién and his band stayed for one more night in Oakleigh forest before moving on.

*

Amber and the boys remained overnight with the elves of Oakleigh forest then turned towards Orlandium on a bright and breezy Harvesthaeme day. They would follow the coast along Mab's Bay, watch out for invaders as they went, hopefully make Orlandium in seven to ten days if the going was good. There was little traffic on the road, elves fleeing from Adammites were making for Belcast'el, Orlandium was too far distant.

One or two things worried them however. As they neared the coast many fishing boats could be seen, all in harbour, none going out to sea or returning with a day's catch. By mutual consent they made their way to a small fishing village, Croftcoats, it clung precariously to the white cliffs surrounding the bay. The view from the cliff top was spectacular, the sea somewhat choppy, but a clear blue sky echoed in its depths.

Not a fishing boat could be spotted at sea. On the horizon however, larger sail-boats could be spied, carracks, with four masts and a flat stern, ships big enough to carry many men.

Warships.

The four made their way down to the village to hear the news. The fishermen were eager to tell them their stories, having been unable to put out to sea for the past weeks, stopped by these massive boats. There were few archers on board, the Adammites preferring sword and shield style fighting, but they had something worse.

The ships held huge ballistae, great wooden crossbows which they fired at the fishermen, often with the ends of the bolts dipped in tar and set aflame. The fishermen were terrified, while those on board the carracks laughed heartily at their deadly new toy. The fishermen told them the ships were headed all along the coast, but mostly for Pennyport to cut off Orlandium from trade. There were dreadful rumours from Pennyport that the port had already been taken by the Adammites.

Amber and the others turned to the main highway to make north for Orlandium to inform the king.

Chapter 6

In Orlandium, King Alexis was sitting in the solar of his castle, explaining to his wife, Queen Neria. 'I have to go, love, I have to lead them. I've done it before and I'll do it again. A leader needs to be seen, not hidden away in a bloody old castle. Those buggers have been seen off our coast, they'll have landed before I can get there.'

He already knew the Adammites had reached the south coast, would take Pennyport, his scouts had informed him. Pennyport was lifeblood to his land, the main importing coastal town, and he would be too late to defend it. It also meant his sailing ships that defended Mab's Bay were either sunk or taken, and he knew the militia at Pennyport were too few to hold it for long against the numbers of ships seen. He hoped it hadn't been a massacre.

He should have listened to the rumours, taken note about the western elven ports, sent more militia down. But truly, he hadn't believed these people had so many ships, nor that they would invade so soon. Where had they got them from? They had invaded so quickly, both Elvinhaeme and Westerling, it was hard to take breath to understand the damage being caused. Those years they had held the Isle of Glasse had obviously been spent creating the paraphernalia of war.

They should have stopped it in its tracks. Why hadn't anyone retaliated when the island was taken over? Why had they all been so blind, so careless? He was as much to blame, had been so used to thinking of any fighting outside the mainland as just petty squabbles, yet good people had died. He should have investigated, they *all* should have ... but they just all kept to their own little corners and stayed safe, refusing to believe anything really bad could happen to their world.

Well, they weren't safe now and he would have to pay the penalty for that lapse.

It was hard to believe he had to go to war. But a king knows his duty, and duty must be done.

Neria, his wife, was a gentle Queen, an elf from Elvinhaeme. 'Can we not talk with these people, reason with them? Find out exactly what they *do* want?' Her large and expressive eyes held concern.

Alexis smiled at her naiveté, part of her charm for him, she never saw the ill in anyone. 'Darling, there is *no* reasoning with these people. They want our lands, they want people like *you* dead. *Neria* - they would kill our daughter, Anna'laeth.' He watched as she stared horrified at him. 'Here, read this ...' He offered her one of the Adammite pamphlets. 'That is the reality of them, it's terrifying.' He put his arms on her shoulders, stared her in the eye. 'Love, I'm leaving you in charge and tomorrow morning I set off with my best troops for Pennyport. I couldn't face my people if I stayed cowardly back here.' He was adamant, he stood determinedly.

She nodded, accepting that he was right, although never in her life before had she come across a situation that couldn't be talked through. But these people - it seemed that was impossible.

She stood straight, threw back her shoulders. 'Well, my heart, if that's the case I'll do my best, you know that. I'll look after Westerling, and I'll be wary, I promise you, But where have they come from these people? Why do they wish this upon us? What evil, cowardly men are these?' Her eyes blazed, she would do her duty, take care of the kingdom on his behalf.

Alexis looked down at his gentle wife with pride. She always amazed him, she seemed so fragile, yet there was inner strength there. 'You've hit it on the head, Neria. They *are* cowards, they are taking over the small undefended towns and our beautiful Temples, killing priestesses. It's time they fought some men with swords and bows, instead of a few elven merchants or farmers. We'll show them, my love, we'll show them.' He sounded braver than he felt.

His daughter came in to the solar at that moment. He kissed the top of her golden-haired head. 'C'mon love,' he said, 'let's play a game or two for the afternoon, have a bit of fun.' He settled down to play card games with the ten year old, his wife watching fondly from her chair. She settled herself too for the afternoon, decided she would complete the tapestry she was making for one of the guest rooms. They spent a quiet but pleasant family afternoon in the warm, sunny, solar.

The following morning, early, he and two hundred knights and foot soldiers set off for Pennyport. They weren't many, but they were all he could muster so quickly.

*

Manecaestr. Date: recent.

Candlemaker's Hall was filling up, plenty of people had arrived to hear the message and the guest speakers, they said there was something special tonight, no one knew what. The young man sat next to a bleary eyed drunk, no other places, the room was full. He was excited, never been to one of these meetings before, didn't really know why he was here, but some of his mates had been before, said it was 'brilliant'.

He only knew he wanted something more in his life, working as bound apprentice under his father for the next few years wasn't enough. His father was a wood turner working for an elf, a master craftsman, beautifully made furniture. It looked like that would be his future too. He had served three years, there were still four long years to go, plus more if he wanted any kind of artistry in his craft. Too long, too damn long for his impatient soul.

But having heard the growling undertones around the town, as well as at his place of work, he decided he was sick of having to graft for an elf, and sick of being the underling. He hadn't the patience or the skill to make a good craftsman, but didn't really know what else to do. He wanted ready money to splash around in the ale house and impress the wenches, have a good time while he was young. He was a simple young man, impatient, impulsive and, at the moment, unhappy with his lot in life.

The stage seemed to be filling with more young men, belligerent looking, angry, black-eyed with hate. He wondered what they hated so much? After the first hesitant speeches, one got up to vent his anger on just about everyone. The young listener wasn't sure what he was angry about, but it sounded good, it sounded how he felt after a few beers, but hadn't found a wench for the night, all keyed up and nowhere to go. He felt a rush of sympathetic blood with the speaker. It was strange, but the air in the Hall seemed to thicken, to darken somehow. He could almost feel it, some power, a power he didn't know he had ...

Then another speaker droned on about 'the movement' and 'the Blazing Sun' which shone through the darkness, would cleanse them all and bring absolution.

He'd no idea at all what that was about, totally over his head. But still, there was something ... something he wanted to touch.

Then a hush came to the crowd. *He* was here tonight, or so they said, word through the grapevine. *He* had to be smuggled in and out, Manecaestr was filled with spies, they said, spies that had to be rooted out and dealt with - the pyre was for them.

Von Adamm walked on to the stage. The crowd stood and cheered, then turned absolutely silent as he raised his hands and bowed his head. He held the silence for a minute before speaking, the young men catching their breaths, wondering what it was all about? He wasn't a prepossessing man, had no airs about him, was neither good- or bad-looking. He seemed just normal. He was just an ordinary bloke up there on the stage, just like them. Then he spoke and the conviction came through, spellbinding the listeners.

'I wish to speak to all of you tonight, and I want all of you to hear. I want you to understand, *I want you to believe*, I want you to grasp what I say with both hands and make it yours.

For you are the future. *You* – humankind. Do you realise the power in your strong human bodies?' He didn't wait for an answer. 'Perhaps you do not, perhaps you are only just beginning to feel your manhood, to believe in yourselves. You are right to have that belief, to trust in yourself and your fellow man. You are here tonight because you are ready to move on, curious as to our cause, wondering what the world is about?'

He looked them all in the eye, a special one to one eye contact. 'I see before me a room filled with young men full of promise, yet men who have to bow down to a master, who spend years apprenticing themselves to say, an elf, or a dwarf or worse, a mage. Intelligent and admirable young men who wait and wait, time going by and the world moving on, yet they still wait for their time to come, they live off meagre wages, yet see power and wealth in the hands of others. And what are those others? *Tell me?*' he questioned, but didn't wait for an answer. 'They are the decadent races, the obsolete races, those whose time has come to an end, for they exploit you, they use you ... yes, *you* ... they reap the rewards of your hard work.

You spend your hours at the forge or the workbench or you break your backs to till the land, while *they* sleep under soft sheets and imbibe wine, the very fruit of *your* labour.' He made as if to share a secret with them all. '*And what then?* These lecherous beings entice our own women to their beds ... they dance and sing, while you toil! They are good for nothing and lazy when you are busy from dawn 'til dusk. *Is that what you want -* your youth stolen from you while your women lie in their arms?'

He shook his head as a groan went around the hall. 'These greedy, fornicating so-called masters supposedly offer you a future, but does that future ever come?' He waited as there was a great shout of '*no!*' around the hall. 'You young men deserve the riches of life now, not some indefinable future when you are too old and infirm to enjoy it.'

He stood, nodding at the hall, his voice steady and reasonable. 'You know you deserve more, you want your rightful place in life, but as yet do not know how to begin. Tonight you have come to the right place, for you have started upon the path of truth, the new strength of your destiny, the cornerstone of your fate.' He paused, perusing each of them, staring them in the eye, man to man, challenging them, challenging their manhood.

'I tell you here and now, you are *men whose time is now*, whose time it is to take the world and shape it in your image. *Your* image, do you hear me? It is time you learned how take your place ... to *rule*. Do you want to rule? ... *of course you do* ... and why? ... because *the world is rightfully yours.'* He paused again, eyed each one, another challenge and a warning to the weak. He knew their response before he continued speaking.

'*Man*, humankind, is ruler of life, the giver of life, the *leader* of his own world ... *if you have the courage*. We, the Adammites should run this world for our own benefit, take what we desire, that is *truth*, that is *fair and right and righteous*.

And let the women of this land also understand who are the true masters, for they are the weaker sex, they too must learn to obey.' He watched, he had them now, appeal to their youth, their self-interest.

'Let the decadent races and the weak women break under the thumb of our power and make *them* work for us .' He raised his voice in anger, 'or *damn them and throw them onto the fire as the waste they are* ...' A great shout rang through the air at this, Von Adamm held his hand for quiet, he had more to say.

'Accept your newfound strength and power, accept it and use it. You only have to reach out and accept the truth of righteousness and of power, accept the Son of the Sun into your lives and feel that strength run through you.' He was well into the fury of his speech now.

He watched as they lapped up his words.

He came to the crunch, the part he had intended, for words alone are nothing, it takes action to change a world.

'Here in Manecaestr tonight, we will no longer wait for the moment to begin our future - for that future is *now*. Your time has come. Tonight we take Manecaestr from the inside, we tear down the walls, destroy the usurpers of our world, and create your new destiny, my sons, *Sons of the Sun*.

We will give you arms, we will teach you to fight, bring out your true strength, for as Sons of the Sun, this mighty and righteous revolution, you will be rewarded and the world will bow down to you and you alone! Mer'edrynn belongs to the Adammites!'

He stopped speaking, yet his eyes challenged the crowd, awaiting an answer. It was done and they would obey.

The hall erupted with cheers. The young man stood clapping, then leapt onto his chair and cheered, the blood rushing through his veins. He felt good, hadn't ever felt this good before, a great rush of power and desire thrumming through him.

Yes, he would show them all, the world belonged to him and his kind only. He wanted the world and he wanted it now! With Von Adamm it was his for the taking. He made for the long lines of men wishing to join Von Adamm and the Cause of Man.

Son of the Sun, oh yes, he liked that. He could imagine its power and heat and strength running through him, invincible, as he ploughed through the ranks and rows of elves or dwarves, slaughtering the bloody lot of them.

Meanwhile, in a corner of the hall sat a dark figure. He sat alone, for although people could see him, none wished to sit close by, a shudder went down most men's spines as they neared him. He had watched and quietly manipulated the proceedings throughout the night. He smiled to himself, Von Adamm had spoken fairly well, had turned a few more minds this night, but it hadn't been brilliant. It was irrelevant though, he was merely a mouthpiece, a human conduit for himself, the true conversion had come from the power he unfolded inside the hall. He needed more, much more, if the world was to be overturned, for the new order to begin.

The war was developing nicely.

The dark shadow wasn't particularly bothered about humans, but they served a purpose, they would rid the world of the elder races. They now believed in death, not their own, but the death of others. That was good, it fulfilled his own purpose. As long as they worshipped death, that would serve, for how can a world survive when belief in death is greater than love of life?

Smiling at the night's work, he wrapped his cloak around him and disappeared from the Hall.

*

Western High Road, Westerling.

It would take the best part of a week to reach Orlandium on foot and it didn't seem as if any public coaches were on the highway. The roads were in fact very quiet, few people travelling, most tucked up in their own homes and villages, probably making a futile attempt to fortify it ready against invasion. The four were also quiet as they walked, they, like the rest wondered if it had all been left until too late?

The stone-filled road rose and fell gently over soft-backed hills, nothing harsh about the landscape here. Occasionally they stopped to gather hedgerow blackberries, firm and juicy. The boys would find a particularly luscious one and offer it to Amber, popping it in to her mouth, watching as she ate. The hedgerows and fields normally held fruit in abundance, and the next couple of months would find the trees filled with flavoursome nuts. Yet, as they passed, they realised the hedgerows were not so full as usual, a little thinner on each bough or twig. It was almost imperceptible, but it was there. They ate as they walked, gathering en route. Dane found species of herbs he didn't recognise to take samples for his medical store.

He had a mage way of doing it; firstly, sight, he looked at the herb and decided its species, then he smelled it, decided on its inner nature. He would touch the petal or the stem or leaf, feel through mage senses and sensitive fingers the rightfulness or otherwise of the herb: potion or poison? Finally he tasted a tiny portion of it, gave a smile or a grimace as he spat it out, with a corresponding 'hmm, so that's it then?' as the flora was mentally classified and boxed, taking note also of the season - young and fresh or old and bitter?

'Very pleasant in spring, I think, a bit tough right now though - and it numbed my tongue!' he expostulated.

The days were still warm, but the nights had turned autumn-cool and they all piled together in Tamlyn's tent, snug and warm in a heap. The four friends and lovers cared only that each was comfortable and made sure everyone had enough blankets.

Early morns brought damp mists, cloaks began to be wrapped around chill bodies. Part of the path meandered through a thick forest, trees loomed up in eerie silence as they walked, chatterless birds huddled under drippy leaves. But the sun would poke through and chase away the damp, continuing its role of ripening the land for one last season before retiring.

'We're too late, aren't we?' asked Amber, suddenly afraid, as they walked. 'We've come too late.'

'What do you mean, dear?' Estrién understood, but wanted her to confirm, to clarify.

'We're at the centre of this, aren't we? I mean, why else would we all have come together? Yet, they're too far ahead of us, I don't know how we can stop it ...' She held out her arms in exasperation. 'I mean, everything's happening *now*, and somehow, we four are trying to fight it, mostly alone, but we are the ones attempting to mobilise people. Get them all off their comfortable backsides before they find themselves strung up under their own beloved apple trees. Somehow we four have to fight these bastards and I'm not sure I know how ...'

'Just keep us all together love, that's the main thing.' Dane smiled down at her. 'We'll work it out between us. Estrién has his amazing sword, I have my magic and the finest staff I could ever hope for, Tamlyn and you weave your own magic and you are both fine warriors - we're a formidable team. But you are the centre of us, Amber, our heart. We don't need battle plans from you, dear, but we do need your faith in us.'

Amber laughed quietly, her eyes bright on all three. 'That, you certainly have. I'm glad I'm with you guys,' she confessed, 'all three of you. Times are changing rapidly and we have need of each other.' She suddenly stopped, turned to each one, Tamlyn included, and kissed each gently on the mouth. 'In Merrie's name, I swear I'll stand by you all.'

Tamlyn bowed gracefully, took her hand in his, 'we stand by you, my Lady. We'll not let you down, I promise, knight's honour.'

'And *I* will never leave you, not until you tell me to go,' continued Estrién, his voice softened by her words. 'You are everything to me, Amber, everything. I'm happy to take on the world on your behalf, just point me in the right direction, my love.' Loving eyes beamed at Amber.

In fact, three pairs of male eyes gazed softly on Amber.

Amber shook herself a little, this was all a bit too heavy. Beautiful, but somewhat overpowering. 'Well, come on then, boys, let's get a move on shall we?' she stated, practically, 'we've got some Adammite ass to kick ...' as she marched along the stony road ahead of them.

Willingly, they followed.

*

King Alexis knew he had a problem as he approached Pennyport. He could see the port from the higher land, it was bloody well filled with the Blazing Sun buggers. He couldn't take the town with what he had, not enough soldiers. If he could wait a day or two, more troops would arrive on foot from the various outposts, but he needed to attack now. It was obvious more ships were arriving with more black-cloaked Adammites. The people of Pennyport were in serious danger.

It wasn't a walled town, it was a port settled on two sides of a river. He kept a small garrison here normally, plenty to keep the peace on a typical day. The worst they ever had to fight were drunken sailors or Tsiganii having a brawl. But times weren't typical. He knew his soldiers must all be dead, poor bastards.

As he neared the hill just north of the town, he formed a tentative battle plan and organised his troops. If he could fight within the confines of the town it would be better, he could fight in small groups, try and take them out little by little. It was foolhardy, and he knew it, but word coming out of the place wasn't good, certainly not for the local townsfolk. He didn't need to send scouts to find out, he could see the burning pyres from afar.

At best he could perhaps harry them for a day or two, keep them occupied, get them angry. Turn that anger towards him instead of the town's people, try to hold out until more of his troops arrived. He made for one of the main roads into the port.

Unfortunately his not so well-thought-out plan was not possible. The Adammite militia were ready and waiting and hurried across the main bridge towards the King and his approaching troops. They had been watching intently for just such an attack. There were hundreds of them, a tide of black-armoured soldiers all bearing the red sun sign, pouring out of Pennyport, all moving in well disciplined lines, all carrying swords and shields, or pikes. Some, but not many archers sent a wave of arrows at the king, he answered with a volley of his own, but immediately had to fall back, to find safer ground. He hadn't bargained for the numbers, there was a massive swarm of them.

He shook his head at the sheer futility of this, he'd rushed in too soon, he knew that now. He knew that where war was concerned, he was a complete greenhorn. His few battles had been against outlaws or marauders, not well-ordered lines of troops. He'd never even seen troops in this kind of formation before, blocks of men, pikestaffs first, all around twenty abreast and at least six ranks deep. They looked formidable, he wondered how it would be possible to break their ranks?

But he also knew those in the town needed his help, that was paramount.

'Holy Mother Merrie,' he thought. 'What am I doing?' But he knew he couldn't, nor wouldn't turn back. This was his land, his own people were down there. He raised his sword high in the air, lifted his shield, his old grandfather's shield, gold lion 'passant' on red background, and called the command to charge.

Alexis was hopelessly outnumbered, he had no idea how long he could carry on. He didn't have the necessary forces, yet he *had* to make a stand. They needed Pennyport, it was part of the lifeblood of Westerling, part of the lifeblood of Mer'edrynn ... it all fitted together. Craft and commerce worked in one big circle, weaving in and out, around itself, the continuing tapestry of life.

Somehow he had to retake Pennyport ... *somehow*. He shook his head in despair.

Where had all these Adammites come from, he wondered? He did not wish to retreat, did not even know if it was possible in any case. He could only try; as the Lady prayer said, he would give his best. That's all it came down to in the end, doing the best you could with whatever you were given, good, bad or indifferent. Take it, use it and make the best of it.

It was in Alexis' nature to fight for his people, for every human, elf, mage, naiad, dryad, dwarf or nymph, his ancestors had cared for them all and so did he. Someone had to stand on behalf of all the little forgotten races that still lived quietly hidden in the forests and the ancient hills. A true king stood for everyone, he didn't let them down. The fight had to begin here ... and, he sighed to himself, probably end here. But it had to be.

For Westerling ... *for Mer'edrynn.*

But he would go out in glory if he could. No one would say he hadn't done his duty. What was his worth if he hadn't tried to save his people? He called his men together, readying the charge, thinking briefly of the wife and child he left at home, hoping they would forgive him. *And perhaps not forget him.*

*

Amber and the group were part way to Orlandium when they met a King's runner on the road, one of many, his swift horse taking him across country to rally troops for the King. He informed them of King Alexis' march to Pennyport, his intended stand against the Adammites.

They turned for Pennyport, annoyed they'd wasted time, they could have gone straight there. By the time they reached the King, Pennyport was taken and several other smaller towns along the coast. What was worse was that many of his own people, citizens of Westerling, predominantly male, had also joined the Adammites.

They heard the battle before they saw it, just across the river, the Adammites fighting the King's forces. It was a nasty sound, the clash of steel, the hate-filled cries of men, anger and horror and pain. And the sound of death, screams cut short and final sobs into the ether.

They watched as they reached the top of a small hill, a pale morning sun glancing off the steel helmets of the troops, a fierce gale blowing in from the sea. The sickly smell of death hung in the air ...

Hundreds of black-clad soldiers in strong straight lines, blocks of sixty-four, eight by eight, were steadily pushing forward, knocking the King's forces back. Estrién took note of how Von Adamm, or the Commander in Charge, had arranged his forces, well disciplined, row upon row, a square of armed and armoured men. Although, there didn't seem to be sight of anyone who could be their leader? He wondered where he could be?

The king's militia appeared to be in groups, milling here and there, unused to such a battle, whereas the Adammite militia was strictly organised, a very professional affair. The King's immediate group of personal knights, his *Corps de Lyons*, better disciplined, was also being pushed back, losing ground. He had lost many troops, he stood in the centre bravely trying to rally them all.

Dane watched as the King struggled, his sword and shield waved in the air, as much a battle cry as a weapon. Dane briefly checked with the others ... *of course* ... what else could they do?

'Come on,' shouted Estrién. 'Let's get down there.'

The four ran down the hill to help the King, knowing they were too few to turn the tide, but they could try, at least try to protect King Alexis. Out came White Star, as Dane lifted his staff. Dane swept a huge arc of fire over one of the lines of troops, Estrién followed up with an arc of the blade. Amber and Tamlyn followed behind, Amber's twin blades spinning and Tamlyn's sabre flashing.

They came from behind, surprising the Adammites, momentarily breaking their rank, throwing out the system, confusing the troops. If they stayed as one they could just - just - break through this group on the king's flank.

They ran as one, they hurled themselves at the Adammites as one, as an arrow hurtles straight through the air and finally breaks through armour and skin when it reaches its goal.

So did Amber and her men break through the ranks. Quickly, efficiently and without pause, onwards and down towards King

Alexis. No stopping, no turning round, keep going, keep moving.

To pause would have meant certain death.

Fire and steel together proved a worthy warrior. Fire flashed on Adammite heads, blasts of lightning on their steel breastplates, White Star blazed and sang, and the steel of Amber and Tamlyn sliced through leather and flesh. Together, they cut a swathe through surprised enemy lines towards the now-retreating king.

Surprise is such a key element in war.

Dane suddenly saw the imminent danger to the king, threw a great flash of amberic lightning at an Adammite swordsman as he made for King Alexis, the king turned just in time, cut him down with his own sword. Estrién cut through the last group of Adammites, a huge figure of eight sweep of White Star, managed to run to the king's side. Together they stood to face the attackers.

'Thank you my friend,' King Alexis shouted to Estrién. 'So they found you. I am glad you are here, but the odds are uncertain. It may be a short friendship.'

Estrién simply lopped the head off yet another attacker. One by one ... *one by one*. Dane threw a wave of fire, a bright and fierce circle, giving them all a little more time, a temporary halt to Adammite troops. He wanted to burn all of them, at least as many as he could before his mana ran out.

King Alexis shouted for his men, screaming more rallying cries and gathering them all together. There weren't many, but they now stood as one group. They turned to face the enemy once more.

They were vastly outnumbered. A horde of Adammites against so few.

Estrién wondered just how good his sword could be ... could it fight so many? Could it hold its promise, would the legends hold true? The enemy looked like a great cloud of hate approaching them. He could only do his best, like King Alexis, he would give what he had. Briefly he spoke with the king, deciding on the best tactics with their dwindled numbers.

He could go in as a spearhead, the others follow in a v shape, split the enemy, work their way through them. It was a plan, of a sort. There was little time for discussion, the next wave were almost upon them. Dane and Estrién moved out first, flashing fire and White Star. Amber and Tamlyn stood with the King's troops.

Tamlyn briefly put his arm around Amber. 'Whatever happens, Amber, I care ... you know that?' She nodded, smiled briefly, warm amber eyes held his own, as her twin swords flashed in the morning sun.

Those well-formed blocks of troops, tight and solid, in front of them ... how ...? Amber didn't consider there was much hope. These damn bastards would end it here, Westerling would go as Elvinhaeme was going. Perhaps the north could help? *No,* Kyneweth had that sewn up, placed - nay given into Adammites' hands. Perhaps that lovable lunatic Lord Black Morus had more up his sleeve than she thought. *Perhaps but probably not.* It didn't matter, it was all unravelling, all going.

All because of some slimy bastard who wanted to destroy everything good. Some shit who preferred death to life.

She had said they were too late ...

She called out to Dane, to Estrién. 'Go carefully, may the Mother be with you.' She saw them both salute her, acknowledge her. 'Merrie's Blessings, my loves ... and to you, Tamlyn,' speaking softly to the elf next to her.

They started the final push, wondering how long it would be before it was all over?

So damn soon, they'd hardly begun to organise a defence against these people, and yet - how damn quickly had these death worshippers overtaken their lands ... their world?

How easy it is for them to give up their lives for their death-god. And equally, how hard it is for a life-loving soul to offer his. That takes courage.

Amber took one last look up at the morning sky, freshly blue, small clouds scudding across, dancing their carefree path. She shook her head at the useless absurdity of it all, so bloody futile, so wasteful ... Then she grabbed her swords and stood ready for King Alexis' command.

For a moment the world seemed still, a hush pervaded the battlefield, perhaps that moment between life and death.

Then the silence was broken, the sound of many hooves from down the valley. 'Not more Adammites?' thought Amber, 'we're finished for certain.'

Yet Tamlyn gave a shout, '*here*!' he called excitedly, waving to the oncoming group.

Horsemen were seen to approach, two hundred or more. These too were clad in black, but the sharp black and silver of the Knights of Floriénne - the Dair Chev'al. Many were archers, they moved forwards and shot a volley at the Adammite troops.

Surprised, they checked their advance, their onward push halted. They tried again, to be met with more volleys of arrows.

Now Estrién shouted with all his might, 'Forward, as one, *move!*' as he dashed in to the fray. He led them towards the Adammites, sweeping great circles with his sword, cutting vast swathes as he had done to reach the King.

Dane stood beside him, matching the flashing sword with great flashes of fire or electrum. When he saw a group of King's troop at his side he blasted the nearest enemy with a freezing shot of ice, enough for the troops to dash in and take advantage of the momentary lull. Then he was back near Estrién again, amberic flashes being sent at the metal breast plates and shields of some of the Adammite troops.

He had no idea how long he could keep this up, but the staff of oak felt marvellous in his hand. It was more powerful than any he had before, and he knew he would keep it until his death, however soon that may be. It was his, as a man's sword is his, so was his oaken staff. And he knew with certainty, that as he aged ... *if* he aged ... his magic would strengthen.

For now, he would strike and strike and strike again. When the mana died down he would rest, leave it in Estrién's capable hands, but until then ...

Estrién simply enjoyed having him by his side, his sword flashing mercilessly back and forth. He almost didn't have to guide it, the great swirling, infinite loops seemingly taken of their own accord, as if it had a life of its own. He could feel its power buzzing, his own strength growing the more he wielded it. It blinded all before him, a great light shining forth on the enemy. He heard Amber behind him, shouting at Adammites, her short-swords going in for the kill, and he laughed to himself knowing *just* where she was aiming those swords.

Bless the woman, he thought, *bless her and may the Goddess keep her*. And Tamlyn, on his right, his sabre taking nasty slices out of Adammite necks. As the king's troops caught up, they went in together, as they had come down the hill, *en quattro*, a death-wielding foursome.

They cut through the lines, the king's troop to their right, the Dair Chev'al dashing around in a semi-circle on their fine and noble steeds, cutting down Adammite foot soldiers with shining swords, or well aimed arrows. They stayed well away from Dane's fire, not wishing to startle the horses any further.

Estrién made for what looked like their leader, a man who seemed to be organising the troops, pointing him out to Dane, it was so difficult to tell when they all wore the same uniform. Dane nodded and shot a massive blast of electrum at the man, then another and another. He turned into a sticky red and grey mess as his blood boiled within and his skin sizzled.

'You blasted mage hater!' Dane screamed. 'Die by my hand, you bastard!' He finished the commander off with flash-fire. The troops around their leader screamed in horror and ran.

Amber took advantage of the cover of them both ahead of her, going for the enemy who came at their flank. Her short-swords whirled in her hands, she jumped and shimmied and twirled out of the way of enemy swords, going down and under, slashing upwards, as she had said she would do. She enjoyed the startled looks on their faces, these so-called men, who would have her as some kind of servant, or perhaps their sex slave if they could. She left them in pools of their own scrotal blood, shrieking in agony.

And Tamlyn, with sabre in one hand and a cruel looking dagger in the other, was heard to sigh very satisfactorily as he took down another Adammite elf-hater. His relief at the sight of his own Dair Chev'al arriving was immense, and he felt proud of his people, his Court.

Slowly the Adammites were pushed back. White Star swung in huge semicircles of death, Dane threw arcs of flash-fire over raised metal shields, burning the bearer's hands and bodies, and the King's men moved in, heartened by the realisation these people *could* be beaten. The Dair Chev'al kept out of the way of the main groups, but dealt a constant semi-circular hail of arrows before finally moving in with flashing sabres or cutlasses.

It turned the tide. Once so assured of themselves, the Adammites found they were now on the run. The battlefield began to turn black with the bodies of Adammites and rivers of red ran across the sweet green fields.

Eventually what was left of the Adammite troops retreated back to Pennyport, their losses becoming too great to sustain. The king made camp on the plain outside the port, awaiting his reinforcements, his troops too exhausted to continue that day into Pennyport. In any case, even with the additional Dair Chev'al, he didn't have enough to take back the town as yet. He approached the newcomers.

'So, you must be Knight Commander Estrién, with the amazing Sword of D'rendiél?' King Alexis gave Estrién an appreciative smile. Estrién nodded, bowed to the king. Alexis spoke gratefully, 'I thank you with all my heart, we were nearly finished there. You wield a marvellous weapon with incredible skill.' He turned to Dane, 'And you Dane, we need more mages. With power like that we can create a great army, with those such as yourself.'

But Dane merely shook his head, 'I only wish there were many more like me, alas we are few.' The king nodded in agreement, even in Orlandium, there were not many mages. Still, he would seek them out. But the king was overwhelmed by the pace at which the Adammites were moving, taking over.

'This Blazing Sun cult is sweeping through the country like a plague,' he told them. 'I'm even finding it among my own men. We've been too soft for too long, we haven't kept up our armies and we don't believe in war. What do we do when we have to fight against these people? They love war, they honour war, they honour death.' He stood wearily, bitterly shaking his head.

'We have to prove that love of life is greater than love of death,' Estrién replied, 'we have to make people realise what they will lose if they let these people take over. My race will go, and there will be no more tree folk, nor dwarves, nor mages. The forests will die. This world, our Mer'edrynn will die, will be lost forever. They will build dark cities of stone where there were once fields and trees. The rivers will become polluted, the fish will die. They will use slaves to till the soil, people who do not have the love of the land in their heart. There will eventually be starvation.

I can see this clearly.' He looked with soulful eyes into the distance.

The king was silent for some moments, realising the truth of Estrién's words. 'That's as may be, you are right. But I'm a simple man, I see people who starve *now*, they need food in their bellies. Cities need a huge amount of food to feed their people, trade is essential. So I'm *not* going back to Orlandium without taking back my port.

We need to harry these people while we wait for reinforcements, they should be here by tomorrow. So we need to get in there now, and make trouble before they revenge their losses upon the townsfolk.' He wondered to himself if any of his Corps de Lyons might have a go.

Amber raised an eyebrow at the group. 'Well, boys, why not? Let's go in, see what we can find, see what mess we can make until reinforcements arrive. I'm game at any rate.' The others nodded, accepting; if Amber thought they could do it, well, they would. Dane said he needed some food, perhaps a healing potion or two from his store in his backpack, he was pretty much drained. But later, he would be ready again. He would also see to some of the wounded in the meantime.

The Dair Chev'al now came riding over, their losses minimal. Tamlyn greeted Kielan and the other Knights.

'Ah, *well met*, my brothers, I thought we were lost. You came at the right time.'

Kielan jumped off his horse, went to hug him as they clasped hands. 'We said we would come, we would not let you down. Now we shall stay until we get the ports back.'

A grateful King Alexis came over. 'Your timing is perfect,' he stated, 'so glad you came.' He held out his hand, amazed at the turn of events. He still lived, would fight another day - and he *would* live. He would see his wife and child once more, *he would*.

Amber and the group planned their evening raid. King Alexis approved, he wanted someone to get into the town and see what was happening as well as to make trouble.

They waited until night, then sneaked into the port. It wasn't a walled city, but it spanned a river, two sides to the city. One side was residential, the other the commercial hub. The Adammites couldn't control all of it. They went in through the residential area, keeping well away from the Adammite Guard now patrolling the streets.

They saw the troops looked downhearted, the life taken out of them after this battle, morale was now low. The Adammites took their anger out on local people, rounding up elves and dwarves, the easiest to identify, women mostly, screams heard throughout the city. Amber and the others knew they could not let this go on for any length of time. Amber's heart was bursting, her indignation intense with every scream she heard. She wanted to rush in and help. The others stopped her, only in the quiet places, the truly dark places could they help. Other than that it would be suicide. She gritted her teeth in anger, but agreed.

They reached the port, full of Adammite ships, the many-masted carracks with the ballistae pointed towards the town, their sails furled. Dane had an idea.

'Let's burn the tar barrels. The sails will soon catch fire, maybe we can destroy the boats - it'll make a mess anyway, keep them busy.'

The others looked shocked at him. 'But Dane, they'll catch us in a moment.'

'True, but not if we have a diversion. C'mon, let's see if the Tsiganii are on their barges, or if they've left ...'

They crept along the crumbling pathway by the river towards where the Tsiganii could usually be found, although tonight there were none to be seen. They followed the river inland, finding them a few miles downstream. A great mass of barges lined the river, all of them empty of goods, when they should have been filled, none were moving when all should have been travelling the waterways. The swarthy inhabitants were anxious and angry.

Dane asked to see someone in charge, telling them he needed a diversion against the invaders.

They were unhappy at first, not wishing to brave the port again, but when Dane explained what he wanted to do, to try to burn the ships, they laughed at the sport of it, and agreed.

'We need trade moving as normal,' they said, 'those bastards have taken our livelihood away. Not only that, they've taken the goods we brought to Pennyport. We'll help. What is it you require?'

'Just give us enough time to set the tar or pitch barrels ablaze, I'll set fire to the sails with my magic. Even if we can't sink the ships, they'll be immobilised, it's enough.'

The angry bargees took their barges back towards the city, left them just short of the port. Then they all went with blazing torches to the port itself, shouting and screaming at the stationed troops. It became pandemonium. The Tsiganii were fearsome fighters themselves, bearing knives and cutlasses, they would not be able to stand a big onslaught, they weren't an army, but they could make a stand.

In fact they too gathered tar barrels and lit them, rolling them toward the Adammite guards at the docks. They collected piles of stones and threw them at the guards, adding to the general chaos.

On board the ships the men hurried to the ballistae, firing into the gathering crowds. For a few minutes their attention was turned to the Tsiganii.

Dane took full advantage as he ran through the port from the opposite end, his mage fire blazing on each and every ship he could reach. He looked on with deep satisfaction as another sail went up and a tar barrel burst into flames. Amber and Tamlyn stuffed rags into tar and attached them to arrows, before Dane lit them, and sent them too into the sails of the boats. By the time they realised that they were being attacked from the other side of the port, there was pandemonium as the sails and barrels were set alight. The Adammites were kept busy trying to throw the barrels off the ships, trying to douse the flames.

It kept them busy all night.

Just as the four had dashed through enemy lines earlier in the day, so did they rush through the harbour, from one end to another, stopping only to light up arrows and for Dane to fling fire through his staff of oak. Eventually they reached the far end of the harbour, their night's work completed.

The Tsiganii ran back to their barges, few Adammites following them, all were desperately trying to save their ships.

Dane and the group snuck out of the harbour, joining the mass rush of the Tsiganii, hidden within the crowd, before turning back through the streets of the residential quarter. Eventually they made their way out, back to the king.

Alexis was laughing, he had seen the mayhem from the hill. '*You* made a mess, Dane, didn't you?' He shook his head, amazed at the versatility of the four. Dane laughed too and explained about the help he'd had from the Tsigani. Alexis said he would remember, take note to thank them, when he next spoke to them.

By morning a large contingent of Westerling troops had arrived. He and Estrién led the joint forces into the town and by evening Pennyport was back in the King's hands.

The Adammites and the turncoats of the town had committed treason.

King Alexis took no prisoners.

The port looked like a disaster area, but it meant many of the Adammite ships were immobilised. He sent troops into each ship to take out any remaining Adammites and to see what was salvageable. The Tsiganii came to see what could be done, they too would help. The shipwrights of Pennyport were eventually given clearance to repair whatever could be repaired, keep them in Westerling hands. King Alexis would add these spoils of war to his own somewhat smaller fleet, play the Adammites at their own game.

The King was truly grateful to the group. 'Come to Orlandium,' he told them, 'we owe you, I assure you, some reparation is due and we are never stingy.' They agreed, and thanked him, they would see him back at Orlandium. Cash was always useful.

But ...'We shall first go to Floriénne,' said Estrién, 'the Dûchesse wishes to see me and I have been given guarantees by the Dair Chev'al that I am not under arrest or anything. I have agreed to go. *It is time.'* His face said otherwise, he didn't really wish to go, but his conscience knew better.

They stayed with the king's troops for some days, helping to clean up, camping with the Dair Chev'al. Dane helped many an injured soldier, magelight waved softly over painful and life-threatening wounds. He was hailed as a miracle worker. It made King Alexis realise he would take mages with him wherever from then on, keep a certain number, however few, with his troops, even if they were just healers. '*Just healers*', he thought to himself - acknowledging they were actually priceless.

Horses were found for the four, riderless from the battlefield, they could be put to good use. And so they rode out eastwards on a fair Harvesthaeme morning, late in the ninth month and the turn of the year.

But a chill wind was coming in from the sea, reminding them there was far to go and dark days were ahead of them.

Chapter 7

News throughout the country was dire. The amalgamation of Adammites and King Kyneweth's forces had taken the north by storm, almost all of Segantium was now in Adammite hands. Kyneweth had built his forces over many years and they were experienced troops, having repelled invaders from the north for decades. Now they were fully part of the Adammite revolution, for that's what it was, a revolution of the world as it stood. They invaded from the Isle of Glasse, their offshore stronghold, yet they came from within. Mer'edrynn was at war with itself, and King Kyneweth was happy to accept this new warrior cult and their new god.

It was even said that Von Adamm himself now resided at Draecastle.

*

Draecastle, north west Segantium.

The fortress at Draecastle looked as it sounded, a dark, forbidding and cold construction. Grey stone met greyed wooden ramparts, weather-beaten and sickly green in places where the sun never reached. A dark, dank moat curved around the castle, only accessible across an enormous drawbridge. It was the epitome of a border castle, easy to shoot arrows from its towers, big enough to hold a small army and probably impregnable. And of course, outer and inner walls, several layers with towers and battlements separated by courtyards until the inner keep was reached. Each guarded more closely than the last, enemies were channelled through the maze of a well defended barbican. The centre with the Great Hall, temple and bedchambers was a veritable virgin's bower - untouched by any outsider for centuries.

A cold blast of wind seemed to howl down passageways throughout most of the year - and there were many passageways. Yet the innermost courtyard was sheltered, summer arrived here as elsewhere, although the dour face of King Kyneweth never acknowledged summer or sunshine.

His wife had died in childbirth ten years previously, the child too, sickly from the first, took ill on a cold winter morn and died unloved and unnamed. Yet he had five other children, all sons, from the ages of twelve to twenty, all good strong stock. He hadn't smiled since his beloved wife had died and he never would again. There were women in his court, he wanted none, he had no desire left. He drank to ease his pain.

But this Mordecai von Adamm, he brought something else to his court - a lust for power. It was new, it was different, and it sufficed. Once more his blood began to soar.

The eldest son, a tall young man with jet black waves of hair, watched his father with contempt. He had never agreed to this amalgamation of forces with these dour and miserable people. Duggan remembered his father as he had been once, so full of life, and love - a rich, hearty man. But for ten years, only a shadow of himself, and now it felt like he was a puppet of these new masters. Like the rest of the Adammites, his father was dressed in black, but then, for ten years he had only worn mourning black. Perhaps that was what had attracted him, perhaps it was as simple as that? He knew he would never understand why his father chose this path.

The new master was speaking. Duggan hated the wretch, piling lies upon lies and turning his father against the people of the realm. There had been elves and dwarves at Court, his own tutor was a dwarf, taught him mathematics and astronomy, some alchemy. A great philosopher was Gourien, a wise man, now banned from Court, hiding somewhere in Segantium. He longed for his sane advice, but his father had turned as bigoted as this miserable bigot who had his father's trust.

Duggan desperately wanted to leave the Court, but was held back by two things. His father wouldn't let him leave - on pain of exile - and the fact that he might just do some good staying here. He had young brothers too, they needed protection. He watched Mordecai von Adamm as he spoke, understanding how he swayed his father. When you watched him speak, he mesmerised you with his eyes, his conviction. But when you turned away, you heard the evil in his voice, at least, *he* did. He hated the man.

King Kyneweth lapped up the man's words, blood that once was cold rushed hot with lust again - the lust for power, the heat of hatred. He hadn't felt so good in years, he finally felt alive. Let this man speak in his Court, his words rang true, he built up a fire in your soul. He listened with reverence as the great man spoke. They stood together in the Haegudsael, the Great Hall of the castle, the place of the stone throne that King Kyneweth's ancient ancestors had all sat upon and ruled their land. He stood listening reverentially to Von Adamm.

Von Adamm spoke quite softly but with surety, a steely conviction, his annunciation crystal clear.

'We will take over the whole of this land, we will reign supreme. Mankind has a right to use Mer'edrynn for his own. We are the very top of the evolutionary tree, they fall before us like swatted insects. They think only of pleasure, of drinking and feasting and fornicating. They live on borrowed time, they are killing themselves with their decadence. No, the land is ours by right.' His words were lofty, his manner dramatic, as an actor facing his audience. He stopped to breathe, before beginning again, speaking directly to the King, fixing him with his hypnotic stare.

He wasn't an imposing creature, he was smallish, slight, of little stature. His looks were plain, one of his hands looked burnt, the skin twisted. Yet he was in no worse condition than any man who had seen battle, there was nothing inherently unpleasant to look at. When he spoke, the conviction came through, the power of the man, he held you in the vice of voice and eyes together. Something about his stare fixed you, stopped you in your tracks. And you believed in what he said.

Right at this moment though, he was obviously annoyed.

'This degenerate group I have heard about is becoming a nuisance. Who are they? I know they are a mix of elves and a mage - but I need to know more. It is thanks to them we have not been able to keep Pennyport, they must be annihilated, put on the pyres of justice and destroyed.' Black eyes blazed with exasperation. 'I am told there is a man outside, he says he knows one of them.' He turned to the guard at the door, gestured imperiously, 'send him in, let us see what he has to say.'

It was quite clear who was now in charge of the castle.

The guard bowed and hurried through the great door.

A tall, handsome man of Sevillon stock strutted through the doorway. He wore leather leggings and a leather cuirass. The belt around his hips held a sabre and a row of daggers. He gave a deep, ceremonial bow. He spoke with a slight accent of Sevillain.

'Sir, my name is Arne and I can at least identify one of these people you wish to know about. He is an ill mannered, sneaking little roué of an elf from the Court of Floriénne. His name is Knight Captain Tamlyn Taenghelin, son of Lord Taenghelin of the same Court. He is without honour and I would be glad to be of your service to get rid of this creature.'

Von Adamm looked appreciatively at the man, he had heard of his prowess with sword and dagger. Yet the name Tamlyn sounded familiar. Where had he seen or heard of him? 'Tell me, what does this Taenghelin look like?' he asked.

The Sevillain sneered. 'Typical, blonde haired, green-eyed, elven stock; a pretty boy with long eyelashes, a seducer of both women and men alike. He is of the Dair Chev'al.'

Von Adamm thought for a while, remembering a summer evening. 'Tell me, does he wear the gold oak leaf on his shoulder and does he play a lute?' Arne nodded, *yes, he does*. 'Then I know who he is, and I know of the others with him. I saw them once in the garden of an inn, a disgusting assorted set, a mage, two elves and a harlot. Let me see ...' he thought back. 'The mage played stupid magic games and the elves sang some sentimental rubbish. The woman ... attractive for a whore ... yes, they were all playing up to her, bees around a honeypot. It was almost impossible to tell who was her lover, perhaps all three were?' His black eyes turned inwards, 'hmm, yes, Amber was her name, the others, I forget - no, wait, Dane, the mage, and the other elf, a strange one, emerald eyes - Strién or something.'

Arne shot out his hand, 'Sir, did you say Amber? What did she look like? Did she have eyes that matched her name and a shock of deep auburn hair?' This was more than coincidence, this was *fate*.

'Yes, she did, a soft voice too, quite attractive for a whore - and she was definitely a whore.'

Arne couldn't believe this. 'I thought she had died in the circus fire. My lord, I can tell you all about her, everything you wish to know ...' He rubbed his hands in glee. Life without Amber had not been good, and the circus was a shadow of what it had been. He'd left Longshanks, made out on his own. He could use this to his advantage. He settled himself to tell everything he knew of her.

Much later, von Adamm spoke to them all. 'I now know who are these irritating little insects. They are in our way and they *must* be destroyed. I want every available man on this. The mage, the elves are to be killed, removed from the face of the world - preferably thrown together on one massive purifying pyre. The harlot will be brought here, to face us, to be brought into line. I have a great fancy to punish this presumptuous hussy, we must make an example of her.' He smiled slyly at King Kyneweth. 'I'm sure you have need of a concubine do you not? She will be most suitable - *after I have finished with her.*'

King Kyneweth wasn't sure, but he would do as von Adamm asked. He seemed to have answers for everything, perhaps his loneliness too?

Spies and agents were sent throughout the land to find Amber and her men.

Young Duggan sat at the side and watched in horror.

Chapter 8

Estrién somewhat unwillingly followed the Dair Chev'al back to Floriénne. They helped with a few mopping up operations to remove the remaining Adammite forces from some of the smaller fishing villages along the coast, these villages being en route to Floriénne. Estrién wanted the Dair Chev'al to come and help with Elvinhaeme, but there were clearly not enough forces yet for that and the Adammites were well dug in, in places such as Hollyporth. He would need far greater numbers to take back Elvinhaeme. He considered that Westerling was always going to be a step too many - at least as yet - for the Adammites, King Alexis was gearing up for war.

But in the future? Who knew?

Once the main fighting at the coast was over, the elven knights wished to return home - and to take their prized possession with them, *the sword* and the elf who had spirited it away from their realm.

It seemed that Estrién had little choice.

The Dair Chev'al surrounded his horse as they traversed the roads, whether as escort or as guards, he couldn't rightly tell. They were friendly enough, and they seemed in awe of him, yet there was a distance. They still had orders to follow, and the orders were paramount. On an evening when they camped they swapped stories and jokes, but still he felt uncomfortable.

It was possibly his imagination, but there seemed hidden undercurrents, he was kept out of the hub. Estrién's heightened senses however felt *something*.

By tacit consent he, Amber and Dane now shared a tent, and while the Dair Chev'al were with them, Tamlyn seemed to constantly be in one or other of their tents for the night. In their own tent alone one night, Estrién quietly spoke to Dane and Amber.

'When we arrive in Floriénne, be on guard. I am not happy. They may speak true, they may not, but I am wary of entering that Court. Maybe it's just the friendly rivalry between Elvinhaeme and Floriénne, but we always used to say they were tricksy elves, so take care.' Both understood, he was, after all, currently Public Enemy Number One in Floriénne. They would keep eyes and ears open, be alert at all times.

They entered Shirewood the following day; a couple of days riding along well tended paths would bring them to Floriénne. It was a realm set wholly within forested lands, both deciduous and coniferous. The elves wanted greenery throughout the year, and a tall fir, whilst being sombre, was still, at least, green. Then of course the shiny green leaves and the red berries of holly added brightness to a cold winter. And naturally, the holm oak grew in abundance, our own glossy evergreen, in a forest mostly dedicated to oaks. The realm was planned to have greenery, berries and preferably blossom throughout the seasons.

On the south facing, sun-catching slopes of sheltered valleys, the elves grew rich and juicy grapes, pinot noir for a warm red wine, Chardonnay for a cool white wine and Muscat for a sweet dessert wine; simple grapes, but they matched the soil and the air. They tended these vines with loving care. They even sold to the fussy Chev'alierre across the water. Tamlyn's father was a great wine grower, his wines famous throughout Mer'edrynn. Soft fruits too were grown here, summer meals were finished off with a delicious dish of strawberries and cream, washed down with a good local Muscat, or perhaps a fine cognac. The elves lived well.

In late summer, as now, the forest was one large leafy canopy, and the elves along with Dane, Amber and Estrién took their horses slowly through. There was no real centre to the realm, only the palace, there were no towns, only small hamlets. Some houses were stone, most were wooden high-roofed lodges, their windows large to let in the light and the forest. Travelling markets were scattered here and there, taking place on designated days and times. In places the trees had been grown so as to weave together to provide shelter, a meeting ground for wood loving folk. Oak trees abounded, some enormous, large enough to have tree houses in them, they could see legs swinging happily along the branches, and happy chatter, the clink of goblets as an elf enjoyed his evening rest.

There were several manor houses with gardens rich in produce. Tamlyn's father owned a very large estate, and was one of the best vintners of the realm. He grew a smoky Muscat grape, in great demand, the resultant sweet wine and the dignified cognac from his vineyard held in high regard. Tamlyn wasn't exactly poor. He told the group they could go visit any time, his family would be glad to see them, put them up for a few nights. He normally lived in the palace, but he still had a room back at his parent's home, complete with childhood toys and embarrassing paraphernalia that his doting mother wouldn't throw out.

'They are lovely people, but I feel stifled when I return, so I only ever stay a day or two. You know what they are like, they worry and obsess about you. Then they disagree with your lifestyle, yet I'm not that much different to my father, he probably remembers his own misspent youth when I'm around. I'm glad to see them, but always glad to get away. They probably think the same about me ...' He pulled a moue with his mouth.

Life doesn't change much, anywhere, anytime. Parents remain parents and children grow up and grow away. *As they should.*

The other three however, looked on him with envy. None had parents to go back to or get annoyed with. Estrién had in fact grown very fond of his uncle, he'd taken him on as a son. And right now, he would have liked a little advice. The man had said too little, too late to him, when he truly needed to know more.

But perhaps there was little more to know; after all, a man forges his own destiny. People make their own choices, fight their own fights, according to their conscience. Advice is welcome, but true knowledge only comes from experience.

The Dair Chev'al were welcomed everywhere - beautiful knights in fine armour on splendid horses are a delightful sight. The young women particularly welcomed them, and Tamlyn and his elven friends spent some very pleasant evenings en route.

But Estrién, Dane and Amber kept themselves a little apart, not that they felt unwelcome, just a little separate. Tamlyn was taken up with, and by, his fellow knights so he was rarely with them. He himself was doing his duty to his Dûchesse. So the three stayed together: strangers in a strange land, as the saying goes.

So it was with a certain trepidation that Estrién entered the Court of Floriénne in the very centre of the realm.

The *hush* began as he approached the main entrance to the palace, or more correctly, the vast palace grounds. There were no high walls, but very large, well tended hedges, each gated. The gates were fine, intricately patterned swirls, like wrought iron, but made of oak. Pennants flew on the gateposts and could be seen on top of many of the buildings.

Chicly dressed people milled about, in and out of the palace park, for that's what it was, there were stalls and small shops here, both outside the grounds and just inside, selling very fine produce. The shops sold wine or silks, jewellery and perfumes, fine leather goods, beautiful, illustrated books, costly spices and coffee and included an armourer's wares and a sword-smith.

The stalls held the very best fruit and vegetables, pottery and elegantly carved woodenware, some ready-made clothing and flowers, a few stalls sold bread, cakes and pies. There were carved wooden tables and chairs outside some of the wine shops, with large gaily coloured umbrellas in the centre of the tables, where elegant elves sat comfortably, toasting the day and each other. One area, under a light wicker canopy, surrounded by hanging baskets and tubs of flowers, was an open air restaurant, people chatting merrily with more clink of goblets.

Similarly, large, richly coloured tents held more goods, and small tables to sit and enjoy their expensive coffee. Everything was grossly overpriced for the 'discerning buyers' of the palace and its environs. Tamlyn explained they held markets throughout Floriénne on different days of the month, and people had small shops or stalls just about everywhere, you just had to know who, or when. If you didn't want to pay these prices, or you didn't have the cash, a mile away most things were cheaper.

Everything about the place suggested wealth, and with it, the self-assurance that only comes from money and security, the knowledge of certainty. Voices spoke loud with confidence.

But strangely, as the knights rode through, and Estrién approached the gates, a hush came to the crowd. They were expecting him, and they all wanted to see this strange and possibly exciting creature - *the thief.* Word had gone ahead.

On his tall bay horse, Estrién felt somewhat conspicuous as they ambled through the gates, the elven guards in their shining armour, saluting them all. It seemed the palace was about a mile further in, keeping the noise of the market well away from its environs.

At first they passed through well tended gardens, a public park behind the small, but select commercial centre. There were tree-lined lawns, fountains, small copses through which streams ran, flowers everywhere, including a sweet smelling rose garden. Statues were placed at strategic spots, some quite erotic, and the very centre of these gardens held a small lake with a huge fountain in the middle, willows wisping into its waters. People were strolling around enjoying the beauty, quietly holding hands, sitting on elegantly carved and curved seats.

Everyone stopped to watch them as they advanced. Estrién felt he was now guarded by two hundred Knights of Floriénne, and they weren't obviously letting him go until he'd seen the Dûchesse. They left the park to ride through a large wooded area, all oaks, various kinds, sessile, common, red oak, turkey oak, the evergreen holm oak, even the slightly smaller evergreen cork oak. It was a cool and peaceful place, and Tamlyn explained that game was nurtured here for their sporting pleasure and their table. Occasionally grouse or pheasant crossed their path, and there was the odd glimpse of antlers through trees.

Through this, and they moved on to well tended vegetable gardens and orchards, the gardeners held in high esteem here in Floriénne. Far to one side, fields of cows and sheep were seen grazing the rich pasture. This produce was for the Court alone. As they came through these, the palace could be seen, the wide pathway surrounded by excellent lawns and now bounded by a tall lavender hedge, the trail smelled beautiful. In fact, all of Floriénne smelled beautiful.

It was indeed, a palace of oak, a solid light-stone base structure, covered with delicate open panelling of intricately carved oak and soaring wooden towers pointing into the sky, pennants flying on every tower. The circular roofs of the towers were oaken, and there appeared to be carved wooden balconies on each floor. A mass of red and yellow adorning the palace walls and balconies could be seen from afar, as they neared they realised these were boxes of begonias and red pelargonium, hanging baskets of trailing flowers.

Now the security became tighter, another high hedge, this time of laurel and privet, solid hedges, elegantly shaped in places, but prickly rosa rugosa with its white and cerise flowers, was allowed to grow profusely through it. The hedge smelled wonderful, and the thorns would deter intruders.

More silver clad guards armed with swords and pikes stood at the entrance gates. These gates were solid oak, nothing could be seen through them, although, once more they were richly carved. As the horsemen approached, the gates opened wide to allow passage of two hundred horses. Estrién wondered where they would all go, but it was clear that here were stable blocks and barracks for the knights, they still had some distance to go to the palace itself.

Nor was the path straight. It wound its way through a maze of hedges, similar to the large hedge outside. Gates led off the hedge, small houses could be seen, for the gardeners and retainers of the palace. The closer they went, the more exotic the flora, olive trees appeared and palms mixed with rich ferns, the occasional tree-lined pond or pretty garden with a statue or fountain. Tubs and urns were filled with flowers and trailing ivy. There was nothing wild here, everything carefully grown, carefully tended. If you wanted the wild wood, you went north, the Foraes Dair went on for hundreds of miles. But here, it was tamed and ordered.

They finally reached the inner palace gates. Here most of the knights dismounted, yet Estrién's group and Tamlyn and his other Knights' Captain remained seated. But as the doors opened to reveal a large and elegant courtyard, with more paths and stables, the knights followed on foot. Estrién felt even more that he was their prisoner. Tamlyn led him to the private Court stables where they dismounted and left the horses in the hands of well-mannered grooms.

'You look pensive, my friend,' he pronounced, 'stop worrying.' That was easier said than done.

Finally he was led into the vast oak-lined Great Hall of the palace, another flower filled room with velvet covered settles, hunting tapestries on the walls and huge windows looking out onto a large and beautiful wooden balcony. Beyond the balcony, more beautiful gardens. filled with terracotta pots, urns, a massive statue of Pan and beds of pale white, pink and mauve flowers, it stretched into the distance. It seemed the Dûchesse was out there, sitting quietly by a fountain, Tamlyn led the way to her.

It also meant there was space for two hundred knights to follow and watch the proceedings. It was clear to Estrién he was not to be trusted. It also ensured he was nowhere near the Vaults to steal some other precious relic.

Nor was she alone, many knights, courtiers as well as lords and ladies of the Court were milling around the gardens, all looking expectantly at him. Tamlyn saw his own father amongst them. He would have given a quick smile and a wave, but protocol forbade, he must greet the Dûchesse first..

For once, Estrién was unsure what to do. At the Temple of Oak, back in Orlandium, he had immediately bent down on one knee and offered his sword in the cause of the Lady Merrie. He had offered it once and would not do so again. Yet he believed this was what they wished, that he should kneel down and lay the sword at the feet of the Grand Dûchesse de Floriénne. He could not do that, it would be tantamount to offering it back to her, admitting it was hers.

It was not, it belonged only to him. Instead, he bowed deeply, the sword remaining on his back. He could hear it humming. Amber, Dane and Tamlyn stood close to him, almost protectively now, even Tamlyn felt the danger. They too bowed to the Dûchesse.

She acknowledged them, nodding her imperious head. As she did so, it seemed to Estrién that her knights closed in a little, ready to do her bidding. Her eye arched at him, and her forefinger beckoned him. He stepped forward, but did not kneel.

'Well, *Knight Commander Estrién*, as I am told you are now called by our priestesses, or *thief,* as I prefer to call you, just what have you to say for yourself?' She was old and stern and had spent the last months in woeful anxiety. She wanted answers, preferably before she threw this impudent upstart into the deepest dungeon and threw away the key. *But*, let him speak.

'I seem to gain new names with regular monotony,' he replied. 'I believe my true name is '*Nim'randuel Soleus D'rendiél Gilsylien Estaran'elvian* ', at least that was the name given me by my dying uncle in the northern Foraes Dair.'

She looked startled. 'King of the Elves - just exactly what do you mean?'

'I haven't the foggiest,' he laughed. 'I'm only repeating the name I was given, nor do I wish a throne of any kind. The sword, however, is mine ...' he looked around at everyone. ' ... *and it remains mine* ...' he spoke loudly. 'I challenge any one of you, or several if you prefer, to dispute me on this. I guarantee you will not live very long. I suggest you ask Knight Captain Tamlyn Taenghelin, along with some of the Dair Chev'al, who were with me on the battlefields outside Pennyport, as to the truth of that.'

He preferred to be on the offensive here, a defensive stance was a waste of time.

Tamlyn stepped forward. 'Without prejudice, my Dûchesse, the sword of D'rendiél is truly his. And he has repaired it, bringing it to its fullest beauty and power.'

The Dûchesse frowned, 'then let me see it, Sir Estrién, display the completed sword to us.'

White Star was now singing in its harness. Estrién slowly drew it forth, he didn't want anyone thinking he was going to attack. It caught the sun and sparkled like a thousand diamonds, the emerald pommel adding its own ghostly hue, momentarily blinding everyone. It was always hard to actually look at it, it blazed upon the eye.

He pointed out the now settled Opalstone, or Elfenstone as Amber knew it. Everything about the sword was magnificent. He moved closer to the Dûchesse, held the sword down, its point to the ground, allowed her examine the sword. The Dûchesse reached out to touch it, to take it from him. He gave a slight shake of his head. 'I am sorry ma'am, you may look, but I cannot allow you to touch it.' A high keening note was coming from the sword, gaining in strength as the Dûchesse's hand came closer. It mellowed as she pulled her hand away. She raised an eyebrow.

'The sword belongs here!' she announced angrily, 'here safely in our realm, it guards us from evil.'

Before she could say more, Estrién butted in. 'No, Your Grace, *the sword belongs in my hand.* It is *I* who will protect you from evil, the evil that pursues us all now, the Adammite revolution. These people intend to take this realm from you, to destroy all elves.' He looked up, his piercing gaze holding everyone, held the sword high in the air. *'Now* is not the time for this to sit idly by, on soft velvet in a glass case in the deepest recesses of an old museum, a useless old relic. *Now* is the time to use this priceless weapon, to wield it on the field of battle, to show these mindless and selfish bastards just what we can do to preserve our world.'

He continued speaking with anger and vehemence. 'And I have already done just that, this sword sings in my hands as I slice these people to shreds, as I will continue to do.' He turned around, speaking to the Dair Chev'al standing behind him, 'You, *fellow Knights*, you joined me in those battles, we showed those bigoted and cruel Adammites what it means to cross Merrie's children. We worked together, eormynn and elf, *as we should.* We took them out and destroyed the fools. We can do it again, but we must work as one, in harmony, as we have always been in harmony.'

'*You still stole it*,' the Dûchesse reminded him, yet she was impressed by his words. '*You should have asked.*' Estrién merely laughed. She nodded, agreeing it would have been impossible. 'and yet, perhaps if you had proved you could open the case, we may have believed you.'

Estrién shook his head, 'Nay, ma'am you would never have allowed me down there.'

That much was true, she would not. *But* ... 'No, you are right, Sir Estrién, you would not have been given the opportunity, we would have considered you a madman or a potential thief. Either way you would have been thrown into the dungeon, or if you were lucky, politely led out of the palace. However ...' she held out her hand, palm upwards, showing Estrién a table on which something lay covered in a white cloth. She nodded to the Seneschal standing close by, who ceremoniously removed the cloth.

Underneath lay the empty case of the Sword of D'rendiél.

'We cannot take you down to the Vaults, you are too dangerous. But here lies the empty case. We are still unable to open it, at least without the Guardians. Prove your point and open it, if you can.' She smiled smugly, knowing she had the advantage. She would have this upstart in irons before long and the sword safely back, if the three Guardians who could supposedly open the case actually could do so.

Estrién shrugged his shoulders. He walked over to the glass case. He did as he had done previously, he slightly touched the edge, then, as if knowing, certain points along the sides - points, it seemed, only he could feel. The top sprang open. White Star made a keening sound again, a sad, weeping sound. It obviously did not wish to return there.

He watched as the Dûchesse's mouth dropped open. Then he smiled, his wide, generous smile, benevolent in his triumph. He turned to his group, to Amber, Dane and Tamlyn. He held out his hand to Amber, she took it. 'Come my friends, we have done our duty, it is time we went ...'

But the Dûchesse stopped him. 'Nay, my Lord, I see, but can barely believe it, I hear the sword singing in your hand, when we here have never heard it. I see the beautiful Opalstone you have placed there, when none of us even knew about it, and *I see it in your eyes.* Your eyes blaze with the same bright green as the emerald pommel of the sword.' She unfurled herself from her seat, silken skirts shimmering and rustling. She stood straight but slight, powerful by nature not body. With an imperious hand she beckoned Estrién. 'It may belong to you, but can you use it? I need to know personally, *I* need to see. Come with me.' She turned and led him out of the gardens.

The knights followed, Estrién was to be guarded at all times. He wondered what she wanted?

She took him across fields towards what was clearly a showground of some sort, a circular amphitheatre with seats all around above a fenced-in tourney ground. Gated tunnels ran off from the central arena, no doubt to underground caves or cellars, perhaps to multiple exits elsewhere in the field.

'You expect me to fight your knights, your Grace?' Estrién asked curiously. 'You are aware that is impossible, I have already killed three of them. Do you enjoy watching the slaughter of your warriors?' He had known there would be something else, the glass case had been too easy.

The Dûchesse shook her head. 'No, Sir Estrién, I have no intention of seeing you kill any more of my people. But I do have something worthy of you and I should like to see you pitted against it.'

Now it was clear that the amphitheatre was filling, people swarming in, including the Dair Chev'al, all looking expectantly at Estrién and the Dûchesse. They were in for some sport and all looked forward to the duel.

Tamlyn came over to Estrién. 'I don't know what they are doing, my friend, I assure you I would not have brought you here if I had known.' He took his hand, peering into his face. 'My sword is yours, I will give any help you need.'

He took out his sword, waved it in the air. 'I stand by Estrién,' he proclaimed to the crowd.

Amber took out her short-swords, also stood next to Estrién, and Dane stepped forwards, took the staff from his back, gave a brief flash of electrum in the air, both gave Estrién their assurance of aid. They would stay by his side no matter what.

Estrién waved them off with a shake of his head. 'I'm fine,' he claimed, 'but I appreciate your kindness. I know you stand by me and that counts fully with me. I know who are my friends. Let us see what happens.' He marched off down to the centre of the arena. He had always known there would be fighting. He would give them a show, if nothing else. He took White Star from his back, it hummed softly as if it hadn't expected this. 'Well, my friend,' he spoke to the sword, 'just you and I. Let us see shall we?' realising that the elves of Floriénne lived up to their reputation. Fair of face, gentle and courteous in manner, but that was a deception. Underneath, they were deadly, rather like Tamlyn. It seemed to Estrién that these people were close cousins to the Fae.

He turned to the now filled stadium, eager faces around him. His friends stood close to the edge, the contrast clear on their faces, frowns and worry lines. He spoke to the crowd.

'It appears you want blood, either mine or some other poor fool's. I have no wish to kill, yet this is your wish. Send in your warriors and let it be done - their blood is on your hands.' He stood straight and firm, raised White Star above him to show readiness. It all felt surreal, false. Out there was a real enemy and they were playing here, studying him, testing his strength and ability. '*What a waste,*' he thought.

He watched as the Dûchesse nodded to someone at the side of the arena, the double gates opened. Eight guards were clearly seen to be pulling something in to the arena, using four plaited dwarven cords, two to each cord This type of rope was made of metal, extruded to flexibility, but strong and flexible. The dwarves were extremely able with metalwork, and this cord was their finest. It was also exceedingly expensive, the elves of Floriénne were showing off their wealth.

But it was surely never meant for this.

Estrién realised immediately and looked on in horror. Two of the plaited cords were around its forelegs, two around it's snout. It looked filthy, as if it had been dragged through mud. What was worse was that its wings were tied together above its body by the metallic cords slotted through holes actually made in the wingspan. The wings were stuck above its back and it would never be able to fly.

He watched, disbelieving that elves could do this.

They pulled it to the centre of the arena, dropped the cords and ran. Estrién looked across into the whirring eyes of a full grown and just awakening dragon.

For a few moments he did nothing, merely inspected the dragon. It was, or would have been, beautiful, it's skin pearlescent, a bright emerald green, the sort that weirdly changes colour when the sun hits it from another angle, purple perhaps. But now most of its skin was covered in mud and it looked shocked as if it had been severely beaten, or drugged, probably both. Estrién could see many arrow piercings in its skin, patches of dried blood, he wondered how many archers it had taken to bring it down? And how much poison? The holes in the wings were festering, poison perhaps had got in to the wings themselves.

The crowd were heard murmuring, they had waited for this. He would either prove himself, or die. Either way was good.

But they did not know Estrién.

The crowd were after a spectacle, and he would give them one. But not the one they sought.

'You bring this poor beast to me bound like this and expect me to slaughter it?' he shouted with rage. 'I will do no such thing, *there is no honour here.*'

The crowd booed sullenly, he wasn't playing along. Let him die then.

The dragon began to stir, awakening from its drugged sleep, incredulous at its captivity. Slowly it gazed around the arena, at its captors. It was clearly in pain and it looked puzzled at the irritating rope binding its head and body. It began shaking off the cord from its snout, looped as it were around it. It struggled and shook its head to and fro, eventually dislodging the cord, immediately opened its mouth to breathe fire. It aimed the fire firstly at the cord still attached to its legs, hoping to rid itself of the discomfort, then pulled back in pain as the metallic rope heated against its skin. Then it shot fire into the sky, frightening everyone. There came a collective scream from the crowd.

It lifted a leg experimentally, the cord loosening, and kicked out, the long metallic line shooting outwards across the arena towards a group of onlookers, missing them by fractions, yet it was still attached. Gasps of shock could be heard amongst the spectators. They were waiting for this new hero to kill the creature before it could attack them, whereas this looked dangerous. *Get on with it man, before we're all killed ...*

Estrién stood in the centre shaking his head. To the crowd's amazement he put White Star back in its scabbard. What was he doing? Wasn't he there to protect them ... ? They watched in horror as he walked over to the dragon, his hands making strange sigils in the air.

He heard a murmuring from the crowd, *'kill ... kill ...kill ...'*

He ignored them and spoke gently. 'Hush, my friend, be still now, I will help.' Deeply he looked into those large round eyes, his hands waving in undulating circles, his voice tender, but commanding. It hurt him, the sight of this glorious beast reduced to a spectacle for blood hungry folk. He wondered how *elves* could do this to such a magnificent beast? What was happening to his world? He bent down and unfastened the cords curling around the legs, a simple matter. The metal cords slotted through the wings however, were quite different, they had been soldered on by a dwarven, or more likely an elven blacksmith. The dragon would eventually get them off, but only by tearing its wings. He could not bear the thought of this marvellous creature with tattered wings flapping uselessly in a vain attempt to rise.

He stood weeping inside. Something evil had entered this land, something that led people to this cruelty. You did not have sport with a dragon, they were magnificent, noble animals, albeit, a dying breed. They lived a world apart, in Draconia, or on the Greylumings, rarely seen in the populated lands. Estrién believed they were to be protected, however fierce they were. If you encroached on their world, or they on yours, and they attacked you, that would be different, you had to defend yourself, or become dragon breakfast. But here ... bound and gagged for sport? ... *No*.

The dragon, mesmerised momentarily by Estrién's innate beast magic, was now getting restless, it shot fire into the air again, although not at him. He spoke softly in its ear, once more making strange sigils in front of its eyes. 'Give me time, my friend,' he said, 'give me a little time and I shall free you.'

He now took White Star from his back. The crowd watched hungrily, at last he was going to kill it, their bloodlust whipping up as they awaited it's slaughter. The chant came again, *'kill ... kill ...kill ...'*

The crowd sighed with collective joy as he jumped up on top of the dragon, their blood thirst ravenous, now was the time, now he would kill it. *'Kill, kill, kill,'* they chanted again. But they watched also in amazement as instead he put the point of the sword inside the metallic cords on the wings, closed his eyes and pulled upwards. White Star sang loudly, almost happily in the afternoon sun, as the strong cord parted. Estrién smiled to himself, the sword truly was as fine as the legends. This kind of cord was as strong as any metal chain and White Star cut through it easily. He pulled the cord out of the holes through the wings. He hoped it would heal, he hoped it could fly. The holes looked terrible.

He jumped off its back, the wings beginning to flutter, as if the dragon was exercising unused muscles. He walked around the front of the dragon, it's eyes following him, almost intelligently, as if it knew, it understood. He patted its hide gently, stroking the rough skin. 'Now go, get out of here, before they come to take you back, go to your nest, your *wyerr*, your family.

Go with Merrie's blessings, my friend,' he shouted, as much to the crowd as to the dragon. He stood back to give the beast room. The crowd watched on. Amber, Dane and Tamlyn were seen to be smiling. It was all they expected of him.

The dragon lifted its wings experimentally, a whoomph in the air as they rose and fell, then with one last look at its benefactor through huge soulful eyes, it took off. The whole crowd ducked to get away from the massive wing span and the crusts of mud that fell from cracked skin as it shot gracefully into the air.

Then there was absolute silence. Estrién walked equally silently, grim-visaged, to the small gate that led upwards and out of the arena, the dragon already a speck in the distance.

He was greeted by the Dûchesse. She bent her head before him. 'I know not who you are, but I am learning. That was magnificent,' she conceded, 'you have qualities I had not dreamed of. You shame us, rightly so. I have made up my mind.' She held her head high, spoke with conviction and the might of her long ruler-ship. She spoke to every elf there.

'I hereby offer every knight, every soldier and every elf in this land in your fight against the injustice of the Adammites. We will aid you in every way we can, I can say no fairer than that. You have full rights of passage throughout this realm, and whatever you require we will do our best to provide.

The Sword of D'rendiél is truly in the right hands and may you continue to wield it well, with the degree of justice , fairness and compassion you have shown today.'

Estrién looked her in the eye. He was furious, but knew he had to hold back, he needed her help. 'Then I suggest you get your knights and militia down to the coast and protect your ports and fishing villages. That is where they will enter, not the Foraes Dair. They have no understanding of the forest and will not come that way, not unless they hack and burn as they go. Do it now, while you have time. And send the Dair Chev'al, as many as you can spare to King Alexis, currently at Pennyport. We need to go westwards, drive out the Adammites from Elvinhaeme.'

He walked away, he could not speak more, he would not offer his sword to them, not now. Later, if necessary, but not until then.

'Please stay the night, my Lord, you are more than welcome,' she continued. 'There are good rooms you can use, you are welcome to stay as long as you need.' The Dûchesse walked by his side as they returned to the palace, treating him as equal. 'You need have no fear, you have proved your worth.'

Proved his worth? Is that what she called it? His eyes briefly questioned his friends, they shook their heads, it was up to him. He realised tact was essential. He wanted to get as far away from here as possible, but ...

'I thank you, Your Grace. A night in a soft bed would be more than welcome, we have spent much time on the road.' Briefly he thought to himself how he would really like to get back to his old home in the north of the Foraes Dair, or ... yes, that little house they had rented in Orlandium. It had been fun, the four of them, but those pleasant days were probably long gone. He continued. 'However, we must go tomorrow, we have a war to fight.' He couldn't leave quickly enough, but there was no need to advertise that. He didn't wish her changing her mind and sending the whole Dair Chev'al on to him. It would be such a waste of Dair Chev'al. Their aid was useful, he could not refuse their help.

But yes, he had a war to wage. He only hoped he was ready for it.

*

Near the Greylumings Mountains.

To the east of Segantium, past the forest of Shirewood where the forest thinned out and became moorland, rose the great Greyluming mountains. At the edge of the mountains, close to a fast flowing river that sang with the icy sharpness of the cold Greylumings, a small tower stood solitary on a rocky outcrop.

The local people, hard headed folk who lived off what they could scavenge from the northern forest and the small herds of mountain goat they tended, left offerings there every now and again, even though the tower was a few days walk away. It seemed a good idea to appease the Lady of the Tower, for she was an enchantress. She had arrived one cold winter night a few years previously, had taken residence. Sometimes an unearthly blue-green light flashed from the windows, lighting the mountainside, unsettling the locals.

She did not speak to them, but would leave a lamp in one of the tower windows when she accepted their offering; food, cloth, wool from the goats. They gave what little they had. If anyone stood at the base of the tower, if all was quiet and there was no wind that day, sometimes, just sometimes, the enchantress could be heard humming. It was a pleasant sound, yet heard rarely. It did not stop the goatherds being afraid of her, for the whole tower was menacing, the sort of feeling that comes only when there is great danger within.

If any had ever looked inside - which they wouldn't - they would have seen a young woman sitting at a loom, weaving, a strange fey look in her eyes. She was very clever, she used natural dyes she had created to dye the wool, had spun the raw rough stuff herself, spun it as fine as any silk. She wove a pattern through the cloth, a story of the world, a story of life. She wove the beauties of Mer'edrynn into the cloth. She had been weaving it for some years, on and off, depending on her mood. Probably it would never be finished.

She wove reds and greens and gold into the cloth, delicate whirls and circles, curlicues of nature, midnight blue and orange settling the sun to sleep, a silver thread for my lady moon, and ... and ...

Sometimes her eyes grew dark with pain, the light in them shone fierce. Sometimes she stopped and stared and her mouth would turn into a big, round O, as she screamed silently, her fists clenched, her body shaking...

... and into the weave she would add a thread, a tiny black thread, misshapen and rough. A thread that warped the beautiful cloth. Not an ordinary black thread that gives texture or depth or drama to the design, it was not a thread of colour, but of singular negativity.

I cannot say all that was in it, but it included nettles and hog weed and the short razor-sharp grasses of the mountainside, the ones that scratch and tear unprotected skin as you walk past. She added deadly nightshade and henbane and poisonous aconites, along with other poisonous foul-smelling herbs and fungi. Her own blood had poured into the mix as she shredded every thorn she could find, and walked for miles to find oak galls to create the dye. She wove them all together with her magic, and spun the result into a misshapen thread of despair. It smelled like a wound gone bad, the smell of corruption and It broke down the other threads, the weave around it, warping the cloth, ruining the beautiful tapestry.

It was a thread of anger and hate and pain. A thread of disease and damage. *A thread of death.*

Her name was Anaïs and she was Amber's younger sister.

*

Tamlyn came over to Estrién. His father had suggested they stay at his manor for a few days, clearly they wished to get away, 'He is disgusted at what happened, you impressed him deeply. We are all welcome there, it's only a couple of hours ride. Let's go tomorrow.'

Estrién and the others accepted gratefully, although they could only stay for a couple of days, there was too much to do. They spent the evening mingling in the Great Hall of the palace, eating dainties proffered on silver platters covered with delicate white lace cloths, drank excellent wines from pure crystal glasses, the sort that sing when you touch to toast. But Estrién could not feel at home here, as Tamlyn did, the earlier hostility would always stay with him.

Tamlyn introduced them to his friends at Court, and his family, proud of his group, his team-mates; many glasses of wine were passed, many toasts were given.

But he seemed quieter, less comfortable than he had been in the past, less cocky and self-assured.

'Life with you has changed me,' he confided to the group when they had a moment alone. 'Estrién, you were glorious out there and I am ashamed of my people for their disrespect to that magnificent beast.'

Estrién shook his head sadly, 'Something is wrong, Tamlyn, there is a power of evil throughout the land now, it invades everywhere, even here. Somehow we must rise above it, cleanse it. These bastard Adammites keep spouting about cleansing our world, yet they are the ones bringing filth and hatred and disease. It isn't just this von Adamm, it's what he represents and the force that drives them.

We four *must* stick together, in harmony, we balance each other.' He looked the other three in the eye, 'we have a force of love between us, we can use that against them. Our youth, and our joy of living must overcome this infection, this cold death-magic. You, Dane ...' he turned to him, 'your magic is pure, that of the forest, of the earth, your dryad heritage adding to your understanding and love of our world. Yours is the force of Mother nature.'

He smiled at Tamlyn, 'and you, Tamlyn, your joie de vivre, your indomitable spirit of good will - don't ever change, we need your happy-go-lucky nature and your sheer charm.' He gazed into his face awhile then finally turned to Amber.

'And you, my dearest heart, where would I be without you? Do you know that whatever it is I do, it is only to make a world fit for you, for our future ... indeed *all of us*,' smiling at the other two. 'You are unique, my love, you can only ever be described as *Amber*, Her essence shines through you, and you complete me. *I vow,* not to those outside, but to you three, my closest friends, I will continue until my very last breath to protect this world of ours, and somehow to set it back on its right track, the harmony that was, is and should always be.'

Tamlyn put a hand on his shoulder, placed his other hand in his, gently kissed his cheek, then bowed his head reverentially before speaking. 'My dearest friend, I have watched you, watched the promise in you. Today, for me, when you faced my people and showed such kindness to that beast, you fulfilled that promise. I think it was one if the reasons I wanted to bring you here, I knew you would not let me down.

I vow that I shall follow you - my sword and my life in your service ... *my king.*' Once more he bowed his head.

Estrién stepped back, a little startled.

The two others nodded, he was right, today Estrién had shown the spirit of courage, generosity and compassion necessary in a king. There was no king of the elves, only a Dûc and a Dûchesse - why? Where was the real king? Estrién just shook his head. 'Stop teasing me, you lot,' he complained, and walked off. But the three spoke together after he had gone, agreed among themselves, Estrién was far more than he thought.

'But I'm not sure I'd want to be Queen,' Amber lamented, hotly contested by Dane and Tamlyn. *She would make a perfect Queen,* they assured her. She shook her head and ran off after Estrién. The last two merely smiled, they knew what they knew and they weren't about to change their opinion.

*

They spent the next couple of days at Tamlyn's comfortable home, travelling through excellently managed vineyards and gardens to a large, comfortable manor house. Like everything in Floriénne, the fine light stone of the house was clad with elegant wooden carvings, there were large windows, and balconies to every main bedroom as well as the impressive dining room and sitting rooms. Like all elven dwellings of Floriénne, the outside and the inside were one, the spring welcomed with delight when meals could be served on the balcony again, or on the beautiful sweeping green lawns.

Equally, Tamlyn's parents greeted them with delight, gracious hosts, as polite and charming as their son. They were profuse in their apologies about the dragon.

'I had absolutely no idea, Sir Estrién,' Lord Taenghelin spoke vehemently, handing him a deliciously cool glass of white wine. 'It disgusted me as much as you, we do not treat such beasts like that. There is something very wrong here now ... we would never have done that in the past. I have to say your beast-sense, or whatever you term it, is excellent. You truly impressed me, on many levels.' He looked round at his son, then spoke again, his voice catching in his throat, 'I have also to say I was proud of my son when he stood by your side in that arena. I saw him offer you his sword. He went, not with the throng, but with his conscience. ... You did the right thing, my boy.' Tamlyn turned a little red in the face, unused to compliments from his father.

Lord Taenghelin held up his wine goblet, *'Vint'ii, vest'ii, vit'ii!'* he toasted.

Tamlyn laughed and repeated the toast, as they all raised their glasses. *'To wine, feasting and life!'* Thank you father.'

They were given an excellent suite of rooms, next to Tamlyn's own, they realised the group was close. It was as if they finally recognised their son had grown up,, accepting them all as equals. They weren't exactly sure about the relationships, but understood it was complex, did not interfere. They treated them to some equally excellent meals and fine wines, and left Tamlyn to enjoy showing his home to his friends.

As they left a couple of days later, Lord Taenghelin spoke a few last words. 'I have enjoyed your company here, all of you. I am glad my son has such friends. Let me say that you are always welcome in my home, and if you are in need of shelter - from whomsoever - come here and it will be provided.' He turned to his son, 'Tamlyn, as you are not likely to be back for some time, I've put a large sum of money in your account, call it business expenses, travelling expenses, whatever. It's not a stipend or an allowance.' He handed him some Promissory notes. 'You can exchange these at the Merchant's Bank for gold, there are branches in all the main cities of Mer'edrynn. Let's say I'm investing in *you*, because without you people, I don't think we've much future. Trade is becoming difficult thanks to those blasted Adammites, I'm relying on you to put a stop to all this foolishness. Go with Merrie's Blessings my son, you and your friends.'

Tamlyn could see his mother nodding agreement, she had actually suggested it to her husband. He shook hands with his father and kissed his mother. 'We'll do our best. It's as you say, father, I have no idea when we can return and I thank you.'

The four mounted their horses and left, Tamlyn as proud of his parents as they were of their son, as he waved a last goodbye.

*

A few uneventful days on the road led them back to Orlandium, where King Alexis had returned in the glory of a battle well-fought. *At least*, he considered, until the Adammites sent even more ships to his main port. He'd left a larger garrison at Pennyport - but worried now about other towns, more troops at Pennyport meant less elsewhere. He let it be known that he was hiring more warriors and would also pay for mercenaries. He was extremely pleased to see Estrién and the group, presented them with a bag of gold.

'I know you wish me to help retake Hollyporth and Westlea, but the Adammites are well-entrenched there. I lost heavily down at Pennyport, I need more troops and those bastards are also coming in through the Bay of Gulls. I have to send reinforcements that way. Thanks to you, Sir Estrién, even the Freowulven are no longer harrying them.' He put up a hand to stop Estrién butting in. 'No, I understand what you have done, Oakleigh forest is precious. It's somewhat unorthodox, but at least it makes them useful and stops them from robbing people on the highway. You are an original thinker, Sir Estrién. And, I believe, a compassionate one - my scouts have told me about your ordeal at Floriénne. But until I train more warriors I'm afraid I cannot help Elvinhaeme. I intend to repair those ships we took at Pennyport, they have good ballistae on them - once we have enough fighters we can attack on two fronts, land and sea. We *can* do it, but it will take time.

What's worse is I am hearing murmurs from within my own city, men joining this damn cult, I could be attacked from within. Frankly, Sir Estrién, I hardly know which way to turn first.' The king sat down heavily on his throne, shaking his head at the uphill struggle he faced.

Amber looked thoughtful, then spoke to the assembly. 'My Lord King, it seems we could carry on attacking and defending, back and forth, ad infinitum. These people seem to grow in numbers each day, almost as if they're breeding. We gain a victory in one place, it's at the expense of somewhere else. To my thinking, there is only one sure method of removing this threat; go to the source and destroy it.

I've heard that this Mordecai Von Adamm is with King Kyneweth at Draecastle. I suggest we four go north, find out whatever we can, make what plans we can to take him out. He will be well guarded, but there is bound to be a way ... *somehow*. Once we've shown the followers that their leader is not invincible, they are sure to collapse.' She stopped, eyed her group. 'What say you guys?'

There was no need to ask, they were all already nodding. The king was uncertain.

'You need more than the four of you, or you go to certain death!'

Estrién agreed, 'We do, but it is not numbers, rather it is abilities. We need more mages with us, and certainly people as versatile as Amber and Tamlyn.' He frowned in thought . '... *A commando unit* in fact, a mixed set of warriors, mages, mercenaries, people with individual skills. Kyneweth has a well-organised and battle hardened army. We haven't the number or quality of troops to march against him. And in any case, Draecastle is almost impregnable from what I hear.

No, we need to be able to sneak into that castle, be able to combat whatever we come up against inside and finally eliminate this Von Adamm who cowardly sits hidden in its well-built walls.'

'That's suicide!' King Alexis wouldn't hear of it. 'You can't do that.'

But the four were already gathering their packs, picking up their weapons. 'We can,' replied Dane, 'We can, and *we will* ...'

As they left the Great Hall, Tamlyn had the last word. 'If we don't try this, we'll die anyway. We are everything he hates. I'd rather die fighting than burn alive on some stinking pyre. Come my friends ... we have work to do and a long path to tread.'

As the four grim-faced fighters left the Hall, the King shook his head in despair. Death, certain death, lay ahead of them.

Perhaps the four were not aware of how rocky and dark the road ahead would be, nor of the dangers and heartbreak awaiting them. But if this world were to heal, all four knew it would take courage and pain and sacrifice.

And above all ... love.

For Merrie's sake ...

End of Book 1

Appendix 1   Calendar

Month *Mer'edrynn* **Associated with:**

January *Endurance* first footing, feasting and friendship

February *Icefall* light in darkness, first love, preparation of the land

March *Shroving* Spring equinox, Mother, sowing and impregnation. To shrive - to make or impose a penance

April *Oestra* quickening, fertility rites

May *Firstfire* Beltane, hawking, courtly love, romance

June *Helios* Lumentide, Midsummer's Day, summertime, weddings, joy

July *Shearing* Heat of the sun, sheep shearing, Male magic, manhood

August *Herneset* Lammas, hunting and the Glorious 12th, hay making, wheat, fulfilment.

September *Harvesthaeme* Autumn Equinox, Michaelmas 29th Carrots & horses! Game, harvests vines, fruition

October *Goldleaf* Halloween or Samhain, ploughing, healing. Female magic

November *Firings* All souls Day, Bonfire, fireworks, burning leaves. Dying, endings, purification

December *Nightturn* Yule 21st, shortest day - the Long Night. Winter. Beginning/endings.

23rd December   the traditional **'Year and a Day'** *Feasting, boxing day, puzzles and games*

Appendix 2

Elvhen – the speech of the elves of Mer'edrynn (mostly spoken in Floriénne)

Ar'amé: of love
Ar'essa: loved one - feminine.
Ar'esson: loved one masculine
Bastedo: Bastard, swear word, of uncertain parentage.
Beainne: Fine and healthy
Bel: lovely
Belcaste: beautiful
bel sil'està: Beautiful to behold, beautiful features. Bonny.
Calice: a chalice or cup.
Cast'el: castle
daêth: meaningful, deep
the Dair Chev'al   the Oaken Knights of Floriénne
Dairhalle, or hall of oak. The oak is the wood elves' sacred tree
Decorum: Correct, straight, of honour
Draconae of dragons
Dûc / Dûchesse   Duke and Duchess, pronounced doochessa
Dulci'aré that which is sweet or soft.
Dulcior: gentle
Dulc'esta mea - term of endearance, 'my sweetness'.
Eormynn   Human.
Elaine; A young woman   **elain'ae**   a tender soul, a gentle person.
'elvian – pertaining to or belonging to one elf.
Elvién: of elves.
En *el'andis,*: in all the world.

En quattro:: Four square, relates to an elven dance, but also four working together as one.

Ent and

Es is

Esil he is

Esel she is.

Estaran the king

Estarian: of the stars, the heavens

Feu: fire or fiery

Foraes dair oaken forest. Shirewood.

Freowulven: (literally) Free Wolves.

Gilsylien: light of the heavens, a holy light.

Haemewagon A small wooden hut on wheels, usually with carvings.

Illucidae: understanding, to make clear.

Illuminae: to bring light.

in perpetuis - forever

Lauralae The laurel tree, a tree of heroes and champions.

Liefl'en: dearest, dear one.

Lumen: Bright,

Lumien: To shine, radiate light.

Lumeneum - (that which is) bright

Mia: my or of mine

Maliaté: wrong, bad

Maliatus: dreadful

méchan - competent

Menaedai: wood spirits, similar to dryads.

Mûcheld slang derogatory and vulgar elven term for someone. Excrement.

Nim: white, reflecting or of reflective nature,

NimEstrién White Star

nix virandem elven phrase, loosely translated as 'sex, or virility, isn't everything.'

Paradais Paradise, also literal - along the lines of the oaks.

Qu'ell That which is …. (masculine)

Qu'elle: that which is … (feminine)

Quattro; group of four

Ran'duel: a shield.

Rosea: of roses. Also, pink, blushed, a ring.

Rugosa or rugosae: ruddy, red faced.

Salixae: The willow tree, a tree of sadness *weeping willow*. Also a painkilling balm.

Sanguinae: of blood

Sentus: To feel, **Sentaé** (I feel)

Sel malia! That hurts!

Si'aré : of my heart 'Qu'elle ben si'are' - an elven statement of love - 'you hold my heart'.

Soleus: The sun or anything associated with the sun, can mean heat or light.

Sol'eteum: touched by the sun.

Sulis : of the sun, solar

Sylvanii: generic term, the tree people, people of the woods

Tué: You, feminine

Tui: You, masculine.

Triumvantis : of great triumph, wonder, a feeling of great pleasure.

Venienté: travel or voyage

'Vint'ii, Vest'ii, vit'ii!' : Wine, feasting and life! An elven toast from Floriénne. (pronounced *ventee, vestee, veetay*)

Bel sil'està lumeneum Bright and bonny

Est ben Elvién: It is good (beautiful/fine) to be elven.

'*Nim'randuel - Soleus D'rendiél - Gilsylien - Estaran'elvian*'
'He who is the White Shield and wields the Sword of Light which shines like the Heavens, is the true King of the Elves

Sulis **estrién** **nim** **lumien** - runes - several meanings: essentially, *'of the sun and the star is the white luminescence.'*

Printed in Poland
by Amazon Fulfillment
Poland Sp. z o.o., Wrocław